"If we go home, it won't be to watch television."

There was a dark edge to his voice that had her pulse pounding. He turned her around, then pulled her to him, so her back was against his chest. His arms encircled her torso. She felt warm and safe, and wildly alive. From the outside, they probably looked like they were simply watching the parade. But to Casey, the air between them was crackling, and his breath was deliciously hot on her skin. He leaned down.

"Here comes Santa," he murmured into her ear. "But I know I'm not getting anything this year."

"Why is that?"

"Because I've been very, very bad." He pressed the hard length of himself against her backside. She sucked in breath.

Every Little Kiss

A White Pine Novel

By

KIM AMOS

FOREVER

NEW YORK   BOSTON

Copyright © 2015 by Lara Zielin
Excerpt from *A Kiss to Build a Dream On* copyright © 2015 by Lara Zielin

Forever
Hachette Book Group
1290 Avenue of the Americas
New York, NY 10104

www.HachetteBookGroup.com

Printed in the United States of America

First Edition: October 2015
10 9 8 7 6 5 4 3 2 1

OPM

Forever is an imprint of Grand Central Publishing.
The Forever name and logo are trademarks of Hachette Book Group, Inc.

The Hachette Speakers Bureau provides a wide range of authors for speaking events. To find out more, go to www.hachettespeakersbureau.com or call (866) 376-6591.

The publisher is not responsible for websites (or their content) that are not owned by the publisher.

ATTENTION CORPORATIONS AND ORGANIZATIONS:

Most Hachette Book Group books are available at quantity discounts with bulk purchase for educational, business, or sales promotional use. For information, please call or write:

Special Markets Department, Hachette Book Group
1290 Avenue of the Americas, New York, NY 10104
Telephone: 1-800-222-6747 Fax: 1-800-477-5925

For Kate and Jenn who give generously, laugh uproariously, and make the world so much more interesting and better. Jenn, thank you for fighting fires and keeping the rest of us safe. You are my hero.

Acknowledgments

Christmas in White Pine has arrived thanks to the Santa-like magic of my amazing editor, Michele Bidelspach. Thank you for leaving the gift of insight and expertise under this writer's tree. That sounds dirty, but it's not, I swear. Thanks as well to my agent, Susanna Einstein, who has expertly steered this series and my writing in general.

I am continually grateful for the wisdom and support of Alex Kourvo. Thank you for having my back. Always. And Rhonda Helms, thanks for getting as excited as I did that this book shared a title with a Bruce Hornsby song. We'll always have the mandolin rain, sister.

When I was first imagining this story and thinking about how to bring a firefighter to White Pine, the awesome crew of Dearborn, Michigan's Station One let me ride along on their calls and ask questions and learn about the profession. Many thanks for your patience and help and, above all, for your service to the community. You put your lives on the line every day, for which I can never say thank you enough.

Finally, three cheers to my husband, Rob, who helps me tweak the hot dish recipes, who plies me with coffee and chocolate when I'm writing, and who played a firefighter himself in the hit student production found only on VHS, *Trial by Fire*. That workout sequence was amazing, dude.

CHAPTER ONE

Casey Tanner had never before had colleagues who played practical jokes. She was used to a corporate watercooler over which smiles were rarely traded. She'd once been so startled when a receptionist cackled loudly while watching an online video about grandmas smoking pot that she'd spilled a non-fat latte across her keyboard.

So it was only slowly, over many long, uncomfortable moments, that Casey wondered if she'd been had. If she'd been punk'd, for lack of a better word.

Because surely the intern with the wide eyes and trembling chin was joking about having just called 911.

"Tell me once more why you thought this was necessary?" Casey asked the young girl—Ellie, if she was remembering the name correctly—whose cropped ginger hair was in disarray around her head. The poor thing could barely be more than a first-year in college.

"The carbon monoxide detector in the basement was

screaming. We should open windows or get everyone out of here *right now.*"

The girl's words might have been a tinge dramatic, but her face was stone serious. If Casey had wanted this to be a hilarious prank, it sure wasn't turning out that way. Cold fear crawled along her spine, but she focused on Ellie and worked to stay calm. Ellie already looked like she might pass out.

"All right," Casey said, "easy does it. I want you to take a deep breath and—"

"I don't want to breathe deeply if the air is poisoned!"

Casey pressed her lips together. She had only just started at Robot Lit, a youth literacy nonprofit, two weeks before. She was still trying to figure out where the extra copier paper was stored, never mind what do to in a carbon monoxide emergency. Ingrid, their director, was out taking her ten-year-old daughter to the doctor, which meant Casey was probably the most senior person in charge. Never mind that she was the newest.

At that moment, though, none of it mattered. If the building was filling with carbon monoxide, she had to get her colleagues out safely. Without causing a panic. Her mind raced.

"Okay, Ellie," she said after a moment. "Most everyone should be on the third floor here. So I want you to calmly—very calmly—let people know that we are being extra careful about our carbon monoxide levels, and folks should stand outside for a bit while the fire department gets here. While you're doing that, I'm going to make absolutely sure the rest of the building is clear. Does that make sense?"

Ellie nodded, her eyes enormous in her small face.

"Don't forget to check the restrooms, okay?"

"Yes."

"And no freaking out, right?"

"Right."

"Say it with me," Casey said, grabbing the young girl's hand. "We're being what?"

"Extra careful."

"And what should folks do?"

"Stand outside."

"Should they panic?"

"No."

"Good. Go tell them."

Casey breathed a small sigh as Ellie walked away, grateful that Robot Lit had only six employees. And there weren't any kids here at the moment. For once, their small staff would be an asset.

Casey grabbed her coat, her eye catching the white of a snow-covered day outside her window. At least if she had to spend time in the cold she'd get to look down Main Street and see all the holiday lights twinkling.

She heard sirens in the distance as she wound her way down to the conference rooms and kitchen on the second floor, looking for anyone as she went. The rooms were empty, so she headed into the lobby on the first floor. All clear. Through the door's wavy glass she spotted Ellie along with the other Robot Lit employees outside, clustered in a small circle. She knew she should join them. Instead, pushing aside a prickle of unease, she descended into the belly of the old warehouse on Main Street, all the way to the basement.

She wasn't going to just let firemen rumble into Robot Lit without knowing what was the matter. It was her job, after all, if Ingrid wasn't there. She would simply find out if the carbon monoxide detector was really going off, or if it was something else entirely.

Careful, a small inner voice cautioned. It was this need to know everything—and, okay, maybe control everything—that had come close to unraveling her life a few short months ago. Casey had screwed up so badly that she'd left a high-paying job in a Minneapolis suburb for a chance at a new start in White Pine and to be closer to her sister, Audrey. Now, she was working at Robot Lit for a fraction of her former salary and living in a creaky Cape Cod instead of her sleek city apartment.

It was all worth it, of course. Casey would do just about anything to atone for her past. She grimaced as she remembered how selfishly she'd acted just a few short months ago, nearly ruining Audrey's chance at true love.

She wasn't about to make that mistake again. She figured she could, however, spare five minutes to figure out what was happening in the basement.

Shrill beeping pierced her ears as she flipped on a small overhead bulb. She inhaled the dank air of dim space. Carbon monoxide was odorless—she wouldn't be able to smell anything—but she took an inventory of her breathing, of her vision, of any pains in her head that could signal toxic levels. At her body's first sign of symptoms, no matter how tiny, she'd be out of there.

Unless she collapsed in a clueless heap first.

Hoping for the best, she followed the beeping to a small box on the wall. The sirens were louder now. The firehouse was just up the street, and the firefighters would be here in no time.

A light was flashing, strobe-bright in the dim space. *Head fine, vision clear*, she thought, accounting for her every breath and movement. Using the flashlight app on her phone, she trained a blaze of light on the panel. There were three lights—green, yellow, and red. But only one of them was flashing.

Yellow.

Service.

The damn thing was low on batteries.

Casey groaned as the thunder of heavy boots came down the stairs. Three firefighters swept into the room, their tanks and gear making them seem like giants. They weren't wearing their oxygen masks, meaning she could see their faces. Two men and a woman.

"What are you doing down here?" the tallest of the two men asked. His hazel eyes were sharp. The bridge of his nose was slightly crooked, like it had been broken in a fight.

"I just wanted to check and make sure things were all right," she said. "I was looking—"

"You should be outside with the others. This is a potentially dangerous situation."

"I know," Casey said, feeling small and silly, "I was trying—"

The fireman shined his flashlight into her eyes. She blinked. "Do you have a headache? Nausea?"

"No, this is all a misunderstanding. The detector is—"

"Did you make the call?"

Frustration needled her. The man hadn't let her finish a sentence yet. "*No,* that's what I'm trying to tell you. An intern called when she thought something was wrong. But the thing is out of batteries. That's all."

She stepped aside so the massive firefighter could take a closer look at the white box on the wall. Underneath the smoky, chalky smell of his gear, Casey detected a scent like wood chips and cinnamon.

The other firefighters stayed a few feet behind, sharing a look that signaled to Casey this wasn't the first time they'd had a false alarm on a carbon monoxide detector.

"Write it up, Lu?" the woman asked. Her dark eyes were striking in her pale face.

The man's name was Lou, Casey realized. It seemed an odd name for him—like calling a bulldog Fluffy.

"When was the last time this device was calibrated?"

"I'm sorry, I have no idea. Lou. Or is it Louis? Louie?" Casey figured she'd better get on this man's good side, and fast.

"Lu is short for lieutenant," he replied, eyes sparking with irritation. Underneath the visor of his helmet, the lines of his face were granite hard.

"Oh." She could feel her cheeks redden. "I'm sorry. Look, I just started here a couple weeks ago."

The lieutenant trained his jaw at the ceiling. His flashlight beam slid down an old copper pipe. "You got a sprinkler system installed?" he asked.

Was he not listening to *anything* she said? She was a brand-new employee. What good was grilling her? It may have been her imagination, but Casey could swear the other two firefighters had just groaned quietly.

"I don't—I couldn't tell you," she stumbled. She checked the time on her phone. The employees had been standing outside for a while in the Minnesota cold, and she figured she ought to herd them down the street to the Rolling Pin and buy them all hot chocolate for their trouble.

"Are we settled here? Can I go back upstairs to the others?"

The lieutenant tore his eyes from the copper pipe and looked around the basement—past the boxes of stationery and the old phone books and an oddly placed plastic Hula-hoop.

"I want to take a closer look at things," he said. "Quinn and Reese, you two head upstairs, check and see that the smoke detectors all have working batteries and the fire exits aren't encumbered. I'll be up in a few."

Casey watched the female firefighter open her mouth, think better of what she was going to say, and close it. Together, the two firefighters tromped back up the steps in their heavy gear.

"So...can I go?" Casey asked, unsure what she was supposed to be doing. The lieutenant frowned, a motion that bunched the chiseled lines of his face. He'd be handsome, Audrey thought, if he wasn't so completely abrupt about everything.

"If you would, I need you to answer a few questions."

Casey shifted, feeling suddenly like she was under investigation. She quickly texted Rolf, their program coordinator.

All clear inside. Take everyone to Rolling Pin. Buy hot choc. I'll be there in a few.

She hit send as the lieutenant made a low rumbling in his throat. The noise involuntarily sent goose bumps up and down her arms.

"You have a smoke detector down here?" he asked, making his way deeper into the basement. He flipped on buzzing overhead lights as he went.

"I don't know," she replied, trailing in his wake.

The lieutenant made the low rumbling in his throat again, and it struck Casey that the sound was of disapproval. Her jaw clenched with irritation. Why were they still down here if this was just a case of low batteries?

Casey tapped her toe on the scuffed cement floor. She watched the lieutenant scan the pipes and boards all around. She caught a flash of blond under his helmet. The lock of hair looked thick and wavy in a way that had her fingertips itching to touch it—at least until he made the low rumble in his throat a third time.

"Can't find a single smoke detector down here. You'll want to change that."

Yes, Your Highness, she thought.

"I'll talk to the director," she said instead.

"And a fire extinguisher. You'll want one of those, too."

"I'll add it to the list."

"What's your name?" He was staring at the pipes on the ceiling again. As if he couldn't be bothered to take time from his all-important inspection to focus on her.

"Casey Tanner."

"What brought you to Robot Lit?"

It's complicated.

"Job change," she said. "I moved down here from Eagan."

She pictured the bare walls of her new house, the naked wood floors, and the stacks of boxes she needed to empty, and held back an overwhelmed sigh. The mountain of work ahead of her was daunting, made more so by the fact that she was desperate to find her Christmas decorations. It was December first already, and not a single ornament was in place, no matter that she had taped a label on every box and listed the contents in Sharpie. But the boxes she'd identified as "Holiday"—inventoried with bullet points like "fake snow, tinsel, Rudolph figures," and more—simply couldn't be found.

"Are you a tutor at Robot Lit?" This time the lieutenant looked straight at her, and for a brief moment the strict lines around his mouth and eyes relaxed. Casey's breath caught unexpectedly.

"I'm an accountant," she managed. "They brought me on

to help get their finances in order. And keep them that way."

She left out the part about taking a huge pay cut to come here and trying to rebuild her relationship with her sister. In other words, the part where she was blind and selfish and in need of a shakeup.

She squared her shoulders, trying to seem more confident than she felt. The lieutenant might have rugged good looks, but she didn't want him knowing anything about her. The way he found every flaw in this building probably translated to finding flaws in people. And Lord knew she had plenty for him to uncover.

She glanced at her phone as a text message from Rolf came in.

Everyone at Rolling Pin. Text when you can.

"Almost finished?" she asked, reading the text message again so she didn't linger too long on the almond shape of the lieutenant's eyes.

"For now," he said. "On our way back up, let's take the elevator. I want to see how the emergency call button is functioning."

Casey blinked. She didn't even know Robot Lit had an elevator. Which was just as well. Small spaces always caused her heart to pound and her head to hurt.

She tamped down the lump of worry. It wasn't as if they were shooting up to the top of the Empire State Building, for crying out loud.

Nevertheless, her throat was dry as she followed the lieutenant into the elevator. Above the collar of his fireman's coat, she caught a glimpse of his neck. The skin was golden enough to have her picturing droplets of honey on a sunny day.

When the doors slid shut behind them, the lieutenant hit

floor three, then punched the brass button with the fireman's
cap on it. The elevator jerked into motion. He kept his finger on the panel, waiting for some kind of response. To take
her mind off the cramped space, Casey studied the fine blond
hairs on the back of the lieutenant's enormous hand. They
looked so delicate in contrast to the rest of him. His spicy
smell was back, so much so that her head was all but filled
with it. She told herself the pounding in her chest was from
the enclosed space.

The lieutenant pressed the fire call button again and
again. No response.

"Has anyone used—" the lieutenant began. But the words
died on his lips when the elevator squawked to a halt, and
they were plunged into darkness.

* * *

Casey couldn't breathe. The blackness was thick and all-
consuming. Blinking, she swiped at the heavy nothingness,
as if to push it away.

"Help!" she cried, pawing at emptiness. "Help us!"

Strong fingers wrapped around her forearm. She looked
down, but couldn't see even an outline of a hand. "Easy
there," came the lieutenant's deep voice. "It's okay."

His unrelenting grip should have offended her. *What right
did he have to touch her?* But instead, it grounded her reeling mind. Fragments of logic pierced through. *I'm in an
elevator. This man is a firefighter.*

Still, her breath was ragged. She couldn't get enough air.
The space pressed against her. She was aware she might be
panting.

"Casey, listen to me." The lieutenant had stepped closer.

She could feel him acutely. "I want you to close your eyes and count to ten."

"We need to get out of here. I have to leave. Why won't the door open? It's time to go." The words were a tangle. The darkness was in her lungs, fighting with all the air. She was beginning to get light-headed.

His grip vanished. She was unmoored, reeling and lost in the smallest space possible. *Come back*, she thought wildly.

Then a flashlight beam sliced through the inky blackness. The lieutenant held it, even as both of his hands came to rest on her shoulders. Heavy and strong. "I'm going to take that breath with you," he said. "Both of us. We're going to do it together." The flashlight cast strange shadows around his eyes. It reminded her of face paint at a carnival.

The hand that wasn't holding the flashlight slid palm-down from her shoulder, along her biceps, all the way to her fingers. He pulled her hand through emptiness until it came to rest on his chest. "Now you'll know if we're breathing together. You'll feel it. In and out, okay? Just like me."

He held her hand tight against his sternum. His heartbeat was there, too, steady underneath his fireman's gear. "In and out," he said. "Easy does it." The rise and fall of his chest was like the waves on Lake Superior—great swells that rolled along, one into the next. She squeezed her eyes closed. She pictured the lake, concentrated on matching her breathing to his.

"Good," he said. The rumble of his voice was so near she could feel it. If his chest was a rolling wave, then his voice was rich sunlight full of heat. "You just keep breathing like that, and I'll keep holding your hand. I'm going to use my other hand here to set down this flashlight, then I'll call for help on my radio. The rest of the fire crew can get us out in no time. I need you to speak and tell me you understand what I'm telling you."

"I understand," she managed. He squeezed her hand. In the cramped space, it should have made her more claustrophobic to be this near to a stranger, touching like this. Yet she wanted to close the last bit of distance between them.

The radio was on the lieutenant's shoulder. He turned his head as he spoke into it.

"Dispatch from unit sixteen, we have an elevator entrapment. It's a single elevator, and we're between floors one and two."

"Dispatch copy. Do you have any injuries on scene?"

"No injuries. There are two other firefighters here also from unit sixteen, responding initially to a carbon monoxide concern. We don't need a cruiser—just an elevator tech."

"Unit sixteen, message received. We'll get a technician en route."

"Copy. Thanks." A pause, then: "Lieutenant to firefighters and unit sixteen, go to channel two."

A crackle of static. "Yeah, Lu. What's up?" It sounded like the female firefighter.

"I'm in an elevator entrapment situation. I called dispatch; they have an elevator tech en route."

"You doing okay?"

"Yeah. Just try to get the stupid elevator going from your end if you can. And somebody wait outside for the elevator tech, help them get to the scene."

"Copy that, Lu. We'll get you out in no time."

"Copy. Thanks, Quinn."

The conversation was over, apparently. The flashlight beam was a tiny lamp in an ocean of black.

"They need to call the elevator company to get those

doors open," the lieutenant said. "They'll get a tech out here, and we'll be out in no time."

How long? Casey trembled, wondering if she'd suffer for minutes or hours.

"My name is Abe Cameron," the lieutenant said after a moment.

Casey's brain fumbled, trying to process how to respond. Where were her manners? She couldn't remember how or what to say. All she knew was that she couldn't think past the four walls pressing so close around her.

"I used to spend a lot of time at Robot Lit," he continued when Casey didn't say anything. "I was tutored here. When I started, I was in fifth grade and could barely read."

The idea had emotion swelling in her chest, though she had no idea what to do with it. "My teacher, Mrs. Wills, brought me to Robot Lit after school one day. They had time to spend with me that she didn't. She really helped. This *place* really helped."

The clouds in her mind broke enough for her to wonder if that was why Abe had been such a stickler in the basement. Because he cared about the place.

For some reason, the idea of Abe being gruff because of affection for Robot Lit calmed her. Moment by moment, Casey became aware of the present, of what was right in front of her, which included Abe's skin against hers. She could picture the blond hairs on his forearms, the tiny pores, the blood warm underneath. His breath was so close. Every exhale was a whisper of reassurance.

Abe's fingers were steady and firm. A working man's hands, Casey thought. Not like the hands of all the other accountants at her last job.

"You're doing great," Abe murmured, leaning forward

and speaking the words into her hair. Casey's breath nearly vanished again, but not from fear. It was the fact that his lips felt mere inches away.

She wasn't used to being this near anyone, let alone a firefighter. She tried to recall the last time she'd been kissed— been held—but the fog of time was too thick. She couldn't glimpse through it.

Casey was suddenly grateful for the darkness so Abe wouldn't see her grimace of shame. There was a word for women like her, she knew. *Spinster.* It might not be the 1800s, but the label fit. *Spinster* even had the right sound to it. The spitting, biting consonants were the perfect reminder that she'd been living a prudish, uptight existence for far too long, batting back the part of her that secretly wanted to break free and live with abandon. With adventure, even.

"Easy now," Abe said. "Just keep relaxing. The tech is coming."

Casey stilled, figuring she must have tensed up just then and Abe had felt it.

"I'm—I'm doing okay," she replied. Her voice sounded small and tinny.

Abe shifted, his leg grazing hers. An unexpected jolt shot through her nerves. There was so much of him, Casey realized. He must be at least six foot four, whereas she was barely five foot five. Unlike her sister, Audrey, she didn't have an athlete's body underneath her clothes. All she had was her medium brown hair and her average figure from being a normal office worker for the past decade.

Here in the darkness, though, maybe it didn't matter. She shifted just slightly, inching closer to Abe. She couldn't be sure, but she thought she heard a soft grunt from him.

Time either slowed way down or sped up. Casey couldn't

tell. She had no idea how long she'd been pressed against Abe when there was a scuffling sound from above them. Casey jerked, wondering if the elevator ties were finally going to give way and they were going to go plunging downward.

"That's just Quinn and Reese working with the tech to open the doors on the floor above us. While they do that, I want you to tell me about a place that you love," Abe said. Was it her imagination, or was he clutching her more tightly? "We're going to picture it together. You're going to tell me all about it."

Tears prickled her eyes. Surely it was the claustrophobia jerking her emotions from one extreme to another. That's why she was getting so worked up over a silly question.

And yet her chest ached as she tried to think about a place she loved—as she tried to think about *anything* she loved, frankly.

There was her sister, of course.

Audrey was generous and kind and beautiful, and Casey had loved her so ferociously it had almost ruined their relationship. Casey's stomach twisted at the memory of how she'd driven a wedge between Audrey and the man Audrey loved, Kieran Callaghan. She'd done it out of fear, out of a need for control, and it had been terrible. Ruinous, even. Fortunately, Audrey and Kieran were married now, and Audrey had forgiven Casey. But Casey wasn't sure if she had yet forgiven herself. She wasn't sure she'd earned it.

Then of course there was Christmas. Since she was a little girl, Casey had adored Christmas with its sparkling tinsel and glittering streets and freshly cut trees and warm cookies and spiced cider.

So, yes, there were things she loved—but a *place* she loved?

The answer seemed impossible. She'd never traveled much outside of Minnesota. Her life up until now had been composed of getting places, of ensuring a specific course on a road to success. She'd never stopped much along the way.

"You're awfully quiet," Abe said. She could hear the smile on his lips as he tried to lighten the moment. As if he somehow understood what a battle this question was.

"I don't…" The words faded into less than a whisper. She had no answer.

"It's okay," Abe said. His hand was on her shoulder again, the other still clasping her fingers against his chest. This man was stronger and steadier and calmer than anyone she'd ever met.

There was a shout above them, and a scraping noise. Casey cringed.

"The place *I* love," Abe said, "is a little German town called Freiburg. The British messed it up in World War Two, gutted it with bombs. But the town was rebuilt with these efficient, logical roads and bike paths that you can take anywhere. There's also a train, and it always runs on time. *Always.* And there's all this green technology through what are called passive houses. They don't require any kind of furnace or device to heat them. They essentially heat themselves. It's efficient. It's incredible."

Casey thrilled at how thoughtful and ordered it sounded. Until a small inner voice reminded her that being logical and ordered was what had almost ruined her life. A straitlaced existence had nearly been her undoing, and she wasn't about to repeat the pattern. She'd moved to White Pine to do the opposite, in fact.

"When were you there?" she managed to ask.

"Never. I've only read about it. I'm saving up to go, but—well, it's a long story."

And based on the shouts and noise above them, there wasn't any time to tell it.

Abe's radio squawked. "Crew to lieutenant. Elevator tech is here. He's going to come in from the top. We'll get you out with the ladder."

"Message received."

"They're coming in through the fire access panel above us," Abe said. "The elevator door to the first floor is just a foot or so away, so they're going to pull us out of the top of this thing, then pull us onto the first floor. Does that make sense?"

"Yes."

Abe's stubbled cheek pressed against hers. The rough feel of it had her muscles weakening. "You're almost there," he said. "Just a few more minutes."

Before she could gather her next thought, Abe dropped her hand and stepped away, just as the panel in the ceiling above them opened. A flashlight beam pierced through, brighter than a hundred camera flashes. Or so Casey thought as she squinted against it.

"There are better places for a party," said the firefighter above them. "This one is kind of hard to get to, and I'm not sure the DJ would fit."

"Get a ladder down here *now*, Reese." Abe's voice was back to being razor sharp. Casey wrapped her arms around herself, thinking she'd liked it much better when he'd murmured.

The flashlight beam bounced as a ladder was lowered into the elevator car. "Reese will hold it from above," Abe said. "I'll grab it down here. Go ahead."

Casey took in the firm set of Abe's lips, the rugged edge

of his jaw, the hardness in his eyes. His kindness, his gentleness, was seeping away—that is, if it had ever been there in the first place.

Not that she was about to stay in the elevator one second longer to wonder. She grasped the sides of the ladder and hauled herself up the rungs until Reese helped her stand on top of the stalled car. Golden light poured onto them from the open doors just a few feet above. Inside the wide doors was the female firefighter.

Casey gulped air, relieved to be away from the confines of the elevator's four walls.

"You hardly have to move now," Reese said, smiling a lopsided grin. "You just raise your arms and Quinn is going to pull you up."

If she had any doubts that Quinn was strong enough, they were gone within seconds. Before she knew it, strong hands had lifted her into the safety of the building. It was all she could do to smile and thank her rescuers. She wanted to collapse onto the floor and kiss the solid ground beneath her feet.

"Casey!" Her director, Ingrid, was racing down the wood-planked hallway to get to her. "Oh my God, Rolf called me just as I was dropping Heidi back off at school. I got here as soon as I could. I was so worried!" Whole sections of Ingrid's white-blonde hair had come loose from her ponytail. A number-two pencil was tucked behind her ear, its yellow wood indented with teeth marks.

"I'm fine," Casey managed. "I just don't like small spaces much."

"What an ordeal. Take the rest of the day off. Please."

"I'm sure I'll be all right."

"Just do it, okay? It'll make me feel better, anyway."

She hugged Casey just as Abe's voice sliced through the commotion. He was directly behind her. "Get the ladder hauled up. Talk to the mechanic. I want it logged in."

"Yes, Lu." The firefighters scurried to get their tasks finished.

"Abe!" Ingrid said, waving at him. "You saved our girl here. Thank you."

Casey was momentarily confused as to how these two were acquainted. Abe had been tutored at Robot Lit years ago. Had he stayed in touch with the staff?

"You guys know each other?" she asked dumbly.

"Abe's a good friend to this place," Ingrid said.

Recognition dawned. Casey hadn't been around nonprofits very much, but she was beginning to understand that *friend* meant donor.

Abe smiled at Ingrid—big enough to show two rows of gloriously straight white teeth. Casey's heart jerked. "Happy to help," he said. "You two take care."

He started off, radioing more commands. He wasn't leaving, was he? The thought had her stomach clenching unexpectedly. Casey gave Ingrid a hang-on-a-minute gesture.

She trotted after Abe. "Thank you," she said, sliding in front of him to stop his forward march. "You kept me calm down there and I'm grateful. You were great. Are great, I mean. At your job, that is." Her brain still felt tangled, her words twisted into each other.

Oh, God, what was she doing? She should have just let him go. She was making an ass of herself.

If Abe minded her babbling, he didn't show it. In fact, his eyes flashed with emotion and, if Casey didn't know better, she'd say that look was filled with warmth. Maybe even something hotter—a light closer to flame.

"Happy to help." Then he tipped his helmet at her and walked away, barking orders at the other firefighters. The sound of his fireman's boots on the warehouse's wood floors grew more and more distant.

The connection she'd felt between them stretched thin as he retreated, like taffy pulled too far apart. She felt a pang of hollowness, an unexpected disappointment. Did he really have to walk away like that? He'd been so comforting, so calming, in the elevator, telling her about Robot Lit and the German city he loved. Underneath all those layers of fireman's gear, she thought she'd glimpsed his tender side, and it left her wanting more.

She thought maybe he'd seen something in her that he wanted more of, too. The way he'd pulled her close, the way he'd murmured into her hair.

Apparently he was just doing his job.

She pulled in a breath. It was just as well. Abe Cameron was a stranger to her. In her frazzled state in the elevator, she'd simply contrived a connection to a man she barely knew. Even worse, she'd turned him into something he clearly wasn't—gentle, caring, even sexy, a *hero*—and when the hard light of day hit her again, she'd been left staring at something that had never been.

It's all for the best. She wasn't looking for someone whose lifelong dream was to visit an orderly German town. Practicality was not on her list of sexy attributes. She had enough of that in her own life, thank you very much.

Which reminded her...

She pulled out her phone and typed an e-mail to herself, a note to get a new fire extinguisher for the basement tomorrow and a new set of batteries for the carbon monoxide alarm. Plus a smoke detector.

She couldn't always shed the responsibilities that seemed to follow her around like a pack of stray dogs, but by God she could shed them when it came to a man. *If* it came to a man, that is.

Which was a big if, considering this was White Pine, and the bachelor selection wasn't exactly brimming.

"I hope those are Abe's digits you're typing into your phone," Ingrid said, standing beside her once more. Ingrid was smiling like she could read every single thought about Abe Cameron that had passed through Casey's brain in the past hour.

"Just the opposite. I'm going to make sure the basement has all the equipment we need so I don't have to see him again."

"Huh. I thought maybe there was a spark there. A little flirty fun, perhaps?"

Casey didn't have the heart to admit she'd thought that, too. For a moment, anyway. Instead, she grabbed Ingrid's arm and plastered on a smile. She reminded herself that this was a fresh start. Maybe she could learn to shelve her responsibilities for a few minutes and get to know her colleagues. Perhaps even develop a friendship here or there.

"We both missed out on the Rolling Pin's hot cocoa this afternoon," she told Ingrid. "How about we pop down for some now. My treat."

"You sure? By the time I'm done asking for extra whipped cream on mine, the up-charge is, like, eight bucks."

Casey grinned. "Maybe I can find a way to file it as a tax deduction."

Ingrid patted her sides. "Maybe I can find a way it won't all end up on my hips."

Laughing, Casey followed Ingrid down the warehouse's

hallway toward the main entrance. She gave herself an imaginary high five. Her colleagues didn't have to know she'd been a stick in the mud for years. They didn't have to know about the embarrassing things she'd done. Not if she worked to show them a different side of herself, anyway.

And when it came to a man, well, Casey knew that she was going to have to find a guy who was her complete opposite. Fun-loving, carefree, adventurous—everything she wanted to be.

She stepped out into the darkening afternoon, the snow swirling and the holiday lights twinkling, and reminded herself she was back in White Pine to change. To be better.

She walked alongside Ingrid to the Rolling Pin and faced the truth.

A man like Abe Cameron would be nothing but trouble.

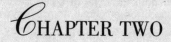

CHAPTER TWO

*T*he morning sun crested over a snow-covered hill, igniting the icy limbs of the cedar trees in a fiery orange glow. Abe Cameron gulped down the cold air, lungs burning as his hiking boots trundled through the fresh powder on the trail. His hands clutched at the straps on his backpack. Sweat dripped down his neck in rivulets that froze almost as soon as they formed.

Three miles in. Five to go. Eight miles every other day along this trail, rain or shine, carrying a backpack filled with weights and a rock or two from along the path, when he felt like throwing them in.

It was the hardest workout Abe could think of. It was also the only one that made sense to him. Because if something was challenging, you did it. It if was tough, you tackled it.

Abe shifted the backpack slightly, ignoring the ache in his shoulders and neck. He'd long ago stopped asking himself how he felt about things. If he focused on the pain, the hurt, the desire to stop, he'd never do anything.

He'd never run into a flame-engulfed building.

He'd never hold the hand of a car-crash victim and tell him to hang on.

He'd never breathe air into the lungs of a drowning victim, willing himself to bring her back.

In White Pine, fire and rescue were wrapped into one, meaning he could get called on everything from a house fire to a sprained ankle. Doing both meant he'd seen his share of broken bodies and tragic situations.

He pushed himself down the trail harder, as if trying to outrun the memories of the middle-of-the-night calls when someone stopped breathing, and the pain in the family members' faces as they helplessly watched him work.

An icy wind blasted his face. He turned into it, welcoming the raw cold. His job should have made him grateful for every day he was alive and healthy. Oddly, it had done the opposite. It had numbed him, in a way, to his life. It could all get taken away so easily, so why get invested?

It was part of why he kept himself cordoned off from any relationships that got too deep or too heavy. He often thought of his love life like those confetti cannons that fire at concerts. They went off with an explosion that took your breath away, and had you thinking the whole world was shimmering—only to realize that it had just been crumpled, wrinkled paper the whole time.

That's just the way it is, he thought—then immediately wondered how he'd gotten so jaded. He didn't much like the hardened cynic who stared back at him every morning from the bathroom mirror.

What might be altogether worse, though, were the ways

in which the reflection was cracking—the ways in which he had to accept that his parents weren't going to be around forever. His dad, especially. It was impossible not to see the fissures in his façade when he thought about it, and to feel as though he might rip apart like a fault line during an earthquake.

He stumbled, nearly losing his footing. He threw out his arms, fighting for balance. When he righted himself, he took a deep gulp of the crystal air. His thoughts were too heavy, too coarse. He knew it. All this existential clamor about feelings was useless. It wouldn't change a damn thing. He should stop right now.

But at the same time, he felt a heavy weariness he couldn't shake. God, but it was exhausting work, living with this reality that life was tenuous, even delicate. It could all end—*poof!*—in a single moment. A fire. A misstep. A piano falling from the sky.

This truth had kept him on the on the edge of his own existence, in a way. It had given him his nickname at the station: Ninety-Eyed. "Eyed" was a homophone for IED. Every relationship he'd ever been in blew up within ninety days. Ninety-*IED*. He did it. He pulled the trigger and he knew it. The guys at the station knew it. And the parade of women through his life certainly knew it—if not at first, then certainly by the time they'd dusted off the rubble and gotten over the shock.

For years, he'd enjoyed the nickname because he'd been happy. Hot sex for a while, then an explosion before things got complicated. But now he was beginning to wonder if he wasn't happy as much as he was…indifferent. It was hard to be too bummed about anything when nothing really mattered.

He grunted, straining under his pack. For the first time in memory, he was experiencing feelings he didn't want to bat down. A tiny spring bubbled inside him every time he thought about Casey Tanner, and he was barely doing a half-assed job of damming it up.

The memory of her soft hand inside his while they were trapped in the elevator had his heart pounding more than it normally would along this section of the trail. He followed a fork to the left into a cluster of birch trees, ducking amid low branches.

If he'd been put off by her reckless decision to go down to the basement when they'd first showed up, he'd warmed to her when she said she was an accountant. He respected the logic of numbers. And then to find out she was working at Robot Lit was an added bonus. The place had been able to teach him to read, had emphasized the wonder of books when most of his teachers had simply shrugged off his struggle for literacy, saying the words would be there when he was ready. Robot Lit mattered to him, and he liked meeting people who felt the same way.

It also didn't hurt when those people had thick auburn hair and wore form-fitting sweaters that emphasized just the right curves.

A pheasant took flight from nearby brushes, startling him into a full stop. His lungs heaved as he watched the bird warble into the air, snow falling like stars from its wings. An ache pressed behind his sternum, and he instinctively brought his gloved hand to his chest.

What the—?

Chest pain. He stilled, trying to pinpoint the source, but he couldn't do it. The soreness was too broad. Surely it was just a little bit of heartburn, he thought. He brushed it off.

After all, the call yesterday had scared him more than he wanted to admit, and he was probably worked up as a result. He'd been extra gruff when his crew arrived because the thought of anyone on the Robot Lit team being in harm's way made his stomach twist. Secretly, he felt bad for turning a low-battery warning on a carbon monoxide detector into a full-blown inspection, especially when that wasn't even his job. Ty Brady was White Pine's fire inspector, and Abe knew he had no business stepping on Ty's toes. That was why Quinn and Reese were irritated about the whole call, though they'd dutifully checked out the building even when they didn't want to. He didn't blame them for being miffed. But he wasn't going to pass up a chance to make Robot Lit as safe as he could.

He started back down the trail, his breath puffing white in the cold. He'd been high-strung about the call to begin with, which was probably why Casey Tanner was affecting him more than she should. They'd shared several minutes in a dark, confused space, and Abe knew better than anyone that trauma could forge bonds with people that normal situations didn't. That was why he'd pulled her closer than he should have, why he'd let his guard down for a few minutes, speaking into her hair and letting his cheek graze hers briefly.

He might like the ladies, sure, but he'd never crossed a professional line. If that was, in fact, what you called what had happened in those twenty minutes he and Casey were in the elevator together.

The problem was, he was still having trouble erasing the picture of her in his mind. Especially when she'd thanked him after it was all over. She'd still been pale and shaken, but her golden brown eyes had been clear and focused. She hadn't felt sorry for herself or milked it for drama. She'd been gracious and grateful and he'd stomped away. Like an asshole.

He didn't want her to know how much he'd enjoyed being trapped in that space with her. Because it was dangerous, this blade of emotion that was pressed against his insides. It hadn't been there with Kaylee, the dance instructor from Burnsville, or Zoe, the freelance photographer who'd texted him some very artful pictures. And he'd liked them both just fine. Zoe had even made it just past the ninety-day mark—she'd gotten to ninety-two—and he hadn't felt it with her, either.

He shook his head, wishing the raw wind could just blow away his thoughts. It would be so much easier that way.

Instead, he pushed himself up a small incline that deposited him into a wide clearing. Above him, the windswept sky was patterned in pale blues and pinks. Ahead, a snow-covered field stretched for miles until it ended in another cluster of woods. He flexed his numb fingers and toes, trying to work more blood into his extremities. He grimaced as a spasm tightened the area underneath his rib cage.

He wondered if he should get it checked out. Chest pain was no joke. Then again, this was probably nothing. Just stress or an overreaction to yesterday's elevator situation.

In the meantime, he blew breath onto his gloved hands and stamped his feet. He'd welcome some warmth to his limbs, all right, but his emotions needed to stay frozen. Abe knew firsthand how dangerous feelings could be. They could cloud your judgment; they could make you think that you had any control at all over this life.

He thumped his chest once. Hard. A warning shot to his heart. *Do your job*, he wanted to say, *and nothing more*. Abe was a confirmed bachelor, he didn't get worked up about women *ever*, and he certainly wasn't going to start with Casey Tanner.

If there was a prickle of disagreement from deep within, Abe ignored it. He focused on the last few miles to his Jeep, the snow and ice as cold as he willed his insides to be.

* * *

The tortillas were burned to a crisp, and the green chili sauce was a mushy mess that Casey Tanner wouldn't feed to a dog. And yet here she was, about to serve up her Mexican casserole at the weekly Knots and Bolts recipe exchange.

She stared across the wide red table at the other women gathered in the cozy, eclectic space behind the local fabric store. Her sister, Audrey, was sipping a white prosecco that sparkled as brightly as the Christmas lights strung along the window behind her. If Audrey had been pretty before, she was stunning now, flush with a bone-deep contentment inspired by her love-filled marriage. Next to Audrey was Willa Olmstead, who ran the White Pine Bed and Breakfast with her husband, Burk. Her swollen feet were clad in reindeer slippers and propped up on a small ottoman. She was passing around pictures of her latest ultrasound. Her first baby, a girl, was due in just a few short weeks on December 30, and she was radiant with expectation.

Nearby in the small kitchenette was Betty Sondheim, who was humming "Jingle Bells" off-key. She had married the local Lutheran pastor, but this hadn't curbed her tendency to speak her mind freely—or swear. "Who took the damn oven mitts?" she hollered, her carol forgotten. "My cornbread is going to overcook if I don't get it out."

"Try the refrigerator," replied Stephanie Munson. "I think

I put them in there." The redheaded mom of twins was often scattered, but she also packed more into a single day than most of the other women accomplished in a week.

"If it gets toasty, we can crumble it up into my homemade flan," Anna Palowski said. Her desserts were often the highlight of the recipe exchanges—as were her stories about her daughter, Juniper, whose recent drum lessons were beating away Anna's sanity.

Casey swallowed, keenly aware she was the only single one in the group. Not to mention the worst cook. The women politely took bites of what she brought each week, but they never slid her leftovers into Tupperware containers the way they did Anna's or Betty's. Even Willa, who supposedly couldn't make a hot dish to save her life when she returned to White Pine after more than a decade, was making casseroles that had the whole group spearing the pan for seconds.

Casey sipped her merlot, frustrated that she wasn't better in the kitchen. It should be easy, really, considering it was following basic steps in order—something her rule-prone mind enjoyed. But somewhere along the line she always got tripped up, whether it was using the wrong kind of cheese (white cheddar and Swiss were decidedly not the same, as it turned out) or putting the hot dish on the wrong oven rack so it charred the first three layers. Her food was an embarrassment tonight next to Betty's golden cornbread and Willa's homemade refried beans and Audrey's fresh guacamole and Stephanie's *arroz con pollo*.

It wasn't just the food, though, that made her shift uncomfortably in the cozy room. It was how far she felt she had to go in order to fit in with these lovely, beautiful women. They were exceptional wives, great cooks, incredible moms, close friends. And Casey was…none of those things. She wouldn't even be here if she wasn't such a mess. It was pity, most likely, that had them inviting her into the group in the first place. She certainly didn't fool herself that it was because of her sunny personality or her bubbly charm. It was because of Audrey, no doubt.

Audrey had let these women into her heart ages ago, and had kept the fires of their friendships kindled no matter what. Casey felt a stab of envy at how easy it seemed for these ladies, how they pointed out food in each other's teeth and wore stretch pants and laughed so hard they cried—or even passed gas. Just one of those things would have Casey sprinting for the door, red-faced with mortification.

Or it would have had the old Casey sprinting, anyway. She thought about her cocoa with Ingrid and her determination to change. Yes, she was trying, but cripes, it felt like work sometimes. It made her muscles tired. Her bones. She looked around the room at the smiling, relaxed women and wondered why it was so hard for her to be like them.

Not that Casey wasn't grateful to the group. She *was*. She'd grown up quickly after her parents had died, taking responsibility for Audrey and working hard at getting ahead. It was just that somewhere along the line she'd lost track of what she was working for. She'd forgotten to value happiness, to value others. As a result, this group was the closest thing she'd ever had to a circle of friends, and she wasn't about to turn her back on such a gift. She just hoped it would get easier, and that one day she wouldn't feel like such a toad among princesses.

"Heard you had some excitement yesterday at your job," Betty said to her, ladling her plate with food as the dishes were passed around. Betty's curly blonde hair was aglow in the soft light.

"False alarm, as it turned out. Just low batteries in Robot Lit's carbon monoxide detector."

Casey silently gave herself props for following through earlier in the day on replacing the detector's batteries, and also buying two smoke alarms and a fire extinguisher.

"I meant the part where you got stuck in an elevator with a fireman," Betty said.

The other women around the table stilled.

"You didn't tell me that!" Audrey said, her brown eyes wide. "And you hate small spaces. Are you all right?"

"I'm fine. It was just an old elevator that stalled out." She eyed Betty. "How did you even know about that?"

"Sometimes I tune into the scanner. Sounded like you and the lieutenant were in there for a good long while."

"I—" Casey stalled, unsure what to say next. They'd been in there for what seemed like hours, even though it had probably only been twenty minutes or so. She could still feel the warmth of his hand around hers, the steady beat of his heart against her fingertips.

"The lieutenant is Abe Cameron, right? Stewart's older brother?" Audrey asked.

"The serious one," Willa said. "Stu was so easygoing and fun. I was on student council with him in high school. Abe would pick him up from school sometimes, and I remember Abe being like—one of the faces on Mount Rushmore or something. So stony and serious."

"The opposite of his parents," Betty said.

"What do you mean?" Casey asked.

"Julia and Pete Cameron were such free spirits. They both painted, and I always loved their work. Now they live up in the White Pine Retirement Village. I hear Pete's memory is going."

Casey blinked with surprise. She couldn't imagine Abe's parents being artists. Military sergeants, maybe. But not painters.

Until she remembered how warm and gentle Abe had been in the elevator. He'd been perfect, really, as she'd panicked in the cramped space. Until the light of day had shone on him again, and Casey figured she must have imagined the compassion he'd shown her.

Or had she? It was maddening to wonder what her addled brain had cooked up and what had been reality.

"What's that look?" Audrey asked, reading Casey all too well. "Did something happen in that elevator?"

Leave it to her sibling to cut to the chase.

"If it did, you're in the clear," Betty said. "Abe is single. At least that's what I hear."

"Abe is always single," Willa said.

"The parade of ladies through his life is impressive," Anna agreed. "Sam knows some of the guys down at the station and I guess he's got quite a reputation."

"Is that good or bad?" Casey asked.

"Very good while it lasts," Betty said with a wink, "since apparently he's quite...*gifted* in certain ways. But then bad when it's over."

"Didn't he go out with Maddie Fronting?" Audrey asked. "I was in a book club with her once, and I feel like she was always talking about this guy who turned her into a gymnast in bed. Twisted her up in all the best ways." She giggled. "That was Abe, right?"

"Probably," Stephanie said, nodding. "He might put all that stony focus to good work in the bedroom, but at the end of the day, he's an unreformed serial monogamist."

"A what?" Casey asked.

"Someone who dates one person seriously for a while. Then breaks up with them and dates someone else—wash, rinse, repeat."

"Did he ask you out?" Audrey asked Casey.

She shook her head. "No, nothing like that. In fact, just the reverse. Abe got me thinking that I should pursue the opposite of him. Someone lighter, more fun-loving."

"Like his brother?"

"Stu's a charmer," Betty said. "Works at that winter gear store, I think."

"I didn't mean Stu necessarily," Casey said. "Just someone with similar attributes. Someone playful. Lively." She bit her lip, unwilling to admit to her rule-bound past, which was why she was thinking about all of this to begin with.

Betty arched a brow. "You sound like you wrote out a whole list."

Casey stared at her untouched casserole. The truth was, she *had* made some mental notes. Okay, more than a few. She had come to White Pine determined to open her heart to others, and there was a tiny ember inside her that was ready to kindle romance, too. Though romance was too nice a word for what she really wanted, which was a tumble in the sack. She'd already begun thinking in earnest about a few ways she wanted to jettison her...inhibitions.

"Oh, you didn't!" Audrey laughed, staring at her. "You actually made a bullet-pointed list, didn't you!" Once again, leave it to Audrey to bare her secrets.

"Not exactly," she said. "I haven't put pen to paper. It's more like I'm thinking about what could be on it."

Willa chuckled. "A serious list to achieve a not-so-serious goal."

"It's not a list—I haven't written it down," Casey protested.

"It's in your head, though," Audrey said, grinning.

"We don't mean to poke fun," Stephanie said, perhaps catching the frown pulling at the corner of Casey's mouth. "We've just been around each other so long we've lost some of our verbal filters."

Another reminder that Casey was the outsider. She set down her fork, no longer hungry.

Audrey bumped her shoulder playfully. "Come on. You have to admit, it is kind of ironic. A serious list so you can have some fun?"

It wasn't serious, though. *It wasn't even a list.* More like it was a mortifying set of thoughts about wanting to get some. Casey knew she should probably be talking about finding Mr. Right, just like all these other women had. But the truth was, she didn't want that. After a lifetime of rule following, not to mention a serious relationship with an even unhappier ending, she wanted something she'd never had before, and it sounded an awful lot like hot sex, no strings attached. Forget a ring. She wanted a *fling*.

"I don't suppose there's any way you'd tell us what's on your li—that is, what you've been thinking about?" Willa asked.

Casey stared at the scorched lump of Mexican hot dish on everyone's plates. It was such a mess. *She* was such a mess.

I'm not like you, she imagined herself saying to the collective group. *You're all happily settled and I want to be un-settled for once.*

"It's okay," Audrey said, coming to Casey's rescue after a moment. "You don't have to share if you don't feel like it."

"The hell she doesn't," Betty said, her gaze sharp. "We share everything here. It's a judgment-free zone. What exactly do you think we won't understand, Casey?"

The degree to which I've screwed up my life.

The fact that I don't want what you all have.

"It's complicated," Casey hedged. "My parameters aren't exactly...wholesome."

Betty hooted. "Even better!"

Somehow, that wasn't helpful.

"Here's an idea," Willa said, patting her round belly. "Why don't we each say something we've done that's a little scandalous. It'll help Casey feel like she can share."

"Right!" Audrey said, brightening. "She hasn't been here long enough to know things like that. Like how you wanted to be fuck buddies with Burk for a while before you guys officially got together."

Willa's eyes widened. "Well. I didn't realize you were going to put it that way, but all right. Should I turn the tables and say how you dropped your panties for Kieran Callaghan in the middle of the day and got busy on a riverbank?"

Now it was Audrey's turn to blush. "I think you just did."

"Sam and I have secret identities," Anna said. "I'm Eva Vespertine and he's Rock Reynolds and we meet sometimes...and role-play."

"Rock Reynolds?" Betty asked. "Seriously?"

"Hey, judgment-free zone, remember? Besides, you have yet to share something scandalous about the good pastor."

Betty grinned. "Fine. I give him massages."

"That's hardly scandalous," Anna said, frowning. "That's called Tuesday night."

"I wasn't finished. I give Randall massages—but I don't use my hands."

"What do you use?" Willa asked, her green eyes glinting with amusement.

"Lots of other parts. Sometimes other...devices. But the rule is no hands."

Stephanie giggled. "Sounds like the opposite of mine. With the twins, Alan and I have had to figure out how to steal quick moments. I put my hands in Alan's pockets all the time, if you know what I mean. Just the other day, the kids asked if I was looking in Daddy's pockets for quarters again."

The group burst out laughing. Casey found herself more relaxed, grateful that these women were helping her feel at home, helping her feel like one of them.

"I appreciate the confessions," she said after a moment. "But I'm not—that is, you all are happily married, and my ideas don't reflect anything long-term."

"Who cares?" Betty asked. "You don't need to be married to have some fun."

"And besides, you never know what will *lead* to marriage," Audrey said.

Casey swallowed. Technically, she supposed anything could happen. But she wasn't pining for a forever mate. Maybe she had at one point, a long time ago. Before she knew better. "I guess that's true," she said, though she didn't actually believe it.

Audrey's brows lifted. "Of course it's true! You're beautiful. You're smart. You're a catch. You'll get married eventually, raise a family—the whole nine yards."

Except I don't want that, she thought. But she'd never say it. Especially not to Audrey.

When their parents had died, Casey had been saddled with the responsibility of raising her younger sister. It wasn't Audrey's fault any more than it had been Casey's, but the reality was that Casey didn't want kids or any additional responsibilities because she'd been there, done that. For a long time she figured she was simply a modern woman and she'd find a man who shared her sensibilities. They'd get married and be enough for each other.

But she just couldn't find a man who shared her thoughts on the matter.

Well, to be fair, it was hard for her to find a man, period. The one she had found for a time, Miles Watson, had broken up with her when he discovered she didn't want kids. "Don't do this again," he'd told her angrily. "Do your next partner a favor and tell him up-front that you don't want everything that comes with commitment."

The bitterness in Miles's words had stung with a fierce pain that took her breath away.

"Aren't I enough?" she asked him. "I thought it was okay, just being us."

After all, he'd told her he'd loved her. She'd met his parents. She'd thought his measured practicality was endearing, that it would mean he'd take care of her always. She'd never seen this cold glint in his eye, or this ferocious curl of his mouth.

"You lied to me," he said, shaking with anger. "It was never supposed to be just us." The way he'd scoffed and stormed away then had forced her to realize what an anomaly she was. Long-term relationships for most people ended in marriage and kids. One right alongside the other.

But not Casey.

Especially lately. If there was part of her that thought she could will herself to want kids, it was getting buried under a burning desire to do the complete opposite.

"We've shared our scandals," Betty said, tapping the red table. "Now it's time for yours, Casey."

"All right." She took a breath. "Here goes. I've been

thinking that if I could only get five presents under my tree this Christmas, what would I want?" The group leaned in. "Like, maybe I get kissed under the mistletoe."

Betty blinked. "That's it? Just kissed?

"Well, obviously it's a really, really good kiss."

"All this talk of scandal," Betty said, "and I thought you were going to give us something good."

"I thought that was good," Casey said, feeling a pinch of hurt.

"Why not spice it up?" Audrey asked. "It's starting in a good place. Why not end it in a good place?"

"Right!" Willa said, hand on her belly. "Like, what if you want to start out kissing under the mistletoe but finish with hot sex in bed?"

Casey giggled. "I was leaving sex for later on the list. But I guess we could move it to number one?"

"Or," Anna said, "what if you make number two about a very specific kind of sex that you want?"

"Good sex?" Casey asked. Miles had been so practical inside the bedroom and out, she'd barely even had that much. Not that she was about to open her mouth and admit it.

"How about role-playing during sex?" Anna asked, winking.

"Thanks, Eva Vespertine, but let's let Casey decide what kind of sexy times she wants," Audrey said.

A flush crept up Casey's neck. Did she even have an answer?

"I guess I wouldn't mind if it was a little…naughty."

"Like with whips?" Stephanie asked.

"No beatings," Casey said firmly. "But funky positions? Handcuffs?" The thought gave her a thrill. Neither of those things would be so bad.

"Let's just leave it at naughty," Audrey said, "and you can decide what fits the definition."

"What else?" Betty asked. Her eyes were glinting with something like delight.

"I was thinking it wouldn't be so bad to have sex on Christmas Day. I mean, since it's a holiday list and all." Plus Christmas was her favorite holiday since everything became beautiful and bright. Plain storefronts were suddenly bedazzled with lights. Normal cardboard boxes transformed when wrapped with extraordinary paper and ribbons. Even a plain girl like Casey felt special on Christmas, felt like the world was full of possibilities. Wouldn't it be amazing to experience that in bed, too?

"How about *lots* of sex on Christmas Day?" Anna offered.

Casey laughed. "Well, I wouldn't say no to it. I'd also like a bunch of orgasms." She left out the part about how she never really had that many during sex before.

"An orgasm for each of the twelve days of Christmas, then," Willa said.

Twelve orgasms. The thought was overwhelming. And wonderful. "Done."

"Which leaves just one more thing on your list," Betty said.

"All good girls and boys on Christmas get toys," Casey said carefully, "and maybe I could get a toy, too. A *special* toy for the bedroom."

"Oooh," Stephanie said, "Alan likes those plugs that—"

"Maybe we just leave it at toys," Betty interrupted, "and let Casey think about what kind would make her happiest?"

"Can we write it down *now*?" Audrey asked. "Make it official?"

Casey nodded. Anna poured more wine. And in the end, Casey's list was this:

All I want for Christmas...

Five ways I want my tree lit this holiday.

1. I want to start out being kissed under the mistletoe, but I want to finish with sex in bed.
2. I want to be naughty, not nice, between the sheets.
3. I want 12 orgasms from sex—one for each of the 12 days of Christmas.
4. I want my stocking stuffed, repeatedly, on Christmas Day.
5. I want toys wrapped with bows—that are all for adults.

"Well, no one can say it's not bold," Anna said, applauding. "I hope you find someone who can deliver your, ah, packages."

"Let's hope it's a big package," Betty said.

"You know," Willa said slowly, "I might know who could help you with your list."

"Abe Cameron certainly comes to mind," Betty said.

"No, *not* him," Casey said. "The opposite of him, remember?"

"I was thinking of that bartender guy," Willa said, looking at Audrey. "The one who thought Audrey was the hottest thing in White Pine until Kieran showed up and dashed his hopes."

"You mean Dave Englund?"

Willa nodded. "The very same. He works at the Wheelhouse and makes asparagus beer every year. Audrey here probably would have gotten in his pants if Kieran hadn't been around."

"Willa!"

"Well, it's true."

"We could go there," Anna said. "Check him out and see if he's still single."

"I'm afraid I'm not going to the bar anytime soon," Willa said, shifting her pregnant belly in her chair, "but I fully support this mission."

"There's no mission," Casey said, feeling embarrassed at all the attention. "It's just a list." She thought about the twelve orgasms and realized it was an ambitious one at that. She couldn't actually find someone who'd fulfill it—could she?

"But you and I could hit the Wheelhouse this Saturday," Audrey said with a playful smile.

Casey briefly thought about protesting, but it was useless. At this point she probably wouldn't refuse her sister anything. Not even an adventure at the Wheelhouse. Casey found herself nodding.

"All right. Fine. We'll go to the Wheelhouse on Saturday."

"Keep Audrey away from that asparagus beer," Willa said pointedly.

"They don't even offer it in December. You can only get it in May. And I only drank too much the *one* time."

"And lucky for all of us, you were vying for Asparagus Queen the next day. We all got to see your hungover pageantry onstage." The women laughed together, and Casey smiled along, even as her shame surged. The day of the pageant, she'd still been trying to manipulate Audrey's life, trying to control where her sister worked and trying to wrench her away from Kieran. It was only when her sister's life was in danger later that night—when she feared her sister might be hurt, even dead—that she vowed to change if given another chance.

Her list was proof she was trying.

Her casserole sat nearly untouched as they cleared plates, then passed around Anna's flan dessert. Casey set her jaw, determined to do better next week. Cooking shouldn't be that hard. It was simply a set of things to accomplish—same as the five things she wanted on her list.

She was lucky to have the opportunity to try any of this. She glanced at the women around her, grateful for their friendship.

They'd taken a chance on her when they barely knew her. Now they knew her better and didn't seem to be recoiling. They were even helping her get her recipes—and maybe even her life—right.

And she'd take every opportunity she could get.

CHAPTER THREE

Abe Cameron looked up at the steely gray clouds overhead. The snow was falling in wet, heavy flakes that seemed to get thicker by the minute. Not that the kids around him seemed to mind. Station One's fire engine was on display in the White Pine Elementary parking lot, and the school's third-grade class was racing around it, marveling as if it were Santa's sleigh.

They tore from the front of the engine to the back, clambered into the open doors, and ogled everything from the oxygen tanks to the hose that was rolled at the front of the truck, near the headlights.

"It's called a front-bumper load," Abe explained to them, "and the hose comes out easier this way. When there's bad weather, we don't have to climb on top of the truck to roll the hose."

He left out the part about it being easier on his back, which always seemed to twinge uncomfortably these days.

And his chest, which had been bothering him since it started aching yesterday.

He debated walking away to call his doctor, but just then, for the hundredth time that day, a pair of small hands pulled on his jacket. "How long have you been a firefighter?" a skinny, spindly kid asked him, eyes full of admiration.

"Long enough to forget I ever did anything else," Abe answered.

The kid grinned up at him, and Abe felt a pang deep down, unrelated to anything happening behind his sternum. *I'm pushing forty and have nothing to show for it*, he thought. *No family, no kids.* He flexed his jaw, thinking of the towheaded toddler who'd been in the station the other day. Reggie had been all of three years old, accompanying his dad, Lambeck, who held the rank of firefighter one. His chubby hands had grasped his dad's helmet, and his sky blue eyes had been round with awe. Abe had watched until the sight of it gnawed at him and he'd pretended to have something else to do.

Lambeck was a good teammate. A hard worker. His commitment to his job didn't get screwed up just because he loved his wife and had a kid. Abe wondered what the hell was wrong with him that his brain was so addled. He'd always liked kids. Some far-off, distant part of him could remember wanting a family. Maybe back when he was a probationary officer getting his underwear stuffed into the microwave by the other guys, and crawling into bed to find his sheets were shorter than they should be.

He gritted his teeth, thinking of the dark calls where he'd seen things he wished he hadn't, like missing body parts and hurt kids and trapped victims. Every year on the job meant a closer view of the worst show in life—the one demonstrating how easily things could get taken away, and how tenuous things were. Even things you cared about.

A picture of his dad flashed through his mind, and he grimaced. Sometimes things could get taken away when there was no emergency at all.

"Hey, Mister Fireman?"

Shit. The kid was still there. Abe strained to stay focused.

"Yeah, buddy?"

"Do you like your job?"

"I do," Abe answered. "It's awesome." The response wasn't bullshit. He loved the organization of the firehouse, from the fire chief all the way down to the fresh-faced probationary firefighters. He loved the order of it, how everyone had a specific task, and how, when it was working right, everyone did their part to make things safer and help people in trouble.

Not that every call was dramatic. Viola Stroud's medical alert tag went off at least once a week, and they'd respond only to find out the old woman was fine, she just wanted to talk. Abe and his crew would make her a sandwich, feed the cat, chat about the weather, and be on their way again. And Hayes Ulfsson contacted them at least once a month to help his prize bull. The damn thing was forever getting its head stuck in the Y of a split trunk at the edge of its field. Abe would tell Hayes the same thing, over and over—his team couldn't respond officially as a unit, but that Abe himself would be over as soon as his shift was done to give the old farmer a hand.

The only problem was, he was beginning to wonder what he was doing all of this *for*. Deep down, he was beginning to wonder if there was more to life than living on a numb periphery and never really getting invested. But what that deeper meaning was, exactly—or how he'd even find it—felt like something hiding behind a thick wall of smoke.

"All right, Lu?" Iris Quinn sidled up to him, studying Abe with a worried expression.

"Fine," he answered quickly. He lifted his chin at the clouds. "Just thinking about the weather. Roads are probably getting slick. I bet we'll be out in it soon."

Quinn blew her bangs off her forehead—a habit the rest of the crew was always teasing her about. Her nickname around the station was Puffy.

"Huh. I figured you were probably still thinking about how you got your lieutenant's ass stuck in that elevator this week." Quinn cackled while Abe just shook his head. He'd been the butt of endless jokes since he'd had to be rescued by his own crew. Which was fine with him. He doled out his fair share of wiseass remarks, and if he could dish it, then he needed to be able to take it.

The part that wasn't fine with him was how the picture of Casey Tanner's golden brown eyes and tumbling auburn hair seemed all but lodged in his mind. No matter how hard he tried, he couldn't wipe them away.

Not that he was about to tell his crew any of that.

"When it's your turn to be rescued, Quinn, I won't taunt you about it. I'll just quietly do my job and that'll be the end of it."

"Like hell you will."

"It'll be embarrassing enough that you'll be handcuffed to the bed."

"With *your mom*."

Abe grinned. He was about to fire back, but fat snow blinded him momentarily. He brushed the flakes away. They were almost in a whiteout.

"Reese around here?" He craned his neck, searching for the young firefighter who was always goofing off, always had to be told what to do ten times.

"Said he had to use the little boys' room."

The wind picked up, sending thick snow blowing sideways. They needed to pack things up with the weather turning so quickly.

"You go find Reese. I'll tell Mrs. Russell to get the kids herded out of here," Abe said.

"On it, Lu. I can get that hose rolled up, too."

"Thanks," he said, marveling—not for the first time—at Quinn's efficiency and capability, the stark opposite of Reese. If he was stuck in a tough situation, there was no one else he'd want by his side. That she was a woman didn't matter to him at all. He sometimes wondered if it mattered overall, though, and if that was why she worked twice as hard as every other firefighter at the station. He'd reprimand anyone he caught harassing her, but he also knew sexism and misogyny didn't have to be so overt. It could be as subtle as an eye roll or a joke the guys, and *only* the guys, shared together.

He had every intention of promoting Quinn to the rank of firefighter two, though. He smiled as he pulled a pigtailed girl out of the truck, thinking about the paperwork on his desk and how happy Quinn would be at the news when it was all filed and done.

He was just closing a side panel when the radio crackled to life.

"Unit sixteen, dispatch to County Road R and Edison Streets, to MVA with no injuries. Fluids leaking from the car—you're needed for a wash-down."

Abe grabbed the radio, already picturing the scene's

busted-up car and its brake fluid and gas spilling onto the road. He and his crew would get the hoses out and wash down the road to keep anything from bursting into flame. "Unit sixteen is clear," he said. "Show us en route."

"Okay. En route at two thirty-nine p.m."

"Load up," he barked at Quinn and Reese, who was finally back from wherever he'd wandered off to.

The third-graders were watching them wide-eyed from across the parking lot. Mrs. Russell waved her thanks, and Abe gave her a quick nod as he buckled himself into the driver's seat and turned on the sirens. His chest squeezed underneath his gear. *Fuck*, he thought. *Not good.*

The engine's red lights reflected on the dark, frigid water as he steered them across the Birch River. Snowflakes pelted the windshield as they wound their way out of town along the service road, past the White Pine Harley dealership and toward County Road R.

Abe readied himself for the scene, even though there were no injuries. That was a good thing, but it was still going to be miserable work, hosing down the road in the freezing cold snow.

Pain smoldered inside him. He climbed out of the fire truck, only to have to lean heavily on its side for a moment. *Is this how I'm going to die?* he wondered suddenly. *Am I going to have a heart attack in the blinding snow?*

"Lu?" Quinn asked. "Jesus, are you okay?"

His gut twisted. Was he okay? Life was short. That much he knew. There was a good chance he'd spent much of his trying to shoulder his way through each day instead of really living it. He'd let plenty of girls into his bed, but he'd never let them sit on his couch and watch his favorite old war movies like *Sands of Iwo Jima* and *Twelve O'Clock High*.

Not that they'd probably want to, but the point was that he hadn't offered.

He was great in an emergency. But in everyday life? Maybe not so much.

"I think I need to get to the hospital," he told Quinn.

She swore softly. "Don't move. I'm going to call for help."

He stayed put. A few yards ahead, through the slanting snow, he could see a car on its side in the snowy ditch. There were two figures standing alongside it.

He wanted to charge the scene and help make it right again, the same as he had a hundred times before. Everything inside was off, though. His heart. His gut. It felt like there was a tectonic shift taking place—as if his muscles were trading places with his bones, and everything was all jumbled up—and he wasn't sure he liked it very much.

He straightened. Maybe he should just ignore whatever was happening.

He was good at that.

But if time was running out, he wanted to do things differently.

The red lights of an approaching ambulance sliced through the blanketing white. When he blinked, the image of Casey Tanner was right there, smiling up at him like she had after they'd been pulled out of the stalled elevator. He shook his head, trying to clear his thoughts.

If he lived through this, he vowed he'd return to Robot Lit. He would see Casey again. He didn't even know if she was single, for crying out loud. For all he knew, she could be dating someone seriously, about to walk down the aisle.

On the other hand, she might be free and clear. And if that was the case—if he didn't die tonight, and there was something between them—it was time to do something about it. *Piss or get off the pot*, as his captain would say.

Abe waved off the white-sheeted gurney and told the EMTs to keep their panties on. He pulled himself into the ambulance by his own accord, determined to live long enough to figure all this out.

* * *

"You're an idiot," the doctor said three hours later, glaring at Abe. "Chest pains for two days, and you don't come in?"

Abe shifted in his paper gown. The air in the clinic was freezing. His balls were shrinking by the minute. "I think HIPAA rules prohibit you from calling me names."

Dr. Nazid leveled a gaze at him. "If the shoe fits."

"I take it this means I'm not going to die?"

"No," the doctor answered, scribbling notes on a sheet of paper, "you have acid reflux. Your stomach acid is getting into your esophagus and irritating it. It's inflamed, and that's giving you your chest pains."

Abe exhaled slowly. His muscles went slack. The idea that he was consoled by the news should have been ridiculous. His life was never at risk, not technically. But he'd *felt* like it had been. For a second there, he thought he'd been standing on the threshold of death, and this news felt like a second chance. A ridiculous one, sure. But the feeling didn't ebb just because Dr. Nazid was writing him a prescription for a daily pill.

I'm going to live, he thought. *I'm a fucking dipshit, but I'm going to live.*

He pulled at the edge of his paper gown. His emotions felt crude and rough—and there were more of them than he was used to. Damned if he wasn't getting worked up about all this. But he didn't stop their flow like he normally would. He uncorked them and sat on the edge of the exam room table, trying to make heads or tails of the turbulent sensations.

Casey Tanner. A raw determination to see her flared in his every muscle. He glanced at his watch, wondering if it was too late to go find her. To ask her out.

Except it was going on ten o'clock, and he had no idea where she lived.

Tomorrow, though. He had the day off. He would find her then. At Robot Lit.

"You okay?" Dr. Nazid asked, ripping a prescription off his pad and handing it to Abe.

Abe straightened. "Believe it or not, I think I am."

CHAPTER FOUR

Casey trotted down Main Street, past cheery wreaths and evergreen roping along light posts, while carols played from speakers outside shop windows. She clutched her shopping bag, trying to enjoy the fact that it was Christmas and lights were twinkling and snowflakes were falling, but frustration weighted her. She'd just spent her lunch hour rushing from store to store, trying to find the perfect holiday gift for Audrey, but all she'd managed to secure was an eggnog-scented candle.

It was worse than lame. It was *terrible*.

Casey puffed up the street toward Robot Lit, feeling like she had no idea what to get her sister anymore. Audrey had everything—a great career, a wonderful husband, a happy home. What could she possibly need from Casey?

In the past, Casey had felt she always knew what to get her sibling. Maybe because she'd been fooling herself into thinking she always knew what Audrey needed. That she knew best. She grimaced. This year, she was lost.

She took a deep breath and told herself maybe this wasn't such a flop. It meant she was approaching things differently, and wasn't that a good thing? She needed to keep trying was all. She'd go online tonight and see if she couldn't find something on one of those cute crafter sites where everything was handmade.

She climbed the stairs to her Robot Lit office, grateful to be warm again, and decided the eggnog candle could go to this afternoon's white elephant party.

A white elephant was an entirely new concept for Casey, but she'd adored it from the second Ingrid explained it the week before. The idea of giving silly gifts to your co-workers in a game-like atmosphere had her laughing to herself as she hung up her coat and got to work wrapping the candle and a Chia Pet in the shape of Elmer Fudd.

Outside her office, she could hear the giggles of the Robot Lit kids. They were hanging out in the great room, the wide space with tables and couches and books where the tutoring took place. Robot Lit had invited whatever kids and volunteers were around that day to participate in the white elephant, making sure to bring extra gifts so everyone had a chance to go home with something.

Pulling a lid off a nearby box, Casey sifted through it, looking for the perfect bow for her Chia Pet and eggnog candle packages. There were hundreds to choose from, and this wasn't even half of it. Casey had been frugal all her life about most things, but when it came to holiday wrapping, she was excessive to a degree that might put the North Pole on notice. In her new home, she'd filled two closets with wrapping supplies, and she had another big plastic bin full of odds and ends she had yet to organize.

That very morning she'd brought in several of her supplies so her colleagues could help themselves to whatever they needed. It had become an impromptu wrapping station of sorts in the great room. Ingrid had asked whether they could keep the station going for a couple more weeks, so they could wrap thank-you gifts for the tutors and interns and even a couple packages for the neediest of their kids. Casey had happily agreed.

Exiting her office, she walked through the warehouse's high-ceilinged hallway toward the great room, where she joined Rolf. He was helping a nine-year-old girl with stick-straight brown hair put massive amounts of tape on a red-and-gold package.

"You guys are going to seal that up better than King Tut's tomb," Casey said.

"As I recall, the archaeologists got in pretty easily," Rolf replied, smiling as he pushed his stylish tortoiseshell glasses farther up his nose.

"There's a curse on everybody who dug up King Tut," the little girl said, covering the wrapping paper with more tape. "They all died."

"All of them?" Rolf asked.

The girl nodded. "Yep. They got snake bites and some of them drowned. One even fell off an elephant."

"That's not true." This was from a pale kid sitting nearby, around the same age. His cheekbones were sharp and his right hand was a claw around a pen—he looked to be scribbling intensely in a journal.

Rolf turned to the boy. "Carter, tell us what you know." He addressed him like an adult, an equal.

"Curses weren't found in King Tut's tomb. Not on the walls or anything, I mean. And most of the people who dug up King Tut lived a long time. One of them died right after, Lord Something or other, but it was because of an infected mosquito bite. Not a stupid curse."

"The curse isn't stupid," the girl shot back, "it's real."

Carter glared at her. His gray eyes were flinty with intensity.

"You know, you guys," Rolf said calmly, "I bet we have a book on King Tut around here somewhere. How about we find it and read it after the white elephant? We can see if the curse is true."

Carter shrugged. "Whatever."

The girl grinned. "Awesome."

Casey marveled at Rolf's easy way with the kids. He was the head of programming, but more often than not you could find him in the great room during their normal tutoring hours—two o'clock to six o'clock every day—just hanging out. Some kids came by for homework help, others came for workshops on storytelling and writing. Some, like Carter, just used the time to put down their thoughts and stories in a journal. The goal of Robot Lit was to foster reading and get kids excited about writing. "Stories change lives," was the motto in the organization's charter. And "Teaching machines to read," was the unofficial adage that the founders had developed years ago. They'd fostered the idea that reading and writing were so important that robots deserved the chance to do it, too, just like humans. So when kids walked in, it looked less like a tutoring center and more like a scientific workshop where the hardest job was to teach robots to read. Kids were easy by comparison.

To that end, there were drawings of robots everywhere,

as well as robot "parts" and robot manuals that the staff had written. The walls were painted bright colors with stencils of gears and lights and electronics. The whole point of the unofficial motto and the name was to ensure kids didn't feel like they were hanging out in an intimidating adult space where they didn't belong. Or someplace where they felt stupid because they needed tutoring, or help with homework. "Our work is serious, but that doesn't mean we have to be," Ingrid had said during one of Casey's interviews. The statement made Casey want to work there immediately. *This is just the place I need*, she thought, inwardly doing cartwheels when Ingrid had offered her the job a few days later. Casey had accepted on the spot. And even though she'd been here only a few weeks, she already felt like the nonprofit was home.

Now, with a table full of white elephant presents nearby, plus holiday music playing and a tippy jack pine in the corner draped with an odd assortment of tinsel and robot parts, Casey couldn't imagine being anywhere else at this exact moment.

"What's that grin about?" Ingrid asked, sliding into the chair next to her. She pulled the number-two pencil from behind her ear and gnawed on the tip—her habit since quitting smoking just a few months earlier. Casey smiled bigger, thinking of the package of pencils she'd gotten her boss, already wrapped and waiting in Casey's office.

"Just thinking about how great this place is. How lucky I am to be here."

The lines around Ingrid's eyes crinkled. She was older than Casey by at least a few years. Her daughter, Heidi, was a handful of a ten-year-old, but even so, there were often days when Ingrid's energy outpaced Casey's by half.

"That's quite a statement, considering you were trapped in our elevator earlier in the week."

"Will everyone please stop reminding me of that already? It's all you people want to talk about."

Ingrid grinned. "Well, you were in there with Abe Cameron, Robot Lit alumnus and supporter, and hunky White Pine firefighter."

Casey pushed away the memory of being close to him, of her frame fitting against his in the dark elevator. "You keep acting like you want there to be something between us. Look, he's a nice guy. Perfectly fine. But not for me."

"You can't possibly know that after a few minutes in an elevator, can you?"

It was more like she'd discovered it in the minutes before and after the elevator incident. In the elevator itself, Abe had been...wonderful, really.

"You saw the way he marched off when it was all over. He wants nothing to do with me. And, I'm sorry to say, I feel the same way about him."

"Because you know him so well after twenty minutes," Ingrid said dryly.

"Are you pushing him on me because he's a donor and you want me to get another gift from him?" she said, waggling her eyebrows.

Ingrid's eyes widened. "What? No. I just know what I saw between you guys the other day. It was a little bit magical."

Casey scoffed. "In that case, let's just say Abe is the Easter Bunny and I go for more of a Santa type."

Ingrid's pale blue eyes grew suddenly wide.

"What?" Casey asked. "What is it?"

Ingrid could barely swallow back laughter. "I think you'd better get out your basket and some Peeps, then," she said in a low, conspiratorial voice. "The Easter Bunny's here, and I think he's look ; for your candy."

Casey stared ast Ingrid, disbelieving, as Abe Cameron walked into the great room carrying a poinsettia in his massive hands. Instead of his fireman's uniform, he was wearing dark jeans and a dark wool coat that stood in stark contrast to his golden blond hair. Around his neck was a brick-red scarf she swore might be cashmere, and on it was a small American flag pin that glinted in the light. A lovely detail, actually.

His hazel eyes locked on hers immediately. Purposefully.

Casey was frozen in his stare. When she didn't move, Ingrid stood. "Hi, Abe. Good to see you out of uniform. I take it this means we don't have another carbon monoxide emergency?"

Abe's mouth twitched. "Not today. No elevator emergencies, either."

"Then you came to have *Goodnight Moon* read to you?"

This time Abe smiled fully. It was like someone flipped on stadium lights in Casey's insides. "I'm a *Cat in the Hat* man myself. Old-school all the way. I was actually wondering if I might have a word with Casey?"

"Sure, of course." Ingrid fixed her with a pointed look. "Why don't you guys go into my office? It'll be a little farther away from the white elephant madness that's about to start."

"Oh, I really can't," Casey replied. "I said I'd be here for the gift exchange, and the wrapping station needs manning...." She trailed off, knowing she sounded ridiculous.

"Rolf and I have it all under control," Ingrid said. She practically hauled Casey to her feet. "Go on. It's all good."

Casey could feel her palms sweating as she and Abe

walked toward Ingrid's corner office. Being this near him again brought back a rush of memories from the elevator. She glanced at his hands, wrapped around the base of the poinsettia, and recalled the warmth of his skin as he held her close.

"This is for you," Abe said, as if he'd caught her look. He handed her the poinsettia when they were in Ingrid's office. The flowers were bright crimson, and the pot was covered in shiny green foil wrapped with a plaid bow. "Don't eat the leaves, though. I hear they're poisonous."

Casey blinked. Had Abe Cameron just made a *joke*?

"That's too bad," she said, setting the plant on Ingrid's desk, "because I love the taste. Mom used to bake poinsettia bread on Christmas morning."

"My grandma had a recipe for poinsettia pudding. She spooned it past her dentures every year until it killed her."

Casey laughed—big and loud. The sound surprised her.

"It's too bad I couldn't get you to laugh like that in the elevator. We could have had a lot more fun."

Was it her imagination, or was there a playful glint in his eye? She felt a rush of excitement.

"You were amazing in that elevator. I would have freaked out without you."

"I feel badly. You wouldn't have even *been* in there if it wasn't for me." He stepped closer. Casey could see the gnarled bridge of his nose, mysterious and sexy at the same time. What had happened there? She noted that his coffee-colored lashes were thick like his hair.

"Is that why you came by with a potted plant? To tell me the elevator was all a big mistake?"

She asked the question teasingly, even though deep down there was part of her that didn't want Abe to say any such thing. In fact, she wanted him to say the opposite—that he'd been replaying their time together in the elevator over and over, same as Casey had.

"I don't make mistakes," Abe said. "I make calculations, and then I correct them when needed."

Was he joking again? "So you're saying you made a measured decision to go into the elevator and bring me along. Meaning the poinsettia is correcting for the fact that the elevator stalled and your crew had to get us out? Do I have that math about right?"

There was a flash of laughter in his hazel eyes. "You're a quick study."

Casey wanted to smile back, but the equation left her stomach churning. It was too close to her own way of thinking—calculating every decision instead of being more free spirited, letting her emotions have more of a say than her brain. She wanted to get away from all that. Even if Abe was joking, the conversation was a reminder that he was offering her more of everything she wanted to be rid of.

"Thanks for the plant, but I should get back," she said, glancing toward the open door. "To the white elephant."

"Wait." Abe's hand reached out and grasped her shoulder. She stilled under his touch. His eyes held hers with an intensity that froze her feet in place.

"They're lighting the town tree this Sunday night. Let's go together, and then I'll buy you a hot chocolate afterward."

Her insides flipped, though she worked to keep her emotions in check. Was he asking her out on a date? Almost reflexively, she opened her mouth to say no. It was a word she was used to in her former life. It would roll off her tongue easily, blocking out so many possibilities.

Abe Cameron was not the guy for her. She had her list,

after all, and there was no way he was going to be able to hit three of the things on it, never mind five.

"I'm not sure..."

The words faded when his hand did that thing again—palming its way from her shoulder, down her biceps, to her hand. Casey wanted to pull away, to tell him to stop, but she couldn't bring herself to shrug him off. In fact, when his fingers grasped hers again, she nearly sighed. It was as if part of her had been missing his touch since the elevator, and somehow this felt like home again.

It made her think that Abe Cameron might be able to hit more items on her list than she thought. What had the ladies at the Knots and Bolts exchange called him? A serial monogamist.

That was the kind of man her list needed, surely.

Except that was crazy.

Wasn't it?

"I—I'm sorry," she stammered, "I really can't."

Abe arched a dark blond brow. "Because you have other plans?"

She wanted to fire back—to tell him her reasons were none of his business and to leave it at that—except she couldn't form the words. She had no excuses. *None.*

Abe was a handsome man with a good job and a long history of getting into women's pants without getting committed. She could do a lot worse.

Then again, she *would* do a lot worse if the wrong man came into her life and brought out all the personality traits that she was trying to change in herself.

"I need to use the weekend to catch up on some work," she said. "It's the end of the fiscal year, and there's a mountain of financials to compile." At least it wasn't a lie.

Abe tilted his head at her. She noticed how perfectly shaped his ears were. The men she dated—okay, *man* if you wanted to count Miles, her one serious relationship—had oversized ears that stuck out at odd angles. Not Abe.

Not that they were dating.

Abe pulled out his wallet. It was rich leather worn smooth and creased with time. It looked friendly. Comfortable.

"How about I make an end-of-year gift, then," he said, pulling out three crisp twenty-dollar bills, "and then technically I'm part of your work. You can lump me in with your fiscal year tally."

Casey nearly smiled. *Nearly.*

"That hardly helps. You're just making more for me to do. Not that we're not grateful for your support. We are. But that's not going to get me out of the office any faster."

"Maybe because the office isn't the problem."

Casey stared at him. "That implies *I'm* the problem."

"To be fair, you *are* overthinking this. But if you insist, then lump me in with your work. Make a connection in your brain and call it good so we can go on a date already."

He grinned then with enough charm to have her smiling back. When had a man ever tried this hard with her? The answer was never.

Still, this was a terrible idea. Abe Cameron was handsome and tempting and all wrong.

She willed her mouth to form the word *no*. To remember how easy it was to utter that one, final syllable.

Oh, but her body wanted to say yes. An electric current hummed between them. Her insides quaked.

"I can't take your money," she said. "You'll have to use an official donation form and submit the gift through the proper channels."

Abe inched closer. Her heart pounded. "Say I do all that. Then will you come to the tree lighting with me?"

"I don't know," she said, hedging. "This whole outing sounds pretty chaste. Will you at least bring some peppermint schnapps to spice up that cocoa you mentioned?"

She wanted to clap her hands over her mouth. Had she actually just uttered those sentences?

"I'll do more than spice it up. I'm a fireman. I know how to handle heat." Abe's voice was coarse and thrilling.

Oh, she really had to get out of there. Talk of heat and spices wasn't helping anything. He put his money and wallet away, and she steeled her resolve, ready to go. That was when—with a small tug—he pulled her against him.

Just like in the elevator. Only now they were in Ingrid's office.

Her protests vanished. They were chest-to-chest again, and the delicious thrill of it had her blood pumping.

What was more, his wool coat was layered with his cinnamon scent. She inhaled, wanting to roll around in it. At this rate, forget five: She had a feeling she could write a list with fifty things on it and Abe Cameron would be able to fulfill them all.

Doubt needled her, though. He might be the right type of player, but was he the right type of person?

She thought of a million more excuses—*I have a meeting* or *There are presents to wrap* or *This probably isn't a good idea*—but they stayed far back in her throat. She didn't even dare ask what he was doing when his hands moved to her lower back, climbing upward. If she spoke, he might stop, and that would be the worst disappointment of all. His fingers raked deliciously over her neck, pausing as they cradled her face.

Now I will end this, she thought when his hands stilled.

Except Abe's skin on her skin felt warm and wonderful.

She suddenly wished she had on more makeup. Had done more with her hair. Had worn something more appealing.

But then again, when had she ever done those things?

Abe stared down at her, his rugged face uncannily handsome. His eyes were full of intensity.

"There's a parade before the tree lighting," he said. "We'll watch that, too."

He wasn't asking.

She should be irritated. Instead, it was electrifying.

"Will Santa be there?" she asked. "A parade without Saint Nick is a deal breaker for me."

"Oh, he'll be there. I'll make sure of it."

"You can do that?"

"I can get Rudolph and wise men and angels, too."

His thumb traced her cheekbone. She thought her skin might ignite. "Angels," she said, "how divine. I didn't realize you were so well connected."

"There's a lot about me you don't know."

"For the record, I was fine to keep it that way. You were the one who showed up to Robot Lit with a poinsettia."

A corner of his mouth lifted. Her insides jumped. "I had a life-altering event and came to see the light. I was like Saul on the road to Damascus."

She smiled. "Are you saying there was divine intervention so you'd ask me out? I didn't know the heavens cared so much."

"Make no mistake. The angels were very clear."

"More angels," she said, her heart pounding. "It really must be Christmastime."

"Every time a bell rings, an angel gets a kiss. Isn't that the expression?" His voice was gravel and silk.

"I don't hear any bells." Her voice was barely a whisper. Was it her imagination, or had his head moved closer? She felt her lips part, her head tilt.

"Wouldn't you know, I don't need any."

And with that, he brought his lips against hers in a smoldering kiss hotter than any fire she'd ever known.

* * *

Kissing Casey Tanner wasn't just good.

It was epic.

She kissed like a fucking cheetah—wild, hungry, and tireless. It was like she'd been caged for too long and she was finally being set free in the jungle again.

I guess that makes me the jungle, Abe thought as he tasted her lips, her tongue. He didn't mind being the jungle at all. Especially not when she twisted against him like that.

He hadn't expected this number cruncher with her hair pulled into a messy bun to be so unpredictably sexy. One minute she was wrapping gifts for a white elephant, and the next she had her hands in his hair and was pulling him toward her like she couldn't get enough.

Dear God. What a bonus.

He certainly hadn't planned it this way.

He'd figured he'd drop off the poinsettia (props to Quinn for telling him to bring it when he stopped by the firehouse before heading down) and ask Casey to the tree lighting, maybe catch a little bit of the holiday parade beforehand. One date. Barely even one, since the lighting would take mere seconds, and the cocoa afterward could be slugged down just as quickly if things were going poorly. He was ty-ing up loose ends, really, shoring up unruly emotions that he wasn't sure what to do with. The heart attack hadn't been real—and surely Casey Tanner wouldn't be real, either. Not in the way he wanted her to be.

But here he was kissing her in the middle of Robot Lit, where anyone at any moment could catch them.

It was unbelievable.

And hot as hell.

When was the last time a woman had surprised him? Hell, when was the last time *anyone* had surprised him, frankly?

The best part about it was that Abe was surprising him-self. He had started to ask himself what he wanted, and the answers weren't as terrifying as he'd thought.

He flicked his tongue over her lips and she moaned softly. Her flavor was beguiling, like honey and something richer. Vanilla, maybe.

He was rock hard. He pressed his erection against her so she knew, without a doubt, what she was doing to him. She hissed in breath. Then pulled him closer.

He was prepared to kick Ingrid's door closed and make out with her for hours when the distant beep sounded in his ears.

They broke apart reluctantly. Casey's lips were shining, her expression still one of hunger. She looked tousled. She looked *perfect*.

The beep kept sounding. He blinked and smelled smoke. And that was when it hit him. Logic broke through his lust-addled brain. It was a smoke detector in the building going off.

And something was already burning.

CHAPTER FIVE

When the smoke alarm sounded, Abe's eyes lost their hungry look so quickly that Casey wondered if she'd imagined their make-out session again—just like she'd perhaps imagined his gentleness in the elevator. But in its place was an urgent concern that was all too real.

"Follow me," he said over the noise. He grabbed her hand and pulled her out of the office. He didn't even pretend to walk. His long lope had her sprinting to keep up.

They tore into the tutoring room, where a handful of kids were pulling on coats and gathering backpacks. Rolf and Ingrid were attempting to herd them all toward the stairs.

Abe pushed past Rolf to yank open the door to the stairwell. When he disappeared momentarily, Casey's heart sank. Had he just left them?

But seconds later, he was back. "The stairwell is clear," he said, chest heaving, "I smell smoke from somewhere, though." He turned to Ingrid. "We need to get these kids out of here. Casey, call nine-one-one—now."

Casey couldn't help but be impressed by the way he took charge as she phoned in the alarm. Moments later, the group descended the stairs. "How fast can your feet go, kids?" Abe called to them. In the air was a whisper of gray smoke that made Casey's eyes water.

Half a minute later, they were all outside in the bright light of day. "Everyone accounted for?" Abe asked Ingrid. Chewing steadfastly on her pencil, Ingrid did a quick head count and nodded.

"All here."

Rolf had just started a snowball fight to distract the kids when they heard the sirens starting down Main Street. The fire station was barely two blocks away.

The benefits of living in a small town, Casey thought. She was about to say as much to Abe, but he was gone. She blinked, looking around, only to catch a glimpse of his dark wool jacket as he went back inside the building.

"What the—?" she muttered.

He might be a firefighter, but he didn't have gear or a hose or anyone with him. Casey glanced down Main Street, where a few of the town's shop owners gathered outside their stores, staring at the fire truck as it pulled in front of Robot Lit.

When the truck stopped, Casey recognized Quinn and Reese, two of the firefighters from earlier in the week. They raced past her to the building's front entrance, just as Abe reemerged. The kids had stopped their snowball fight to stare at the shining engine and the firefighters gathering together.

"It was a smudge of a fire in the basement," Abe said. "I hit it with a fire extinguisher."

Relief washed over her. The blaze was out.

"Go ahead and check to make sure it's clear. When you do, I want you to note everything." Something in Abe's voice made her tune in more closely. "The fire started in a pile of papers that weren't there when we made the call a few days ago. It looked like someone dumped a box."

"Dumped it and lit it?" Quinn asked, staring up at Abe from underneath her fireman's helmet.

"We don't know until we document and log everything. Just to be safe, secure the scene. And call Ty Brady. He should know about this."

"There was a fire extinguisher down there? There wasn't before," Reese said. For the first time, Casey realized just how young he was. He couldn't be that much over twenty.

"Good attention to detail," Abe said. "Robot Lit got a fire extinguisher recently and new smoke detectors. Without them, we wouldn't have gotten everyone out as quickly. And you'd be battling that blaze right now with hoses."

Pride washed over Casey. She'd grumbled about installing all of it the day after Abe had shown up at Robot Lit, but it might just have kept everyone safe.

"They worked fast on that," Reese said. She wasn't sure if he sounded impressed or bummed that he hadn't been able to fight a fire that day.

"They did," Abe agreed, catching her eye. Casey's cheeks heated, no matter that the rest of her was frozen from being out in the snow and cold without a coat.

"I think it might be a while before we can get back into the building," Ingrid said, sidling up to her. "You want to take the kids down to the Rolling Pin and call parents from there?"

"I'll go anywhere it's warm," Casey said, her teeth chattering.

They had just grabbed Rolf and started herding the kids down the sidewalk when Casey felt something heavy descend on her shoulders. She turned.

Abe was right there. And he'd draped his coat over her. His spicy smell was wonderfully close.

"Take it," he said. "You're freezing."

"I'm fine—the Rolling Pin is just up the street." The rest of the group was already moving on without her. She should shirk off Abe's coat and join them.

Except for the fact that she was already warmer, and part of her was thinking she didn't want to take his coat off—ever.

He leaned in, his arm snaking around her. She froze. Was he going to kiss her again? Out in public like this?

Instead, he reached into his coat pocket and pulled out his cell and wallet. "I can't trust you with my credit cards. You might rack up charges for Internet porn."

He was as stone-faced as ever. Even when a brittle wind whipped past them, he barely flinched. Casey burrowed deeper into his coat, feigning disinterest. "It's your phone I would want more. I could have texted all your contacts to tell them you were being treated for erectile dysfunction."

Abe stepped closer, towering above her. "We both know I don't have that problem," he growled into her ear. His breath was deliciously warm. Casey's knees weakened. Then, to her surprise, he nipped her lobe before pulling away.

Oh, he was good. Practiced. The thought made her muscles tighten.

"The inspector may need to contact you about the fire," he said, pressing buttons on his phone. "I'll need your digits to pass along."

"You sure it's not so you can text me what time you're going to pick me up for our chaste date on Sunday?"

She flipped her hair.

Since when did she flip her hair?

"Absolutely not," Abe said, holding up a hand solemnly. "I'm a professional."

"A professional fibber, maybe." She grinned.

"Digits please, miss. As an public servant of Dane County, I can tell you it's obstruction if you don't provide them."

Casey laughed. "Then you may have to handcuff me and take me away."

At the word *handcuff*, something dangerous and wild flashed across Abe's face. It was a look that had desire surging just under her skin. She thought of the five things on her Christmas list and how she was decidedly ready for something more adventurous.

She was beginning to believe Abe could certainly check them off. The Knots and Bolts crew had seemed to indicate he was capable. And if what they said was true, then he wouldn't want any kind of long-term commitment, never mind a ring or a family.

Which meant Abe Cameron was suddenly a very good candidate for her five things. If only he was a little more easygoing. A little more fun. Someone who wouldn't have her tripping over her old ways.

This man is the opposite of what you need, an inner voice reminded her. *In every possible way.*

Except he didn't feel that way. Not right now, anyway, with his ruggedly handsome face staring down at her and the feel of his breath still lingering on her skin.

"Phone number." He spoke the words firmly.

She gave it to him. When he slid the phone back into his pocket, he rewarded her with the tiniest of smiles. "See you Sunday."

"See you then," she said, and headed off to the Rolling Pin with Abe's heavy coat pulled around her body.

She couldn't be sure, but she thought she could feel his eyes on her back long after she'd started walking away.

CHAPTER SIX

That Saturday afternoon, Audrey was huffing with exasperation as she helped Casey haul a four-foot concolor fir tree into her home.

"Can I please just call Kieran? He can be here in two minutes and he'll have the thing up in three."

"We're almost there," Casey replied, lifting the trunk higher. Sap smeared against her jacket. "Just up the steps and into the house."

"That's the hardest part," Audrey grumbled. "You didn't even shovel your sidewalk."

"I know, I know. I'm used to living in an apartment."

"All this snow just makes everything worse."

"Think of it like a workout," Casey said. "Like this is one of those circuit-training things you make all your clients do."

"If this were actually a workout, I'd be out of a job within a week."

Nevertheless, Audrey lifted her end with grace and

strength, and they started up the steps. Across the bundled boughs, Casey watched her sister, feeling a surge of pride. Audrey had started a small personal training business in White Pine, and it was booming. She'd been a gym teacher and coach for years at the high school, so parents and teachers and community members already knew her and were excited to work with her. She did all this on top of working with Kieran at the Harley dealership, where they'd changed the whole culture of the place to be more welcoming to women, and they'd watched profits burgeon as a result. Business was good for her sister, and Casey couldn't be happier. She just wished Audrey would ease up on the complaining a little.

"You always make me do stuff I don't want to," her sister said, fumbling with the front door.

Casey bit back laughter. It was as if Audrey was eight and she was eleven, and she was forcing her little sister to sit still while she brushed Audrey's hair or demanded she be the student while Casey played teacher and "graded her homework."

Her sister had put up with so much. And had loved Casey anyway.

They maneuvered the tree into the living room and propped it up in the corner. "I can do the rest," Casey said, shrugging out of her jacket. "You sit down and I'll make you some spiced cider."

"God, *finally*," Audrey said with mock drama. She pulled out one of the white stools around the island in the kitchen and collapsed into it. "I may need sustenance as well. In the form of sugar cookies, if you've got them."

Casey grabbed the nearby Santa tin. She pulled off the lid to reveal rows of trees, stars, ornaments, and snowmen, all covered with frosting and sprinkles. She'd made extra the weekend before when she couldn't decorate, since the boxes with all her holiday trimmings were still missing.

Audrey grabbed a snowman and bit off the head. She tucked her glossy auburn hair—*so much thicker and lovelier than mine*, Casey thought—behind an ear and looked around. "The place is really coming together. I love the paint color you chose in here."

"Apple Blossom," Casey said, recalling all too easily the cans she'd hauled up the steps and onto a tarp so she could paint what were formerly beige-colored walls. In her previous life, she would have left the beige. So many things about her used to be beige, after all. Her clothes. Her car. For years, she'd allowed that to be fine. But the truth was, there was a deep-set part of her that loved bright colors. That loved sparkle, even. She'd just buried it under years of practicality because, growing up, when you're living on a shoestring and trying to raise your little sister by yourself, you take what you get, not what you want.

But then there was the night of the asparagus festival, when Casey realized that all that practicality had done more than define her—it had turned her into someone she didn't want to be.

Within a week, she'd given notice at her job. Within two weeks, she'd bought her first pair of shoes that weren't brown or black. They were purple. And the heel was taller than an inch.

Casey heated the cider and pulled out two mugs. They were each a dull muddy color. She'd purchased them years ago. *I should replace these, too*, she thought. The idea excited her and exasperated her all at once. She was trying to change so she'd never repeat the mistakes of her past, and she'd come so far. But staring at the mugs made her realize how far there was to go.

When will I know when I'm there? She wondered.

"Hey. Are you listening?" Audrey asked.

"What? Sorry." Casey's head jerked up. "What'd I miss?"

Audrey broke off another snowman's head. "I was asking what time you want to hit the Wheelhouse tonight."

Right. The bar. "I'm supposed to say hi to...what's the guy's name?"

"Dave Englund. He was in my class. All through junior high and high school."

Casey wondered what he looked like. She tried to picture him, but the only image in her mind was of Abe Cameron.

She still hadn't told her sister about kissing the firefighter. Frankly, she wasn't sure how to tell her.

"You're introducing me to a *younger man*," Casey said instead.

"Three years. It'll cause a scandal in town, no doubt."

"They'll brand me with a letter C. For 'cougar.'"

Audrey laughed, a rich, lovely sound that filled up the kitchen. Casey smiled. For years, she had treated her sister like a project, something to be managed. Now she wanted to kick herself for missing out on so much. *Like just hanging out*, she thought. No agenda. No strategy.

Just two sisters.

"What will you wear now that you're a cougar?"

"Something skin tight, no doubt," Casey said. "My heels should be at least three inches tall."

"Chandelier earrings," Audrey said, nodding. "And fake nails."

"Nails so long I can't even use my phone."

"You'll have to ask Dave Englund to text for you."

Casey mimicked batting eyes at the bartender. "Er, Dave, I hate to ask you this, but can you text my sister for me and tell her I'm having a terrible time and she should come rescue me?"

The two women laughed together. Just outside the kitchen window, neighborhood kids ran past with sleds in tow, headed for a nearby hill. The smell of freshly cut pine from the new tree enveloped them. Casey wanted to hit the pause button in her head and let this happy moment stretch forever. This was what she'd been missing in her life before. This was what she'd been working so hard to achieve.

She just hoped she could keep experiencing these blips of happiness. Deep down, she was secretly terrified by the idea that she'd mess up again and Audrey wouldn't want anything to do with her. Of course, Audrey had promised her that wasn't the case. "Forgiveness isn't something you ladle out once and then it's over," Audrey had said the first time they'd walked into the Knots and Bolts recipe exchange together. "It's a renewable resource." She'd winked at Casey. "Besides, you might need to forgive *me* for something soon. Like making you join this club."

Casey had felt small and out of place during that first Knots and Bolts meeting. She still felt that way these days, but not as much. It was a small price to pay, though. You did things that were uncomfortable when you tried to change. If it was easy, then you weren't changing.

Right?

The cider heating on the stove interrupted her thoughts. Casey focused on pouring it into their mugs. The rich, spicy smell steamed all around them.

"Oh, man," Audrey said, wrapping both hands around the ceramic, "this is such a treat. A freshly cut tree and cider and cookies on a snowy day. It reminds me of when we were kids and you'd string popcorn together because we never had any tinsel. We wound up eating more of it than we hung."

"I'm surprised we didn't get sick," she said, recalling the scrawny pine tree she'd cut down behind the high school one year. Aunt Lodi, the girls' caregiver after their parents had died, never seemed to have time to get a tree between shifts at the nursing home and long stints at the bar. So Casey had picked one out herself in the middle of a snowy, windswept field. She'd found a rusty saw in the garage and brought it with her, though she probably could have used scissors on the trunk, the tree was so anemic. But she and Audrey had hauled it home anyway and stuck it in an old coffee can. It had started to list while they'd decorated it with popcorn and paper ornaments they'd made. Together, they'd managed to keep it from toppling over completely.

When Aunt Lodi had finally come home that night, the girls expected her to be irritated. She usually was. But instead she'd actually smiled, and then had gone to the basement to retrieve a moldy-smelling cardboard box rattling with ancient ornaments. Together, the three of them had hung as many as the little tree would bear.

In the end, the scrawny thing had been transformed, just like so many other things on Christmas. Right then, Casey realized that included herself and Audrey and Aunt Lodi as they sat there and stared at the skinny branches and mangy needles. For a moment, they were a normal family appreciating the season with a beautiful tree in their home. Casey's heart wasn't bottomless with bone-deep grief over the loss of her parents, and Audrey wasn't crying herself to sleep every night, and Aunt Lodi wasn't lying to them about having extra shifts at the nursing home, when they all knew she was headed to the bar. Christmas was magical that way. For a little while, even just a few minutes, the dazzle and twinkle of it covered everything else, and the whole world was aglow.

"You were a good big sister," Audrey said, as if the exact same memory were flashing through her own mind. "You still are."

Casey took a breath. She didn't know about that. The reality of their holiday was that they were just poor kids with some cheap popcorn, a listing tree, and, in Casey's mind, too much of feeling like everything was up to her. That everything depended on her. Tears pricked her eyes. "Sometimes I don't feel that way."

"Then sometimes you're ridiculous."

Casey laughed in spite of the overwhelming emotions. She had done her best. It was flawed, but her sister loved her anyway. And always would. Christmas would always have *some* magic to it, even if everything didn't remain glittering and perfect forever.

"You want to hear something even more ridiculous?" Casey asked.

"Always."

She took a deep breath. She had to share her news with her sister. She had to tell *someone*. "Abe Cameron kissed me. And I kissed him back."

Audrey's molasses-colored eyes grew wide. "Are you serious? When did this happen? We've been together for hours. This should have been the *first thing* you said to me today."

Audrey reached across the counter and smacked Casey's arm in mock fury.

"I can't believe I'm not getting more credit here. I almost didn't tell you at all."

"What? Why?"

Because of the list. Because I'm not sure he's right for me. Because I don't want to mess things up again.

"Because you have Kieran," she opted instead. "You two are so happy and you have it all figured out. I'm just—well, I'm not there." It was a partial truth, anyway.

Audrey sat back. "Are you forgetting the part where Kieran was a total jerk and I could barely stand him? He nearly fired me from my job. And I was so bullheaded, thinking he was the exact same guy he'd been when we first met. I was determined to believe he'd never change."

She knew Kieran and Audrey's road to being together hadn't been easy. But it was still hard for her to believe that her sister could empathize with Casey's current situation.

"You got there in the end, though. Being together, finding love."

Something out of reach for Casey because she knew that most men who wanted love and marriage wanted kids, too.

Audrey's eyes sparkled with deep happiness. "We did. And so will you."

Casey shook her head. "I doubt it. And even if I did, it wouldn't be with Abe Cameron. Though he wants to take me out on Sunday."

"A date? Casey! How are you telling me all this now?" Casey got another arm smack.

"It's complicated."

Audrey leaned forward. "Why?"

He's all wrong for me. But I still want to bang him. "He's just not my type," she said instead.

"But?"

"There are no buts."

"Abe Cameron has a butt," Audrey said, smiling. "I've seen it. It's not half bad. So, technically, there *are* butts."

Casey almost spit out her spiced cider. "I'm not talking about those butts. Or about his butt. I just mean…"

She fumbled for the words. Deep down, she was fearful of getting involved with someone all over again, believing that they had a future together, only to find out that she wasn't enough on her own. That she was part of a bigger package that involved responsibilities she'd already shouldered. Plus, being with the wrong man might bring out her type A tendencies, and she'd turn into a controlling freak all over again.

"Ideally I'd want to check things off the list with someone who's less uptight. Who can help me loosen up a little."

"You don't think that Abe might loosen up in the bedroom?"

Casey thought about Abe's sculpted firefighter's body, the way he'd held her face in his hands as he'd pressed into her at Robot Lit.

"I don't know. There's a lot to him, that's for sure."

Audrey stared at her over the top of her mug. "Care to elaborate?"

"I'm saying that he's very…thickheaded."

Audrey squealed and nearly fell off her stool. "Oh my God, I thought he just kissed you! Are you telling me you *saw* it?"

"No. I just kind of felt it. Through his jeans. And my jeans."

"But there was a lot there?"

She shivered at the memory. "Yes. Plenty."

Audrey squealed again. "Maybe that should be how you decide."

"Decide what?"

"Who gets to tackle your list. Between Abe and Dave Englund, you just pick whoever has the biggest—"

"Audrey! Stop!"

This time Audrey laughed so hard she *did* fall off the barstool. Only Casey couldn't help her because she was too busy holding on to the counter and trying not to topple over herself.

CHAPTER SEVEN

$\mathcal{A}$be sloshed his beer as he got to his feet, but it hardly mattered. He whooped as the Minnesota Wild took the ice. Next to him, Stu hollered and stomped.

"The Red Wings suck," he said.

"The Red Wings definitely suck," Abe agreed as the Detroit team skated out to more jeers than applause. Abe smiled. He loved that about hockey. It was raw and surly and just the right amount of bloody.

The brothers took their seats again when the first period officially started. They clinked plastic beer cups and toasted a Wild victory.

Abe settled in, his eyes on the goalie. It was the position he'd played in high school, well enough so that he'd gotten a scholarship to the University of Minnesota Duluth. His freshman year, a puck had come flying at him during a practice, cracking his nose in a few places and breaking it. At the time he'd laughed it off—he counted it as a kind of a badge of honor. These days, though, he sometimes wished for his old, straight nose. It might help him feel like less of a hulking gargoyle next to, say, certain brunettes who worked at Robot Lit.

Not that the ladies seemed to mind his appearance overall. Especially when he was such a good listener, using his seriousness as the sounding board against which they could bare everything. Especially when it led to the bedroom. That was where he could really shine, exploring and fine-tuning until he knew just where to press and lick and thrust. He might not be particularly outgoing or conventionally handsome, but he'd learned how to be masterful where it counted—and that had kept him exceptionally occupied.

It was a comforting thought. There had never been a shortage of women for him and there wouldn't be in the future—not unless he wanted there to be.

And he didn't.

Not exactly.

Sure, thinking about his date with Casey on Sunday—*tomorrow*—gave him an unexpected sear of excitement. And, fine, he hadn't really been able to stop picturing her since they'd made out last week. Her soft moans, her hands in his hair, and her jeans pressed against his had made it one of his hottest make-out sessions ever.

But there was always another make-out session to be had, he reminded himself. Especially if it went south with Casey.

Never mind that he respected the hell out of the way she hadn't panicked at the Robot Lit fire alarm. She'd helped get the kids out of the building and to safety. Plus she'd already installed smoke detectors and fire extinguishers in the basement. Without both, the blaze could have been something else entirely. Something else much worse.

He rubbed his hand over the stubble on his chin, wondering if that had been the intent. The fire had just begun to blaze when he'd gotten to it. The smoke was thick, but not too hot. The blaze was conveniently located next to an old, dry wood post. It would have ignited easily if he hadn't gotten there. He hadn't smelled accelerant, but the pile of papers hadn't needed it. Not technically. A single match could get it going.

And yet, the whole thing was odd. Why burn a pile of paper if you were going to start a fire? It was hardly efficient. He had tried puzzling it out, but in the end that wasn't his role. Ty Brady would shake out all the details—eventually. He had only just begun his assessment.

Abe ground his teeth. If someone had tried to harm Robot Lit, he wanted Ty to find them, and he wanted them prosecuted to the fullest extent of the law.

"Clipping!" Stu shouted, jumping to his feet.

Abe blinked, realizing he'd been lost in thought and had missed much of the first period. The ref was sending one of the Red Wings players to the penalty box.

"See you in two minutes, meathead!" Stu yelled.

"Damn straight," he said, trying to catch up.

Stu took his seat again. "Detroit plays dirty."

As far as Abe could tell, each team had the same number of penalties so far. He didn't argue, though. "How's Arnie's?" he asked instead.

His brother worked at Arnie's Ski and Snow in the winter, and at the Birch River canoe livery in the summer.

"Same," Stu said.

"You still working the register?"

"Yep."

Abe's jaw clenched. Sometimes, getting Stu to talk about

anything besides hockey and video games was a herculean challenge.

"Any chance you'll get into management this year? Maybe sales?"

Stu turned away from the game to focus on Abe. This close, Abe could see so much of his parents in his little brother. He had their mom's smile, big and wide. He had their dad's eyes, dark green and curious. And he had a mix of their hair color—a honey shade that was darker than Abe's blond, but not quite brown.

"Is this the part where you quiz me on my lifestyle choices?" Stu asked.

Apparently, his brother also got his parents' artistic temperament. Or at least the part that didn't want a regular day job.

"I don't want to lecture," Abe answered honestly. "I just hate to see you pissing your talent away at that ski shop. And at the canoe livery."

"I like both gigs."

"You liked delivering pizzas."

"What wasn't to love? Driving around. Meeting people. Free 'za at the end of the night."

"You can do better."

Stu crossed his arms. He was leaner than Abe, his limbs longer. "I don't know if I want to do better. I'm pretty happy."

Abe studied his younger brother, wondering how happiness could come to Stu so easily. It didn't much matter what Stu did, he always seemed content. How was it that Abe had become the opposite, kicking against his own peace of mind for years?

He could almost feel the phantom pains in his chest.

He debated telling Stu about them—about how it had been enough to make him ask Casey Tanner out on a date—but in the end he just swallowed more beer instead.

"Mom was asking about you, by the way," Stu said. "When I saw her last week she showed me a new painting she did."

"What's it like?"

"It's a Sasquatch with its head up its ass. She titled it *Stu's Older Brother*."

"Very funny."

"It's actually a rugged landscape. Lots of sharp rocks. You'll like it. And I'm glad she's making time to paint."

Abe nodded. It was part of the reason he helped pay for his parents' rent at the White Pine Retirement Village. It meant they could have freedom and independence, which they liked, but support, too. Just in case they needed help getting groceries, for example, or if his dad left and forgot where he was going—which happened more and more these days as his dementia worsened.

The upside was that he was able to support his parents in a tangible way that felt good. The downside was that it put his Freiburg plans on hold for . . . well, a long time, anyway. Abe had wanted to take pictures of Freiburg's metamorphosis and bring them back for his parents to paint. His folks had met there when they were in college during a foreign exchange program. They hadn't been back since.

"Getting old sucks," he said.

"The alternative is even worse," Stu replied.

Fair enough. But it still made him grimace every time he thought about losing his dad in stages—like water wearing away stone until there was nothing left.

The Wild goalie blocked a slap shot, and Abe whooped.

If he reached far enough back, he could remember his dad introducing him to the ice all those years ago. He had no idea where his dad had unearthed skates, but the fit wasn't half bad. Together, they'd walked over to Loon Lake, which had pond hockey rinks that anyone could use when the teams weren't practicing or playing.

"Just go slow, little man," his dad had told him when Abe had first wobbled onto the ice. "Easy does it. Stay loose."

Abe could remember asking if he'd fall. His dad had laughed and lit a cigarette. "Little man, we all fall. That's just part of it."

If Abe was rigid in everyday life, on the ice he was just the opposite. It was so freeing; he was limber in a way he felt he couldn't be otherwise. He went back to the pond hockey rinks day after day. That year, his dad had painted him as a dark silhouette skating against a pale winter sky. The painting hung in his parents' apartment to this day.

"So you think we'll do Christmas Eve over at the retirement village, like last year?" Stu asked at the start of the third period. The Wild were ahead, two to one.

"It's probably easiest. But this time let's bring the food. The dinner they served in the main dining room last Christmas was awful."

"God, yes. It tasted like Band-Aids."

"It smelled like Band-Aids."

"I'll bring the turkey," Abe said, "if you want to bring the sides."

"Deal."

Abe could already picture his parents' apartment—the tiny, overstuffed kitchen, the living room with its smattering of macramé and newspapers, the little bedroom with the handmade quilt. His mom would probably brew mint tea.

Abe would uncork a bottle of wine with dinner. They'd eat on the same plates they'd had growing up, and his mom would probably try to get him and Stu to curl up in sleeping bags on their cramped living room floor, like they were twelve again.

Hell, they might even do it.

Because who knew how many more Christmases they'd have together?

Abe frowned, hating how tentative everything seemed lately. And that his usual tactic of holding himself at arm's length from all of it wasn't working anymore. Briefly, he debated asking Stu about how to be happier, how to be more easygoing. Stu's apartment by the river might be cramped and damp, but he was content with it. And where Abe would keep one woman in his bed for ninety days max, Stu was always welcoming scores of women into his life for as long as they wanted to stay. To be fair, it was usually until they found out there were other ladies in Stu's mix, but, somehow, it all worked for his little brother.

The Wild scored again, and Abe leaped to his feet, cheering. All he wanted to do was focus on being here, rooting for his favorite team with his brother in tow. And of course there was the prospect of tomorrow, of seeing Casey Tanner for the tree lighting, which had his gut twisting in ways that he wasn't used to.

Briefly, he debated telling Stu about her, but a fight on the ice distracted him, and he lost track of it until the ride home. He almost opened his mouth as they headed out of Saint Paul, back to White Pine, but instead he asked his brother if he wanted to stop for burgers.

Casey Tanner was his secret—at least for now. He wasn't sure what to expect when he saw her tomorrow, and on the

off chance it was terrible, he wouldn't have to explain to
his brother what happened. He could just move on to seeing
someone else.

Inside the A&W, when his brother asked him if he had
someplace to be, Abe was surprised to find he'd been staring
at his watch, counting the hours until the tree lighting.

"No, just trying to figure out if I missed a special airing
of *The Bridge on the River Kwai*," he said. Stu shrugged
and tore into his second burger. Abe shifted his arm so he
wouldn't see his watch face and start thinking about Casey
all over again.

* * *

Casey smiled and tried not to stare at Dave Englund's dark
hair and the toned muscles as he poured her and Audrey each
a pint of his new seasonal winter ale. Audrey rounded out
the introductions while Dave manned the tap.

"Casey lives in White Pine now, working down at Robot
Lit, the tutoring place in town."

"Nice," he said. "It must be so rewarding working with
the kids."

"It is," Casey answered, "though mostly I'm focused on
spreadsheets. I'm an accountant."

"Oh," Dave said, sliding the glasses across the polished
bar. A thick post hammered through the top of his left ear
glinted in the light. "That's—well, that's cool, too."

"Another new tattoo?" Audrey asked, grabbing Dave's
forearm. Casey stared at the swirls and patterns into which
were etched chef's knives and whisks and even an asparagus
stalk.

"The pint glass. For the new ales," Dave said.

Audrey smiled. "Dave's taken to expressing himself through body art and beer," she said.

"So you made this?" Casey asked, lifting her pint and staring at the light-gold liquid.

"You bet. There's a little bit of orange in there, to brighten it up. See if you can taste it."

She and Audrey clinked glasses and took their first sips while the jukebox cranked out "American Pie" by Don McLean. Casey was ready to love a beer that matched her favorite season, but the moment the first drop hit her tongue, she had to force herself to swallow it down.

"It's delicious!" Audrey said. "It tastes just like Christmas."

Christmas in a wheat field, Casey thought. The spicy cloves and the orange were great in theory, but the yeasty flavor of the beer was throwing everything off. She seemed to be the only one with that opinion, though. Just about everyone at the bar was drinking it, and her sister had guzzled nearly half the pint in her first sip.

Audrey elbowed her and she realized Dave was staring at her. No doubt waiting for her to say something. "I—that's—spicy," she finally managed.

She wanted to kick herself. The winter ale, even if she didn't like it, was at least clever. And if Dave could be clever about beer, chances are he could be clever about other things, too. His tattoos and piercings made him unconventional anyway, and there was a chance that translated to being unconventional between the sheets.

Someone down the bar flagged him and Dave lifted his chin in response. "Excuse me while I take care of some other customers. Good to meet you, Casey. See you around, Audrey."

Casey watched his muscled form, poured into an extra-hot form-fitting black T-shirt, retreat down the bar and tried to muster up a pang of regret. She'd just blown it with someone who could have ushered some fun into her life. Apparently Audrey thought so, too. She gave her a sideways kick at the bar.

"For heaven's sake! Couldn't you have *pretended* to like his beer? Your face looked like you'd swallowed an entire bag of Sour Patch Kids."

"I'm sorry! I wanted to like it. But it tastes like he crossed Malt-O-Meal with stollen bread."

Audrey eyes widened. "It does not. It's really good."

"You're right. It tastes more like a fruit cake had sex with a potato roll."

Audrey clapped her hand over her mouth, trying to keep the laughter at bay. But it was useless. It sputtered out until the two of them were cracking up together.

"You're terrible!" Audrey said. "Dave is a really nice guy."

"Without question," she agreed. "But his winter ale is not nice. It's definitely on the naughty list." She lifted up her glass. "Lump of coal for you," she said to her still-full pint.

Audrey rolled her eyes. "If he comes back, can you just pretend to like it? Here, dump some in my glass so it looks like you actually drank a bit."

Casey dutifully poured ale into her younger sister's glass, feeling small. Dave was creative and hardworking, so what was her problem? Why wasn't she even trying?

Abe Cameron.

She turned her head, thinking she saw him in her peripheral vision. Her heart raced until she realized it was just a burly farmer whose hair was close to the same color.

Her ears strained, and it took her a moment to understand

why, until she figured out that she was hoping to hear Abe's rumbling voice over the Wheelhouse's jukebox.

Which was, of course, foolishness. She needed a man like Dave, not a man like Abe.

Right?

The answer was that she needed to get laid already. She needed to get something checked off her list already. She needed to prove to herself she was changing.

She was almost ready to call Dave over and try again—to see if she couldn't force herself to light a spark between them—when Quinn, the firefighter who'd pulled her out of the elevator and responded to the fire at Robot Lit, grabbed the next seat over at the bar.

"Hey," Casey said. "Fancy meeting you here."

Quinn studied her for a moment until recognition dawned. "Oh, right! You're the lady from the elevator."

Casey stuck out her hand. "Casey Tanner. I didn't get to thank you personally for coming to my rescue. Or for responding to the Robot Lit fire."

"Iris Quinn. Happy to meet you." She blew her dark bangs off her forehead.

Casey blinked. "I'm sorry, I thought Quinn was your first name. Iris is lovely, though."

"My mom's favorite flower. I go by either, really. Quinn's fine."

"In that case, Quinn, it's nice to meet you."

"You, too. Busy week at your place, eh?"

"What are the odds we'd have an elevator break *and* a fire? This is my sister, by the way. Audrey Callaghan."

Audrey leaned over and shook the firefighter's hand. "Thanks for saving my sister. She's usually a lot more careful about getting into dark places with strange men."

Casey shot her sister a warning glare.

"No offense, but I wish you'd been a farting dog or an old man with bad breath," Quinn said. "We would have let Abe suffer in that elevator for a while longer. Since we knew he was in there with a pretty lady, though, we got him out quick."

Casey laughed. "Thanks for the speedy rescue."

"It wasn't that hard, once we got the mechan—"

Quinn's words died on her lips when Dave appeared, ready to take her order. Her long-lashed eyes traveled from his tattooed forearms, up his chest, to the very top of his dark hair before settling back on his face.

"What can I get you?" he asked, seemingly oblivious to her long look.

"I..." She paused for a second, as if needing to regroup. "I hear you've got a seasonal beer on tap."

"He brewed it himself," Audrey chimed in. "It's delicious."

"You made it? Really?"

"Dave here makes the seasonal asparagus ale, too," Audrey said. "Also the bomb."

"I love that stuff," Quinn said, her dark eyes sparkling. "I never knew the brewer would be the bartender, too."

"Dave the bartender, meet Quinn the firefighter," Casey said.

Dave smiled. To Casey, he looked like he was standing up just a little bit straighter. "I wish I could make the special flavors year round. I have to keep it to every once in a while. For now, anyway." He glanced over at the edge of the bar, where a runner had just placed some freshly fried cheese curds. "Listen, some food's up and I need to tend to some customers here, but once I'm done, let me get you that beer because you should have a drink in your hand if you're going to be on a first-name basis with me."

"That sounds great," Quinn said. "The beer part, I mean. Not the part where you leave. I mean...never mind."

Dave laughed. She could have sworn Quinn clutched the bar to keep herself upright. "Be right back," he said, giving her a wink.

Quinn turned to the sisters when he was gone. "Ugh. A cute bartender shows up and I get so flustered he probably thinks I'm cognitively challenged."

Casey studied the young woman's heart-shaped face, her enormous dark eyes, and her strong, athletic fireman's build. *Challenged* was probably not what Dave was thinking at all. *Hot* would be more like it.

Hotter than Casey, certainly. She looked down at her boring black sweater and her plain jeans. She was still so practical, even when she was trying not to be. Audrey, in contrast, had on a suede knee-length skirt with a flirty cream-colored top. On the other side, Quinn sported a snug black shirt and black leather pants. *She looks like a total firefighting badass*, Casey thought with a small twinge of jealousy.

Not that she suddenly wanted to challenge Quinn for Dave the bartender's attentions. It was just that she wanted so badly for someone to be utterly captivated by her.

She glanced at her unfinished beer, wondering if it had been a fool's errand to have made a list in the first place. She could feel her cheeks pinking with the brazenness of it. The sheer balls she and the Knots and Bolts group had to spell out everything they did like that!

Suddenly, Abe Cameron was back in her brain, and she shifted on the barstool.

"Hey," Audrey said, "you okay? You look flushed all of a sudden."

"I'm fine," Casey said. "I'm thinking about the fire at Robot Lit is all." It was a terrible lie. She could see the doubt in her sister's face. To her relief, Quinn took the bait.

"Lu's got an investigator looking into it. He'll probably ask you whether you can think of anyone who would want to harm the place. Maybe a disgruntled employee or something?"

"I barely know everyone's names," Casey said. "I haven't been there long enough to have a clue. My boss, Ingrid, will, though. It was her mom who started the place. She's been there since the beginning."

Quinn nodded. "The investigator will be in touch. Keep an eye out in the meantime."

"Keep an eye out for a certain tall, handsome bartender, you mean?" Casey asked, watching Dave approach them, a pint of winter ale in hand.

"If you are God-fearing women, please start praying that I don't say anything ridiculous," Quinn muttered.

Based on the grin Dave was sporting, Quinn could probably start speaking Icelandic and Dave would be happy about it. So long as she was still talking to *him*.

The way Dave's eyes were locked on to Quinn's, Casey knew that Audrey's hopes of getting her together with the well-meaning bartender had failed. Which was just as well. It was hard to fall for a brewer—or an artisan of any kind— if you didn't like what they made.

The night would be a total bust, Casey thought, if she weren't so grateful to her sister for trying at all. For coming out and attempting to introduce her to people and helping Casey feel part of the community.

She squeezed her sister's hand. "You want to go back to my place and watch a Christmas movie? I have *Miracle on 34th Street* and *It's a Wonderful Life*."

"Best pickup line I've heard all night. As long as there are more cookies."

"Cookies and popcorn and a chardonnay in the fridge."

"Sold!" Audrey said. She leaned in and dropped her voice. "I also feel like we're doing a good deed here, letting Dave focus on his new friend, Quinn. Look at the way he's zoned in on her."

"She can't stop *smiling*," Casey whispered.

"Maybe that was why we were meant to be here tonight," Audrey mused as Casey pulled out her wallet to leave money on the bar. "To introduce those two. We can leave feeling good."

Casey studied her beautiful, well-meaning sister and her heart swelled.

Casey might not have been lucky in love tonight the way she was thinking—but she was lucky in a different way. The relationship she was happiest about and most grateful for was right there with her as they exited the bar.

There was also the fact that they'd ruled out Dave Englund as potential list fodder, which left her with Abe Cameron as the only viable option.

The thought warmed her more than she thought it would as she and Audrey headed out into the frozen night.

CHAPTER EIGHT

There may not have been much of a spark between Dave Englund and herself, but nevertheless Casey was still thinking about fire the next morning. Something about the Robot Lit blaze wasn't right. She mulled over the details as she pawed through the unpacked boxes in her house, searching for her Christmas items.

She'd started enough bonfires and blazes in the fireplace to know that lighting paper wasn't always a guarantee something would burn. You needed kindling, maybe even something more.

So why had someone lit the paper, and only the paper, to start the blaze? It was a half-assed job if it had been arson. Which didn't make much sense. Didn't arsonists want to be successful?

Then again, it could have just been a fluke. A pile of papers got tipped over and...maybe there was an exposed wire somewhere? Except Casey had been down there the day before installing the smoke detectors and fire extinguisher, and there were no papers strewn about, no sparking wires laid bare.

Puzzled, she plunged her hands into packing peanuts, hoping to land on an ornament, a wise man, an Abominable Snowman—anything. But all she felt were the squeaky Styrofoam bits. She sat back on her heels, frustrated by her search and frustrated by the fire. Things weren't adding up on either account. Her ornaments and tinsel and sleigh bells should *be* here. And if someone had really lit the Robot Lit fire, they'd done a piss-poor job of it. So why go through all the hassle of starting a fire at all?

She took a deep breath and tried to bring her heart rate back to normal. Down the hall in the living room, holiday music played softly. She looked at all the boxes stacked in her guest room and figured she should give up on the ornament search and just unpack everything already. She knew where everything needed to go—she'd figured it out on graph paper the day she bought her house—and now she was ready to tackle it all.

If there was part of her that had been procrastinating because she'd wondered if she'd fit in in White Pine, it was fading. The relationships with her colleagues at Robot Lit, with the Knots and Bolts crew, and with Audrey were beginning to feel like rope she'd been braided into. It was getting harder and harder to unwind her existence from theirs.

There was a time when the idea would have terrified her.

Now, it delighted her.

She placed a book on the nearby shelf, and gave herself a mental high five. One down, and too many to count to go.

As if cheering in response, her cell phone buzzed once next to her. A text.

I need my coat. I suppose I could get it from you today at the tree lighting.

Casey stared at it for a minute before bursting into laughter. *Abe.* It was either the worst way to ask someone to accompany you to something—or the most hilarious. She could picture Abe's stone face as he typed it. A prickle of excitement traveled down her spine.

If I said I gave your coat to needy children, would you still want to go?

A pause. Then:

No. But I wouldn't deprive you of my company. I'm selfless like that.

Casey giggled.

What time do you want to pick me up?

Who said I was picking you up?

You did. When you gave me your coat.

You hold me to my word. I'll hold you period.

Casey's hands trembled slightly.

I'd rather be picked up than held if we're still talking about the lighting.

Right. Pick you up at 3 to catch the parade. Lighting is at 4.

OK. Don't try to pull into driveway. It's not shoveled.

Why not?

My butler didn't get around to it.

I can help. I'm good at shoveling.

Casey smiled.

I'm ok. And btw, doesn't the fire truck need to be in the parade?

Yes. But I don't have to be on it. I'm the lieutenant.

Not a captain, then. Too bad.

Why is that?

I can't call you O captain my captain.

Are you trying to seduce me with poetry?

Casey cracked up, the sound echoing in the quiet of her home. She knew she should type no, but instead, she typed the opposite:

Yes.

It's working.

Her muscles tensed. How had texting turned into such a thrilling thing? She sent Abe her address. He asked if he should look for a cardboard box at that street number. She told him she'd upgraded to a shipping crate.

Good for you.

And then, as quickly as it had started, it was over.

Casey stared at her phone, her breathing shallow. Her body was taut and achy. What was Abe Cameron doing to her? How had texting turned her inside out?

She set down her phone. From the living room, the strains of "All I Want for Christmas Is You" floated through the air. Casey rocked her hips to the chorus, humming along to the lyrics about wishing for a person—not a present—for the holiday.

In her mind she painted a picture of Abe holding her by the Christmas tree. His strong arms would encircle her, his warmth would encompass her. And the ornaments—when she found them and hung them—would sparkle like snowflakes in the sun.

She shook her head. She needed to stop fantasizing about Abe already, unless it was as him checking things off her holiday list. The thought didn't repulse her anymore, though. Not by a long shot. She'd left the bar last night with him front and center in her brain. He was even strong enough to override the memory of that awful Christmas ale.

She glanced at her watch. She had three hours before Abe got here.

She was determined to be as pulled together as possible.

Meaning in three hours, she was going to unpack everything she possibly could, find her missing decorations, hang them, shovel the drive, shower, and get ready.

Casey liked nothing more than a challenge. She tore into the box at her feet and got to work.

* * *

Abe checked the address before he knocked again. Supposedly this was the right place, but no one was answering. He thumped on the front door one more time and listened. He could hear the strains of holiday music playing. He glanced through the window beside the door and saw a candle burning, as well as one of Robot Lit's fund-raising brochures. This was likely Casey's house, and it looked like someone should be there—so why wasn't she answering?

Behind him, a car drove past on the road—a young couple in a minivan. The car's undercarriage was clotted with clumps of snow and slush. Abe glanced at his own Jeep, bright and clean in spite of the weather. He was fastidious about his car getting washed frequently.

Abe glanced down at his snow-covered boots. Casey was right about her driveway not being shoveled. In fact, her cozy little Cape Cod had a curved sidewalk that looked like it hadn't been touched since *November*. His boots were covered in powder.

He rang the doorbell once more, but still got no answer. Disappointment weighted his insides. Had she forgotten about him? After texting early this afternoon, he figured the date was locked in. He'd been looking forward to it.

Maybe she just had to run out for something quickly, he thought. The idea gained traction in his mind after a moment or two. Willing himself to believe it, he trudged back through the snow to his car. If Casey was out running late somewhere, he'd just keep himself busy until she returned.

Grabbing a shovel from the back of the Jeep, he started carving a path along the sidewalk. He hurtled great piles of snow off the cement, his muscles burning with the effort. God, but he liked this part of winter. Battling the elements reminded him that he was a survivor, that this is what humankind had done for years, that he was part of a long line of Homo sapiens who had worked for millennia to keep the cold at bay and to carve out a comfortable existence amid the ice and snow.

He felt so good when he finished the sidewalk that he started in on the driveway. It wasn't a big one—just a little patch of blacktop, really—and he was making good progress when he heard his name.

He stopped his work and turned back toward the house. Framed in the doorway with golden light all around her was Casey. And she was wearing... shorts and a tank top. He had to blink to make sure he wasn't imagining the summer-like outfit on her. Or the fact that her legs looked long enough to wrap around him. Twice.

Holy shit.

"Oh my God, how long have you been out here?" she gasped. "I'm so sorry, I got in the shower late, and I must not have heard the door...." She was wringing her hands. Leaning the shovel against his car, he started back up the now-clear sidewalk.

"Please, come in. And to think you were out here *working*. Look at all you did! I've been meaning to shovel. I'm so used to apartment living that I forget about it, but I—"

He was close enough to her now to see the moisture still beading on her skin. Her dark brown hair clung to her shoulders in damp tendrils. He could smell a simple, clean fragrance that had him wanting to pull her close.

"Please, come in," she said. She held the door wide, and he stepped into her home, which smelled like sugar cookies and fresh pine and frosting. He inhaled deeply.

In the living room just to the right of the door, there was an undecorated tree shoved in the corner. It was still bound in twine, its stump resting on the hardwood floor. Straight ahead was a cheerily colored kitchen, and then a small hallway to the left.

"Nice place," he said, and meant it. The floors were bright and clean, the furniture classic, the colors warm without being overpowering. He went to take off his boots, but she waved her hands.

"No, no need for that. Please, keep them on. Make yourself comfortable. I'll be ten minutes, max. Can I get you anything?"

Scarlet color was working its way up her neck. She shifted from one foot to the other. She was mortified, he realized. It didn't stop him from appreciating the way the red brought out her collarbones, two long and delicate lines under her tank top straps. He wanted to run his hands across them.

"I'm fine," he said instead. "Lester Lawsick organizes this thing, and he's always running late with the animals."

She looked at him quizzically. "Who's Lester? And what animals?"

Right. She was still new to town.

"Lester's the large-animal vet. He always tries to get some goats into the holiday parade, or a llama from Vick Henderson's place. It's usually a mess. Means the parade never starts on time. And then the lighting is late, too."

"Oh," she said. At the top of her tank was a dusting of freckles. He had to consciously keep his eyes trained on hers to keep from staring at the smattering of color on her smooth, pale skin.

"Please, have a seat. I'll be ready shortly."

She padded toward the kitchen and down the hallway. He watched her retreat, thinking of how soft she looked. Her sister, Audrey, was athlete-hard and toned, but Casey was rounder and smoother in a way that had his cock thickening. He forced himself to take a calming breath. He wasn't going to get worked up before they were even out the door. Not if he could help himself, anyway.

Wiping the snow off his boots, he walked over to the tree in the living room. It was starting to brown, and he wondered how long it had been here. The thing needed water—and soon.

"You got a stand?" he called down the hallway. "I'll get this tree sorted out for you if you want." He heard the click of a door, maybe a closet, and the sound of a drawer opening. He tried not to wonder whether she was naked, or if she was pulling on a pair of panties right this minute.

"My poor tree. I can't find the stand, but I haven't caved in to buy a new one yet. I keep thinking it's going to turn up any minute." There was the sound of more shuffling. "I'm going to run my blow dryer for a few minutes. Sorry."

The electric whir started up before he could answer. He stared at the tree as the noise filled the cozy house, thinking that White Pine Hardware would have tree stands. And Main Street was only about a minute away if he floored it in his sturdy Jeep. He figured he could take the side streets in to avoid the parade traffic, double-park while he got the stand, and be back before Casey even noticed he was gone.

He hesitated for only the briefest of seconds. Shoveling Casey out *and* fixing her tree might be a little presumptuous, but he couldn't deny the pleasure it gave him. He'd always liked helping people. He just wasn't prepared for how much he liked helping *her*.

He told himself it was what anyone would do. Casey was adjusting to small-town life and home ownership, after all. He was just being friendly. It was no big deal.

Nevertheless, he was already grinning as he pulled the front door closed behind him with a soft click.

CHAPTER NINE

The feeling of being dazed was a new one for Casey, but that was the only way she could describe the stupefied brain sludge that currently had complete hold of her. It kept her mouth open slightly, her eyes wide, and her heart thumping with disbelief.

Abe Cameron had not only shoveled her sidewalk and driveway, he had bought a stand for her and fixed her tree in place, all before she'd been able to put on clothes and dry her hair.

She wanted to pinch herself. Surely she was imagining this. The fog of impossibility that was rolling over her would dissipate if she could just bring herself to accept that she had conjured all this up. Because surely she hadn't gotten so wrapped up in unpacking that she'd totally spaced what time it was. And definitely she hadn't hopped into the shower late, then heard the scrape of a shovel just outside her front door when she'd turned off the water. Certainly she hadn't thrown on the first thing she could find, which was barely any clothes at all, and no way had she opened the door to find that Abe Cameron had shoveled not only her sidewalk but her driveway as well.

It was all more fiction than fact, right? Because Casey was always on time. She always took care of her responsibilities. She didn't lose things like tree stands and she always had Christmas *handled*.

Except when she didn't.

Except this year, when she was trying to be more laid-back and fun-loving, and she'd moved to a whole different town and everything felt topsy-turvy, especially the fact that she couldn't even find a gift for Audrey, for crying out loud, when she always knew exactly what to get her sister.

Thank God she had Abe Cameron helping take care of all the stuff she was slacking on.

The thought had her stomach fluttering. Maybe it wasn't so bad that Abe was responsible and serious. She certainly couldn't remember Miles putting her Christmas tree in a stand. Heck, she couldn't even remember Miles helping wash dishes after she'd cooked him dinner. And here was Abe, shoveling her walk and putting up her tree before they'd even had their first date.

The thought had tears pricking her eyes unexpectedly. She blinked them away, horrified that she was getting so worked up about this. Surely a little help couldn't mean so much?

But the truth was, it was the first time in forever that someone had stood by her side and shared any kind of burden. It wasn't a huge load, but it was a load nonetheless.

And it made her happier than she'd ever thought it could.

Now, standing outside of Hair We Are on Main Street, Abe put a steaming cup of mulled cider in her hand. The greetings of "Merry Christmas!" and "Happy holidays!" sounded from folks all around them. When his eyes found hers he gave her if not a smile, then a look that said he didn't hate being here with her. A look that said he might even be having a fine time. His black North Face jacket and black fleece hat made the strong lines of his face even stronger, and she couldn't help but stare a little.

Okay, a lot.

"The cider doesn't rule out us getting cocoa at the Rolling Pin later," he said. "Unless you're having a bad time and just want to leave."

"How will you know?"

"I'll have you fill out a little scorecard and rank the date so far. Anything less than a seven and I usually pull the plug."

"I don't think you have to worry. Between the tree stand and the shoveling, you're doing okay."

"Just okay?"

"I don't want you to get overconfident."

He winked at her as a brisk wind flapped the awnings on Main Street's storefronts. The sun was already sinking, the sky darkening all around them. Lights twinkled and flickered—from the glowing wreath on the door of Loon Call Antiques to the smiling snowman in front of the library. The whole world sparkled enough to take her breath away.

A man in a down coat with the fingers of an adorable, chubby toddler in one hand and a bright red package from White Pine Hardware in the other stopped in front of them. He shifted the package so he could stop and shake Abe's hand. "Heya, Lu," he said. "Happy holidays." He gave Casey a pointed look she couldn't quite read.

When Abe didn't introduce her right away, she stuck out her hand.

"I'm Casey Tanner."

"Saul Lambeck. Good to meet you. And this is Reggie. Say hi, buddy."

The kid garbled something incomprehensible, his wide eyes taking in all the lights and sounds. He stamped his feet, clearly impatient for the parade to be underway.

"We just came from doing some Christmas shopping," Lambeck said. "Reggie was doing fine until I told him there were going to be tractors down at the parade. He busted out of the hardware store screaming his head off. The kid's *insane* for tractors."

Abe remained stonily silent. The seconds ticked by uncomfortably. "At least he hasn't asked to change his name to John Deere," Casey offered finally.

"I have about a month then, I figure." Lambeck said, grinning. Abe had yet to say a word.

"Well, see you around, Lu. Enjoy the parade. Nice to meet you, Casey."

When he was gone, Casey rounded on Abe. "What the heck was that? Why were so you rude to him?"

"I wasn't."

"You completely ignored him!"

"I didn't." Abe's jaw barely moved.

"Come on. You hardly spoke just then. Don't tell me it's because you're selectively mute now."

She was startled by the intensity that was suddenly blazing in Abe's hazel eyes as he faced her fully. "Listen," he said, "firefighters are worse than a ladies' sewing circle when it comes to gossip. If I'd said one word just then, Lambeck would have read something into it. About being with you. I've learned just to stay quiet."

Casey straightened. "You've had practice at this."

Of course he had. She knew his reputation. Abe Cameron liked the ladies. His crew had probably seen him with hundreds of them. So why was she letting it irritate her?

"I've had practice taking shit for it," Abe said, his jaw flexing. "And I don't feel like being gossiped about right now."

Casey snorted. "Abe, the whole town is here at this parade tonight. This wasn't exactly the best event to take me to if you wanted privacy."

Abe glowered. "I don't work with the whole town. I don't do twenty-four-hour shifts with the whole town. I don't have to eat meals with the whole town."

He surprised her by stepping in closer and whispering into her ear. "Most times I'm out with someone, I don't care. Not about the girl, and not about what I say, or what the other firefighters say. Tonight, I wanted to be careful."

His breath was warm, deliciously so, as his cheek pressed against hers. She nearly lost her footing. Was he telling her he hadn't said anything because he *liked* her?

Before she could think of anything to say in reply, he pulled away and pointed down the street.

"Here comes the first float," he said. A giant papier mâché train coated in lights was headed their way. It was being hauled on a trailer with WHITE PINE MODEL RAILROADERS painted in bold letters on the side. Steam billowed out of the top of the float, and the crowd cheered. Casey grinned, feeling like a little kid.

The train was followed by a trio of dancing Mrs. Clauses. They shimmied and kicked to "Rockin' Around the Christmas Tree" and flung candy canes into the crowds. Kids raced into the street to grab the candy before the next float—an enormous John Deere tractor with Santa waving from the top.

"That's Red Updike," Abe said. "He does the Halloween corn maze every year out at his place."

"Too bad there's no such thing as a Christmas corn maze," Casey mused, watching the huge tractor roll past. "It could be in the shape of Rudolph and be lit by lights and have holiday trees scattered all throughout."

"Sounds wonderful," Abe said, flashing a smile. "But farmers have to pull in the crop before then. Leave it out too long and it gets too dry. Too much grain loss."

"Thanks, Farmer Buzzkill."

Abe leaned in, and his closeness had her toes curling in her boots. "Just providing facts, ma'am. Don't you want to know why a holiday corn maze doesn't exist?"

Her eyes slipped to his mouth, remembering how it felt against hers. "Not really. I was just trying to imagine it."

"And now you can set your expectations accordingly. Farmer Buzzkill is your friend."

"Does Farmer Buzzkill get a scorecard, too?"

Abe shook his head, his perfect ears tucked snugly under his black cap. "He's in the agriculturally immune category. It's in the fine print on the back."

He was as deadpan as ever, but Casey found herself laughing. Not to mention noticing how the lights reflected in his hazel eyes, igniting the flecks of gold there.

He was watching her watch him. For a moment the world stilled, the parade faded, and it was just the two of them. *Fireworks on Christmas*, Casey thought as her body lit up with a tingling, exploding sensation that flamed through her skin and muscles.

Abe's golden brows drew together. The darkening of his face was from frustration, she realized. She wondered if he wanted to kiss her again, right here at the parade, but was holding off because more firefighters could be nearby. Nevertheless, her insides thrilled at the notion. Making out with the fire lieutenant at the holiday parade! What would the Knots and Bolts crew say? In that moment she didn't care.

Instead of kissing her, Abe grasped her mittened hand in his gloved one. He squeezed gently. It was sweet enough to have her skin sparking with the contact, even through the layers of fabric. Holding hands felt like their secret. A linking that was all their own.

Right then, she couldn't deny that she felt a pull toward Abe that felt as natural as gravity. It was like a force that had always been there, something you'd study in physics and write equations for. The X of Y equals the force at which CT meets AC.

It was strong enough to remind her of the list. She smiled to herself, thinking how fun it would be to challenge him on all five counts. God, but could she be that direct? Would she come out and just ask him "Hey, I want twelve orgasms, can you give them to me?" She swallowed, realizing she'd never gotten that far. She'd never even thought about how to present the list to a possible...candidate.

She glanced at Abe, thinking about everything he'd done for her already, and wondering if there were *five more very important things* he could give her. She recalled feeling the length of him at Robot Lit and shivered.

"Here comes the rig," Abe said, jarring her back to the here and now. She blinked, reminding herself that this was only a first date, and she shouldn't yet be thinking about tumbling into bed with Abe.

Or should she?

The possibility made her light-headed. She needed to

think about this later, when she was home alone, not when Abe was right here and they were surrounded by half the town. She struggled to focus on the shining fire engine rolling slowly toward them, sirens blipping and lights flashing. Quinn was driving, and Reese was throwing candy out the passenger-side window.

"You don't mind if they see you with me?"

Abe shook his head. "No. Of course not. I just don't want to *talk* to any of them. I refuse to add fuel to their fire, no pun intended."

"Don't you wish you were up there?" Casey asked, watching the enormous vehicle.

"I rode in it for years. It's nice to be down here for once."

"How long have you worked for the fire department?"

"I went in not too long after college. I was holding down an IT job right after graduation, but it didn't take me too long to figure out I hated coding software and loved helping people."

The fire truck was followed by the White Pine High School marching band. They were belting out a brassy rendition of the Beach Boys' "Little Saint Nick."

"What about you?" Abe asked over the music. "Did you know you always wanted to be an accountant?"

"Pretty much. It was logical, anyway. I liked math. I was organized."

"Can you tone down the enthusiasm? It's making me uncomfortable."

Casey laughed. "God, I know. I sound so boring. It's just that for a long time, what I wanted wasn't an option. Not when I was just trying to get what I needed."

"How do you mean?"

"My sister and I were on our own a lot growing up. I

think I stopped asking myself pretty early on whether I liked something. If it got me from point A to point B, I just did it. If it meant Audrey and I survived, I didn't think, I just acted."

"Sounds like you had a lot of responsibility on your shoulders."

"Looking back, there are days that I wonder how it all even worked out. We didn't go hungry or get pregnant. Audrey and I both got college educations. I'm so grateful."

She took a sip of cider, worried she was rambling. But Abe was leaning in, tuned into her every word. "And how about now?"

"What do you mean?"

"Are you giving yourself a little more slack to enjoy things?"

There was a playful note in his voice that thrilled her.

"Probably more than I should be," she said, thinking of all the ways she wanted to loosen up and have fun. And all the ways Abe Cameron could help her do just that. She turned away slightly, worried her face was the picture of open hunger.

"You have a younger sibling, too, right?" she asked, trying to change the subject. "Stu?"

Abe nodded. "He's a pain in my ass. Takes after my folks more than I do. They're artists, and he's more—free thinking that way."

"Are your folks still around?" she asked, pretending Betty hadn't told her precisely where they were.

"Up at the White Pine Retirement Village. My dad…" He trailed off, his Adam's apple working.

"Is he okay?" Casey asked. Pain flashed across Abe's face.

"His memory is going," Abe said, staring down the street, his jawline hard. "It's slow. It's relentless. A tough combo."

A wave of compassion crashed over her. "Oh, I'm so sorry, Abe." She squeezed his hand. "That must be so difficult."

He nodded, his mouth grim. "They call it the long good-bye for a reason. He has good days, though. Lots of them. And he still tries to paint. The fact that he even wants to pick up a brush is great. He's got that, got my mom. So it's not as bad as it could be."

Casey wished she could wrap her arms around Abe and pull him close. His pain was so raw, like an open wound. "And there's no cure? Nothing the doctors can do?"

From the parade came the sound of sleigh bells and singing. It was too happy, suddenly, too festive.

"No, there's no cure. There have been advancements recently, but by the time they figure something out, it will be too late for my dad."

Casey used the hand Abe wasn't holding to touch his face. She wanted to pull him close, to kiss the worry away from his eyes.

Her brain fired a warning, reminding her that feeling too much with Abe wasn't what she was looking for. She didn't want to learn all this, did she?

"All right, enough," Abe said, as if her thoughts were spelled out on her forehead. He pulled away from the hand that was cupping his face. Casey shoved it back into her coat pocket. "I can't be the only one sharing things here. What about you? What about your folks?"

Let the sad tales continue, Casey thought. "My parents died when my sister and I were young. My aunt Lodi raised us, but she moved to Arizona when we went to college. She passed away a few years back."

"I'm sorry to hear that."

Casey nodded. "She never wanted kids, and when two young girls landed in her lap, I'm not sure she knew what do to."

Abe studied her. "So you had to grow up fast and shoulder what she couldn't."

Casey felt like he was staring straight into her heart. "It's practically a Lifetime movie," she said, trying to lighten the moment. Because the loss still stung—so much so that there were days Casey wondered if the pain would ever go away. She would do anything to never feel such a deep hurt again.

"You should feel proud," Abe said, his eyes serious. "Audrey is settled and happy. Christ, I feel proud and I had jack shit to do with the fact that Stu is just fine. He's a good kid."

"Kid? What's the age difference between you guys?"

"Isn't it impolite to ask someone their age?" Abe asked.

"I'll tell you mine if you tell me yours."

A smattering of candy canes landed at their feet. "I'll be forty this spring. You?"

"I'm thirty-four."

"This is quite an age gap."

"Do we need to get you home in time for *Matlock*?"

"If we go home, it won't be to watch television." There was a dark edge to his voice that had her pulse pounding. He turned her around, then pulled her to him, so her back was against his chest. His arms encircled her torso. She felt warm and wildly alive. From the outside, to any prying eyes, they probably looked like they were simply watching the parade. But to Casey, the air between them was crackling. His breath was deliciously hot on her skin. He leaned down.

"Here comes Santa," he murmured into her ear. "But I know I'm not getting anything this year."

"Why is that?"

"Because I've been very, very bad." He pressed the hard length of himself against her backside. She sucked in breath.

God, there was so much of him. It had been years and years since Miles, and she wondered if her anatomy would be able to... accommodate it all. If they ever got that far. If she let herself tell him about the list.

A picture of him towering over her in bed flashed into her mind. Hot skin. Twisted sheets. Loud cries.

She had to battle back the urge to grind against him in public. Instead, she pulled away slightly, leaving a whisper of space between their two bodies.

"Is it something I said?" he asked.

"There are families here. And possibly more firefighters. I'd hate to give them the impression this parade was NC-Seventeen."

"Is that as bad as you think I can get?" he asked, low and gravelly. "That's barely above R."

"I hadn't given it much thought," she lied.

"In this case, thinking might be overrated."

Her eyes were on his lips again. "What's the alternative?"

"There's action, for one. Taking it. *Giving* it."

The very center of her was about to melt. Good grief, he was going to undo her while they were standing in front of the whole darn town.

The part of her that didn't mind the idea was getting bigger by the minute. *A fling with Abe Cameron.* She rolled the idea around in her head until she was dizzy with it.

But they were enveloped in the crowd at present. Firefighters or no, they'd be the talk of the town if they didn't put some space between each other.

"How about the fire at Robot Lit?" she asked, desperate to move the conversation away from how much she wanted him at that very moment. "Have you given any *thought* to that?"

She could feel him stiffen, but not from desire. From something else. Nervousness, perhaps. Or concern.

"I've got the inspector on it." She could hear a note of frustration in his voice, and she wondered if he was as perplexed about the blaze as she was. She turned around to face him.

"Kind of weird, overturning a box of paper if you're an arsonist," she said, testing him out on the subject. "Wouldn't you—I don't know—soak some rags in gasoline or something?"

Abe's golden-green eyes tracked across her face. "I was thinking the same thing. Accelerants can leave a pretty big footprint, though. They're easier to detect. So I can see why an arsonist might not use them. Or maybe it wasn't arson at all. It could have just been a fluke."

"But I was down there the day before, installing the fire alarms and the extinguisher. And there were no random papers in a pile. I would have cleaned them up."

"So why light a blaze if you know it might not be successful?" Abe asked, more to himself.

"You'd be doing it for some reason other than to set a building on fire."

"But that makes no sense."

"Not yet," Casey agreed, "but I could always go check things out tomorrow when I'm back at work. Have a look around and see what I find."

Abe shook his head. "We secured that scene. It's technically under investigation. Ty Brady is lead, and you shouldn't go anywhere near it."

Casey frowned. She was aware that the spectators all around them were breaking up. The parade was over. It was time to head down the block for the tree lighting. Only she and Abe didn't move.

"It's my place of work," she insisted. "Surely I can poke around a bit."

"That's like saying you should be allowed into a crime scene investigation because you walk your dog on the same street every day."

"It's just that the idea that anyone would try to burn that place down makes me crazy."

Abe nodded. "True. But we have to let the professionals do their jobs."

Casey exhaled with frustration. "This is the first job I've ever had that actually, you know, makes a difference. I can't stand the idea of someone trying to undo all that good work."

Abe moved his gloved hand to her face. He traced the outline of her cheekbone with his thumb. "Neither of us gets to fix this, even though we both want to."

His touch made her shiver. His words were a punch to her heart.

"Then what's left to do?" she asked, her voice barely a whisper.

"I can think of at least one thing."

He kissed her then, just as the White Pine holiday tree down the block blazed to life.

* * *

An hour later, Casey was back in Abe's Jeep, sweat collecting at the base of her spine as her body overheated with nervous energy. She should ask Abe inside when he dropped her off. She should tell him she wanted him.

The thought was ludicrous. And thrilling. She twisted in her seat.

"You doing okay over there?" Abe glanced at her as he steered his Jeep past the parade traffic, taking side streets away from the congested downtown.

"Oh, fine," she lied, forcing a smile. *It's just that I'm trying to figure out how to ask you to sleep with me.* "Just remembering how wonderful the parade was."

Abe gave her a wink, and she nearly put her head in her hands. What was she playing at? There was no way she could do this. There was no way to open up her mouth and tell Abe she wanted him, no strings attached—just a night of fun because, dammit, she was a fun-loving girl.

She wondered if every fun-loving girl felt as nervous as she did right then. She wondered if she was getting sick.

Her house was so close now. She took a breath, working up the energy to ask him to come inside, but then realized she hadn't even worn anything sexy underneath her jeans and sweater. Just her plain cream-colored bra and her normal cotton panties. Fine, sure, but not fling worthy. What would Abe think when he peeled off her clothes? He'd probably stare at her boring old underthings on her boring old body and burst into laughter.

Casey swallowed. No, the way to do this wasn't to just invite Abe inside spontaneously. She'd have to think about this, have to plan it out more. She'd need to set rules and get organized and ponder how to execute it perfectly.

Except that's the opposite of a fling, a small voice inside chided.

Oh, but she wanted black lacy underwear and fuck-me red lipstick and stilettos as long and sharp as carpenter's nails. She should at least try for those elements so she didn't screw this up. She needed to plot it all out perfectly, to reduce the risk of failure.

She clenched her hands, wondering if she was the only woman in the world who calculated a fling.

Her mind was so consumed with how to get Abe Cameron into her bed that she barely registered that the Jeep had pulled into her driveway. How long had they been sitting there? She turned her head from the window, only to find Abe staring at her.

"Everything all right?" he asked. His brows were drawn together with concern.

"Never better," she said, forcing a smile that felt as fake as flashy tinsel. "I had a wonderful time. Thank you."

She knew she sounded hollow. *It's just because I'm trying to figure out how to sleep with you*, she imagined blurting. Instead she stayed silent, her posture as rigid as molded plastic.

Abe's fingers twitched, and Casey wondered if he might reach out and twine a piece of her auburn hair in his fingers. Or maybe he'd put his hands on her shoulders again, and pull her close. But he did neither of those things, and Casey couldn't force herself to bend to him. Her brain was muddled and she felt sticky with sweat. Desire was undoing her—and undoing their romantic evening.

It was the height of irony.

"I—this was so fun," she stammered. "Let's do it. Again, I mean. Let's do this kind of thing at a subsequent time that we arrange..." She trailed off, horrified and unable to finish the imploding sentence.

Abe smiled then, and some of the tension drained out of the Jeep. His eyes flickered over her lips, her neck. "We can arrange a subsequent time, sure," he said, low and impossibly sexy.

He leaned closer, and Casey could feel his hunger for another kiss. Hell, she could feel her own hunger for a delicious make-out session that steamed up the windows.

Except she wasn't sure she could trust herself to *just* make out. She wanted more, dammit. Lots more, starting with Abe in her bedroom, fucking her until she couldn't see straight. But she couldn't go there tonight. Not with her stupid bra and her boring panties and—God, her sheets had stars on them, since the only set she'd unpacked so far was her oldest, most threadbare set.

Wasn't this the whole point, though? To do something risky when the conditions weren't completely ideal?

Oh, she wanted to. She wanted to throw her arms around him and drag him through the front door and do unspeakable things until they both collapsed.

But she had to make it right, first. *Exactly, precisely right.*

She swallowed, realizing that in trying to have a fling, she was actually creating more rules. More boundaries and more parameters. She was her own worst enemy, doing the opposite of what she'd set out to do.

But when her heart slammed against her ribs, she knew there was more to it than that.

She needed Abe to say yes to *everything* on the list. Not just one thing, but *all five things*. She required more than one night with him. If he fucked her and never saw her again, she would never complete her list.

She needed to ensure total, complete success. It was calculated, yes. But it was also better than a quick lay and an empty bed the next morning. She didn't need Abe Cameron to stick around forever, but she needed him for more than just one night.

And in order to achieve that, she could not ask Abe in. Not yet. Even though her muscles were twitching and her lips were ready to press themselves against his, she had to steel her resolve and back away. Heat surged through her, and she knew she was going to lose it if she didn't exit stage left. Pronto.

"See you soon," she said too brightly, opening the Jeep door and hopping out.

If she saw Abe's eyes darken with confusion, she ignored it. If she saw his hand reach for her, she twisted away.

And before she could change her mind, she was racing to the front door, not looking back.

CHAPTER TEN

The next day before work, Abe could hardly concentrate. He kept replaying last night's date with Casey in his mind, wondering what in the world had happened. It had been the most enjoyable date he'd had in ages—at least until she'd frozen up at the end. It was like a blizzard had come through and smoldered the spark between them, leaving him to shovel out from under it while trying to make sense of the whole thing.

Only he *couldn't* make sense of it. The only thing he knew was that he'd been having fun last night. He liked Casey Tanner. But the way she'd bolted from the Jeep left a gnawing doubt about whether she liked him back.

He groaned, feeling like he was fifteen again and wondering if the pretty girl in algebra thought he was cute, too.

His phone rang and for a brief moment he brightened, thinking it was Casey. Maybe she was calling to tell him she wanted to see him again after all. But when he saw the number, he just groaned. It was Hayes Ulfsson, and his damn bull was in the damn tree again.

Abe headed over to the farm before work to help the farmer out. In a distracted moment, the animal's sharp back hoof nearly connected with his gut. "I'll make prime rib out of you." He glowered at the muscled black beast.

"He'd sure be tough," the old farmer said. "He'd make you work for every damn bite."

Abe kicked a frozen turd. "This gets less and less fun, Hayes. I'm doing this on my off time, you know. Any chance you can keep him in the barn more?"

"Too close to the cows."

The farmer had left it at that, content to have Abe volunteer to help him once again.

After freeing the bull, Abe arrived at the firehouse and started in on some paperwork, glad to see Lambeck wasn't in. He didn't have the energy to tamp down rumors today.

He scribbled on a handful of forms, only to keep glancing at his phone. He wanted Casey to call, and also wondered if he should call her instead. Probably he shouldn't. He didn't want to look desperate. It hadn't even been twenty-four hours since he'd seen her.

He frowned. He didn't like this indecisiveness. It wasn't him.

He tried not to think about the way her body had felt against his while they'd watched the parade the night before. Her warm scent had him wanting to lick parts of her that were covered in winter layers. Her sparkling smile as the parade had marched by had his chest aching with something he couldn't place.

He glanced at his phone again. The screen showed the time and nothing else. Not a text, not a voice mail.

And why wouldn't it? Casey was probably busy at Robot Lit, working her numbers and helping the kids there. She had a life. And a good one at that. Her home wasn't big, but it wasn't a shoebox, either. It was just off Main Street in an old neighborhood that he'd always liked. Her furnishings had been tasteful—maybe even expensive by the looks of it. On the bookshelf, he'd spotted a picture of Casey hugging her sister, Audrey, who was wearing a wedding dress. They both looked pink-cheeked and radiant.

He wondered if Audrey's marriage had been what prompted Casey to move back to White Pine. He'd have to ask her that. Along with a thousand other questions that were hustling through his brain. What were her favorite movies? What books did she like to read? Had she ever been abroad? He thought about his dream trip to Freiburg and his mind suddenly flashed to Casey walking with him on the clean, straight streets. They would take pictures for his folks together, then hold hands on the platform as the train rumbled into the station, precisely on time. He'd help her into her seat, and her golden brown eyes would glitter at him. *Danke*, she'd say, and he'd kiss her, even though the Germans probably frowned on public affection.

Panic surged. *Jesus, what was even happening to him?* He pushed his chair away from his lieutenant's desk. Sitting around and fantasizing about Casey Tanner would not do. It was ridiculous. Stupid. Especially when she'd bolted from the date last night like she couldn't get away fast enough. He knew plenty of girls who would kill to stick around when he wanted them to. It was no use getting worked up about one who didn't.

Still, he wondered if he should phone Stu. "When is it cool to call a girl again after a date, especially if she didn't seem that into you at the end?" He pictured himself asking the question and Stu laughing on the other end. His brother was his opposite—he *loved* love—and always had a woman in his bed whom he claimed to adore. Often two. Girls fawned over him, and he opened his heart to them readily. He just never seemed inclined to make them stay if they wanted to leave. And often they did when he couldn't love just one of them at a time.

"Lunch is ready, Lu," Reese said from his office doorway, jarring him back to the here and now. The kid's navy pants and navy polo with Station One's emblem on the chest were all spattered with grease.

"What the hell did you make?" Abe asked, taking in the kid's skinny frame, his unruly, sandy hair.

"Hamburgers. Fried 'em up for the whole crew."

Abe could already picture the black hockey puck of beef on a dry bun. This was what happened when his team took on different duties each shift. The upside was that it enabled them to get a range of experiences—like being able to drive the engine versus always riding in the rescue wagon. But the downside was that it meant the crew often did things at which they weren't skilled. Like cooking, in Reese's case.

"You guys go on without me. I'm going to pop down to the Rolling Pin to grab a doughnut."

Reese shrugged. "Sure thing, Lu," he said, and returned to the kitchen.

Abe grabbed his coat and set off. Ten minutes later, he was walking back on Main Street from downtown, two custard-filled long johns sitting like rocks in his gut. He'd just taken a tentative sip of his steaming hot coffee when the sight of smoke stopped him in his tracks. A thin, gray stream rose from one of the windows at Leroy's auto repair place, just up the street from the firehouse.

"Dammit," he swore. He tossed his cup into a nearby snowbank, vowing to go back and get it later. He sprinted toward Leroy's, reaching for his phone. He fumbled with the device, trying to dial the firehouse as he ran.

"Station One. This is firefighter Iris Quinn. How can I help you?"

"Quinn, it's Abe," he huffed, still running. "Get the engine started now. There's smoke at Leroy's place. It's coming out the east-facing garage window."

"Copy, Lu. We'll be right there."

Abe shoved the phone into his pocket just as he reached the front of the abandoned building, its weathered brick façade pale in the afternoon light. A rusted tow truck rested in the driveway, snow up to its wheel wells. Darting to the nearest window, Abe strained for a look through the garage door's dusty glass. The sound of sirens from the firehouse reached him as he squinted to make out what he was seeing.

The smoke was coming from a small pile of papers and some strips of cardboard on the cracked cement floor. Small flames licked the edges of the pile. It was a small fire for now—but potentially deadly if it hit the right accelerant.

Just like the Robot Lit fire, he thought.

Straining, he attempted to open the rusted garage door, but it wouldn't lift. That had him wondering how the person who'd started the fire had gotten in and out of the building in the first place. He pressed his face against the window again, and that was when he saw it—a hooded figure exiting out a warped back door.

Abe's heart hammered. *Got you*, he thought.

The sirens were louder than ever as Abe sprinted around the side of the structure. The figure was headed west, away from downtown, but was close enough to catch sight of Abe's form coming toward him. Like a deer bolting from a gunshot, the figure jumped into flight, arms and legs pumping furiously.

"Stop!" Abe cried, giving chase. "You'll only make it worse if you run!"

Nonplussed, the person ran faster, up the street. The small shoulders hunched with effort. To Abe's dismay, his quarry darted across the street toward Robot Lit, white sneakers flashing.

It's just a kid, Abe realized, pushing himself harder. He was only a few paces behind as the kid flew into the Robot Lit lobby and bolted up the stairs two at a time—all the way to the third floor.

He knows where he's going, Abe thought as his quads strained to carry him along. He didn't let up, but burst into the great room on the kid's heels, his chest heaving as he threw open the door.

"Stop!" he bellowed. The tutoring groups clustered around tables froze. Abe pointed a finger at the figure at the far end of the room. He was trying to sneak off into the nearby hallway. "Freeze right now. Then turn around and walk slowly toward me." Abe made his voice as deep and authoritative as he could. He needed to scare the shit out of this kid so he'd do whatever he told him to. "Now."

The kid straightened and turned—and that was when Abe's stomach dropped. He was maybe ten years old, if that. *Just a boy*, Abe thought. The kid's lean face was too hard for his young age. His skin was pale but his gray eyes were sharp. He was scared—but maybe mad, too. Or defiant. Or *something* that made him light fires to burn off whatever intensity was flaming inside him.

"You're not a cop." The boy lifted his chin.

Abe's resolve hardened. Young or not, the kid had started a fire. And Abe needed to ensure that that stopped. Immediately.

"I'm Lieutenant Abe Cameron and I'm with the White Pine Fire Department. I don't need to be a cop to get you down to the station." He worked to make his words tough and even. Authoritative but not scary enough so the kid bolted again. "So I need you to come on over to me, nice and slow."

"I didn't do anything," the kid said.

"That may be. But you and I are going to have a talk about it nonetheless."

"There's nothing to say."

Abe's patience frayed slightly. "I saw you in Leroy's old place. Where there's a fire burning right now. I'd say that means we have quite a lot to discuss."

"You can't prove anything."

Abe inched forward. He kept his eyes on the kid's lean face, all the while calculating how to grab hold of him before the kid ran again.

"Come on," Abe said. "I'm not the police. Just a fireman."

The kid's pale face whitened another shade. Abe's stomach twisted. This kid looked downright tortured.

"What's your name, son?" he asked.

The boy looked at his shoes, then back at Abe. He didn't say anything.

"All right. Let's make a deal. If you come my way and agree to talk, it'll just be you and me. But if you run again, I'll have the cops track you down, and once the police are involved, this is a whole different matter."

The kid stared at him, and Abe met his gaze head-on. "It seems like you know this place," Abe continued, "and I bet at least a few people in this room here recognize you. So you won't be hard to find. For the cops, I mean. That's a lot of trouble, though. So what do you say to you and I just start talking now?"

The kid's expression crumpled, and Abe's gut wrenched. What was so bad in this kid's life that he had to light fires?

"Fine," the kid said.

Abe exhaled. The young boy took a step in Abe's direction—but then, at the last minute, swiveled on his heel. He was going to run for it again.

Dammit, Abe thought, leaping into pursuit.

Straining, he just managed to grab a handful of hoodie before the boy could get his feet under him.

"Let me go!" the kid yelled. "You're hurting me!"

Frustration washed over Abe. He was holding on to the kid's *sweatshirt*, for crying out loud.

The kid twisted, desperate to break free, but Abe held fast. Behind him, the reading room attendees were scattering. He could hear chairs scraping on the hardwood. Maybe the tutors were getting the kids out of there so they didn't get swept up in any drama.

"Settle down, son. Easy does it."

In response, the kid opened his mouth and let out a full-on scream. Abe struggled just to hang on as the kid fought and kicked. Dimly, he heard doors slamming and heels on hardwood.

"Little help here!" Abe called out, hoping one of the Robot Lit staffers would come to his aid. Maybe even Casey.

"Abe! What in the world?" Ingrid was rushing toward them, white blonde hair streaming behind her.

"Help me," the kid pleaded, his eyes brimming with tears. "This man chased me."

"You bet I did. And we both know why."

"Ingrid, help. I'm so scared."

"Not as scared as you'll be when the police book you for lighting Robot Lit and Leroy's on fire," Abe said.

Ingrid's eyes widened in surprise. She turned to the kid. "Carter, is this true?"

Instead of answering, Carter kicked at Abe furiously. Abe was just about to pin the kid's arms behind his back when the kid's toe collided with Abe's groin, inches away from his nuts. The air whooshed from Abe's lungs at the close call. He spotted Casey then, standing a few feet away, her mouth slightly open.

Abe swallowed back a string of curse words. "Ingrid, handle him. I need to call the cops."

"Carter, into the conference room now," Ingrid said firmly. As she led him away, Abe pulled out his phone and called dispatch. By the time he was done explaining the situation and was assured the police were en route, Casey was at his side.

He caught her glancing at his crotch, even though she pretended not to. "Need an ice pack?"

"It was only a close call. I'll be fine."

"Police on their way?"

"As we speak."

She shifted, seemingly reluctant to leave him. Unlike last night, when it was as if she couldn't wait to get away from him.

"You think Carter started the Robot Lit fire?" she asked after a moment.

Abe blew out a breath. "Well, I caught him mid-blaze at Leroy's, and he ran here."

"In other words, it was him."

There was concern in her brown eyes. "It would make sense based on all the things that confused us before," he said. "It would mean the blaze here was amateur. Young. A kid messing around, versus a seasoned arsonist. Same next door."

She reached out and put her fingers on his forearm. The contact, even through layers of clothing, had his every muscle tightening.

"Carter's a good kid. As far as I can tell, anyway. He's here a lot, and I just wanted to say—you know, go easy on him."

Abe glanced down the hallway to the frosted conference room door. The dark shapes of Ingrid and Carter moved on the other side. In the distance, he could hear sirens wailing. No doubt the cops, since Quinn and the other firefighters would have put out the tiny auto shop blaze in moments. In his mind, he could still see the smoke wafting up from Leroy's, could still feel the air burning in his lungs as he chased Carter into Robot Lit.

"There are programs for kids like Carter," he said. "He's all of what—ten?"

Casey nodded. "He was recently placed in foster care," she said quietly. "Rolf told me his mom went into rehab. He'd been coming here off and on before that happened. Now, it's like he's here every minute he can be."

Abe clenched his jaw. He knew that feeling. He knew firsthand what an oasis Robot Lit could be when it felt like nothing else was going right.

"The cops won't—take him away, will they?" Casey's forehead wrinkled. Abe imagined kissing away all the fine lines.

"No, nothing like that. They'll talk to him. Get a statement from me. They'll want to talk to his foster parents or his social worker. Maybe both."

"But someone will help him?"

He thought briefly that her concern for the kid should have bothered him—he had just lit a blaze and run, after all—but it did the opposite. It moved him.

"We've got specialists we can refer through the fire department. Sometimes, though, depending on the case, a bunch of us just sit down with the kid in question and try to get to the bottom of why they did it. Try to help them see there's other ways to manage their feelings."

Casey nodded. The sirens were close now, wailing in the Robot Lit parking lot. The cops would be on them in a few moments.

"I can keep you appraised, if you want," Abe said, surprising himself. He wasn't one to share information about a case. But he found he wanted any chance he could get to talk to Casey again. "Probably makes sense to keep Robot Lit in the circle of adults who are informed and trying to counsel him."

She brightened. "I'd be grateful. Ingrid, too." For a second she looked like she was going to throw her arms around his neck, maybe even kiss him, but the moment passed, and she stayed rooted to the spot.

Damn. Had he done something on the date to offend her and cool things off between them? He hoped not.

At least he had an excuse to contact her again, though.

He could hear footsteps and voices in the stairwell. "I should go meet the officers before they head into the conference room. I'll be in touch."

Casey smiled. "Good," she said, and if Abe didn't know

better, he'd say she sounded excited about the prospect of hearing from him again.

Which left his brain more rattled than he'd like to admit. His head suddenly ached. He was good at reading women, dammit. So why was Casey Tanner throwing him for a loop? Irritation flared. He reminded himself there were other fish in the sea, and he didn't have to sit here getting worked up about someone who had him off his game so thoroughly.

But the idea rang hollow. He wanted to know what was going on with Casey. He wanted to know where they stood.

He ground his jaw, determined to think about it later. For now, he had police to talk to—and a young boy to deal with.

CHAPTER ELEVEN

I need a plan to get Abe Cameron into bed with me,"
Casey whispered to her sister the next evening. They were in
Audrey's kitchen trying to perfect a meat-and-potatoes hot
dish for the upcoming fund-raiser at the Lutheran church.
Local cooks could enter dishes, and then community members paid a small fee to taste and vote on the recipes. The
proceeds went to buy toys for kids who otherwise wouldn't
get them at Christmastime. The entire Knots and Bolts crew
was participating in lieu of their meeting that Thursday, and
Casey had begged her sister to help her make something that
wasn't overcooked or flat-out disgusting.

Audrey arched a brow as she blended sweet corn with
cream and butter on the stove. "Wow. I take it that means
your date went well?"

"Shh," Casey said, glancing toward the living room,
where Kieran was reading a book of poetry. Turns out the
Harley biker had a soft side for verse, which was one of the

many things that Casey had been surprised to learn about him. It had also been one of the many things that had made her feel even worse for trying to keep Kieran and Audrey apart for so long.

Audrey left the stove to turn up a small set of speakers that were plugged into her phone. The sound of "Rockin' Around the Christmas Tree" filled the small kitchen.

"That should do it," she said with a smile. "Now, spill."

Casey set down the potato she was peeling. "The date was good. Really good, actually."

"So why not have another and see what happens?" Audrey said, tossing a pinch of salt into the creamed corn. "Why do you need some big plan?"

"Because of the list our group came up with the other night. I mean, I want to make sure Abe is up for it. For *all* of it."

Audrey turned the burner down and wiped her hands on her apron. Her movements were confident, secure. The actions of a woman who was happy and loved her life right here, in this very house. Casey felt a twist of envy. She wanted happiness, too—just a different brand.

"Don't you want to make sure you like him first?" Audrey asked. "Like, *really* like him if you're going to sleep with him?"

"I like him well enough," Casey said, thinking of Abe's brawny shoulders, his hard jaw, his uncanny nose. "I just need a way to approach him with the list. Something that's not ridiculous and that doesn't make him run for the hills."

"What list is this?" Kieran Callaghan leaned in the kitchen doorway, his wide mouth grinning at Casey like he'd just overheard everything and was pretending not to.

"Casey's got the hots for Abe Cameron," Audrey said, sidling up to Kieran. She gave him a quick kiss on the cheek, but he grabbed her apron and pulled her in for more. Casey marveled at their playful ease, even as she fumed at her sister for blabbing about her attraction to Abe.

"Stop playing tonsil hockey already and help me, will you?" she asked, picking her potato back up. Brown ovals flew off her spud as she tried not to pay too much attention to Audrey and Kieran's make-out session. She was delighted her sister was happy, but she wished they could tone it down once in a while

Finally, they broke apart. Kieran walked over to the sink and picked up an unpeeled potato. His dark red hair glinted under the kitchen lights as he stood next to Casey. The potato looked small in his massive hands.

"You ever think about throwing yourself at Abe and seeing what happens?" he asked, grabbing an extra peeler and setting to work beside her.

Casey frowned. "Not really. I think the parameters should be clear from the start."

"Oh? And what parameters are those?"

Casey bit her lip. She couldn't really tell Kieran about her five things, could she?

"We helped Casey make a booty list," Audrey chimed in.

"Audrey!"

"Well, we did. And it's good. It's five things she wants this Christmas. And let me just say, you can't get these things at the mall."

"Ah. And you think all-American firefighter Abe Cameron should know about said list before you do...anything."

Casey nodded. She didn't want Abe thinking if she slept with him she was pining for a relationship—or anything close to one. She just wanted some fun. She also wanted to make sure he stuck around long enough to give her *all* five things and not just a one-night stand. It was a fine line, and how to walk it, never mind say any of it, was beyond her.

"I still don't get it," Audrey said. "Why not just let nature take its course? If you get the five things on the list, great. If not, you go your separate ways."

"I guess I'm trying to calculate the odds," Casey confessed. *What if he says no? What if he doesn't want anything to do with the list? What if I look stupid?* "I guess I just want a high probability of success."

"Jeez, talk about spontaneous," Audrey said.

Casey's heart sank at her sister's dry tone. The whole thing *was* a series of computations, it was true. Her efforts to be more fun-loving and free were coming up against her accountant's personality. Still, she *was* trying. More than that, she was beginning to lust after Abe so much that if he said no, she was beginning to worry it might sting more than she wanted it to.

"You could just tell him," Kieran offered. "Give him the list and say, 'Here. I want to do these things. You?' And then see how he responds."

"Seriously?" Audrey asked. "But what does Abe get out of the deal?"

Kieran smirked. "Other than sex with a hot woman with no strings attached? You mean *apart from that*?"

Casey blushed and kept peeling, unsure what to say.

"All right, but does she slip him a note?" Audrey asked. "Send him a text? Ask him in person?"

"The less of a paper trail the better," Casey said, dumping the now-peeled potatoes in boiling water. "At least that would be my preference."

"I agree," Kieran said, nodding. "Ask him in person. Do you have another date set up?"

"Not yet. But he's sent me a few texts about Carter Weaver, this kid he caught at a fire yesterday at Leroy's. Carter confessed to setting the Robot Lit fire, too. He's only ten years old, so it's not like they want to lock him up or something. The kid needs help."

"So the next time he texts you about Carter, say something along the lines of 'Great. Let's discuss this in person at my house over drinks.' And when he comes over, you proposition him."

Casey blinked. Kieran made it sound so simple. Just invite Abe over and—wham, bam, thank you, ma'am. Ideally, anyway.

Audrey left the potatoes to stand next to Casey. She linked arms with her sister. "I still don't understand. If you like Abe, why don't you just *date* him? See where it goes? You might get a lot more than just what's on your list."

I don't want more than what's on the list. I don't want a relationship. Casey bit back the words. Casey would never want her sister to think she didn't want these things because of Audrey. "I think the best thing for me is to just live a little. For now."

"You know," Kieran said thoughtfully, "I think Thursday's panel of judges includes a certain local fireman."

Casey nearly dropped the knife she was holding. "You mean Abe Cameron is going to taste what we're making right now?" Even with Audrey helping her, the idea of Abe downing her cooking was mortifying. There was still a high probability it would congeal into a tasteless blob and she'd have to serve it, red-faced and humiliated.

"Don't freak out—it's going to be good," Audrey said, handing Casey a block of cheddar cheese to grate.

"Even if it's not," Kieran said, "you'll both be in the same room, and that will give you a chance to talk. You can invite him over to your place afterward. Tell him you have something to discuss. Carter What's-his-name. Either way, you'll get him inside and you can tell him what you want. Boom. Done and done."

Casey grated a mound of cheese, thinking it sounded like a decent idea. Or, if not decent, then passable. A lot like her hot dish.

It might not win first place, but if it did the job, then she'd call it a victory.

"You think I can pull this off?" she asked them both.

Kieran popped a hunk of cheese into his mouth and smiled his lopsided grin. "I think we're as anxious to find out as you are."

Casey sprinkled the cheese on top of the casserole pan, into which Audrey had dumped the potatoes, the corn, some browned hamburger, sautéed onions, and a can of cream of mushroom soup.

"This had better work," she said, not sure if she meant the recipe, or what she was about to ask Abe on Thursday.

It would be a small miracle if she could pull off both.

CHAPTER TWELVE

Abe stared at the wrinkled face of Evelyn Beauford. "You want us to what?" he asked, certain he'd misheard the elderly woman.

"Take your shirts off," she said. "Except you, dear." She nodded to Quinn. "You can keep yours on."

Abe shifted in his metal folding chair in the basement of the White Pine Lutheran Church. The room was filled with the smells of baked goods and casseroles. Christmas lights twinkled along the edge of the ceiling, and a tree with a large, golden angel was shining from the corner. His stomach rumbled, even as his brain tried to process why Evelyn Beauford was asking him to strip in the house of God.

"We thought we were judges," he said, kicking Reese under the table as the probationary fought back laughter. "We didn't think we were—on display."

"You're not, sweetheart," Evelyn said, patting Abe's tough hand with her own padded one. "But we sold far more tickets to this thing when we said some of the judges were shirtless firefighters. I'm sure you understand. It's for a good cause."

He had to kick Quinn next. She was laughing so hard she was losing her breath. Lambeck tossed a wadded-up paper napkin at him. "Come on, Lu. You heard the lady. It's for a good cause. Don't you want your new girlfriend to see how hot you are?"

"I'm just trying to save everyone from seeing your man boobs," Abe fired back. Lambeck grinned, and pulled his shirt over his head. His toned chest hardly sported man boobs. The ridges of his six-pack were as well defined as the sturdy casserole pans all around them. He could have sworn he heard Evelyn Beauford utter a tiny squeal of delight.

Abe shook his head. He wasn't opposed to going shirtless—he had a body he'd chiseled out of a whole lot of hard work and sweat—but he wasn't much for surprises. And he certainly didn't like things being sprung on his *crew*. But since the three other firefighters seemed game—Lambeck was already letting Evelyn's friend Freida pat his biceps—he shrugged it off. He was just glad the mayor sitting at the far end of their judges' table, Robert Mackelson, hadn't been asked to go shirtless as well. In that case there *would* be man boobs.

Knowing Evelyn's eyes were trained on his chest, Abe pulled off his navy blue T-shirt with Station One emblazoned on the front. "Feel free to flex while you chew," she said, winking at him.

Quinn sat back in her chair, smug. "For once, I'm glad I'm a girl."

"You mean because that bartender wanted into your lady parts?" Reese asked, miming sex by putting his index finger through an O of fingers on his other hand.

"Haven't seen *that* move since middle school," Abe said to Reese.

Quinn snapped straight up. She poked Reese's bare chest, which was pale and lean compared to the other firefighters'. "Cut it. I don't want to hear you say one more word about him."

Turned out Abe wasn't the only one catching shit for being seen with someone new.

"Why, because you banged him and then walked away, and now you don't have anyone to have sex with?"

Quinn's face went so dark Abe was worried she was going to erupt. He knew that look. It usually happened when someone took her last yogurt from the fridge, but occasionally he'd seen it on a call, when they'd exhausted themselves and just couldn't save someone. It was the tender side of the bear, and this bear didn't like getting poked.

"Can it, Reese," Abe said. "No trash talk in the house of the Lord."

"Yes, Lu," Reese mumbled.

Abe made a note to ask Quinn about the bartender later, to see if she wanted to unload anything. In private. In the meantime, Evelyn Beauford placed herself in front of the panel of five judges—four firefighters and the mayor—and slid her eyes over the firemen's bare chests every chance she could get. "We're just about ready to open the church doors to the community," she said. "Some of their dishes are already here, dropped off in advance. But most of the food will be coming down those stairs with the cooks themselves. They will serve the judges first and then leave the rest for the townsfolk to eat. Pencils and scorecards are there on the table. You will decide together which dishes get third, second, and first place. Sound dandy?"

Everyone nodded. "Wonderful!" Evelyn said, and turned on her white sneakers to go unleash the community on the unsuspecting judges.

Within minutes, the basement was packed with people, loud voices echoing off the white-bricked walls. Abe had five small plates shoved in front of him before he could think.

"That's a key lime pie," said a raven-haired woman who leaned her hip on the table just so, to angle in. Sherri Sheridan. Her eyes swept unabashedly from Abe's face to his bare chest, and then lower. "It's made with real limes, not the imitation stuff."

"You raid a pirate ship for fresh limes in the middle of winter?" Abe asked, taking in the woman's long lashes, her full mouth. He'd been on the debate team with Sherri once, and thought he remembered that mouth. He thought she'd gotten married and moved away for a while. Apparently she was back now. No ring that he could tell. He speared the pie but didn't bring it to his lips.

"No ships, but I drove up to Minneapolis for my fruit. Lots of booty involved either way." She winked then, long and slow, and Abe felt a grin start to spread on his face.

"Sherri, dessert is supposed to arrive at the judges' table *last*. You didn't wait your turn." A frowning Evelyn had elbowed into the tight-packed table. Reese was shoving food into his face like he hadn't eaten in a month, not even writing anything on the scorecards.

"Sometimes you want the sweet things first," Sherri said. "Yolo and all that."

"Yo what now?" Evelyn asked.

"Nothing," Sherri said, waving a hand that sported long, lacquered nails. "I'll remember the rules next time. And for

the record, it's what's at the *bottom* of the pie that's sweet-
est." She glanced pointedly at the edge of the plate, where
her initials were written. All the other entrants' initials were
written on their dishes, too.

S.S., Abe read, thinking that was appropriate. She was
like a ship all right, cutting through the chop to get what she
wanted. Then he saw it. Sticking out from underneath her
initials was a small corner of paper.

A note. For him.

With a final grin she walked away, her ass moving like
it still had things to say. Abe watched appreciatively for a
second, then pulled out the piece of paper from underneath
the plate. The old adrenaline was back—the rush of meeting
someone new and wondering if he could get her into bed.
Wondering how long it would be before he tired of her. He
stared at her number, at the heart that was round and bubbly enough to have been drawn by a twelve-year-old, and the
rush went cold. It turned to ash somewhere deep in his gut.

A picture of Casey was suddenly in his mind.

Shit. Why did she have to be everywhere, when a couple
weeks ago she hadn't been anywhere? He tucked the number
quickly away, muttering under his breath.

"I saw that number at the bar," Quinn said between bites
of food, "on a bathroom stall."

Abe ate the pie so he didn't have to reply. Quinn was giving him a hard time, and he didn't feel like taking the bait.
A few weeks ago, he would have thrown a smart-ass remark
right back at her, then jumped over the table and taken Sherri
back to his place without thinking. He would have peeled off
Sherri's skinny jeans and let those long nails rip tracks up
his back. He would have worked his *Ninety-Eyed* name with
pride.

Now, though, the idea was tinged with a gray edge, colorless and empty. What he wanted to do was see Casey. He pushed the pie aside and dug into a macaroni salad instead.

He chewed, thinking about his texts with Casey over the last few days. Mostly, they'd been about the situation with Carter. Abe had told her how the boy's social worker had been firm but sympathetic after the fires, asking Carter questions about his feelings, his foster family, and his school—all to try to get at what was behind Carter wanting to see things burn. Abe and Officer Niequist had headed down to talk with Carter's school counselor, Amy Strand. She'd indicated Carter was a good student whose only parent, a single mother, had recently checked herself into rehab for prescription pill addiction. Without any family close by, she'd agreed to let Carter go to foster care temporarily. Carter's mom was slated for reevaluation at the end of the month, when her stint in rehab ended. In the meantime, both Casey and Ingrid had made sure to say that Robot Lit's doors were still open to Carter, and that they wanted him to keep writing. That it was a safer way to express what he was feeling than fire.

The texts hadn't been exactly flirty. Or playful. But Abe hadn't minded. He'd felt as though he and Casey had been trying to solve a problem together, and he liked that. Their communication was substantive. Meaningful. He glanced at the key lime pie. His communication with Casey was the opposite of an empty dessert.

The question was, where was any of this headed? Abe swallowed the last of the macaroni salad, rating it a four out of five on the scorecard. Then he pulled in a plate of casserole that looked like someone had dumped melted cheese on one of Reese's hamburgers.

Women like Sherri were easy to figure out. They were

simple. Casey was a lot more complex, but he found he didn't mind. He'd never shied away from a challenge, after all.

Like this hot dish.

He took a small forkful. He stared at the lumpy mess for a moment. Then he thought *What the hell*, and swallowed it down. To his surprise, it had a sweet and salty undertone to it—some kind of corn thing—and it was seasoned with a hint of spice, just a tiny whisper of heat. Damned if this hot dish wasn't *good*. Abe almost smiled, thinking the casserole was just like him. A little rough in some aspects, but all right if you give it a chance.

Like him, if *Casey* would give him a chance.

He shook his head. What a ridiculous thought. It was the chest pains talking. They'd made him desperate to settle on someone, when in reality he probably just needed to lighten up.

He slid the plate aside, but not before writing 5 on the scorecard.

Quinn elbowed him. "Careful," she muttered, "everyone here is going to think you've reformed." She blew her bangs off her forehead.

"What are you talking about, Puffy?" Abe asked, reaching for asparagus soup next.

"You blow off the cougar and then rate your girlfriend's dish the highest? It's textbook."

"I don't have a girlfriend. And what do you mean?"

"Duh, Einstein," she said, pointing to the edge of the paper plate. And that was when Abe saw the initials. *C.T.*

Casey Tanner.

And right then, he felt it. More precisely, he felt *her*. In the hot-packed room with all the overpowering food scents, it was hard to find her, hard to know where exactly to look. More than anything, though, he knew she was here, and he wanted to see her.

He stood, leaning his hands on the judges' table as he peered over the heads of the crowd.

When a pair of molasses-brown eyes near the Christmas tree found his, something locked into place. He grinned. She was wearing a bright red off-the-shoulder shirt, with a thin little belt around her middle. More color on her than usual, but it made her look like a present he wanted to unwrap.

Her eyes were big and round, staring at his shirtless chest. He flexed, and swore she swallowed. He flicked his head in a come-here motion. As she wove her way through the crowd, his stomach rumbled.

He wanted more of her hot dish.

And then, when that was done, he wanted more of *her*.

* * *

Casey had watched Abe flirt with a black-haired bombshell and swore to herself that propositioning him was off the table. What was she thinking, trying to snag a firefighter with abs you could grate cheese on? She might want Abe, it was true, but so did lots of other women.

Disappointment had needled her. But so had something else. Frustration, maybe. Not at Abe, but at herself. Was she really going to give up on her list so easily? Was she really going to get knocked off her game by a pie-serving floozy in skinny jeans?

That was right about the time she'd caught his eye and he'd motioned her over. She'd started across the floor on unsteady feet. What would she say once she got to the table?

Would she actually follow through with inviting him to her place?

Now, Betty elbowed into her side as she made her way through the crowd.

"Somebody liked your casserole," Betty sing-songed, a ring in her voice like triumph, like she'd bet on the underdog and come out with a pocketful of winnings.

"How can you possibly know that?"

"I saw him eat it. Devour it, really. Wasn't much to look at, but he sure licked his plate clean."

Why was it that every time Betty talked to her, she felt like she was being teased? No fair that a pastor's wife could be the saltiest one of them all. "Thanks for the heads-up."

Betty smiled so big her whole face crunched. "I'm proud of you, kiddo. You have a look on your face like you're going to go get something you want. I hope it includes letting Abe check a few items off your Christmas list?"

Casey stared. Betty's eyes were too warm for her to be teasing. It was more like Betty was asking her if she was going to fish or cut bait.

"You never mince words, do you?"

"Not if I can help it."

Casey stopped. Bodies jostled around them. Abe was mere feet away. She was close enough to see the contours of muscle underneath his tight skin. It brought to mind terms she'd learned in grade-school geography. *Moraine. Caldera. Fault line.* She bet she could find an example of every one of those things on Abe.

"I'm going to invite him over to my house after the event."

Once the words were out there, it seemed more true. Betty swatted Casey's ass.

"That's the spirit."

"Thanks?"

"You can thank me next Thursday at the Knots and Bolts meeting. Maybe by telling us all how it went?"

Casey gave her a sideways glance. They both knew Betty didn't need to phrase it as a question. Casey would tell them all what had happened. Betty would no doubt find a clever way to pull it out of her.

Casey barely had time to blink before Betty had retreated back into the crowd. She returned her focus to Abe, who was shirtless and surrounded by plates of food and not paying them any attention. He was looking straight at her.

She squared her shoulders.

It was time to ask him over for a drink.

It was time to take some action on her list.

CHAPTER THIRTEEN

$\mathcal{T}$wo hours later, Casey was pouring wine with shaking hands, unable to believe that not only had Abe accepted her invitation to come over, but also that she'd somehow won the third-place ribbon in tonight's fund-raiser. She'd tried to press the silky fabric into Audrey's hands, but her sister would have none of it. "I only helped a little. *You* earned that ribbon."

Casey wasn't so sure. She had almost added cream of celery soup to the hot dish instead of cream of mushroom, and she'd baked it at 450 degrees instead of 400. So it was clearly not a perfect outcome. But she was the one who'd suggested a dash or two of Tabasco, just to spice it up. And she had added more cheese than the recipe called for, because what could go wrong there?

In the end, the answer was nothing. And the fund-raiser had taken in more than a thousand dollars to help buy kids Christmas presents.

Now, as she carried the wine into the living room, where Abe was sitting, she was wondering if her luck would hold for the rest of the night. Namely so she could ask the firefighter in her living room to sleep with her.

And hear him say yes. That last part being key.

"So Evelyn Beauford has a wild side after all," she said, handing Abe his glass. He reached for it, his fingertips brushing hers. Electricity sparked on her skin. She nearly spilled the liquid everywhere.

"She got what she wanted tonight," Abe said.

"I suppose she's coordinated enough fund-raisers and charity events in this town to think about herself for one minute," Casey said, seating herself next to Abe on the couch. Close, but not too close. "It's not like she asked for a million dollars."

"No. Just some half-naked firefighters."

Casey smiled. Abe lifted his wine. "To getting what you want," he said, and Casey shivered slightly as she clinked her glass with his.

If only Abe knew what *she* wanted.

"Ingrid, Rolf, and I are going to speak to Carter tomorrow," she said, trying to focus. She had asked Abe over under the guise of talking about next steps with the troubled boy. She might want to skip the talking and go straight to bed, but it was important to ensure that they talked about Carter getting the help he needed.

"He always comes in on Fridays, and we were going to see if he might share his journals with us. It might shed light on what he's going through."

Abe nodded. "Good idea. And it will help him know that Robot Lit still cares about him. I think a lot of places would have thrown him out after what he did."

Casey studied the rich red hues of her cabernet. She'd thought about serving Abe beer or Scotch, but decided against it because she drank neither, and she didn't want it to seem like she'd bought something in anticipation of him coming over, even though that was precisely what she had done. She took a sip of the bold, oaky flavor and decided it was plenty manly enough.

"We are being cautious," she said, shifting her thoughts back to Robot Lit. "Carter has to be under Rolf's observation when he's in the building. He can't even go to the bathroom by himself. But Ingrid and I talked about it. We don't want to take away the only thing that he has. And right now, sad as it is to say, we think that might be the nonprofit."

Abe leaned forward a few inches. To Casey it felt like he had crossed the Mississippi, or the desert, or some other unfathomable border that brought his scent stronger, his warmth closer. If she leaned in, too, their bodies would almost be touching.

"It's a lot of years ago now, but when Ingrid's mom ran the place, I was the same way. My parents were great—are great, actually—but they're artists, and they didn't understand the struggle I was having to read. They were more the 'Oh, it'll come when it comes' type. But in the meantime, I didn't understand anything that was happening at school. I was falling behind. I was just a kid, but I'm pretty sure I was depressed. Or something like it."

"Was it dyslexia?" Casey asked.

Abe nodded. "Mild, but yeah. I felt like such a freak, but Robot Lit made it okay for me to be who I was. They worked with me. Met me where I was at. The fact that you're doing the same thing with Carter now"—he shook his head—"it's incredible."

"I know the kind of pressure kids can have heaped on them," Casey agreed, thinking of her own past. "They need help sometimes. Not just punishment."

Abe surprised her by grabbing her hand. He raked his thumb over her knuckles. She inhaled sharply.

"You're a good person," he said, his hazel eyes dropping to her lips. "So if I did anything the other night to offend you, I apologize."

Casey blinked, trying to concentrate as Abe's fingers played with her own. "You mean the night of the Christmas tree lighting?"

"You raced out of my car like you couldn't get away from me fast enough. Not to mention," he added playfully, "you didn't even complete my survey so I'd know where I went wrong."

Because I was worried I'd throw myself at you, she thought.

"It's—well, I did leave quickly. But not for the reasons you think."

Abe raised a brow. "Oh?"

Casey set her wine on the table. Abe followed suit.

"It's because…" she trailed off. She'd practiced this part, dammit. She should have this down. Only her words were mixed up and jumbled, like the ingredients in her casserole.

She tamped down her nerves and worked to find her accountant's composure. "I found myself very attracted to you," she said after a moment. God, she sounded like a robot. "That's why I left. I was worried I'd do something foolish."

A smile lifted the corner of Abe's mouth. Cripes, she wanted to kiss that corner. "That's bad news," he said. "If you find yourself attracted to me again, there's nowhere else to go. You're home and I'm right here."

Casey could see the sliver of an opening in his words. It wasn't great, but she'd have to take it.

Here goes everything, she thought.

"We could make the best of it," she said slowly, letting her fingers play along Abe's knuckles. "We could have some fun together, I mean. Nothing serious. Just...fun."

She'd said *fun* twice. He was going to think she was talking about a bouncy castle, for crying out loud.

Her words hung there for a moment. She stared at Abe's blond hair, threaded through with gold, and his hazel eyes, like a field of grass after fall's first frost. She could still picture his wide chest, bare and brazen at the fund-raiser, and how she'd longed to taste his skin more than any of the dishes there. Her whole being trembled as she imagined his arms around her, his lips against hers, his weight on top of her as they came together. Her center heated.

"Fun can mean a lot of things," he said, inching closer to her on the couch. "Care to elaborate?" He pushed back a strand of her hair. He was so gentle. Too gentle. She wanted him rough.

Impulsively, she grabbed his hand and brought her mouth down on his index finger. His eyes widened as she began to suck. And then he growled in a way that had her nerves tingling. She moved her tongue around, having no idea what she was doing. She'd never sucked anyone's fingers before. Heck, she'd never sucked a man's *anything* before. Not even Miles's. But Abe seemed to like it. He closed his eyes briefly, and then used his other hand to palm his way up her ribs.

A moment later, he pulled his fingers out of her mouth and left his hand an inch away from her breasts. She could feel her nipples tightening, could feel them straining for his touch.

"You didn't answer my question."

He acted like he was going to cease all making out and touching until she spelled it out.

"I want you," Casey said, her words more breathless than she'd expected. "I hear you're a player, and, as it turns out, I'm in the mood to play."

She studied Abe's chiseled face for a reaction, but his features didn't betray anything. So she barreled forward. "I would like some specific things done to me. It's not a long list, but it's *my* list, and I wondered if you wanted to take a stab at it. It's no-strings-attached sex. Two adults agreeing that the arrangement can work and deciding to do it. Nothing more."

Abe's fingers teased their way a millimeter closer to her breasts. She nearly groaned.

"What's on your list?" he asked, his voice even lower than it had been minutes ago.

"Nothing I'm sure you haven't tackled a thousand times," she said. She tried to sound authoritative, like she did this all the time. "I want to start out kissing, but have it lead to sex. I want the sex to be rough. I want twelve orgasms out of said sex." She could feel her face burning but she kept going. "I want the sex to happen a lot, specifically on Christmas Day. And I want some adult toys involved."

A muscle worked in Abe's jaw. She searched his face for a clue to his thoughts but couldn't find one. The man was iron and ice.

And muscle and skin, she thought hungrily.

"Do you want all twelve orgasms in one sitting?" he asked finally.

This was his question? All the tense silence for that? Casey actually giggled. She clasped a hand over her mouth.

"No," she said through her fingers, "I just want to say that I've had twelve. With someone else. Not, you know, by my own doing."

Abe's hazel eyes narrowed. "You've never had twelve orgasms with anyone else?"

Casey dropped her hand. She supposed she'd have to be honest if she wanted a chance at this arrangement happening.

"No. I've only ever really dated one guy seriously. And he wasn't exactly...a creative type."

"Are you a virgin?"

She might as well be. "Technically, no. I've had sex. Not good sex, but I've had it."

This seemed to pique Abe's interest. "And me because...?"

Casey dropped her bullshit filter as far down as it would go. "I want you. I hear you...might have some experience to offer. Plus there's chemistry here. I want what I want, and you seem like the guy who could give it."

"But nothing more than what's on the list?"

Was it her imagination, or was there a hopeful note in there somewhere? Like maybe Abe wanted more? But of course that couldn't be true. And even if he did want more, Casey wasn't about to give it. Because where would it end? If they took it all the way, it would end in disaster. She'd been down that road before, and she wasn't going to repeat her mistakes. She'd lived too much of her life being constricted by things. Now it was time to be free.

"Nothing more than what's on the list," she said firmly.

"I may have to take issue with your categories, though," Abe said slowly, his hand inching upward again.

He rubbed his thumb over her nipple and she arched back, savoring the feel of his fingers on her. He brought his lips to her throat, warm and strong. He licked the length of her neck.

He could stop here, she thought, *and it would be the most wild and alive thing that's ever happened to me.*

Except then he slipped his hand underneath her red shirt and his palms slid along her ribs, to her back. In one quick motion he'd unhooked her bra, and then his fingers were on her breasts, expertly rolling along her left nipple and then her right, and the vibration from his touch echoed in every single one of her cells.

"Oh my God," she whispered.

"No," he said, the heat of his words on her skin, his breath setting her insides aflame, "that was earlier in the Lutheran church."

She could barely hear him. She was losing her train of thought entirely. Her brain was in shutdown mode, letting a more primitive part of her body take over. She loved it. The visceral no-thoughts-only-feelings tide carrying her away was the most freeing thing she'd ever known.

They were doing this. He was saying yes.

Or at least that was what she thought until Abe started talking again.

"See, the problem is," he said, nipping along her clavicles and neck while his hands continued their magical course, "I'm not sure what happens in this arrangement if I do *this*." In one swift motion, he tugged on the edge of her shirt and lifted it over her head. Her bra, already unhooked, came off with the wad of clothing.

She straightened, surprised to suddenly be sitting in front of him topless on the couch. While he was still clothed.

Casey brought a self-conscious hand to her chest. The

lights were still on, she realized. Was he seeing too much of her? "Uh, is there cause for concern?"

Abe smiled, then pulled her hand away from her body gently. She was bared to him once again. His gold-flecked eyes gazed into hers, and she wondered at the tenderness there. Wasn't this supposed to be rough? Emotionless? She swallowed back the nervousness, and tried to imagine all the things he was going to do to her. Once he got done asking questions, that is.

"I'm just trying to understand the boundaries," he said, staring at her breasts, the tenderness in his eyes transforming to something closer to hunger. "Your plan is ill defined."

"I don't see how."

He pulled her to him then, quick and rough, and her whole body ignited with feeling. His mouth was hot, his tongue penetrating and tangling with hers in a way that had her imagining twisted silk and knotted sheets. He broke the kiss to push her back on the couch. She'd hardly opened her eyes before she closed them again, savoring the solid weight of him on her. Her hands grasped his shoulders, taking in the feel of his knotted muscles underneath his fireman's shirt. But then he broke from her grasp and slid down, so that his lips were suddenly on her breasts.

She gasped as his mouth landed on her right nipple, his other hand working perfectly over her left breast. It felt as if a string of fireworks was connected from her chest to her innermost parts. She cried out at the thrilling sensation. Abe sucked and nipped her tender skin. She plunged her hands into his blond hair, twining her fingers in its thickness, trying to anchor herself to the here and now. His mouth found her left nipple, giving it equal attention. She bit her lip to keep from shouting at the ceiling again.

By degrees, Abe pulled away from her skin. His eyes met hers. "That wasn't on your list," he said, low and gravelly. She wondered suddenly what it would feel like to have the vibrations of his words on her breasts, to have him talk in that charcoal-and-fire voice of his while he was against her chest. She shook off the thought, trying to concentrate on what he was saying.

"Not technically it wasn't," she said, "but you could infer that it's *leading* to things that are on my list."

He kissed the tip of each breast gently. "I'm just saying, there are a lot of loopholes." His warm breath heated her skin.

"I think you're being too literal," she said, shifting underneath him. The hard length of him was right there. She lifted her hips. He closed his eyes, swallowing visibly.

"You're the one with the rules," he growled, his hands unbuttoning her jeans almost before she realized it. He yanked them off her raised hips, leaving her on her back on the couch in nothing but a red lace thong. He cocked a brow. "A lot of thought went into this. Clearly. But maybe not enough."

"The only thing I'm *thinking* is that you're wearing too many clothes." She sat up, trying to lift off his shirt, but he pulled back.

"Oh, no you don't," he said, pushing her back down. He kneed apart her legs, and settled between them. The heat of him was delicious. She wondered if maybe they'd make out some more, and then he'd climb off and undress slowly. Maybe he'd give her a little show. She shivered, thinking of his bare skin, his rippled muscles.

"We need to close these loopholes," he said, trailing his hand from her knee, up to her thigh, then higher still. He snapped the band of her underwear. It bit her skin deliciously. *Do that again*, she thought. But he went one better. He slipped his fingers underneath the seam of the thong, touching her folds.

"Oh!" she cried out. Her back arched.

"Stay with me," he said, a smile on his lips as he kissed her. "We're still discussing this."

"I don't want to discuss anything."

"But I do." His finger trailed over her clitoris, down her folds and up again. She writhed against him. She was wet and wanting. She'd never hungered for anything like she hungered for Abe Cameron inside of her.

"There are technicalities we need to broach," he said. His knee guided her legs apart farther. She let him. She'd let him tie her up if he wanted. He pushed aside the minimal fabric of her thong for more access. She moaned.

"Are you going to talk or fuck me?" she asked. The bold question felt dangerous, felt right.

"That's just it," Abe said. "What if I do this instead?" He guided a finger into her, and her whole world went dark. She was blindfolded and underwater and knew nothing except the feeling of him gliding in and out of her. It didn't matter that it wasn't his penis. It was the most glorious thing she'd ever felt. Better than the nights alone with her vibrator. Better than the no-frills sex she'd had with Miles. Better than anything she'd imagined up until this point.

"Where is this on your list, Casey?" he growled into her ear. He rested more of his weight against her, angling himself perfectly. She opened her legs wider, grasping at his back for grounding. "Where does this fit?"

She couldn't answer. It was like being in the elevator all over again, only this time pleasure was shutting her down, not fear. He inserted another finger. Then another. She hissed in breath. He was stretching her. *Imagine what his penis will do*, she thought wildly. It was a flash of logic before she went under again, drowning in the sensations churning in the foundation of her body, building and building, until she was sure everything would come crumbling down around her.

His teeth bit her skin, his hand crashed against her. "I *will* make you come," he said, his lips right up against her ear, his rock-hard shaft grinding against her bare thigh. "I'll make you come so hard you forget where you are. And you won't know what to do with it on your *list*."

It was as if her body wanted the challenge, and was all too ready to meet it. The minute he uttered the words, she broke. Her orgasm stampeded out of the pent-up amalgamation that was her body—her skin, her cells, her bones, her marrow all flung themselves to the far reaches of feeling, barreling into the sensation as a ship might meet an oncoming wave.

She heard a noise and realized vaguely that she was making it. She wished she could say she was crying out like they did in the movies, but it was more like she was howling. She was animalistic, clawing at his shoulders, letting these wild nerves carry her deeper into the tangled forest of her own pleasure. She wailed and imagined moonlight and sharp branches, teeth and claws, shivering grasses and dangerous shadows.

Abe plunged into the primitive place with her. "Yes," he hissed, his movements in synch with her pulsing, his breath in time with her own ragged lungs. "Go deep, go hard." He didn't let up, he kept pace with her rocking pleasure, demanding her body give everything it had. He drove her, he pushed her—his body anchoring her and flinging her off some reckless cliff at the same time. She tumbled headfirst into it, savoring the wild falling sensation, letting everything go light and dark as she spun downward through her sparking pleasure.

She arched and twisted and yelled for what seemed like full minutes and also no time at all. By and by, the shadows retreated from her periphery, and the light slowly lost its edge, returning to the warm glow of her living room. She came back to her body, remembered she was on her couch. Naked. With Abe Cameron. She opened her eyes.

His hand had quieted. He was staring at her with a cross between amusement and something else. Awe, maybe. She was dazed, wondering if she had somehow imagined all this. Had she really just let herself come undone so fully, so unabashedly in front of a man she hardly knew?

Of course, that was sort of the point. She'd just taken the first step toward getting some things checked off her list.

Or not, as Abe seemed to want to remind her. "That was anomalous," he said, easing some of his weight off of her. She felt the absence of him keenly. He made up for it by kissing her shoulder, her clavicle. "That was not on your list. It can't count as one of the twelve orgasms, since it didn't result from sex."

She sighed contentedly, hardly caring. "I'm not sure it matters," she murmured.

"It means everything on your list is still unchecked."

"Do we need to get hung up on a technicality?"

"Possibly."

"Why?"

"You constructed this plan. So if I'm going to be part of it, I want it to be clear-cut."

If. Like he was on the fence, still deciding. Even after

what they'd just done. Her heart hammered. Maybe he would, after all, just walk away from her after one brief encounter.

"It's easy to rectify," she said, trying keep the worry off her face. Even her concern couldn't stop her hunger from building for him already, all over again. "Let's have sex. Now. And when I come from *that*, it will count." She placed her hand on Abe's groin. His thickness jumped at her touch. But instead of surrendering to her and taking her to bed, he clenched his jaw. Everything in him tensed.

"It's more than tempting," he said, "but there's still too much gray area for my taste." Abe smiled, but there a sharp note in his tone—a sliver in a sea of silk. He sat up and handed over her pants and shirt, everything crumpled and wrinkled.

"So let's work on it together," she said, putting a hand on his arm. "Come on." Playful. Light. *Just stay here and keep having fun*, she thought. She fiddled with her clothes but didn't put them on.

"Don't get me wrong. I liked tonight. A lot. I'm just saying, the list is imperfect. Incomplete."

"So?"

"So, it means that if I do something to you and it's not on the list, where does that leave us? Tonight, for example."

"I'm not sure it matters. Think of the list more like guidelines than rules. Like the pirate code." She smiled but he didn't return it. Her neck prickled with unease. She didn't understand why he was so frustrated.

Audrey's words came back to her then, about how she should just throw away the list and see what might happen with Abe. But no, she didn't want that. And a player like Abe surely couldn't want that from her, either.

"What if," she said slowly, "I modify the list a bit? Make sure we've got more...*specifics* covered? Would that help?"

He ran a hand over his jaw. "I'm not sure—" He stopped himself. Took a deep breath. Casey watched him, unable to decipher what was really going on with him, what thoughts were churning just underneath the surface.

"That's a good idea," he said finally. "Precisely what I was thinking." He stood to his feet and pulled on his clothes. She watched, wishing they were headed toward her bedroom instead.

She grabbed a nearby throw blanket and wrapped it around herself. She stood next to him.

"You look like you just got out of the pool," he said. The bridge of his crooked nose crinkled as he grinned.

"I feel like I just got dunked into the ocean, then left on the beach."

Abe stepped close. He ran a finger across her cheekbone, to the edge of her face, around the lobe of her ear. She shivered with the impossible deliciousness of it.

"If you wanted, you could..." he trailed off, his eyes not moving from hers.

"What?" she asked, her heart pounding. *He wanted to take her back to the bedroom.* Surely that was it. He hadn't had enough of her yet.

He shook his head. "I was just going to say that if you wanted to text me the revised list, that would be fine. Once you get more specific."

I thought I was specific, she mused as he kissed her and melted her on the spot. His kiss was a perfect mix of soft and spicy. How did he know how to *do* that? Before she could think to ask, he had pulled on his coat and grabbed his keys and was heading for the door.

"See you soon," he said, his boots crunching cold snow as he walked into the December darkness.

Once again, it wasn't a question.

When the door closed behind him, Casey leaned against it, feeling spent. And confused. Had Abe really just refused sex with her, claiming to want more... guidelines?

Her list was supposed to be a road map, nothing more. She was glad she'd left out the part where the entire Knots and Bolts crew helped craft it.

The question of whether Abe actually wanted her nagged at a corner of her brain. Had he said all that about the loopholes just so he didn't have to get entangled with her? It was a distinct possibility. And yet it hadn't seemed that way when he'd looked at her. And certainly not when he'd touched her.

So why had he left her tonight?

She chewed her lip, wondering how in the world she was going to fix her list to satisfy him. Satisfy *them*, when it came down to it. Abe touching her had been an explosion of feeling she'd never known before, and she would do just about anything to get it to happen again.

She walked to her pile of clothes, her muscles deliciously slack, thinking that she would paint a precisely detailed picture of her needs for Abe, down to every last position and possibility. He'd have no wiggle room.

Her heart constricted. And if he balked then, she'd know he didn't want her.

Either that, or he wanted *more*.

She blinked. Was there a possibility he was finding flaws in her list so he wouldn't have to play by the rules at all? So that they could have an actual... relationship and not a to-do list?

No. She pushed the thought aside. That was nuts. Abe Cameron didn't want a relationship. That was why she'd propositioned him in the first place.

The reality was that the rule-prone firefighter just wanted more... well, rules. And that was fine with her. She could get very, very detailed indeed.

Casey smiled as she flipped off lights and carried her tired body to her bedroom, thinking that she couldn't wait to introduce Abe to her bed. She flipped back the covers, where her crisp, freshly washed sheets had been at the ready. There had been scented candles on top of the nightstand, and body oil tucked into the top drawer, along with a multi-pack of condoms.

More for next time, she thought, yawning as her body relaxed into the sheets. She tried to think of the ways her list could be more specific, tried to get her mind humming with options to shore up the loopholes, but her ideas were blurry and unspecific. She couldn't get ahold of them.

Except for one, sharp and clear, as sleep overtook her:

What happened tonight might not have even been on her list, but Abe Cameron had made her feel extraordinary.

CHAPTER FOURTEEN

The next morning, the streets were quiet and muffled from a fresh dusting of snow as Abe drove to the White Pine Retirement Village to see his folks. Outside all was peaceful, but inside Abe's head, the noise was as loud as one of his station's engines.

The previous night with Casey Tanner had been a jumbled series of contrasts he couldn't make sense of. Wild and restrained. Sleek and barbed. Flaming hot and ash cold.

And *he'd* caused the variations. Casey had been specific and focused about what she'd wanted. But he'd made their night so muddy it would be a miracle if he ever saw straight through the whole situation.

Never mind that what he could still see, clear as day, were Casey's breasts, tight and high as he ran his tongue over them, her back arching as she came in his hands. She'd fallen apart so beautifully that his chest had ached all over again from something he couldn't put his finger on.

What was even happening to him?

He slammed an open palm against the steering wheel, hating how edgy and indecisive he felt. He was never this way about women. He always knew what to do, always knew what he wanted.

But not this time.

He steered his Jeep into the village's parking lot and pulled into a parking space. The lemon yellow structure with white trim rose cheerily above the snow. He spotted a Christmas tree decorated with colored lights through the large bay window at the front. Cardinals darted into and out of the bird feeder on the main lawn. Their crimson wings flashed against the surrounding white.

Abe killed the engine and took a deep breath. He was going to have to get his thoughts together about Casey Tanner.

But that was just it. He didn't know *what* to think.

On any other woman at any other time, her list of five things would have been the greatest invitation of his life. *I am a beautiful woman, and here are five sexy things I want, no strings attached. Give them to me.* He could imagine his former self clicking his heels and saluting. Yes ma'am. Ninety-Eyed here, proud to do my duty for the good of all.

But Casey was different. And, yeah, maybe it was the phantom chest pains talking and, fine, so he was pushing forty and thinking about whether or not he should get his shit together and start a family. But it was more than just that.

Casey was smart and funny, resourceful and kind. He loved that she didn't want to throw Carter under the bus for those fires, and that she was trying to help him. He respected the hell out of how she'd pulled herself—and her sister, for that matter—from an unfortunate situation and made sure they turned out okay. He dug her logical, practical mind, which was so much like his own.

And when it came down to it, he admired how she'd been bold enough to write down a list and say, "This is what I want." So many of the women he'd been with would put a screen over their lust, as if he couldn't see right through it. They'd talk about wanting to take it slow, and then they'd jump him on the second date. They'd pretend to be shocked in the bedroom when he tried a different position or two, even when he could see their eyes narrowing with want.

Casey did away with all that. She was honest. She was straightforward. And Abe should be meeting everything on her list with aplomb.

Except he couldn't.

He sighed as he pushed open the car door, thinking that her list was like Dr. Frankenstein's monster—wonderful and horrible at the same time.

It wasn't that he didn't want to do those things with Casey.

It was that he didn't want to do *only* those things with Casey.

He pulled open the door of the village, and signed in at the front desk. A nurse with square glasses smiled at him, said something about the weather. He could barely respond. His mind was still on the damn list. He saw that list in the curve of the furniture in the cozy meeting room, where families and village residents sat and chatted. He saw the list in the sparkle of the snow beyond the large, wide-paned windows. He saw the list in the stacks of books and games piled in the library, where a faux fire crackled happily.

The list was everywhere.

And at the same time it was nowhere. He'd made sure of that, because he'd told Casey to change it.

As he ascended the elevator to his parents' apartment, he wanted to kick himself. Last night he'd thought finding the loopholes in the damn thing was the smartest thing he'd ever done. He'd pinpointed them so that he wouldn't have to be chained to her rules. He wanted to put a wrench in her game and hint at the possibilities of them as something more than just those five things.

But he'd pushed it too far. And now she was going to alter the list to make it expanded and specific. In other words, iron clad. He'd see her again and her five things would practically be a notarized legal document, with clearly stated facts there'd be no way to get around.

Once he was presented with that, he'd have to tell her if he was in or out.

He'd have to decide if he could give her what she wanted—and only what she wanted—or if he'd need to walk away because he wanted *more*.

The thought was jarring.

Was it possible he wanted an actual relationship with Casey Tanner?

He turned over the notion in his brain.

Not ninety days. Not a hundred and ninety days. But as long as she'd give him.

His gut twisted. The answer was yes. It was the first time he'd ever felt this way about anyone. And he'd never been more miserable. No wonder he'd been single for so long.

He rang his folks' bell, wondering what in the world he was going to do. Was there any way he could convince Casey to commit to him when all she wanted was five things? He respected her choice to create her list. And yet he wanted to shatter those five things and tear through to her heart, begging her to trust him with it.

His mom opened the door, took one look at his face, and pulled him into a hug. "Oh, Abe. Come on in and tell me all about it."

Abe hugged his mom back and almost smiled. How did parents always know?

* * *

Half an hour later, Abe was sitting with mint tea steaming from a mug, and his mom's paint-splattered hand was patting his gently. His dad had been cutting up a ginger snap with a spoon moments before, until Abe had reached over to help. "Let me get that for you," he'd offered. When his dad had started to protest, they all decided to cut their cookies with spoons. Now the floor was littered with crumbs from their clumsy efforts, but their cookies were in bite-sized chunks and, more importantly, his dad was happy.

Abe allowed the happiness to be enough. Even though his dad was already more childlike now than the last time Abe had visited. Even though his eyes had a paleness to them that hadn't been there before, like his gaze was becoming as misty as his brain.

It would continue to get worse, Abe knew. Happiness would come only in blips, in flashes. He would hold on to whatever he could get.

"What's happening at work?" his mom asked, distracting him. Flyaway hairs from her gray-blond ponytail curled around her lined face. "Everything okay there?"

She was trying to get at the root of what had been eating at him when he showed up. But she was too polite to ask about it directly.

"Things are okay. I caught a kid lighting fires. He's young. Just ten."

"My." His mom's face fell. "That *is* hard. What will you do?"

Abe fiddled with the string on his tea bag. "A group of us are going to meet with his guidance counselor, his social worker, his foster parents, maybe. The nonprofit where he set the first fire—they're going to be in the mix as well. The idea is to talk to him, give him some counseling, to help him deal with his issues differently."

"Have you done this kind of thing before?"

"Sort of. Kids play with fire, you know? I've talked to lots of dumb teenagers who weren't using their heads and almost got hurt. Little kids, too, who didn't understand what they were doing. But this feels different. This kid feels—on the edge of something, you know? Like, if we don't get this right, we might lose our chance at helping him. Period."

Behind his mom, the curtains rustled slightly as the heating ducts blew warm air into the room. Abe should have been sweltering, but instead he felt clammy. Most arson was committed by kids who were eighteen or younger. Anger was always a motivator, but the fury was usually a result of something else. Abuse, maybe, or humiliation, like if Carter was being bullied at school. Given Carter's family history and the fact that he was now in foster care, anything could be driving him to burn.

"You sound so concerned," his mom said. "Do you know this boy well?"

"Hardly at all. But this friend I have at Robot Lit—she's going to ask him if she can take a peek at his journals, see what's going on."

"Ah." Her tone was like a detective who'd just found the

clue she needed at a crime scene. "Tell me more about this friend."

"Who is this?" his dad asked, suddenly taking interest in their conversation.

"Someone I met recently," Abe said, avoiding his mom's all-knowing gaze. "She works at that place I used to go to as a kid. Robot Lit."

"With the tables. You used the tables."

Abe nodded. Now that his dad's word retrieval was getting worse, he often substituted "table" to mean just about anything. "They have lots of books and they help kids to read and write. It's a great organization."

"And your friend? What's her name?" His mom wasn't letting him off the hook.

"Casey. She's an accountant there." *And I like her. More than I should. Only I can't figure out what to do about it.* He clenched his fists, wishing he could confess everything. Only the words stayed lodged in his throat.

His mom stood up, probably sensing his frustration. She knew him better than himself, some days. "Pete, you want to come with me while I show Abe my new painting?"

"No, that's all right. I have the—the table here. And I'll just do that." He motioned to his unfinished cookie and tea.

"Holler if you need anything," Mom said, kissing the top of Dad's head. To Abe, she said, "Come on, then. Let me show you what I've been working on."

He followed her down a short hallway lined with family pictures. Abe and Stu in swim trunks, leaping off the edge of a dock. Mom and Dad, grinning at the camera with their arms looped around each other's necks. A family portrait the year they'd driven all the way down to the Grand Canyon. In the background, the red stone layers were stacked in jagged pieces, slicing and sloping their way into the horizon.

Abe's mom led the way to a small second bedroom at the end of the hallway. Light poured in from south-facing windows. Along the wall was a smattering of canvases resting on easels. A small desk was cluttered with tubes and brushes sticking out of Mason jars. Abe smelled oil and paint thinner and thought of his childhood, sitting at his parents' sides and watching them translate the world to a small square—a bit of life, frozen and beautiful and timeless. His dad painted less now that dementia had become more symptomatic, but his mom had kept on. He wondered if pictures of Freiburg would help his dad, would jog his memory back to a place he had loved. Back to a place where he'd *found* love.

"Is this the latest one?" Abe asked, staring at a painting of a small boy flying a kite on the beach. The sand was gray, the sky was churning. The waves were frothing and roiling against a jagged shoreline. It was downright ominous. But the boy was steadfast—holding his kite aloft, the red of the windswept toy like a scarlet burst among all the muted colors. There was an expression on the boy's face like a cross between joy and longing.

"Finished it just a day ago," Mom said with a small smile. "Do you like it?"

Abe stared at it, feeling the bite of the wind, the tension of the string, the shimmy of the kite above. He could all but hear the roar of the waves. "It's beautiful, Mom. Stunning."

"I call it *Abe Aloft*."

He raised his eyes from the canvas. "Why is my name in the title?"

His mom was backlit by the winter sun. He could hardly

see her face. "Because you anchor us to the shore so we can fly."

Abe shook his head. He was used to his mom's poetic language. She was an artist, through and through. But he didn't know what in the world that meant.

"Care to elaborate?"

"You're so literal, Abe. Why not just stare at the painting and think about the title and see what comes to mind?"

This was what his parents had been asking him to do since he was in diapers. To them, there were no answers to things. Not literally. Just gauzy ideas that you could maybe put a loose wire-frame around.

Abe had grown up without much faith in their abstracts. He liked knowing what the rules were, where the boundaries stood. When it was getting dark and other kids' parents called them in for dinner, Abe found himself still wandering in the deepening dusk, longing for a normal meal like the other kids might eat, maybe even the chance to watch some television afterward. His parents, not great about time in general and distrustful of most electronics back then, threw granola bars on the table and Popsicles into the freezer. There was always peanut butter and jelly for Abe and Stu to make sandwiches. But there wasn't much routine, much order.

Some kids thrive in that environment. His brother, Stu, for example.

But not Abe.

Reason number four thousand, eight hundred and ten why Robot Lit had been a godsend.

He studied the painting. The longing on the kid's face. The way his lean arms struggled to hold on to the string. *Abe Aloft.*

Shit. He had no freaking clue.

"Can you just tell me, Mom? I'm not good at this."

His mom moved closer to him. "Without you, son, so many of us would lose our anchor. All the people you help every day in your job. Your dad and I here in this retirement home. Even those good people down at that literacy place. You help us all."

She looked up at him, her eyes shining with emotion. It made his heart swell and thump. "That's not—"

"No, don't minimize it," she interrupted. "You do that, you know. You tell yourself it's your job or it's your duty or whatever. But it's not. You don't *have* to help everyone the way you do. And I'm grateful, Abe. Your dad, too. Even if he can't say it. We both—I just don't know where we'd be if you weren't giving us the chance to live here. For me, taking care of your dad—well, it would be quite a lot more exhausting than it already is."

He took his mom's hand. "Are you guys doing okay? Do you need anything?"

"See? This is what I mean. You're holding the kite string, even now."

Abe didn't know what to say to that. It was simply how he was wired. "You need to let me know if there's something missing. Anything. More help, more money. Whatever. Okay?"

His mom pressed her shoulder into him. "For now, we're fine. More than fine. The village helps when I need them to. Your dad is comfortable. It's all we can ask."

Abe struggled to reconcile that version of his dad with the one who had been fearless when he was growing up, who'd taken him to the ice rink to skate, who had once spent an entire week salvaging wood scraps so he could build Abe and Stu a fort.

"It's awful," he said finally, "this disease."

His mom nodded. "It is."

Abe thought about his ninety-day pattern, wondering if he acted that way because he knew how tenuous things were when you loved something deeply. "Don't you get mad or frustrated or anything?" he asked his mom. "Do you ever wish this all just—hadn't happened?"

"The disease? Sure. I absolutely wish Pete didn't have dementia. But I'm also thankful to be here, and to be one of the last things he'll ever remember. Your dad has been the great love of my life. I'd hold his hand through anything, and be honored to do so."

The truth of it tore at his heart. Being in love meant risking being hurt. The prospect and the reward were intertwined.

He turned back to the painting. "The longing on the kid's face. What's that all about?"

"Ah," his mom said, smiling, "you caught that."

"Is it supposed to mean something?"

"It all means something, honey. In this case, maybe he's just looking at that kite and thinking he wants to be up there, too. Flying, instead of steering."

"How's that even possible?"

His mom laughed. "Literal again! I love you, Abe, but art interpretation will never be your strong suit."

"I could have told you that when I was five."

His mom chuckled. "This girl you mentioned earlier. What's going on there?"

Nothing. Everything.

"She's nice. I like her."

His mom raised an eyebrow. "Will she last for a bit?" The subtext wasn't missed by Abe: *Unlike all your other girlfriends.*

"That might be more up to her than me."

"Nonsense. You woo her. You romance her. You get her to see your good qualities if you like her."

"I didn't know my love life was so clear-cut."

"I'm only saying you might want to open yourself up a bit, honey. She's the kite, you know?"

"Wait, a *woman* is the kite now?"

"Possibly."

Abe rubbed his forehead. "I'm confused. Can't we just go cut more cookies with spoons?"

His mom laughed and hugged him. "We can. Come on."

As they left the room, Abe glanced over his shoulder one last time at the painting. The kite shimmered on the canvas, bright and beguiling. A lot like Casey, actually.

She liked being up there, in the wild wind. But how could he launch himself into the air and meet her in the clouds? She was impossible to reach, it seemed, and there was only a thin string connecting them.

He could try, though. For once, he could put himself on that beach and believe that there was more for him than cold sand and freezing foam and pelting rain. There was a kite. It was Casey. And he could reach it.

Abe Aloft.

It was starting to make a little more sense.

CHAPTER FIFTEEN

Casey tapped gently on Ingrid's office door. "Got a sec?"

Ingrid glanced up from her computer and pulled a gnawed number-two pencil from between her teeth. "Come on in," she said, blinking as if she were trying to focus.

Casey wondered if her own eyes had the same bleary look. She'd thrown herself into her work this morning as well—in large part to distract herself from the constant stream of Abe-related thoughts coursing through her brain. Namely the way the curve of his biceps flashed in her head, the way her skin tingled at the memory of his hands on her, and the ways she couldn't quite read the emotion in his eyes when he'd pointed out the loopholes on her list.

The list. It was priority number one when she got home. Fixing it would sort out her scrambled brain—at least a little.

In the meantime, though, they had their big talk with Carter this afternoon, and she found her stomach knotting at the thought. Asking a ten-year-old kid to share his personal journal was no small thing.

"I was just thinking about this afternoon," Casey said, dropping herself into a chair across from Ingrid's desk. Framed artwork from Ingrid's daughter brightened the walls around her. "Rolf knows Carter so well, and you have so much more experience with kids. I want to be involved—I want to contribute—but I'm wondering what I can even *do* when we talk to him."

She was an accountant, after all. She cared about Robot Lit and she cared about its kids, but she had to admit she might be in over her head.

Ingrid smiled at her. "You've already done the best thing. It was your idea to have Carter share his journals. Clearly you're invested. That makes a difference. Carter needs to know he's surrounded by adults who care."

"I *do* care. Absolutely. But I'm—it's not like I have kids. I don't know if I'm qualified for this."

Ingrid laughed, her light blue eyes sparkling. "None of us are qualified when it comes to kids. They're complicated and difficult and there's no manual. We're all just making it up and hoping for the best."

"That's not true," Casey protested. "You're a great parent. And you're amazing with the students here. Rolf, too."

"And you're approaching this whole situation from a place we never would," Ingrid said. "You're thinking about data, about what information we might have to get at Carter's motives. That's great logic. I need more of that. If it were up to me, I'd probably hand Carter one of my jacked-up pencils and tell him to draw his feelings and we'd be here for days."

Casey chewed her bottom lip. She wanted to believe Ingrid, and she desperately wanted to help Carter. She just wanted to make sure she wasn't going to mess the whole thing up.

"There's no reason to be insecure," Ingrid said, watching Casey closely. "Just because you don't have kids doesn't mean you don't have the right stuff to counsel and help them. If I thought otherwise, I'd ask you to bow out."

Casey shook her head. It was hard not to think about Audrey and all the ways she'd tried—and failed—to do right by her little sister growing up. She'd been too hard, too strict. She'd often acted out of fear, out of desperation, but even now she worried there was still more iron inside her—and that all that cold, metal emotion would find its way to the surface with Carter. She pretended to study the art on the walls, wondering if old Casey would come roaring out of her this afternoon, and if she'd ruin more relationships—not to mention the fragile heart of one troubled little boy.

"Penny for your thoughts," Ingrid said gently.

Casey waved a hand. "Nothing. It's silly. I'm..."

Terrified. Insecure.

"I just want to make sure I'm a help, not a hindrance," she finished.

"You're the only one who has any concerns in that respect," Ingrid said. "But if I don't think you're up for it at any point, I'll ask you to leave it to Rolf and me. You have my word."

Casey nodded. "Thanks. I appreciate you understanding. And being so supportive. I really do love this place."

"I know. And this place loves you. So much so that it tried to trap you in an elevator and never let you go."

Casey groaned. "Enough with the elevator already. This dead horse has been beaten, battered, and fried up on a plate."

"You know that's my way of bringing up Abe, though."

Casey rolled her eyes. "Jeez. You don't say."

"So? Aren't you going to take the bait and tell me how it's going with everyone's favorite firefighter?"

Casey sat back in her chair, trying to formulate an answer. "We're having fun. It's nothing serious."

"How much fun?"

Casey felt her neck heat. "That's—never mind."

Ingrid grinned. "I did that once in college. Rex Warrington the Third, if you can believe that name. We would call each other late at night, usually after parties. We never hung out, never went to dinner. We just…well, you know. It was college."

Except I'm in my mid-thirties, Casey thought. She wondered briefly if she was too old to be doing this, then dismissed the idea. She was too old *not* to be doing this.

"When did you meet Neil?" Casey asked, referring to Ingrid's husband, a bow-tie-wearing attorney who often surprised Ingrid at work with flowers or a homemade lunch.

"I had gone to a party with this law school student I was seeing," Ingrid said, her blue eyes fixed on an image Casey couldn't see, "and the room was lousy with wannabe lawyers. It was all red wine and Scotch and pretentious chatter, and I kept wondering where the beer was stashed. At some point I decided the cheese platter was more interesting than my date, and I was pretty much making out with it. That's when this guy came up to me and asked if he could cut in."

She smiled, her skin pinking with the memory, even now. "I told him to wait his turn because the Brie had just signed my dance card, and the cheddar wanted a spin next. They were *wheels*, after all, I said. And this guy, he laughs like I just made the funniest joke he ever heard.

"He was wearing a bow tie, even back then, and I remember thinking that was nice—that he wasn't another dude in a striped polo shirt. He took one look at my untouched wineglass and my plate full of crackers and told me there was a bar around the corner with good burgers, and asked if I wanted to go with him. I said yes. Just like that. I left my date without another word. Neil and I were married a year later."

Casey smiled, even as she envied the simplicity of it, the bone-deep knowing of something, even after a few moments. She wondered what that must feel like, how someone could grasp such an impossible thing so quickly.

Involuntarily, her body recalled the delicious shiver of Abe touching her. *That's what it feels like*, a voice inside her whispered.

But of course that couldn't be. Could it? Their connection was just physical. He was her Rex Warrington III, not her Neil.

After all, he wasn't the kind of guy who wanted commitment. And if he did—well, that was even worse. Commitment could only lead to heartbreak when the end of the storybook read differently for them both. Hers was a child-free happy ending. No doubt his was filled with blond-haired, hazel-eyed cherubs who wanted to grow up to be firefighters, too.

At the end of the day, there were simply too many potential obstacles between them. Best to keep it simple. Best to stick to the list.

She stood up, brushing the thought aside. "I love that you and Neil clicked so quickly," she told Ingrid. "It's a great story."

"Because I didn't fight it," Ingrid said. The romantic note in her voice was gone, her eyes were suddenly sharp. "I let it be what it was."

"And what was that, exactly?"

"It was perfect. And I didn't try to tell myself it was a rock, when I knew it was a diamond."

Underneath the words, Casey sensed there was a warning, a caution for her. As if she was supposed to connect the dots between Abe and Neil somehow, which felt a lot like trying to link two opposite things: an ant and a skyscraper, for example. The distance was incomprehensible. Unfathomable, really.

"See you at three o'clock with Carter," she said, forcing her voice to be light. Just two colleagues discussing business.

"You bet. There's no need to worry about anything. It'll all be fine."

She suspected Ingrid was talking about more than just Carter again and hinting at some deeper meaning about Abe. Ducking her head, Casey left before Ingrid could get another word in. What with all Ingrid's platitudes plus the conversation with Abe last night, her head was beginning to hurt. She wanted to be done talking.

In fact, she was more than ready for everyone to stop yammering so she could get laid already.

* * *

A few hours later, whatever anxiety had been riddling Casey vanished under waves of compassion for Carter. He showed up pale-faced and practically shivering in the great room. He wore a black T-shirt and jeans with stringy hems and full of holes. His thin face and gray eyes looked as worn as weather-beaten wood. A battered journal was clutched to his side, a pen shoved into the notebook's spirals.

The first thing Casey did when she laid eyes on him was to get him comfortable on the sofa and make him some hot cocoa. She handed it to him while Rolf and Ingrid made small talk, trying to put him at ease.

Arsonist or not, she wasn't going to have him shaking the whole time, for pity's sake. "You need anything else?" she asked him as he clutched the warm ceramic, his eyes round with gratitude.

"N-no, thank you," he managed.

She took her seat across from him and tried to smile. She hoped it didn't come across like a creepy grimace.

Rolf started the official conversation with a small throat-clearing. "We've known you for a while, Carter," he said, pushing his glasses upward, "and you've been such a model student. Hardworking. Attentive. Engaged. We're here today to ask if there's anything going on, since these fires seem so out of character for you. Something that maybe you feel like you could tell us but no one else."

Rolf leaned forward, his chin resting on his hands. Carter dropped his gaze to his cocoa. "I don't think so," he said softly.

"So you just lit those fires for no reason?" Ingrid asked.

"The cops already asked me all this stuff," Carter said. He raised his eyes to Ingrid's and there was such pain there. *Anguish* was the word that popped into Casey's mind.

"You're in a foster home now, is that right?" Rolf asked, trying to get the same answer a different way. "Tell us about it."

Carter shrugged, dropped his eyes again. "It's fine." He was white-knuckling his mug.

"Who's in your new home? What are their names?" This was from Ingrid.

"Scotty is the dad and Bridget is the mom. They have another kid, Luke. He's like, thirteen or something."

Carter's shoulders rounded, as if he were trying to pull his thoughts farther into himself. He was so skinny. Casey wondered if there was any food in the kitchen she could give him.

Rolf asked questions about the foster family and about school, and Carter answered dutifully, but he didn't say anything revelatory. Did anyone hurt him? No. Did anyone say unkind words to him? No. Were things okay at school? Yes. Did he have any friends? Yes.

Casey eyed the journal while they talked. Its battered cover was crisscrossed with creases and lines, like a map she couldn't read. "Carter, can I take a look at that notebook?" she asked, when Ingrid stood to take a break and to get the boy more cocoa. He handed it over slowly, tentatively. This thing meant something to him, that much was clear.

"I'll be super careful," Casey said, giving him a small smile. "And I won't go anywhere with it. I'll read it right here, okay?"

Carter nodded. His gray eyes were so sad, Casey wished she could take the pain away—but she'd settle for second best, which was figuring out where the pain came from.

She turned the ink-covered pages carefully, and started to read.

Kyle has Batman Legos and we played with them today. Mrs. Finn gave us math homework. It's hard but I like math, it's better than social studies.

Brayden ripped his pants on the slide at school. It was

sooo funny! Sonja likes him and said "it doesn't matter" and Chad Foster made kissing noises.

It went on like this for pages—little snippets of a kid's life like snapshots of a moment. The substitute teacher who had fingernails so long they called her the Claw. The librarian who gave him *The Strange Case of Origami Yoda* to read, and he tore through it in a day. Hayden Idris's birthday party, which was held up in Burnsville at an indoor trampoline facility, and Carter thinking he was going to throw up from the combination of cake and bouncing.

When he got to foster care, the sentences got shorter:

Spaghetti for dinner. Math homework. Miss mom.

Casey studied the prose. It was stuttered, sure, but there weren't any red flags that she could see. She let out a small sigh of frustration and kept going.

Read The Castle Behind Thorns. *Good book. Saw a crow. Luke got to drink soda at dinner but not me.*

Thanksgiving. Had some turkey. Crow flew by. Scotty watched football.

Casey turned the page slowly, wondering at the sudden appearance of the crows. Was it because it was fall and they were flocking together as the weather turned? Or was it something else?

Got an A on math test. Tried to build a snow fort at recess. Crow.

Casey clenched her jaw. Crows were so common, why flag them? Something else must be going on. She checked the dates in the journal.

Crow sightings started about a week into foster care, she realized. She flipped to the last page of the journal. It was there, just the day before. *Crow in the sky.*

Casey closed the notebook and sat there for a moment,

collecting her thoughts. Carter was hunched into the couch, the empty cocoa mug on the table. The bright walls of Robot Lit looked jarring against his pale, drawn face.

"Carter," she said slowly, trying to make her voice casual, "you like to read, isn't that right?"

He nodded. Casey smiled. "Me, too. And there's this book I read one time that really stuck with me. It's about this farm, with all these animals. They gang up against the farmer and they overthrow him. And the animals are all like, 'We're going to run this farm better than that farmer ever did.' But can you guess what the problem was with the situation?"

Carter's gray eyes were sharp. He was listening intently. "They didn't run the farm any better with the farmer gone?"

"Exactly. You could say things even got worse. And the thing that was so great about the book was that it was actually sort of based on a true story about a really complicated, confusing political situation in Russia. Super far away, you know? But this author, he made me understand it because he used animals."

Carter blinked rapidly. His hands fisted against his sides.

"It's smart, really," Casey continued. She glanced quickly at Ingrid and hoped her eyes communicated *Pay attention*. "It's kind of like a code. Like a secret message. What does each animal mean? What is this author trying to say?"

Carter had gone a shade whiter, which Casey hadn't thought was possible, given how pale he was to begin with. Casey wanted to give him a blanket, but she knew if she didn't continue talking about the crow right now, she might lose him. He was caught off guard, which wasn't a bad thing. No time to think up a lie, no time to dodge it. She had to get to the heart of the crow—now.

She took a deep breath. "Carter, you're not in trouble for writing anything in your journal. It was really brave of you to agree to share it with us. Not everyone would do that."

"There's nothing in there," he said, an edge in his voice that hadn't been there before.

"There's a crow," Casey said gently. "A crow that you start seeing in November. And you saw it again—what, just yesterday?"

Carter went still on the couch.

"What does the crow mean? Who is the crow?" Her heart thundered. *Tell us*, she pleaded silently.

He shook his head. "Nothing. No one."

Casey leaned forward through the tension-thick air. Ingrid and Rolf were silent, but their eyes were pleading with Carter to tell the truth. "We can help you," Casey said. "You're not alone, okay? You just need to help us understand what the crow means."

"It doesn't mean anything. It's just a stupid crow I keep seeing in the sky. Or in a tree. Or whatever. It's dumb."

"It's not," Casey said, hearing the fear in Carter's voice. She wanted to reach out and grab his hand. "It's not dumb. Is the crow hurting you? Is the crow a person who is harming you?"

Carter stood suddenly. Ingrid, Rolf and Casey followed suit. "I don't want to talk about this," he said. He snatched his journal from Casey's hands. "You can't make me."

"You're right, we can't," Ingrid said, palms facing upward. Open. Nonaggressive. "We can't force you to say anything. But we're going to need to bring this up to the police and your guidance counselor at school."

Carter's brow furrowed. He was getting angry. The crow was the spark that kindled his anger—and made him burn fires. Casey knew it as surely as she knew her name.

"So what? It doesn't matter. Everyone at the school is dumb. The police are stupid, too."

"They're just trying to help you," Rolf said. "We're all just trying to help you."

Carter whipped his head away. He swiped a palm across his eyes. Casey's heart constricted inside her chest. What had the crow done to this boy? And how would they ever find out?

"You don't have to tell us right this minute," Casey said. "How about we get a snack and just chill for a little bit?" Carter exhaled visibly. Ingrid gave Casey a small nod that said *Good thinking; don't push too hard*. Together, the four of them bundled up and hit the Rolling Pin for donuts.

Fifteen minutes later, Carter relaxed visibly as he ate. The blade of his defensiveness dulled slightly. When he looked up at Casey and actually smiled—powdered sugar smeared on one gaunt cheek—it nearly took her breath away. She felt something rising inside her, and realized it was protectiveness. She took a sip of her coffee as holiday shoppers scurried by outside, thinking of Audrey's present and how she hadn't found it yet. She *would* find it, though, and it would be just the thing. And maybe she hadn't found the crow yet, either, but she would uncover it, too. Come hell or high water, she would get to the bottom of what the crow was all about and help this boy.

She straightened in her chair.

She would expose that crow and rip its damn wings off.

CHAPTER SIXTEEN

*T*hat weekend, Casey gave in. She bit the bullet and decided to buy all new holiday ornaments, seeing as how hers were probably still with the movers, maybe in a box in Pasadena somewhere.

Her stomach twisted with the idea that her collection of ornaments was gone. She blinked back tears and told herself not to get overly sentimental about things. *You can't take it with you*—wasn't that the expression?

Even so, her heart sank as she faced the reality she'd never glimpse anything in her holiday collection again.

She'd never see the tinfoil-and-cardboard star Audrey had made her when they were both in college, dead broke and unable to buy anything for each other. She'd never again hold the snow globe she got in Duluth, with Paul Bunyan and Babe the Blue Ox standing vigilant in the permanent blizzard. Her cow wearing reindeer antlers was gone forever.

Swallowing the stubborn lump in her throat, she pulled

on her down jacket. Buying new ornaments felt like giving up, which was why she supposed she'd waited so long to do it. But with only two weeks left until Christmas, she needed to get something up or risk missing the season entirely. And that felt unacceptable, like a defeat worse than losing her ornaments altogether.

The morning was mild, the sun low in the pale blue sky, and Casey decided to walk downtown instead of drive. Besides, she hadn't shoveled her driveway or sidewalk since Abe had done it, and it would take her a good half hour to get her car out.

At the thought of Abe, she shivered—but not because of the cold. He was a memory so vivid and visceral she felt like he was standing next to her, breathing on her skin all over again.

Which wouldn't be so bad.

And then his hands could do that thing again, the one that had her back arching like a cat, and his mouth could nibble at her like she was a gingersnap cookie and—

She shook her head. Before they could do anything more, she needed to revise her list. She had to get more specific. She pulled her scarf up over her cheeks so no one would see her blush as she thought about how in the world she was going to do this. Moreover, *should* she even do this?

Her list was just fine, really. There was something unsettling about Abe wanting to change it. Why was he so bent on poking holes in it?

And yet, did it matter? The way he'd made her feel... good grief. If she needed to spell out more parameters for him to touch her again, to make her explode with feeling, so be it. Her boots crunched snow as she walked and pondered.

The first item was so cut and dried she could hardly imagine how to make it more clear. *I want to start out being kissed under the mistletoe, but I want to finish with sex in bed.*

She'd paraphrased that one for Abe, but it hardly mattered. *I want to start out kissing, but have it lead to sex.*

Okay, fine. She'd circle back to that one in a minute. Maybe there were others that were easier.

I want to be naughty, not nice, between the sheets.

Casey bit her lip. This one could probably stand some fleshing out. She'd paraphrased this by telling Abe she wanted rough sex. Not that she wanted a whole BDSM experience or anything—though hats off to anyone who did. In her case, however, she didn't necessarily need whips and chains and leather to get off. All she wanted was a little… excitement. So how to make that clearer without taking all the fun out of it?

I want to be tied up during sex.

She pondered that: Her hands bound to the headboard, and Abe taking his sweet time with whatever he wanted to do.

Or he could not take his time.

The point was he could do anything and she would be… bound to endure it. Pun intended.

The idea was hot enough to make her think she could melt the snow all around her. Good grief, she'd be lucky to make it to the hardware store without needing to plunge herself into a snowbank to cool off.

She increased her pace, in part so she could make herself think that her elevated heart rate was the result of physical exercise.

All right, she thought. *I'll change the second item on my list to:* I want to be tied up during sex. *That should cover it.*

The next item on her list lodged itself in her frontal lobe like it had been eagerly waiting its turn.

I want twelve orgasms out of said sex.

As Abe had so thoroughly pointed out the other night, she could get twelve orgasms many ways, not just from sex. Which was fine by her. So maybe she just trimmed the sentence. *I want twelve orgasms.* One for each of the twelve days of Christmas.

It didn't much matter to her what the road map was for getting there. Abe could do that thing with his hands all day long and she'd be delighted. She'd light up like a freaking Christmas tree.

Meaning that one was covered as well.

Next one.

I want my stocking stuffed, repeatedly, on Christmas Day.

In this case, maybe she could make sure to note that the sex didn't have to be Christmas Day *only*. They could have tons of sex anytime, really, and it would be great by her.

She loosened her scarf slightly as her face heated to an uncomfortable temperature. *I want my stocking stuffed, repeatedly, on any day, but especially Christmas Day.*

That should be an adequate change.

Leaving only one more.

I want toys wrapped with bows—that are all for adults.

How could she make that any clearer? She couldn't, was the answer. That one and the first one, *I want to start out kissing, but have it lead to sex*, were about as cut and dried as anything could be. If Abe found a way to poke holes in those rules, then he was going to be doing it for a reason other than clarity. He would be doing it as an excuse.

Maybe because he didn't want the list at all.

Maybe because he wanted *more* than the list.

Casey's muscles tensed. Either way, she wasn't going to worry about that right now. She'd cross that bridge when she presented the revised list to Abe. If he balked then, well, she'd get to the root of it and figure it out at that point.

In the meantime, she thought she'd done a pretty good editorial job. No matter that it had gotten her hot and bothered as she walked. She could feel sweat on her forehead and the back of her neck as she stepped into White Pine Hardware. A lawn reindeer raised and lowered its head in greeting. A red SALE sign was taped to the reindeer's back. NOW ONLY $199.00! She considered the purchase briefly before realizing she couldn't haul a lawn reindeer home, thanks to the fact that she'd walked. She swore she heard her wallet sigh with relief.

Dabbing her forehead with the back of her sleeve, Casey picked up a shopping basket and headed for the Christmas aisles toward the back of the store. She passed endcaps filled with shovels and sidewalk salt, gloves and hand-warmers and thick-soled boots. She had paused at a display of flameless candles and extra-long extension cords, wondering if she needed either—or both—when her back stiffened.

The grating rumble of Abe's voice was in her ears, on her skin, making it suddenly hard to hold on to her basket. "As a fireman, I can tell you flameless candles have a much higher safety rating than regular candles. In case that influences your purchasing decision."

She turned, chin tilted upward to take in Abe's winter coat, his cashmere scarf, his sexy stubble from not yet having shaved today. He was unbearably handsome. She worked to keep her face expressionless. "And what about people who want candles *and* excitement? What do you say to them?"

He took a step closer. His cinnamon scent reached her. She trembled slightly.

"Fire's not the only way to get thrills," he said.

She wanted to press her fingertips to his throat, to feel the rumble there as he spoke. Instead, she licked her lips. His sharp eyes watched her.

"Where can I find those thrills?" she asked. "Are they here at the hardware store on a Saturday morning?"

"You tell me," Abe said. He brought a hand to her forehead. His fingers were deliciously warm. "You're looking a little—peaked. Everything okay?"

Casey bit her lip self-consciously. If only Abe knew it was the thought of him and the damn list that had her all riled up.

"I—I'm fine," she said, forcing a smile and willing herself to cool down already. "I just walked here and put on too many layers."

"Let me give you a ride home, then. When you're all done shopping for candles and...?"

"A gift for Audrey if I can find it. Not to mention Christmas stuff. I've finally resigned myself to the fact that my ornaments are lost. They never made it to the new house."

Abe smiled sympathetically. "Need to swing by the Wheelhouse for a farewell beer? Godspeed, old ornaments, and all that?"

Casey laughed. "Little early for that, don't you think?"

"It's five o'clock somewhere," Abe said. He glanced at the thick watch on his wrist. It gave Casey an excuse to stare at the downy blond hairs on his arm, to think about how those hairs had brushed against her skin when they'd been tangled on her couch together. Her body started to heat up all over again, and she wanted to kick herself.

Was it completely impossible to be a normal temperature around Abe?

"I don't think I should put any booze in my body just yet," Casey said. "But thanks."

"So we'll drink Coke instead. A dry send-off is still a send-off."

He smiled, his golden-green eyes locked on to hers. Her insides knotted uncomfortably. The friendliness in his gaze had her shifting. She wanted him to back her into a shelf and put a hand up her shirt. She wanted him to knee her legs apart and lick her neck, right here in the store. The scalding idea of his lust was so much more tolerable than the idea that he liked her and wanted to spend time with her.

Because Casey didn't want to be liked. She wanted to be fucked. She wanted to be taken every which way until Sunday and then some.

But nothing more. No feelings, for crying out loud.

Feelings led to complications. And complications led to hurt.

Her chest tightened as she remembered the way Miles had stormed off, and the anger in his eyes at her desire to be childless. He'd looked at her like she was *wrong*. Like she was a freak of nature.

Miles hadn't exactly been a passionate love affair, but he'd still wounded her deeply when he'd left. His practicality had matched hers. She hadn't thought for a second he'd go off and shock her, especially not by doing something as irrational as fleeing. She didn't think there was a single topic they couldn't tackle with logic, with reason.

It turned out there was, and she'd gone and found it like she was digging for buried treasure.

The memories froze her blood. She felt queasy.

The truth was, she'd endured enough loss in her life. Her parents weren't supposed to leave her, but they had. Miles wasn't supposed to race away, either, but he was gone.

Casey wasn't about to take any more risks.

She lifted her chin. Miles had been wrong about one thing: She wasn't a freak. She simply knew what she wanted.

"Why don't we just head to my place," she said, low and full of meaning. "I've given my list some...thought. Some revision, even."

Abe arched a brow, but didn't immediately respond. She waited, her heart hammering. Was he going to say no? Her concern that he'd found flaws in the list just to put her off came roaring back.

But then why would he want to give her a ride home if he didn't like her, didn't want her? She held her breath, waiting.

"I'll be over by the power tools when you're done shopping for ornaments," he said, his eyes raking over her body. "Come find me."

"How appropriate," Casey said, inching closer. "Power tools. And after that, screws?"

Abe gave her ass a quick, hard smack. "I'd say let's find out," he growled.

* * *

An hour later, Abe was helping cart bags full of tinsel, ornaments, lights, nativity scenes, and faux snow up Casey's sidewalk. His steps were even, but his mind was racing. He wanted more from Casey than her list, but he had no idea how to get her to think of him as anything but a hot lay.

Not that being a hot lay was *awful*. He could do a lot

worse than putting his hands on her soft body, coaxing pleasure from her in waves that overtook them both.

His groin tightened, his lust aroused. He wanted Casey Tanner, there was no doubt. But he didn't want her just physically. He wanted her mentally and emotionally and...well, every little piece of her he could grasp. In sum, he wanted *all* of her.

Abe set the plastic bags on the kitchen table and went back for the next load. She'd nearly bought the whole store, her warm brown eyes shimmering with joy as she shopped. She'd confided in him that she loved Christmas, loved decorating, and it had been a blow when her ornaments had gone missing in the move.

"What company did you use?" he asked as they'd checked out, bags filling to the brim.

"Northwestern Movers." She'd frowned at the name, and he'd made a mental note. If he could, he wanted to try to help her get back what she'd lost.

In the meantime, he stood in her cheery green kitchen, surrounded by Christmas décor, and watched her paw through her bags with delight. Her smile was infectious, her laugh bubbling. He couldn't help but grin as she put a wooden Santa on the windowsill.

Abe gathered up all the lights he could carry and headed for the tree. "Where are you going?" Casey called after him.

"I'm going to trim your tree." He paused for a moment and gave her a wink. "And no, that's not a euphemism."

Casey laughed, throaty and loud. The sound filled the house, and his chest tightened. He shouldn't be feeling so much for her. It was a dead end. She wanted her list, and that was it.

Except he couldn't just shut himself off. He'd had a

switch inside him for as long as he could remember—but when it came to Casey Tanner, the damn thing just didn't work.

To distract himself, he unwound lights and an extension cord and got to work. He wasn't sure when, but at some point he was humming along with Christmas music—*when had Casey put that on?*—and the scent of something warm and spicy filled the air. He plugged in the lights, and the tree glowed in a kaleidoscope of colors. He heard a small gasp, and when he turned around, Casey was staring wide-eyed, a smile on her face. She was holding two ceramic mugs filled with steaming liquid. Hot cider. He crossed the small room to take both from her before she lost her grip. Her expression was downright dazed.

"I've always hated doing the lights," she said. "I mean, I love the result, but the lights are always such a pain. Thank you."

"Are there more?" Abe asked, setting the mugs on the coffee table. "Lights, I mean. If you want, I can put them up outside. I think you cleaned out the hardware store's stock."

Casey bit her lip. "I got so excited. I pictured the house covered in white lights."

"*National Lampoon* style?"

"Maybe not quite that many."

"Let me help, then. I'll do outside."

Casey stepped closer. "You've already helped," she said. She gazed up at him, her eyes liquid enough to melt his insides. He liked her desire, but he also liked this side of her, too, this whisper of vulnerability. Like his help meant so much to her. Little things that maybe made her feel special. He leaned down and kissed her cheek, a soft brush with his lips that had her trembling.

"I bought mistletoe," she murmured. She linked her arms around his neck, pressed her body against his. He swallowed, hardening for her. He wanted more than just her body.

God, but he'd take her body. If that was what he could get.

He brought his lips down on hers, and she responded with a hot little moan that set his skin on fire. She pressed herself into every surface of him, shimmying into all the curves and nooks and lines where they would be closest. He braced himself, worried he might lose it right there. Instead, he sucked in a deep breath and let his hands slide along her buttery skin, let his lips taste her sugar cookie scent. He would devour her if he could. He'd nibble her for days and hope never to get to the end.

She broke from him then, her eyes dazed. Her lips were kiss-swollen, her breath heavy. "I want you," she said. And then, after a moment, she smiled and added "please."

His heart lurched. Right then, he knew that he desired Casey Tanner with everything he had, but the only way to her heart was through her rules. Her parameters.

"Have you revised the list?" he asked, like he cared about what it actually said. "Is it clearer?"

"Crystal," she murmured, her fingers trailing up his arm. "The first item still stands, though."

"Remind me which one that is."

To his surprise, Casey turned on her heel and left the room. He heard the rustle of a bag, and then she returned. She held a plastic bundle of mistletoe in her hand. "Start here," she said, gesturing to the plant. "End there." She jerked her head toward her bedroom.

Simple enough. He would do as she asked, and in the

process he'd pry open Casey Tanner's heart little by little, inch by inch. He'd do exactly what she wanted, and in the end, he'd make her want more than just his body.

He pulled her to him, hard and fast. She gasped, and he covered the sound with his mouth. He kissed her like he was dying—breaking and cracking and she was the only thing that could bring him back to life.

Maybe a little bit of it was true. He didn't want to think what would happen if he failed. He tipped his head back when she put a hand on his groin.

And with that, every single thought emptied out of Abe's mind entirely.

* * *

Casey realized she still had the mistletoe in her hand when Abe picked her up and carried her to her bedroom like she was a seventeenth-century maiden and he was about to deflower her.

Which might not technically be the case, but the nervous churning in her stomach was worse than it had been when she'd lost her virginity to Miles. He'd been methodical and thorough. He'd been...fine, when it came down to it. Not rough, not hurried. But it certainly hadn't been this relentless—a jungle drum of feeling, pounding deep inside, and Casey holding tight to the edge of something she couldn't see or explain.

The springs of her mattress squeaked as Abe's enormous form followed her onto the bed. Oh, but there was so much of him. She thought of how big Abe was when she'd felt him, and she worried she might crack in half. Then thought maybe she didn't care if she did.

She let her legs fall to the sides as Abe settled between them, grinding into her with a delicious rhythm that reminded her of a thoroughbred galloping, pounding along the track in a blur of muscle and sweat.

She lifted her hips to meet his. His hands grabbed her ass, pulled her tight against his body. She saw stars, she panted like she was thirsty and would never drink again. She found her name on his lips. "Abe."

"Tell me what you want," he said, his hands unbuttoning her jeans, sliding them off her so she was down to her panties. Pink cotton. Unplanned. She hated it and then didn't care because Abe was pulling them off her. Plus she still had the condoms and the body oil and she still had Abe Cameron in her bed, asking her what she wanted.

"You," she said, untucking his shirt and sliding her hands over the muscles of his back. "I want you naked. No fair last time you got to keep all your clothes on."

"You *did* get more specific, didn't you?" he said, lifting himself so he could pull his T-shirt off. His skin was golden, his abs like smooth stones at the bottom of a stream. She placed her fingertips on him and he hissed in breath.

"Now you," he said, and lifted off her sweatshirt in a single tug. Her bra was plain white—it didn't match her discarded panties and it was boring as hell, but from the way Abe was staring at her breasts, it was a wonder she wasn't wearing a Victoria's Secret negligee. Lowering his head, he kissed his way from her belly to her breasts, his hands palming her sides as he moved slowly upward.

Casey twined her fingers in his dark blond hair. She moaned as his rough whiskers rubbed against her flesh. "You're still wearing too many clothes," she said, trying to find logic in the drunken pleasure that was threatening to overtake her. "Pants off. And"—she paused, licking her lips—"I want to watch."

Abe lifted his head. His face was blank—too empty. There was a question mark in the air, hanging over them. What had she said? But then it was gone as Abe lifted himself off her. The absence of his flesh, of his heat, had goose bumps forming along her skin.

He climbed off the bed and stood. The late-morning light slanted in from behind the gauzy curtains. Casey itched to trail her fingers along the dark gold hairs on his chest. She watched, hardly breathing, as he undid his pants, taking his boxers with them, then kicking everything away.

He stood like a marbled statue, hands on his hips, baring himself to her. His thick penis, rock hard, pointed directly at her. His stance said *Here I am; this is my flesh.*

So why were his eyes the thing she couldn't stop staring at? The light was too filmy, his face angled into shadow. She fought to read his expression but couldn't.

Blazing in her mind's eye was the Christmas tree he'd painstakingly lit. The sidewalk he'd shoveled. The way he'd listened to her plea for Carter at Robot Lit. Her heart filled up her rib cage to bursting. Clouds shifted outside, and the light brightened in the room. And there, she could finally see— Abe's eyes were on her, locked and laser-focused and heating up emotions that bubbled like a tar pit. Not just lust, but something deeper, something older, like the bones of dinosaurs that made petroleum.

Except that's not what this is, Casey thought desperately.

She sat up and unhooked her own bra. Abe made a noise deep in his throat as she ran her hands along her own body. "I can do this," she said with a small smile, touching her own nipples, "or you can."

He closed the distance between them in a fraction of a second. The back of Casey's head hit the pillow before she could blink. He was between her legs, the tip of him poised at her damp entrance, hovering there. His mouth bore down on her right nipple, then her left, sucking and biting on the thin, glorious line between pleasure and pain. She cried out, wrapping her legs around him.

He was gone, then. She had only begun to protest when he found her—or his *mouth* found her. His lips were between her legs, licking and kissing her folds, pushing apart her thighs to give him more access. She opened herself as far as she could go. He settled in, sliding a finger inside her, the notes of a Christmas song floating in the back of her brain. Her thoughts were far away, but the feeling of being this close to Abe Cameron was the most solid thing she'd ever known.

"Tell me what it's like," he murmured into her skin. The words vibrated deep inside. Casey clawed at the inside of her skull, trying to find the words.

"It's beautiful," she gasped, her body glowing like her Christmas tree—only hotter, brighter. She could hear an electric hum building in her nerves, and wondered if Abe caught the sound, too. It was in perfect harmony with the Christmas song—notes and bells and chords and a symphony that filled her up.

"You're what's beautiful, Casey," Abe said. His voice was the music's bass, sliding along the lowest register. The perfect pitch to reach her. "You are exquisite." He slid a third finger into her and she joined her voice to all the sounds. Her orgasm broke apart like the universe opening up. She arched her back and let the galaxy of feeling sweep over her with a million million stars.

"I've got you, baby." Abe's fingers worked inside her as light flickered all around. She lost herself in the moment, knowing that Abe had her, knowing he would catch her as she settled back into the present. Slowly, as the world became real again, he kissed his way back up her body. His lips met hers and she could taste herself on them. She'd never known anything like that. Her body heated all over again.

But before she could demand anything from him, he was there. It was as if he knew what she wanted before she did. He found a condom and rolled it on. Then his tip was at her center, his weight carefully positioned. Slowly, achingly, he eased himself in. She gasped, biting his shoulder. There was so much of him. She inhaled, trying to breathe, even as the edges of the world warped.

"Am I hurting you?" His golden-green eyes found hers. His hand held her cheek.

"N-no. It feels...*everywhere*. I feel you in every single part of me."

Abe kissed her, his mouth joining hers at the same time the rest of him slid into place. She swallowed back a cry. She was stretched to breaking, but on that particular edge, things were so new, so glorious, she wondered if it was possible to know them again.

She hoped it was. She wanted to repeat this experience. Forever.

She blinked. *No*, she thought. *Not forever. Just until my list is checked off.*

Abe rocked against her, and her mind imploded on itself, every thought vanishing with the perfection of his hips squaring with hers, his lips murmuring words into her skin, his hands finding her center all over again. She relaxed into the tide of his rhythm, imagining waves crashing and surf roaring.

"You feel incredible," he said, his breath in her ear. He ground against her anew, and she came apart all over again, her orgasm overtaking her so quickly she hardly had time to clutch Abe and hold on.

His name was on her lips, over and over. She opened her eyes in the hottest, whitest part of her pleasure and found him staring back at her, his eyes so filled with emotion that she wondered if he was tumbling through the same waves that she was. Their gazes locked as she contracted around him. He pulled her tighter against his massive form. His breath went ragged, his skin was aflame everywhere she touched.

He came with her name in his throat—a torn-up sound like a call she wanted to answer. She imagined crying his name in response. She pictured two wolves on opposite cliffs, howling their desperation for one another, deep into the night.

But of course that was foolishness. There were no wolves here. Only two people who had agreed to a checklist.

She closed her eyes, and held herself back from reaching for Abe when he rolled off of her. He kissed her shoulder, and she wanted desperately to curl into him. But instead, she turned onto her side. *This was only physical*, she reminded herself. The thought was hard and plastic, like her brand-new ornaments. She lay still, not daring to move or even to think, until sleep overtook her.

CHAPTER SEVENTEEN

*C*asey woke up feeling emptied out—in a good way. She stretched, wondering at the time. The light was bright against her curtains, and she could hear the shouts of neighborhood kids playing in the snow.

She reached over, curious if Abe was still there, but came up only with a handful of cold sheets. *It's a good thing he left*, she thought, swallowing back disappointment. *It's less complicated that way.*

Never mind the tug in her stomach that wanted him all over again.

Her rag-doll body was testament to the fact that she'd enjoyed herself yesterday—several times, in fact, as the afternoon faded and the night rolled around them like a blanket. She was solidly on her way to checking most of those orgasms off her list. That part was amazing, but so was the fact that Abe had helped her get her ornaments and lights home, that he'd stayed and put all those lights on the tree, and that she'd been able to talk with him about Christmas, about work, about everything.

It was magnetic and confusing all at the same time. She didn't want to *converse* with Abe, for crying out loud. Did she? But every time they talked, she wound up laughing and enjoying herself. And technically she didn't need him to do any of the things around the house he was so good at, either—shoveling, putting up lights, getting a stand for her tree. But at the same time, she was so grateful for the result, and for the feeling that someone had her back.

It was brand new to her, this idea of having help in her life. For so long she'd shouldered every responsibility for herself and Audrey both. Audrey had of course tried to do what she could, but she was younger and just couldn't manage much, especially in those early years with Aunt Lodi. Casey had always done everything. By and large, she'd made things work—or mostly had, anyway—and it had been just fine.

She bit her lip, wondering what it would feel like to have a real partner in life. Someone she'd help, and who would aid her in return. Not like Miles, who seemed interested in only *his* end of things.

Was that even possible?

It seemed like a luxury too rich even to contemplate, like a yacht or a private home on a remote tropical island.

She shook her head, and that was when the scent reached her. Bacon. She sat up straighter. Bacon and...coffee?

She crawled off the bed and threw on clothes, padding her way down the short hallway to the kitchen. The strains of more Christmas music reached her. When she rounded the corner, there was Abe—in jeans and his white T-shirt, holding a spatula and cooking in her kitchen.

"Hope you don't mind. I made pancakes," he said, his golden blond hair tousled and impossibly sexy. "And you had some bacon in there. Plus I brewed us coffee."

He grinned and her heart hammered. Casey blinked with surprise. *He shouldn't be invading my kitchen; this wasn't on the list*—but she found she didn't care. She was nothing except delighted. She could feel a grin spreading before she could stop it.

"Smart move. I'm starving."

"We worked up an appetite," he said, winking.

Casey feigned indifference. "I guess. It was kind of average for me."

Abe grabbed a mug from next to the sink—*He already knows where the mugs are*, Casey thought—laughing while he filled it with fresh coffee. "If that's true, then that's some bell curve."

"Do you have a problem with my curves?"

"Never. I'm *all* about those curves, bell or otherwise."

She smiled as she pulled out a stool at the kitchen counter and took a seat.

"How do you take your coffee?" Abe asked, holding up her mug.

"Black. Like my heart."

He arched a brow, handing her the warm ceramic. "Breakfast will be ready soon. I'm sure your other lovers had it prepared much more quickly. But bear with me."

Casey snorted, then sipped her coffee and watched Abe find his way around her kitchen like he'd been there a hundred times before.

Because he's done this a hundred times before, just not in my kitchen.

The thought was so sharp it sliced through her mind before she could stop it. Because of course Abe would be practiced at making breakfast after a bout of hot sex. He had a long history of getting into—and out of—women's beds.

Casey pushed her disarranged hair back from her face. She forced a smile and told herself it didn't matter. That prickle of whatever it was in her belly—*Not jealousy; that's ridiculous*—would go away if she just sipped her coffee and watched Abe work.

Except the prickle only got worse. It was changing into jabbing needles every time she thought about his hands on other women, his skin against theirs, his whispers in their ears. Desperate to imagine anything except Abe spreading the whole town's legs, Casey brought up Robot Lit.

"So, Rolf and Ingrid and I met with Carter on Friday, and he even brought his journal."

Abe transferred sizzling bacon to a paper towel. "Good for you guys, getting him down there to talk. Did he say anything particularly useful?"

"He wouldn't admit anything was amiss at school or in foster care. But when I read his journal, there was this crow that kept coming up."

"A drawing, or what?"

"No, like text about seeing it. It started in November, about a week into foster care, and he was still spotting it as of a couple days ago. When I asked him about it, he kind of shut down. I think it's a clue to what's going on inside of him, but he won't open up about it. We're going to share it with his school counselors, maybe even the police."

"Smart thinking. I wonder if we could all sit down with him and try to get to the bottom of it."

"I could ask Ingrid if we could set up a meeting with all the concerned parties. Maybe at the school? Get you there from the firehouse, some Robot Lit staff, his foster parents, and see what he says."

"If someone is hurting him, that's the group that can help get to the bottom of it."

Abe handed over a plate with bacon and pancakes piled high. "It's hard to see kids in trouble like that," he said, serving himself as well. He pulled up the stool across from her so they sat facing one another. "I don't think people are born bad, but I think there's only a small window of time where kids can get pulled out of a tailspin. Carter's right there."

Casey speared her food. "You sound like you've given a lot of thought to the idea," she said. "Carter. Kids in general."

Abe stilled. "I suppose I have. Especially recently. I had a health scare that got me mulling it all over."

"Is your health issue serious?" Casey asked, her stomach tightening with enough concern to surprise her.

"No. Just the opposite. Heartburn. Even so, it made me start thinking about what I wanted."

"And my list came to the top of your mind?" Casey asked, grinning.

Abe smiled back, tenderly enough to have her throat tightening. The hard lines of his face were softened in the morning light. She wanted to put her hands on his chiseled cheekbones and kiss him.

"This has been fun," he said. "There's no doubt about that."

Casey tilted her head. Something in his tone was different. "Why do I feel like there's a 'but' at the end of that sentence?"

Abe set down his fork and folded his hands. Casey shifted. The air in the room felt charged, but not with sexual tension. With something else she couldn't put her finger on.

"I like your list, Casey. It's fun. It's very, very enjoyable. But I also like you. A lot."

Casey's stopped. She forced herself to swallow the hunk of pancake in her throat. "I like you, too," she said lightly, trying to brush past the meaning she heard in his voice. "It would be hard to sleep together if we didn't at least like each other."

"It's more than that, though," Abe said quietly.

"Fine," she said, winking. "I really like you. Is that better?"

"I'm not joking." His voice was strong and even.

No, she thought. *Don't say this. Don't ruin what we've got going on.*

"Let me take you to dinner," Abe said, leaning closer. "*White Christmas* is onstage up in Saint Paul. Live. We'll go to dinner beforehand, then we'll see the musical. You love Christmas, and I'll get you to love Manny's, my favorite steak house."

He smiled, but Casey couldn't return it. He was asking her for a date. For more than what was on the list. She placed her palms on the counter to steady herself.

"And after that?" she asked quietly. "We have a date and let's say we get close. Then you want—what? What did your health scare convince you that you needed?"

"Nothing. All I'm asking is—"

"For something more than what we have now. Are you picturing a wife? Some kids? A minivan and baseball practice with Timmy?"

She hated the hurt that flashed across Abe's face. He tried to hide it, but she'd caught it, and it had slashed at her heart. Even though she'd wanted her words to be brutal. To make her point.

"You're jumping the gun. I'm not here with a ring. All I wanted was a date. Is that such a problem?"

"It is most definitely a problem."

"Why?" Abe asked, his eyes flickering across her face. "Why is it so repulsive to you that we could have more than what's on your to-do list?"

Because I've been locked into commitments my entire life. Because I already raised my family. And because in the end this can only hurt us both.

Casey took a deep breath. "I can't give you what you want, Abe. Not if you're standing here telling me that suddenly you've had a health scare and you're looking to settle down."

"It's not just that," Abe said, his hand reaching out and covering hers. She tried to recoil but found she couldn't. "It's not just some random knee-jerk reaction. I want to be with *you*. Just you."

Casey's stomach plummeted. She fought the urge to tear at her throat, where the words *Me, too* were dangerously close to bursting forth. "You can't feel that. We barely know each other."

"I know enough. I'm not saying we have to buy a house and elope and start a family. But I want you to give me a chance. Give me more than five things on a list."

Casey swallowed hard. "But you'd want kids, right? Eventually?"

Abe's jaw flexed. "We don't have to think about that right now."

"Except why start the race if you know at the finish line there's only heartbreak? Because I don't want kids, Abe. I raised my sister and I'm done. I love her more than anything, but I don't want to spend my whole life bringing up kids."

She pulled her hand away gently, hating the frigid motion

of it, hating the fist tightening with pain at the base of her gut. This shouldn't be hard. There shouldn't be tears pricking at the edges of her eyes.

"This is good, Casey. *We're* good. There's something here, and you can't tell me you don't feel it. What happened between us in that bed isn't typical. And don't sit there and say it was just a good fuck. I *know* you felt it."

The protest died on Casey's lips. Abe was right. She had felt something more than pleasure with him. There had been a moment when emotion had poured into her, filled her to bursting, and she'd experienced something beyond just an orgasm, just a hot lay. It was affection for this man. It was a lucid, light string connecting them both—delicate and steel-strong at the same time. It was the fibers of something like love.

Except, no. She shook her head. "It doesn't matter. We want different things. We can feel whatever we want to but it doesn't change things. Practically speaking, we're a mismatch."

Abe grimaced. "Practicality again. You say you want to let loose, but here you are, making more rules."

"I thought you'd appreciate that. You're the one with the dream vacation to Freiburg."

"I'm not the one fucking up something good," he said.

"I just wanted the fucking part," Casey said. "Not the other stuff."

Abe shoved his stool away from the counter and stood. His eyes were dark with emotion. "Fine. Be a smart-ass about it."

She caught herself before she could reach out to stop him. *Let him go,* she told herself. It was for the best. Even her aunt Lodi said sometimes relationships were like Band-Aids—

best to rip them off and get it over with than drag out the pain, thinking it was somehow gentler that way.

Never mind that this wasn't supposed to be a relationship. Or anything like it. It was just supposed to be a list.

Sunlight striped the room, too bright and too warm for the cold ache that spread through Casey's body. She heard Abe pulling on his boots and coat, the faint jingle of keys as he grabbed them off the hallway table.

She wanted him to slam the front door. She expected it, braced herself for it. But instead he pulled it shut with a soft click.

It ripped her worse than if he'd shattered the molding in a hot fury. The sound was a knife. It slayed her with its gentle care.

* * *

Abe drove straight to Stu's house, the radio blasting and his Jeep wheels fishtailing on the powdery back roads.

He slammed a fist on the dash, uttering a string of curse words. He could kick himself for being such an idiot. Why had he pushed so hard for a date the second he and Casey had tumbled out of bed? What the fuck was wrong with him? He should have known better. He *did* know better, but he'd let his feelings interfere.

Dammit, he should have backed off, given her list more time. Given *her* more time. Patience never was his strong suit; his mom would say so in a heartbeat. God, but he was stupid. He was furious at Casey for being an idiot as well. Sitting there and denying she felt anything for him when he *knew* she did. He could see it in her face when they were in bed together, he could feel it in the way she bent to his touch, in how her eyes followed him everywhere he went in that kitchen.

Both of them numbskulls. Jesus, but they deserved each other. He turned up the radio another notch, the squeal of an electric guitar and the thud of drums drowning out the furious thoughts raging in his head. He focused on the slate gray of the road, the icy blue of the sky, and the fridge full of beers his brother would have when he got there. Stu might not have much, but he always had alcohol.

Thank fucking God.

* * *

Abe was three beers in when Stu finally tucked himself into the chair across from Abe. "Either spill it or I'm cutting off the booze," his brother said.

Abe stared at the amber glass of his beer bottle. Dancing bears on Grateful Dead posters leered at him from nearby walls. The faint sounds of a Phish song floated through the air. "I blew it," he said finally. "I jumped the gun with someone I was seeing. Kind of seeing. And everything just—exploded."

Stu leaned back, folded his arms. "Who is she? And when did you decide monogamy was your style?"

Abe watched the condensation on the bottle. "Her name is Casey and I didn't decide to be monogamous. I liked her is all. No, not liked. *Like*, present tense."

"So what happened?" Stu asked. He was leaning in now, interested. This was new territory for them both.

Abe explained the list, and his stumble that morning. "I don't know why I pushed," he said, taking another swig of beer.

"Because you've got your rules, too," Stu said. As if it were entirely obvious.

"What the hell does that mean?"

"When you see something in your head, like the way you think it should be, you can't not interfere."

"Example?"

"Every single time you got benched for arguing with the ref when they made a call on the ice you didn't agree with."

Abe flicked the bottle cap at his brother. "No way. Every hockey kid does that. I was young."

"Fine. How about crawling up my ass every time you see me because you think I should have a different job?"

"Because you're smart. You *should* have a different job."

"Never mind that I'm happy."

"So you say. Got any other examples? These are lame."

"Didn't you just tell me you kept your firefighters on a call at Robot Lit to do what amounted to a fire inspection, even though that's not your job?"

Abe opened his mouth to protest, then closed it again. He stared at the faux grain of Stu's cheap table. One example he could argue with. But three? And Stu looked like he could keep going.

"I just like things the way I like them," he said after a moment. "Is that so wrong?"

"Only when those things fly in the face of what someone *else* wants. Like your gal here. She was pretty clear about what she was after from the get-go. You agreed to the terms—then changed your mind. Not cool."

"But I *like*—"

"Doesn't matter. You switched up on her. And now you're irritated that things didn't go well. Surprise, surprise."

Abe clenched his jaw. He hated that his younger brother had a point—but maybe the kid was right. The issue might not be that he wanted more from Casey, it might be that he was putting his needs before hers.

"But don't I get a say in any of this?" he asked, hating the bitter tone in his own voice.

"I think you had your say," Stu replied.

Abe drew a breath, then released it. He was frustrated with Casey without thinking about how he'd turned the tables on her. He was just barreling ahead with his own desires. But didn't his wants count for *anything*?

"So what do I do?" Abe asked. "How do I fix this?"

"Seems to me you go back to her list," Stu said with a small shrug. "That's what she wants."

The idea left a bad taste in Abe's mouth. "But Casey and I could be so much more than just a hot fuck."

"Dude, you're not getting it. What does *she* want?"

"A hot fuck."

"So give it to her. Make her happy. Stop thinking about yourself and you might get somewhere."

Abe shifted. "I don't know if I can be satisfied with scraps when I want the entire meal."

"It's either that or go hungry, brother."

Abe rubbed a hand over his jaw. He wasn't sure about this situation at all.

Could he make do with crumbs when he wanted *all* of Casey? He swore softly. This was why he'd stayed away from relationships for so long. They were needlessly complicated. If Casey would just do what he wanted, this would all be settled.

Of course, Stu's point was that Abe should do what *she* wanted.

"So I just do what's on the list and nothing more?"

"Bingo," Stu said, grinning.

It seemed awful. And right. Awfully right.

"When the hell did you get so wise?" he asked Stu.

Stu grinned. "Delivering pizzas, bro. Natch."

CHAPTER EIGHTEEN

The damn house was like a shrine to Abe. This was the thought rolling around in Casey's brain by Tuesday morning as she got ready for work. Ever since Saturday, she'd been trying to avoid seeing Abe in every single object that surrounded her, but there he was: in the branches of the Christmas tree he'd put up, in the reflection of the lights he'd strung, in the cushions of the couch where he'd touched her, and in the sheets of her bed, where he'd had her believing she was lit with gold flame, inside and out.

She'd forced herself to tear off the bedding and throw it into the washer because Abe's cinnamon-and-smoke smell had been omnipresent when she'd tried to sleep. With every breath, he was there. It was a presence with more weight than a shadow and yet not fully realized—just enough to tease her and have her imagining his hands on her all over again, his lips working deliciously across her flesh.

"Crap," she muttered, setting her coffee down on the

counter and wondering how she was going to fake her way through the workday again. Even her stupid mug had her thinking about him, picturing the way he'd handed it to her with a wink after she told him she took it black, like her heart.

Maybe it wasn't such a joke after all. Her heart was feeling downright rotten, rancid with the knowledge that Abe had summoned the courage to tell her he wanted more from her and she'd shot him down. No, not just shot— she'd lobbed grenades and missiles at his idea, then set off a nuclear-level explosion just to make sure to blow the notion to bits.

And now, here it was Tuesday and she was heading straight into a meeting with him to talk about Carter. She'd have to see him at the school today and pretend that her very bones weren't aching for him, a soreness so deep there were moments she wondered if she could stand up.

What have I done? She asked herself this question for the hundredth time. And, like always, the same statement followed it:

I couldn't have done it any differently.

Because there was no future for Abe and her. None. She wanted to be free, and he wanted commitment. She wanted pleasure, he wanted kids.

The idea of them together was impossible. Or, if not impossible, then certainly implausible. No matter what part of her was yearning for Abe—and God knew it wasn't a small part—they could only end up hurting each other. Casey understood what kind of a danger she posed when she felt too much, when she couldn't control her emotions. It was a slippery, dangerous slope. And not only that, they wanted completely different things from their futures.

She swallowed, staring at the green walls of her kitchen.

Even if she would—even if she *could*—risk letting her emotions run unbridled for Abe, they'd never outpace the inevitable fracturing that would crack them apart when Abe wanted children and she didn't.

It was the flag in the ground. It was the unmovable barrier. It was enough to separate them forever.

She sighed. She supposed she should be grateful for what she'd been given, and not regret what was never meant to be. At least she'd had a little excitement in the sack for once.

She tried to tell herself it was enough, though her body was weary with the thought. Fighting off the craving for Abe Cameron was exhausting. Worse, it was no longer just carnal. She wasn't just having to battle back her flesh; she was tamping down way-deep, didn't-even-know-she-had-them emotions. She was trying to sever a link between her and Abe that was no longer a spider's thread, but a steel cable.

"Stupid list," she muttered. She was beginning to wish she and the Knots and Bolts crew had never created it in the first place.

She took another sip of coffee.

Black, like her moldy, worthless heart.

* * *

Later that morning, Casey sat in the school counselor's office looking everywhere but at Abe Cameron. She took in the motivational print showing a boundless ocean at sunset and the words SEE POSSIBILITIES, NOT LIMITATIONS. She studied the maroon carpet, flattened by the feet of so many students over so many years. And she listened to the sound of Ingrid, next to her, gnawing on the wood of a pencil, while on her other side Rolf pushed up his glasses and took a deep breath.

Carter's counselor, Amy Strand, glanced at her watch. It was thin and silver, and Casey appreciated that it was the wind-up kind. Old school. She wondered if Amy twisted its little dial every morning. "Just a few more minutes," Amy said, trying to smile past the fact that Carter's foster parents were late. Next to her, Carter was slumped in his chair. His feet kicked at the legs of a small table until Carter's social worker, Kellie Sampson, quietly asked him to stop.

Finally, the door opened and Carter's foster parents entered. "Sorry we're late," the man said—Scotty, if Casey remembered correctly. "I was wrangling a workers' dispute. And those aren't things you can just walk out of." He was wearing a gray suit nearly the same tone as the one on his wife, Bridget. They both carried briefcases.

"Scotty's with a firm that represents the Canadian Auto Workers," Bridget said. "I'm a lawyer, too, but my cases usually involve mineral rights instead of workers' rights."

They smiled with white, even teeth. They weren't large people, but something about them seemed to take up every last ounce of space in the room. Their presence sucked at Casey's air, pulling it away from her body. She felt immediately smaller, more pressed into her own self. She glanced at Carter and saw that he'd stopped kicking the table. In fact, he looked like he'd stopped moving entirely.

Amy made formal introductions all around. "I'm so glad we have the opportunity to talk with Carter as a group," she said. She turned to the boy. "Carter, everyone in this room cares about you. It's important to say that at the outset. The people gathered here want what's best for you."

The social worker, Kellie, nodded her head in agreement. Her dark curls bounced. "You should feel free to tell us about anything that's bothering you. Everything you say in this room is safe."

Except it didn't feel safe. Not to Casey, anyway. Maybe not to Carter, either, who just nodded and kept his eyes on the floor.

"Carter, you were very brave the other day," Ingrid said, "sharing your journal with us. We know how hard you work to get your thoughts down at Robot Lit."

The crow, Casey pleaded with him silently, *just tell us about the crow*.

But Carter remained mute.

"Nothing you say will get you in trouble," Abe said. "We don't think you're a bad person, Carter. But we do think there's something in your life that's making you want to burn stuff. We were hoping today you might tell us about it."

Casey glanced around at the faces in the room. God, they were all leaned in, poised and waiting for Carter to tell them what was the matter. A big group suddenly seemed like a terrible idea. Too many giants focused on one troubled ant. But there was nothing she could do about it now.

"Can you tell us about the crow?" Casey asked after a moment. "The one you wrote about?"

Carter raised his eyes to hers and there was a pleading there that tore at her heart. She wanted so much to help him, but she had no idea how. Not unless he opened up to her.

"I don't believe it's an actual crow," she said. "I think it's a symbol. But unless you give us a hint, Carter, it's just a word on a piece of paper."

Carter didn't move. Or speak. He just locked on to Casey with his eyes, which she knew were sending a message she couldn't read.

"Or it could be an actual crow, I suppose," Scotty said.

His short brown hair was threaded through with gray. He ran a hand through it distractedly. "I guess that's the lawyer in me, arguing all sides."

"It's not a literal crow," Casey said. Sharper than she meant to. She tried for a conciliatory smile. *All friends here*, she hoped it said. Even if it was bullshit. She couldn't put her finger on it, but something about these people got under her skin.

Next to her, Rolf sat up straighter. "Hey, what if you wrote it down, Carter?" The boy turned his head. "Like, just get a pen and write down the key to the code. Pretend you're at Robot Lit and it's any old day."

Carter shrugged. "Yeah," he said, "okay."

Just like that. God bless Rolf.

Casey exhaled a breath she felt like she'd been holding since last Friday.

"Here you go," Amy said, handing Carter a pad of paper and a pen with White Pine Middle School printed on the side. "I'll take your note when you're done."

Carter shook his head. "No. *She* gets to read it. Only her." He pointed the pen at Casey.

Casey's stomach felt like it dropped through the worn carpet, all the way into the building's basement. Carter was trusting her. Except he didn't realize she was the wrong person for the job. There were professionals in this room, for crying out loud, and she was just an accountant who didn't even want kids. She started to protest, but closed her mouth before anything escaped. Her heart swelled with something like courage. If Carter wanted to share his secret with her, then she wasn't going to fight it. Whatever it took to find the crow and shoot it out of the sky, that was what she'd do.

"Of course," she said. "Anything you want."

Carter crooked his arm around the pad and lowered his head. He was a comma of a fortress. Casey wondered if he could even see what he was writing. Finally, there was a tearing sound. He sat up straight and handed Casey not a full sheet of paper, but a fraction of a corner. It was a tiny piece, barely a scrap.

What could he have possibly written on such a fragment?

"Thanks," she said, curling her fingers around the white paper. The room swiveled to focus on her. She was frozen, unsure what to do.

"So?" Bridget asked, sitting up straighter. "Are you going to read it?"

Casey bristled at the impatient tone. Then she turned her back to the group and pulled apart the small, white remnant. Inside was one word.

Caw.

Casey stared at the three letters. Was this a joke? Why write down what a crow says when—

Casey stiffened suddenly. She understood the message. Or at least she thought she did.

"Well?" asked Scotty.

Casey turned back around, hoping her face was as blank as she was trying to make it.

"It was empty," she lied. "Carter didn't write a thing."

* * *

Casey could feel clammy sweat break on her forehead. Lying had never been her strong suit. She'd done a terrible job of it when Audrey had confronted her directly about Kieran all those months ago, and it hadn't been hard for her sister to determine that Casey was all-out fibbing.

Casey recalled the sickening twist in her stomach when Audrey had uncovered her treachery. The whole world had gone thick and sluggish with the wrongness of it. Time had slowed down, and Casey was forced to endure the endless eternity of the moment when Audrey had known that *her own sister* had bribed Kieran to leave town and never see Audrey again. It was Casey's fault, Casey's doing, and she'd wrapped her arms around the responsibility of it, pulled it in tight and owned it, knowing that if she didn't, she'd repeat the same mistakes again.

Since then she'd tried so hard to be honest, to be up-front and change, but now here she was again, lying her fool head off. She just hoped the universe would forgive her because it was for a good cause.

"If you change your mind and decide to write something, I'm always here," she said directly to Carter. She threw the boy a look that she hoped said *Trust me*. If he was smart enough to give her a code to his puzzle, then she hoped he was smart enough to know when she was playing the game.

The boy dropped his gray eyes. His battered tennis shoes toed the table again. "Okay," he said.

"Well, then," Kellie said, pushing a dark curl off her forehead, "since the crow seems like it's off the table for now, we should probably talk about some restitution options for Carter. You did damage to those buildings, and it's important you take responsibility for that. Do you agree?"

Carter nodded. His whole body looked tense enough to snap.

Casey could barely sit still as Abe offered up some community service hours at the fire station, and Ingrid said there was always volunteer work to be done at Robot Lit. After a short discussion, the group agreed to fifty hours of community service—twenty-five at Robot Lit and twenty-five at the fire station—beginning the next week.

When they told him how much time he'd have to spend at both places, Carter actually looked relaxed for the first time all day.

The group stood, pulling on winter coats and shaking hands all around. They'd meet in two more weeks, they all agreed, to talk about how Carter's community service was progressing, and to see if they could address the crow again. Casey clenched her teeth, willing herself to carry her secret for just a few minutes longer.

She took her time with her coat, aware that Abe's eyes were on her, watching her. She hoped he couldn't see her trembling hands, hoped he didn't notice her sweaty neck.

She forced a smile when Scotty and Bridget shook her hand on their way out of the office. "Good to meet you," they said. Both of them clamped her fingers so hard she wondered if they were trying to squeeze out the truth of what the note said.

"Good to meet you, too," she lied.

"See you at home tonight, buddy," Scotty said to Carter.

Carter nodded, but kept quiet.

Kellie was headed out the door behind Carter's foster parents, but Casey grabbed the social worker's arm. "Got a sec?" she whispered.

"Of course. What can I do for you?"

It's not what I need, she thought, *it's what Carter needs*. In a flash, she closed the door shut, sealing the group—minus Carter's foster parents—into the room.

"Carter's note wasn't blank," she said quickly. The room quieted. Everyone stopped pulling on gloves and hats. "But it provided a clue that I wasn't comfortable reading in front of the entire group."

"Which was?" Kellie asked.

"Caw, like what a crow says, but it could also mean Canadian Auto Workers. Is that right, Carter?"

Casey crossed the floor quickly, crouching next to Carter, who looked like he might topple out of his chair at any moment. "It's okay," she reassured him. "I made sure we could talk without your foster parents in the room, in case it was a clue about them. About Scotty, in particular. Was I wrong?"

The kid's eyes were round with a sadness that ripped apart her insides. He shook his head no. She'd read the clue correctly.

Impulsively, she grabbed the kid's hand. She expected him to pull away from her, but he didn't. Instead, he looked grateful.

"What do the Canadian Auto Workers mean to you?" she asked. "Is there something about Scotty's job that upsets you?"

"No," Carter whispered. His skinny frame was nearly swallowed by the chair. "It's the way he says it. It's *wrong*. He should say the letters—C-A-W—but instead he calls it 'Caw.' He goes around the house, caw this and caw that and sounds like a crow. That's how he became the crow."

"Can you tell us why you wrote about him?" Rolf asked. "Why you put him in your journals?"

"I didn't want him to read my pages and know I was talking about him. In case he ever found them."

"But there was more to it than that," Casey said, squeezing his hand. "Wasn't there? When you wrote that you saw the crow, it was code for more than just *seeing* Scotty, right?" She hated the question, and her insides shook at the possible answers. *He touched you. He beat you.*

Carter nodded. "I did it on the days when I didn't get food."

The whole room stiffened. "You're saying they made you go hungry?" Kellie said, her voice tight with what Casey could only imagine was shock and anger.

"At dinner sometimes, yeah. They'd eat like normal, but I could only have so many bites. Two or something. I never knew when—like, there wasn't any way I could tell if they'd do it. Some days I could eat. Others, I could only have one or two bites."

Casey saw spots of darkness in her peripheral vision. She was sickened and furious and heartbroken—all at once. She longed to wrap Carter into a hug. Instead she nodded, trying to reassure him that he was doing great, that telling this group the truth was his way forward.

"And it was just Scotty who did this, or did Bridget do it, too?" This question from Amy, who had grabbed a pen and was starting to write all this down.

"Scotty sort of decides it. I don't know how. He just says how many bites I get some nights. Bridget and Luke just pretend like nothing is even happening."

"Were you afraid to tell us for a certain reason?" Kellie asked. Casey noticed she left the question intentionally vague, but the subtext was vivid in Casey's mind: *Were you afraid to tell us because you were worried Scotty would hurt you?*

Carter bit his lip. "I just didn't want it to get worse. Maybe they'd stop letting me eat at all."

"If there are other things you can tell us," Casey said, "if it went beyond not getting food, you need to let us know."

Carter shook his head. "No. They gave me my own bedroom with an Iron Man bedspread. I wanted to like them. I thought maybe I did something wrong. I was so mad at myself."

There was the anger. Casey had to swallow back tears. Carter wasn't even mad at Scotty for withholding food. He was mad at himself, believing he'd done something to deserve it.

"You didn't do anything wrong, kiddo," she said. "Okay? You need to know that. If Scotty and his family aren't giving you food, it's not right. And it's not your fault. Can you understand that?"

Carter nodded. "I guess."

Casey looked around the room. *What happens now?* She wanted to yell the question, then forgo the answer by finding Carter's foster parents and starving *them* for a change. Instead, she found Abe's eyes and locked on to them. His gaze held her steady, helped calm her pounding heart.

"I'll call Child Protective Services," Kellie said, pulling out her cell phone. "We'll open this up for investigation."

"What will happen to Carter in the meantime?" Casey asked.

Kellie exhaled. "Well, it's really in CPS's hands for the time being. They'll talk to Scotty and Bridget. Probably Luke, too."

"But he can't stay with them while that happens, can he?" Casey asked. "Not if they're withholding food from him, for crying out loud."

"It will depend on what CPS finds. What they decide."

"I'll take him." Casey blurted the words before she could think. For a moment she swore she saw them hovering in a cartoon bubble in the air, just in front of her face. *I'll take him.* She debated popping the bubble, letting the words fall to the ground and then scrambling to clean them up, saying it was a mistake, she never should have said such a thing. But she didn't want that. So she stayed quiet and let the phrase hang there: *I'll take him.*

"That's kind of you, Casey," Kelly said, "but if CPS decides he should be removed from foster care—and it's a big if—he'll need to go to a home that's been approved, inspected, and where the parents have filled out the right paperwork with the state."

She felt her face heat. Of course she couldn't just take Carter home with her like some puppy. It didn't work like that. What was she even thinking?

She nodded. "I—yes, of course." She blinked back mortified tears. Everyone must think she was such a fool.

But then there was the pressure of small fingers on hers, and she realized Carter had squeezed *her* hand this time—just a little bit. "Thanks anyways," he whispered, and her heart folded in on itself, an origami shape of affection for this young boy who was dealing with so much.

"Folks, if you could excuse us, Kellie and I may need to speak with Carter privately about the next steps." Amy set down her notebook. The face of her old-school watch glinted in the late-morning light.

Abe nodded. He reached out and extended his hand to help Casey up from the floor, where she was still kneeling in front of Carter. The sureness of her palm against his was a welcome support.

"Will you call at least one of us?" Casey asked. "With any updates?"

"You have my cell," Ingrid offered. "I'll take a call night or day."

"Will do," Kellie agreed.

From his seat in the chair, Carter glanced up.

"See you at Robot Lit, okay, bud?" Casey said.

Carter gave her a whisper of a smile. "See you."

With Ingrid and Rolf leading the way, the four of them stepped out of the middle school offices and into the hallway. Casey noted that the ever-present smell of paste and hot lunch hadn't changed in two decades.

"Can I have a word?" Abe asked, pulling gently on Casey's sleeve.

She stilled. Her mind reeled, thinking of their fight in the kitchen. Part of her wanted to refuse, to tell him there was nothing to talk about. Except there was no fight left in her—not even enough to tell him she didn't want to talk.

She waved at Ingrid and Rolf. "I'll catch up with you at the office," she said.

Ingrid nodded, though she raised an eyebrow. As if she sensed the conversation between Casey and Abe was going to be about more than just the weather.

Abe turned to her. Behind him, a row of red lockers stretched down the hallway.

"That was rough in there," he said. "You did great."

"Thanks," she said, even as she wished she'd been able to do something more tangible for Carter. She couldn't take him home, it was true, but leaving him in the hands of CPS didn't seem right, either. Not that she had any choice in the matter. It was out of her control.

She waited, wondering if the conversation was over, if Abe had held her back simply to compliment her. But no, there was a shadow on his face that hinted at emotions churning just below his chiseled exterior.

"I wanted to apologize for the other day," Abe said finally. "About the way I handled things." He ran a hand along the back of his neck. "You've been very clear about what you wanted from the beginning. I agreed to your terms, then changed course on you. That wasn't fair."

Casey could feel her eyes widen. Out of all the things she expected him to say, an apology was almost dead last.

"I know I don't exactly deserve it, but if you'd give me another chance, I'd like to try the list again. *Just* the list, nothing more. No loopholes, no modifications."

Casey opened her mouth, but Abe held up a hand. "Before you go telling me no, I promise I won't ask for more when the list is complete. I've thought about this since Saturday, and I'm not using this as a trick. I like you, it's true. But I also like your list, and I'm good for some checked boxes if that's still what you want."

Casey wasn't sure what to say. Which was just as well, since a bell sounded, loud enough to drown out whatever she might have uttered. Doors swung open and kids poured into the hallway, swarming past them. They were suddenly two islands in a chaotic, energetic stream.

"Let me think about it," she said, raising her voice over the thunder of the middle schoolers. "I'll text you."

Abe smiled. No teeth, just a pull at the corner of his perfect lips. But it was enough to have Casey remembering what his mouth could do—*had* done—to her.

"Ingrid was my ride," she said as Abe turned to go. "Any chance you can give me a lift back to Robot Lit?"

Abe arched a brow. "If I was an asshole," he said playfully, "I'd tell you I needed your answer first."

Casey almost smiled. "If *I* was an asshole, I'd tell you my answer was no."

"I'd better give you that ride, then." He grinned at her then—big and wide—and Casey found her pulse pounding louder than the kids all around her.

I will think about this, she vowed. *I will not just jump back into bed with Abe.*

Her brain fought to hold on to reason and logic, even as her skin was already whispering yes.

CHAPTER NINETEEN

That evening, Casey had finished decorating her tree, swept up errant pine needles, scrubbed the sink, and was beginning to think about cleaning out the fridge when Ingrid called. "Finally," she said, grabbing for her phone. She'd been waiting for word about Carter since they'd all met in the counselor's office that morning.

"Tell me," she said, not even bothering with a hello.

"They took him to the doctor's office," Ingrid said, "and he was right on the edge of being malnourished. The parents denied not feeding him, but CPS got it out of their teenager, Luke. They'd been letting him go hungry, the assholes. Of course the parents changed their story then, saying it was to discipline Carter. Suddenly he was unruly and surly, not doing his homework, that kind of thing. No one's buying it, though. They're messed up, but at least they won't be able to foster any more kids."

Casey reached out to the counter to steady herself. She

thought she might be sick. "And Carter?" she managed to ask. "Is he okay?"

"Placed with a different family for now. His mom gets out of rehab in another couple weeks. With any luck, he'll be back with her soon."

"Cripes," Casey said, shaking her head, "what the heck is wrong with people? No wonder Carter was burning shit up. I'm surprised he wasn't stealing as well. Just so he wouldn't starve."

"He's a good kid placed in a bad situation. I'm cautiously optimistic that things will turn around from here."

"Me too," Casey said. Deep down, though, she could feel a small pang of disappointment where part of her had been hoping *she* could help Carter. That somehow Kellie would decide to place him with Casey—even just for a short while—and she'd give him the stability he needed until his mom was back on her feet.

Of course that was silly. She didn't want kids.

But Carter wasn't hers, she reminded herself. He was just someone in a tough spot who needed help. And the idea of coming to his aid, or even to the aid of kids like him, had her heart filled with something she couldn't put her finger on. Hope? Want? Happiness? Whatever it was, it gave her such a lightness and a peace that she wondered if she wasn't floating a bit.

She was startled back to the present by a sound on the other end of the phone. "You'll have to excuse me, I have a Disney princess tugging on my pants and a husband who's just made dinner. See you tomorrow?"

"You bet. Thanks for the call, Ingrid."

After they hung up, Casey stood in her kitchen, pondering what in the world was happening to her. Surely being a fos-

ter parent wasn't in her cards—or was it? She didn't have
the answer. So instead she simply let the newfound lightness
envelop her, buoying her mind and body. She smiled and
wondered, for the briefest of seconds, if she wasn't about to
hit her head on the ceiling.

* * *

That Thursday, the Knots and Bolts recipe exchange decided
to let someone else do the cooking for once. The group met
at the Paul Bunyan Diner, the six of them crushed into a corner booth, to hold an informal baby shower for Willa.

"I need something fried, stat," the mom-to-be said, grabbing a menu. "And if I can get that with a side of chocolate
ice cream, that would be great."

She brushed a lock of dark blonde hair away from her
face with swollen fingers. Casey felt a pang of sympathy
as Willa shifted, trying to get comfortable. Her protruding
stomach bumped the table, even though she was seated on
the end, feet propped on a chair in the aisle. Her position
probably violated some kind of fire code, but it wasn't as
if their waitress, Pauline, who'd worked there for years
and knew them all by name, was going to say anything
about it.

"I craved sour stuff with Juniper," Anna said. "I'd pile
lemons into my water, or suck on them straight. I drank but-
termilk right from the carton. I think Sam was disgusted,
even though he never said anything."

"Smart man, staying quiet," Betty said. "When he carries
a baby for nine months, *then* he can judge."

"Alan had to learn how to make curry because I wanted it
so often," Stephanie said. "I don't think he minded, though.

I'm usually averse to spicy food, so the fact that we were having it regularly had him over the moon."

"I definitely crave Charleston Chews. I think it's a texture thing," Betty confessed. The whole table stared at her.

"Are you—?"

"Oh my God, you and Randall—"

Betty paled, then shook her head. "No, I'm not *pregnant*. I meant when I get my period I crave Charleston Chews." She waved her hands, as if trying to erase the misunderstanding. "Randall got smart and started buying them in bulk. He thinks I don't know he hides them in the wheel well in his trunk. But right about the time I want one, he's got it right there." Betty smiled, soft and gentle in contrast to the rusted saws and cookware tacked to the diner's walls.

"I like how bubbly you get when you talk about Randall," Stephanie said.

Betty immediately stiffened. "I do not get *bubbly*."

"It's not a bad thing," Audrey said. "Even if it's not precisely bubbly, you get happy, at least. Which is great."

Betty looked down at her menu, her cheeks pinking uncharacteristically. "I am happy." Her words low, heavy with feeling.

Casey stared down at her hands, wishing that for once she could have that same sentiment, too. That someone out there—maybe by the name of Abe Cameron—could feel so much for her that one day she'd tell a whole tableful of ladies all about it.

Of course, it was a shadow-thin fantasy. There was no future for her and Abe Cameron when they wanted such different things.

"You're the best thing that ever happened to that pastor," Willa said, bringing Casey back to the here and now.

"Believe me. His sermons are so much better now that he's getting laid."

They all stared at her for a moment.

"Sorry," Willa said, grimacing. "It's the pregnancy." She shifted and, as she did, she emitted a tiny fart. The whole table quieted. "This is the part where you call out the fact that I just passed gas, Betty. In public. Because I'm a human blimp."

Betty pressed her lips together, trying not to smile. "Should I also say it smells like rotten broccoli?"

"More like a compost pile in the summer."

"Gross!" Stephanie said, waving her napkin in front of her nose. "How are we supposed to even eat now?"

Willa giggled. "No problem. Whatever you don't finish, I will."

"You're going to finish us all if you fart again," Betty said.

Casey covered her mouth to keep from barking out laughter. She barely succeeded as the other women collapsed into fits of giggles. After a few minutes, they settled down, gave their orders to Pauline, and then handed Willa their shower presents. The table was piled with enough pink to wallpaper a nursery.

Willa pulled off the wrapping paper for the gifts, one by one, to reveal a slew of thoughtful, handmade items. Betty had knitted the baby a blanket as well as a stuffed bear wearing a green cardigan with impossibly delicate buttons. Anna had purchased a pile of classic children's books, and had tied them up by knotting onesies together. Stephanie had put chocolate, coffee, bath salts, and a neck massager into a basket for a mommy survival kit. And Audrey had purchased a package from Click Here, the local photography studio.

Whenever Willa felt ready, she and Burk could take their tiny arrival in for a family portrait. In addition to the photo package was lip gloss and a brand-new compact, to help the new mom look her best.

Casey could feel crimson embarrassment creeping along her neck as her turn came. She tried not to read too much into the gift that Willa was about to open. It didn't mean she was completely awful at every single thing having to do with babies and relationships. All it meant was that she should have asked Audrey for help shopping for this thing.

Right?

Willa tugged open Casey's gift and, to her credit, her smile never faltered. Not even as she pulled out a generic pack of washable breast pads and what looked like a miniature baster, but was actually a tool used to pull snot out of kids' noses.

"It was on your registry—" Casey started, trying to explain. She wanted to say she had no idea that everyone else was going to pull together the most creative gifts in the history of female pregnancy ever. She wanted to put words to the fact that this was her first shower and she didn't know what she was doing. But instead, she just plastered on a smile.

"Thank you," Willa said, "these are going to be so useful."

Not memorable. Not special. Not cherished. *Useful.*

Casey caught Audrey's eye, and her sister gave her a little smile. *Next time I'm not going near a baby store without her*, Casey thought.

But there was an ache inside her that persisted, even as she tried to brush it aside. She couldn't shake the feeling of longing—of wanting to be loved as wholly and completely as the women around her were, and the overwhelming disappointment that came from knowing it wasn't in the cards.

She could wish and wish for her path and Abe's to be different, for them to twist together on the road to happily ever after, but it was useless. Casey was never going to be his, and she was never going to have that look on her face that Betty Lindholm was wearing right now.

Pauline brought their dinners and she tore into her hamburger, trying to distract herself with food, not realizing that, lo and behold, there was dessert. Audrey had baked a cake— complete with fondant ribbons and *Welcome Baby Olmstead* swirled on it, for heaven's sake—and Pauline brought it out after the plates had been cleared.

As she speared a hunk of frosting, something in Casey felt off, like a house after an earthquake that's suddenly no longer square with its foundation. She'd felt like she was part of this group, and she'd let them help with her stupid list, but even after all that, they still had lives that were fundamentally different from hers. They had committed relationships, which led to weddings. Showers. Marriage. Kids.

None of it was for her. And while it was one thing to feel like a freak when it came to a recipe klatch, what would happen when it was Audrey's turn to have a family? She pressed the tines of her fork against the plate, trying to imagine stumbling through a shower for her sister, screwing up everything along the way, and then not knowing even how to *relate* to Audrey as she plunged into parenthood. Casey would try, of course. She would paint nursery walls and change diapers and take Audrey's overtired two-in-the-morning phone calls. She'd do anything for her sister.

But that didn't mean she'd do it right. Her emotions

weren't to be trusted, after all. What if she screwed up something with the baby, God forbid, like she had with Kieran and Audrey? And even if she didn't, she'd still never fit into the mommy culture, never truly understand it or connect with it.

Casey swallowed. She'd tried so hard to change her life, but fundamentally she just couldn't change who she was. It wasn't a bad thing, but it was a heartbreaking thing, because it left her feeling not just alone—but actually lonely.

She pushed her plate away, trying not to dwell on it. Because if Audrey had a kid, then her job was to be supportive. Period. Her feelings didn't matter.

But that didn't mean they didn't *exist*.

Casey muddled through the rest of the shower, forced a laugh when Betty joked about naming the baby Burka, and fairly bolted out the door after the farewell hugs were complete.

Moments later, she stood by her car, breathing in the brittle air and watching the night-black water of the Birch River ripple by.

Since moving to White Pine a few months ago, she'd experienced moments of uncertainty and of doubt. But she hadn't, until now, been discouraged.

About her friends. About her sister. Even about Abe— someone she might want to care for, but couldn't, because he wanted kids in the end, too.

She'd just unlocked her car when she heard footsteps behind her. "Hey, speedy! What's the hurry?"

She turned to see Audrey jogging toward her, long legs eating up the distance before Casey could slip inside her vehicle and drive away. Audrey's breath puffed in the cold, and her brown eyes reflected the glittering Christmas lights strung along Main Street. "You in a race to be the first one out of here?" Audrey asked.

A thousand fibs crossed Casey's lips. How it had been a long day and she wanted to put her feet up. How she had things to do at home. How Ingrid had asked her to work on a project that was due tomorrow and she needed to tackle it.

She opened her mouth to utter one of the excuses—any of them, actually—and found herself bursting into tears instead.

She clapped a hand over her mouth, mortified. She tried to swallow back the tears, but only ended up hiccupping sobs instead.

She tried to turn away, to hide her face, but couldn't move before Audrey had thrown her arms around her and pulled her close.

"Oh my God! Are you okay? What's *wrong*?"

Casey fought to regain her composure. She shouldn't be standing here crying in a parking lot. But the tears just kept coming, leaking onto Audrey's down jacket as her sister rubbed her back and told her it was going to be okay.

Casey's whole head hurt as she wondeed if that was the truth. Was everything going to work out, or was Casey destined to be on the outskirts of their happy group, never really knowing love or commitment just because she didn't want kids? Would it affect not only her friendships, but the heart of her relationship with her sister as well?

"Hand me the keys," Audrey said after a minute. She released Casey and held out her hands.

"What? Why?" Casey asked, wiping her nose.

"We're going to the Wheelhouse. I'll drive. We're getting you a drink and you're going to tell me what's going on. And no bullshit. You looked like a ghost during that baby shower, and I'm *not* going to believe you if you tell me it was from the smell of Willa's farts."

Casey didn't have the energy to argue. She handed over her keys and got into her own passenger seat. Audrey started the car and, a few minutes later, they were motoring across the Birch River, passing over geese clustered along the banks, their bills tucked deep into their downy wings.

Casey wondered why they were still here, why they'd stayed the winter in White Pine. She wondered if she'd fly away if she had wings that would take her anywhere.

But where could she go? The problem with any destination was that Casey would have to face herself when she got there.

* * *

Ten minutes later, they were seated at the bar and Dave Englund was handing her a bubbling drink the color of warm honey. It was garnished with a lime like an exclamation point of color. "A dark and stormy," he said, "to match your mood."

"It doesn't *look* dark and stormy," Casey said, hating the little-kid pout in her voice. Part of her was miffed that, when they'd arrived, Audrey had blabbed to Dave that Casey had just been crying, and needed the perfect drink.

She barely wanted her sister to know she'd been bawling, much less their *bartender*. At the same time, she didn't hate that she was here, with the smooth wood of the bar under her palms and the comfort of her sister next to her, and Dave smiling like a friend might.

As if she belonged here.

"The black rum's the trick to that drink," Dave said, muscles bulging from underneath the sleeves of his T-shirt. "I think it's supposed to be reminiscent of a churning ocean or something."

"Just imagine you're in Key West and the clouds are rolling in," Audrey said. She'd ordered the Christmas ale once again, and was sucking it down like she was dehydrated.

"You guys want some cheese curds or something?" Dave asked.

Audrey put a hand on her stomach. "No, thanks. I just ate enough baby shower cake for three." She gave him a small smile. "But maybe we could get an update about you and that firefighter, Quinn."

Dave's easygoing bartender demeanor instantly hardened. His dark eyes flashed with hurt. "I wish I could tell you. We went on some dates. I thought things were fine, but she stopped returning my phone calls."

"What, just like that?" Audrey asked.

"Yeah, pretty much. I thought things were cool. But apparently she had a different viewpoint."

Audrey shook her head, her ponytail bouncing. "Sorry, Dave. That sucks."

Dave's jaw flexed. From the look on his face, he thought so, too.

Two weeks ago, Casey might have tried again with Dave, maybe leaned forward to stir up some sparks between them. But now the idea seemed ludicrous. The only person she had on her mind was Abe. He was the only one she *wanted* on her mind.

"I'll check on you guys in a little while. In the meantime, enjoy." Dave left them to attend to another set of customers. Audrey drummed her fingers on the bar.

"That's too bad about Quinn," she said. "I wonder what happened."

Maybe she realized Dave wanted kids and she didn't. Maybe she realized she had tried to change, but she still didn't fit in anywhere.

The thoughts stung hard enough to make Casey's eyes smart all over again.

"For heaven's sake," Audrey said. "Will you please tell me what's wrong?"

Casey hated that her sister was having to drag all this out of her. She should be brave enough just to speak honestly about what was going on. Except confusion had her words lodged somewhere in her throat.

She had to try, though. If she wanted to salvage any kind of relationship with her sister, she had to be honest.

"I slept with Abe Cameron," she said finally. She figured it was as good a place as any to start.

Audrey's eyes widened. Then her mouth cracked into a huge grin. "You told him about the list? And he agreed?"

Casey played with her straw. "Kind of. I mean, yes, he agreed. But then, after we slept together, he told me he wanted more."

Audrey's grin spread. "You don't say."

"You shouldn't smile. This isn't a good thing."

"What? Why not? He likes you, Casey. How is that not awesome?"

"Because we want different things. At the time he said he wanted a relationship, and he even admitted to wanting kids. But I don't—it's not where I see my life heading."

Audrey tilted her head. Her brown eyes searched Casey's. "Where *do* you see your life heading?"

"I don't know. But I don't think pushing a baby stroller is in the cards."

"Why not? I mean, if you found the right person?"

Casey sucked down a big gulp of her drink. *Liquid courage.* She was going to need it. "Growing up for us wasn't easy," she said. "Aunt Lodi did her best, but you know as well as I do what we went through. I shouldered a lot. We both did. And now, I just feel like I kind of want less responsibility in my life, not more. Does that make sense?"

Audrey blinked. "You're saying you don't want kids because of our childhood? That was ages ago."

"But it put me on a very specific path. And it's not that I don't want responsibility, it's that I don't want responsibility to define me. For years, I took on so much, and look where it got me. Alone. Rigid. Trying to control everything, being a total bitch, and—eventually—I was working my ass off to split you and Kieran apart. I don't ever want to go back there."

Audrey shifted. "I get that, for sure. If you don't want to have kids, that's your choice, and I support it. I'll stand by you, no matter what you decide. But why do I get the feeling that's not all there is to what's bothering you?"

Casey sighed. "Because you're right. If I don't have kids, that means I'm not like you and your friends. It means I don't want the white picket fence and the happy, perfect family package. I'll always be different."

Audrey arched a dark brow. "If you think any of us are perfect, then you haven't seen Stephanie's twins draw on the walls with Sharpies, or me after Kieran leaves ice cream out on the counter all night." She smiled, but Casey couldn't return it.

"That's just it, though. There might be tiny aberrations here and there, but fundamentally I'm not the same. And I can't change that."

"So?"

"So then I'll always be an outsider."

Audrey sat back. "Are you looking for reasons to not be friends with us?"

"What? *No.*"

"Because if we're being honest here, then these all sound like excuses, Casey. Friendships don't just happen, they take work. You think I liked Willa when she marched back into town two years ago with her nose in the air, like she was so much better than all of us? I didn't. But I kept at it—we both did—because she deserved a shot.

"If you want to find reasons not to be part of the recipe exchange, they're there. For all of us. But don't show me a handful of bullshit and pretend it's gold."

"I'm trying to tell you how I feel," Casey said, her irritation rising. "It's not bullshit."

"Is too," Audrey said. "The recipe exchange isn't the problem."

The words spiked Casey's heart. The implication was clear. If the recipe exchange wasn't the problem, *Casey* was. Casey gripped her drink to keep her hands from shaking.

"The recipe exchange is oil and I'm water," Casey said, thinking of Betty's radiant face and Willa's swollen belly. "You can't blame physics when they don't mix. It's how the universe is constructed."

"No, I think you're the oil here," Audrey said, "because you're being deliberately slick."

"How so?"

"You came to White Pine because you wanted a new start. You said you didn't want to be on the same path of responsibility and rigidity you were before. Fine. But everything you're saying right now is *rooted* in rigidity and control. You don't want to give the recipe exchange a shot.

You don't want to give Abe a shot. You don't want to give kids a shot."

Audrey held up a hand when Casey tried to interrupt. "Kids are a complicated choice, and I'm not trying to pressure you into changing your mind on that front. What I am saying, though, is that you came here wanting to change. You made a booty list like it was proof you could release your inner wild child. But now, think about it. That list has brought a good man into your life, who you're determined to push away. Moving here has brought a group of women into your life, who you're determined to stay removed from."

"I *have* to push Abe away."

"Why?"

"Because I know how the story ends. You're right that he's a good man, and he deserves to get what he wants. He told me that's kids, Audrey. Which I don't want. So how can we be compatible long term? Don't you see?"

Audrey reached out and touched Casey's shoulder. "Maybe there's a way around all this."

Casey shook her head. She knew from experience. There wasn't.

"You know," Audrey said slowly, "you had a lot of responsibility when we were kids. And you had a lot of fear, too. More fear, I think, than anything else. These days, you've tried to disguise it as other things, like inhibition, maybe. But it's still just fear."

Casey stared at the bar's polished wood. She could all but feel terror twining her gut like nettles. Audrey was right. It was still there.

"I don't want to screw up again," she whispered. "I lost a relationship once over the whole kid thing. Not that he was some great love, but—still, it was awful. And of course

Mom and Dad, and then I came so close to losing you just a few months ago. Now, I'm just trying not to let everything fall apart again." The tears were back again, collecting at the corners of her eyes. She tried not to let them fall.

"Oh, Casey." Audrey wrapped her arms around her sister. "Things fall apart. It's part of what being human is all about. But being afraid of mistakes, of hurt, doesn't justify sitting back and letting what you want slip away. You *have* to talk to Abe."

"And tell him...what?"

"That you care for him. That you want to try and work it out, even if you don't want kids."

"But that will only lead to—"

"*Stop*. Stop saying that. You don't know that. Maybe that's how one relationship of yours ended a long time ago. But maybe this is different."

Casey swallowed. This didn't seem possible. "It's so risky," she whispered.

Audrey nodded. "That's what love is. It's one big, huge risk. A great leap off a cliff, and it's not always going to be a smooth drop until the end. You're going to hit some stuff on the way down. The people who love you—who really love you—won't care about the bumps."

"But why jump at all?"

"Because it's fun. It makes life worthwhile."

"It sounds awful."

"Sometimes it's that, too. Listen, you don't have to jump. But you also can't stand on the edge and tell everyone you're having a blast on the way down, when we can all see you haven't moved."

Audrey pulled back. She took a sip of beer. Casey tucked her hair behind her ears, trying to regain her composure. She felt like she'd just stepped out of a wind tunnel. Her emotions were battered and buffeted.

After a moment, Audrey touched her shoulder. "When you get a better handle on things, sit down with Abe and be honest. Even if you end up in different places, it's better that you get there by telling the truth."

Casey tossed back the last of her drink.

She didn't have to be honest with Abe. He had agreed to her list, after all. If that was what she wanted, she'd get it.

But she wasn't at all sure she wanted just her list anymore.

She thought about watching the parade with Abe, shopping for Christmas decorations with him, and watching him cook breakfast in her kitchen. She'd been so deeply content in those moments, it was hard to think about reverting to a list of only five things.

Crammed in alongside the picture of Abe in her mind was Carter, and all the kids like him who needed help. She might not want her own kids, it was true. But maybe that didn't mean she had to reject supporting and loving any kids, ever.

"I'll talk to him," she said finally. "But first can we have another round?"

Audrey smiled. "We can have three if you want. You've earned it."

"Maybe I should get something besides a dark and stormy. I feel slightly better. Maybe there's a different drink out there for me."

"Sex on the beach? That is, if things go well with Abe?"

Casey laughed. "It's better than a mudslide."

"Or a rusty nail."

"I could get a tequila sunrise," Casey mused. "It's night

right now, technically, but maybe I can convince myself to look forward to what's ahead."

"That's called something else," Audrey said.

"Yeah?"

"It's called a glass half full. You're practically an optimist already."

CHAPTER TWENTY

*V*iola Stroud was missing her dentures, which made her story about her deceased husband's black Packard all the harder to understand. Abe and Quinn were standing in the old woman's small kitchen, trying to follow along.

"Drobe da Bacard da churb on Drismab," Viola said, nodding emphatically. Her white hair was fine and thin, tufted out from her head like a wispy halo. Behind her, faded flowered wallpaper lined the walls. Abe and Quinn glanced at each other, trying to translate what the elderly woman had just said.

"Oh, I'm sure it was such a nice drive on Christmas morning," Quinn said suddenly, grasping the old woman's meaning. "Do you want us to find your teeth for you? And maybe feed Mr. Mittens?"

Her gray cat was twining around their boots, meowing. Viola had an in-home caregiver stop by three days each week to clean and cook food and help out generally. And on the other days, she had the White Pine Fire Department, since she used her medical alert tag liberally.

Abe had debated telling her that she should only call in emergencies, but so far he hadn't been able to summon the words. As long as they weren't on another call, it was no sweat off anyone's back to stop by and see her. She was a widow, after all.

She'd lost her husband two years ago to a heart attack. He'd slumped over while watching the evening news. Abe had been on the call, in fact.

That dreary night, Viola's face had been a flat sheet—shock had made her featureless, like there weren't any muscles in her cheeks or jaw or brow. Abe had let her ride in the ambulance. His team had worked on her husband the whole way, even though it was clear he was gone, snuffed out before they even got there. They kept the resuscitation going for Viola's sake, because no one wanted to tell her the truth.

In the hospital, he'd let the doctors take over. He'd let them break the bad news to the old woman. At the time he'd told himself this was why you didn't love anyone or let them in. Because it crushed you, in the end. He could see it on Viola's face that very night. She was a ghost, a shadow of herself, without her better half.

Two years on, Abe knew Viola was still a shell in a way, bumbling through every day like it was a cobwebbed maze. But she was happiest when she talked about her husband—when that happened, her eyes focused, her voice brightened.

Any light she had left, it was because of him, Abe realized. Eighty years in, and he was still with her, helping her through the days that remained. Even if he wasn't physically present.

Maybe that was what love did, he thought. It gave you strength, even when it was seemingly gone.

He swallowed hard, trying not to think about Casey. But there she was. He felt more for her than he had for anyone, ever. So much that he was willing to risk the pain that came with caring for someone with your whole self. Not just one balloon on the beach, he thought, picturing his mom's painting, but two.

Even if it was just for a moment. Even if it was just for the five things on her list, he would float alongside her. He wanted more, of course. He wanted a lifetime. But he'd take what he could get. He'd live out the rest of his life in dim gray if it meant he could have a little of her light blazing alongside him for a few brief moments.

They fed Mr. Mittens, then found Viola's dentures in a small glass next to her bedside. Once her teeth were in place, they made her a sandwich and poured her a glass of milk. Abe grabbed Viola's hand when she was done eating. He should remind her of the rules, tell her she shouldn't use her medical alert signal all the time. "You call us if you need anything," he said instead. "Anything at all."

* * *

Abe and Quinn were uncharacteristically quiet on the ride back to the station. Usually they'd be ribbing each other, debating about a quick stop at the Rolling Pin, or trying to think about what pranks to pull on Reese.

Instead, Quinn was turned toward the window, blowing her bangs out of her face with soft sighs. Abe had Casey on the brain, and knew he probably looked tired. Hell, maybe he was.

"Penny for your thoughts," he said, after the silence had stretched too long. One of them had to say something.

Quinn shrugged. "Just thinking about how differently two people can see the same thing. Like, I'm looking at that Viola lady and thinking she's so lonely, and it's so sad. But maybe she's sitting there thinking she had the fullest, bestest life ever, and she's feeling sorry for *me* because I'm alone—"

Quinn cut herself off. This wasn't how firefighters talked. "Fuck it," she said, shoving her shoulders back.

Abe threw her a knowing look. "If Reese was here or Lambeck, I'd let it go. But it's just you and me. I'm not going to say anything to anybody if you want to talk about...whatever you've got on your mind."

Quinn tensed. Then threw up her hands. "Fine. The gossip mill already knows I went on a couple dates with that bartender, Dave. And it was going fine, but I bailed."

"Why? He mess up?"

"No, that's just it. He was perfect. Too perfect. And I freaked out."

Abe took a deep breath, thinking of all the women he'd shoved to the back burner because of fear. Too many to count.

"Why do you think you did that?" he asked.

Quinn shrugged. "I think I'm broken. Because the thing is, Dave was good. Really good. And not just in bed, although—shit, never mind. Point is, there was part of me that didn't want to mess it up. I was scared I'd ruin it somehow. So I bailed."

Abe gripped the steering wheel. Usually he'd just clam up and nod at whoever was talking—it was safer that way in the firehouse—but this time he wasn't about to let Quinn hang there alone, twisting in the wind. "I've got the opposite problem," he said, trying to catch her eye. "I like a woman who doesn't like me back. Or, at least, she likes me enough for five things."

"What does that mean?"

Abe confided Casey's list to Quinn, and her eyes grew rounder with each number. "Color me shocked. I never would have guessed she had a list like that."

Abe chuckled. "Me either."

"And you're not going to try and talk her into more than those five things?"

"Nope. I did that, and it didn't end so well. I'm at a place now where I like her so much, I'm willing to give her what she wants and end it there."

"God, that's pathetic."

"I know."

"But it's romantic, too. I'll deny ever having said that, by the way."

"Romantic is you walking up to Dave Englund's house with a six-pack and telling him you acted like a jerk."

"That's humiliating."

"Same difference, some days."

Quinn gave a dry laugh. "I'm so used to running, I don't think I'd know what to do if I was in more than one spot for a while."

"You've been at the station for years now. What are you talking about?"

"It's a metaphor, dumbass. For my heart?"

"Don't call me dumbass. I'm your superior."

"Superior dumbass, then." Quinn grinned, and Abe was relieved to see that some of the tension had vanished from her face.

"You're scrubbing the toilets, just for that."

"You're buying me a cruller at the Rolling Pin first."

Abe pretended to be put out. But he smiled as he stood in line at the Rolling Pin.

And then he bought her a whole box of donuts instead of just one.

* * *

Saturday afternoon, Casey was pacing the floor of her house, staring at her phone. Abe had texted her, asking if he'd could come over, and, God help her, she'd said yes.

After their talk at the school, she knew that meant Abe wasn't coming over for a sandwich and a chat. At the same time, she wasn't sure she wanted to just leap into bed with him. There was so much she wanted to tell him. Since Thursday, she'd had tentative phrases rattling against the underside of her cranium:

I'm scared to feel too much for you.

I don't want kids, but I want you, and I don't know where that leaves us.

I'd jump with you, if it meant we'd be together when we fell.

She stopped in front of her Christmas tree, the lights blurring in front of her eyes. How in the world was she going to say any of that when Abe had just proclaimed his dedication to the five things on her list? What if he didn't want to hear any of it?

But of course she knew he would be open to every single word. He had told her he cared about her, and, more than that, she could feel it when they were in bed together. The sex had been mind-blowing and not just because he had a huge penis and knew his way around a woman's body. It

had been glorious because they cared about one another—
perhaps more than either of them realized.

The doorbell rang and she squared her shoulders. It was
time to pull on her big-girl panties and be brave about expos-
ing not just her body, but her feelings, too. It was the only
way forward.

Except, when she pulled the door open, Abe was standing
there, shirt open in the winter weather, baring his sculpted
abs and holding a pair of handcuffs. He looked like a cal-
endar model. Maybe for November, since he was yummy
enough to serve up for Thanksgiving.

He stepped inside and kicked the door closed with one
foot. Then he was pressing Casey against the wall, his frame
towering over hers and his eyes locked on to her face.

"I'm sorry I fucked up," he said, kneeing apart her legs
and shoving a deliciously muscled thigh in between them. She
barely had time to comprehend what was happening. But her
body knew all too well. It heated from the inside out, and she
swore she could hear the air crackling with electricity.

She struggled to remember what she wanted to talk about
with Abe, even as she licked her lips. God, but she was hungry for this man.

"Abe, I have to tell you—"

"Nothing. You don't owe me a single explanation or piece
of information. You told me what you wanted, Casey. And I
aim to give it to you."

Before she could blink, he shrugged off his shirt. His
naked torso was smooth and honey colored. Her fingers
itched to run the length of it, from the dark blond hairs near
his pecs to the trail that ended just below his waist.

Then she heard a click, and realized he'd locked one
of her wrists into the handcuffs. Her heart pounded.

Excitement—and a little bit of fear—twisted through her. She pulled in air, trying to think.

"We should…" She said but trailed off. The idea of a heart-to-heart chat right now seemed ridiculous. How could she stop the stampede of desire that was roaring through them both? She couldn't. More than that, she wouldn't.

Her list was like a fire, flaming in her mind's eye.

Maybe her five things weren't *all* she wanted, but right now, at this moment, they were a dessert too rich and delicious to resist. Her thoughts were carnal and base, but she didn't care. Abe was willing to give her the list.

And, God help her, she wanted it.

If part of her felt like a coward for bending to her desire above all else, she pushed it aside. There would be plenty of time to talk. Right now, she would do the opposite of talk. She would shut up and let Abe do what he wanted.

Because it was what *she* wanted.

"We should go to the bedroom," she said finally. "And you should lead the way."

Abe grabbed her wrist, the handcuff dangling loose. He twisted her arm behind her back—not roughly, but the sharp movement had her panting. His voice was low in her ear. "No, you lead the way," he said, and marched her down the hallway like she'd just been arrested. It was thrilling enough to cause her legs to tremble. She wondered for a brief second if she'd even make it to the bed.

* * *

Moments later, Abe had Casey's arms stretched overhead. She was handcuffed to the headboard, her back against the bedding. Her heart thundered in her ears. She was shirtless—he'd pulled off her top and unhooked her bra before she could think. Now, her blood was hot, just on the edge of boiling. Her chest rose and fell like she'd been running.

Abe unbuttoned her jeans and slid them off her while she could only watch. She was naked, fully exposed, and every muscle in her body felt tight enough to snap. She was thrilled to her core, but something else, too. Nervous? Scared? Maybe all of it.

She bit her lip, wondering what Abe's next move would be. She pictured him taking her every way he wanted while she was powerless to stop him.

Abe tugged his clothes off. He was thick and hard, and the sight of his penis ignited a throbbing deep inside. Casey sucked in air as he knelt between her thighs, towering over her.

He grasped her nipples in his fingers, pinching slightly. She lost her breath.

"Do you like that?" A mischievous smile flashed on his face.

"Yes," she breathed. "Oh, yes."

He turned her to her side and spanked her once. Not hard, but she felt her eyes widen with surprise nonetheless.

"And that?" he asked. "Did you like that?"

She nodded, her heart pounding.

"Tell me," he demanded.

"I liked it," she said, thrilling at his authority.

He turned her so she was fully on her back again. He shoved her thighs apart with his hands. His eyes glinted with desire.

This is it, she thought. *He will take me with everything he has, and it will be thrilling.*

She was ready.

And yet, she strained against the handcuffs. "Wait," she said, not sure why she was stopping him. Abe pulled back.

"Is everything okay?" he asked. His eyes had gone from hungry to concerned in the space of half a second.

"Yes, of course, it's fine. I just—I don't know. If you wanted to take your time, I'm not—that is—"

He shut her up with a kiss so deep and long she wondered that time itself didn't stop. His hands stroked her as gently as his tongue. His fingers were everywhere on her, while she pulled against her handcuffs, wishing she could plunge her hands into his hair, wishing she could feel his cock. The desire—the yearning—was as almost as delicious as his touch.

When he finally broke the kiss, Abe leaned back to study her figure. He ran his hands along her legs, all the way up her thighs and over her belly. His hands were slow. When his eyes found hers, they were full of an emotion she couldn't place.

"You are gorgeous," he murmured, lowering himself so his lips were on her skin. He kissed her clavicle, her sternum, the tips of her breasts. He mouth lingered on her nipples sweetly.

Oh, she liked this pace. She liked this *even better*.

She had thought being tied up would lead to a rough, hot ball of excitement that ricocheted through them both. Instead, Abe was so soft, so adoring, that she felt more like a bride on her wedding night.

The idea should be incongruous. Disjointed.

But instead, it was incredibly right.

Something bright and aching began to spread through her. Something she had never felt before. Abe lowered his head, pushing her thighs still farther apart.

"You are perfect," he said, trailing kisses down her belly,

to her inner thigh, and then to her very center. She gasped as his mouth and tongue worked their perfect magic on her folds, on her clit.

She cried out, arching her back to give him more access. To give him all of her.

For a moment, he replaced his lips and tongue with the precise movements of his fingers. "Am I hurting you?" he asked, his eyes flickering across her body. "Are you all right? Do your arms ache?"

His concern made her heart constrict. "I—no. This is…"

She fumbled for the words. *This is not what I expected.*

She'd thought this would be white hot, bone-jarring sex that would make her scream and claw. Instead, she felt like she was on the verge of tears, feeling so much for the soft way Abe held her and pleasured her.

His hands still working on her center, Abe kissed his way back up her body. "If the handcuffs are too much, let me know," he murmured into her neck. "I don't want to hurt you. Ever. I care about you so much."

She strained against the handcuffs, wanting to put her arms around him, wanting to pull his head to her and kiss him. But she couldn't. She trembled instead, spinning with confusion. This rowdy, hot fuck was turning into anything but.

And that was a good thing.

Abe kissed her, and as he did, she pressed her chest against his. Skin on skin, heartbeat on heartbeat. "Abe," she murmured.

"I'm right here," he said, the tip of his penis straining against her center. "Tell me what you need."

The answer was so simple, it startled her. "You," she said. "I need you."

Abe reached for the bedside table, grabbed a condom,

and rolled it on. She watched, her mouth all but watering in anticipation. When he slid inside her, it was a sweet connection that filled her with light and song. She could have burst from happiness, from the rightness of it. Her whole body contorted with pleasure.

And with something else, too. "Abe," she said, crying his name as this strange current swept her away. She was about to be taken under by this unfamiliar tide—until she realized precisely what it was.

It was vulnerability. Every single cell in her whole body was exposed to Abe Cameron right how. There wasn't a single part of her he didn't have access to. She thought he could claim her physically any way he wanted. Now she knew he could claim her heart as well.

He pulled her bottom upward, burying himself deep inside her. She was lost in the perfection of the surrender. With her hands locked to the headboard, she was powerless to control what he did. Then again, she wondered if she'd ever had any control at all.

She'd had her list, her rules. But Abe Cameron had defied all of them, from the start.

He was defying them now, in fact.

And it was perfect.

"I've got you," he panted into her skin. "I've got you, always."

She knew it was true. With those words, she could leap off the cliff and trust he'd be right there. With those words, she could believe they might have a chance, come what may.

She broke in his arms then. She came in a spinning, billowing ecstasy that brought to mind summer nights and hot stars. She strained against the handcuffs, rattled them against the headboard, and clenched his body with her thighs. Abe was right there, tuned to her every movement, riding her with perfect synchronicity.

He shouted her name when he came. The sound of it was a gunshot tearing through them both. The raw need there was terrible and wonderful to hear. Abe's orgasm overtook her almost as much as her own. She lost track of everything except the threads of pleasure that knotted them together. They could be apart for the rest of their lives but she would always feel this connection, this twining.

When he was fully spent, he unlocked the handcuffs and pulled her close. Her body folded itself into the valleys and plains of his shape, two puzzle pieces fitting together perfectly. He kissed the top of her head, his arms wrapped protectively around her. "Are you all right?" he murmured.

She could barely contain the emotions that wanted to burst forth. For the first time in her life, it seemed, she was more than all right. She was happy. Deliriously so.

She kissed him and prayed her body told him what she still was struggling to find the words to say.

$\mathscr{C}$HAPTER TWENTY-ONE

$\mathscr{A}$be Cameron had just pulled Casey more tightly against him, relishing the feel of her body against his, when his phone began vibrating incessantly. He squeezed his eyes closed, trying to ignore it. This moment was perfect—Casey in his arms was perfect—and he wanted to stretch it out as long as possible. His heart was hammering, pounding out the message that this was the woman he cared for above all else. It didn't matter if she was tied up or unbound—he would want her with everything he had, forever.

He was in love with Casey Tanner.

Not that he could tell her that, of course. To her, he was just a means to a list. He knew this, understood the cold, bare truth of it. Nevertheless, he wanted to hold her against him for a few moments longer and pretend she returned his feelings.

Only the buzzing of his phone wouldn't quit. It was a hive of bees and he wanted to throw rocks at it. But that would just create a swarm. With a groan of frustration, he peeled himself away from Casey and fumbled for the device in the pocket of his jeans. His stomach sank when he saw it was dispatch.

"Yeah?" he asked, walking into the hallway—stark naked—so he wouldn't disturb Casey.

"I've got a mandatory callback, Abe. A large warehouse fire at 4230 Brainerd Ave. Smoke showing at the initial call. Backup needed."

Abe's whole body went stiff. "I'm on my way," he said, and clicked end.

Casey sat up drowsily as he threw on his clothes. "Where are you going?" she asked. She was so beautiful, with the light slanting in behind her, hair cascading over her shoulders. He would give anything to have the entire day in bed with her.

"There's a fire. I have to go."

She blinked. "But you're off duty."

"We're a small unit. They call us in if the responding team needs support." He tried not to think about Reese, so excited by his first real fire that he could mess something up. He took a breath, told himself the kid would remember his training.

Casey was wide awake now, clutching the sheets as Abe finished dressing. Her eyes were round and hollow-looking. Abe realized it was fear.

She was scared for him.

The idea surged through him. She wouldn't look that way if she didn't care for him. Right?

Now wasn't the time to figure it out, though.

He kissed her. A quick pressure that barely skimmed the surface. If he did anything more, he'd put his job—and his team—at risk.

"I'm sorry. I have to go."

"Abe." His name on her lips came out cracked. Her mouth moved in almost imperceptible twitches, trying to form the words. "Be careful," she said finally. "Maybe call me when it's all over?"

He exhaled. Something inside told him she'd wanted to say more, but he didn't have time to pry it out. Instead, he nodded. "I'll call when it's all over." Then he turned and left, his boots echoing on the bare floors.

He was grim and white-knuckled as he drove away in his Jeep. His emotions were pounding through him, his heart was surging in his chest. He'd feared this for so long: the reality of having something to lose for once. Being in love made the stakes so much higher in any emergency.

He could lose an arm. A leg. He could be burned beyond recognition.

And what then?

Would his love endure? Would *hers*? Because deep down, he knew what she felt for him. There was no disguising it when she was handcuffed to the bed, laid bare in front of him. It was on her skin, in her cries, as surely as if it had been written down on a sheet of paper.

But it might not be enough. He understood that.

His heart hammered. Could he survive any fire, any emergency, knowing she might not be there when it was all over?

This would be the test, then.

He loved Casey Tanner.

Now he'd find out if love could survive the flames and heat, and whether she'd be there if he made it out again.

* * *

Casey sprinted into Knots and Bolts, the cold December air following her into the store. "Betty!" she called. The fabric was lined up like books on a shelf, row after row of neat bolts. She felt dizzy, suddenly, among all the colors and patterns.

"Coming!" Betty's voice floated from the back room. Casey didn't wait. She sprinted through the aisle and into the cozy space where the recipe group usually met.

Betty's eyes widened as Casey barreled into the room. "Scanner!" Casey sputtered, realizing she probably sounded mad. "Turn it on!"

She wondered what she looked like, having tumbled out of bed after Abe. He'd left in his Jeep for the fire, and she'd thought about following him, until she realized she'd be a hazard in the midst of a raging fire. What would she even do? Stand around and watch?

Instead, she remembered Betty had a scanner, and she'd hightailed it over to Knots and Bolts.

"Casey, what in the world? Sit down; let me get you something. What's wrong?"

Casey walked unsteadily to the big red table where she usually passed around the remains of her charred and useless hot dish. Now, she placed her hands on top of the wood and imagined drawing strength from all the women who had gathered here, who had let her share this space with them.

Betty grabbed a bottle of Irish whiskey from a nearby cupboard and poured some into a mug. "Sit down," she commanded, "and drink this."

Casey accepted the mug with shaking hands. "Can you just turn on the scanner?" she asked. "I need information about the fire."

"What fire?"

"The one Abe was just called to. He was off duty, but then said something about a fire needing backup. It must have been bad, then, right?" She pulled in ragged breaths, hating how weak she sounded. But that was exactly how she felt—like she'd had her legs kicked out from under her and was now a dribbling mess.

Betty pulled out the chair next to Casey. "Listen, I'm no expert, but Abe is a lieutenant. He's been in this job for years. You worrying about him is sweet, but turning on that scanner won't change a thing. It'll just ratchet you up even more."

Casey glanced around the room, hoping maybe the device was on a counter somewhere and she could just flip it on. But all she saw were empty counters and tall windows looking out onto blankets of white snow.

"He could be in *danger*," Casey said, setting down her mug. "He could be in trouble."

"And what would you do about it if that were the case?"

Casey opened her mouth, then closed it. She had no earthly idea. She couldn't save him. She was powerless to help. "I just..." She wasn't sure how to finish.

I just had the most incredible experience of my life in bed with Abe.

I just figured out I feel so much for him.

I just don't want him to be in danger.

I need to find out if there's a chance for us.

I just can't stand the idea of losing someone else I care about.

And there it was. The stabbing hurt of losing her parents when she was young came knifing back. A terrible car accident and—*wham*—her whole life had taken a different course. Now, with Abe, she risked being hurt all over again.

What if she loved him and he *died*? What if he got taken away, too?

She hung her head, her eyes trained on the liquor. Her muscles felt pummeled, beaten. Maybe her boundaries with Abe were never about kids. Or commitment.

Maybe this had only ever been about protecting herself from the ultimate hurt, the ultimate pain. In the end, maybe Audrey was right.

Casey was making excuses. She was pushing people away. She was telling herself she was trying new things and becoming a different person, but really she was still standing on the edge of the cliff, afraid to jump. The pain of the fall might be unbearable.

"Oh, Betty," she said, glancing up. She could feel the tears pooling in her eyes. "I've made such a terrible mistake."

Betty poked her tongue in her cheek. "Guess that makes you human like the rest of us, then."

Casey groaned. "I'm serious. This is big. Abe Cameron could die in that fire and I'd have to live with the fact that I didn't figure things out sooner."

"What things?"

"That I care for him. That I—that I—love him." The words stumbled out. *She loved Abe Cameron.* It was an unbendable truth. She'd been trying to run from it, trying to avoid it. Now that she'd said it, however, it was as if she could finally acknowledge that she wasn't standing on a protected island, but rather in the middle of a tumbling avalanche that was sweeping her akimbo into something entirely new and wild.

"You don't say." Betty was entirely nonplussed.

"Betty. You're not being very helpful. Will you please just turn on the scanner?"

"No, I won't. Because it won't do any good. Honey, whatever happens in that fire happens. That's a brutal truth that I hate saying to you, but it's true. Abe chose this career. He picked it and that's that. He could go into that fire and never come out. Same as Randall could cross the street and get hit by a truck."

The sharp edge of the words tore at Casey's heart. "I can't stand the idea. I *can't*."

"You don't have to. But if you love this man, you will. Because life will be more miserable if you don't."

She could hear Audrey's words from their heart-to-heart at the bar, and knew she cared enough about Abe to stop being terrified. She was willing to believe that maybe the mountain of their differences wasn't immovable. Maybe all it took was them scaling the mountain together.

She rubbed her forehead. "He has to come out of that fire. He must. He told me he'd call me after it was over."

Betty reached out her hand, palm up. "Then I'll stay with you until he rings. Long as you need, okay?"

Casey stared at the hand, at the offering of friendship. She took it and squeezed. "Thank you," she said to Betty. "Thanks for being here for me."

Betty smiled. "You just like me for my Irish whiskey."

"It doesn't hurt, that's for sure."

"Well, drink up. We have a long afternoon in front of us."

Casey drained the last of her mug and watched Betty pour another shot. Then she took out her cell and laid it on the red table, praying with her whole heart that it would ring soon.

* * *

Abe cursed the property owner as he battled his way through thickening smoke to the second story of the warehouse. Above him, heads had been removed on the automatic sprinkler system and the pipes scrapped by scavengers. Below him, piles of rags, bundled in twine and burlap, sat like hulking monsters that could ignite at any minute.

The very location of the fire had been what had precipitated the mandatory callback. The fact that they were doing battle in the abandoned cloth company's warehouse had automatically required more personnel. Even now, the thick, greasy smoke pointed to a fire burning hot with oil and chemicals. The company had left this place when it went out of business, never cleaning up the waste and the piles of oily rags, and now something had set part of it ablaze.

"Shit," he muttered, trying to get to the heart of the fire. It was on the second story, at the top of the stairs. Branching off to the left and right were hallways, each leading to different rooms in the warehouse. The fire looked to be in the left-side hallway and, based on the amount of smoke, it still seemed small, relatively manageable. That is, if they could just get their hoses close enough to it. From the outside, chain-link fences and piles of old tires had blocked the trucks from pulling up on the side of the building where the smoke was pouring out. When Abe had arrived, his team had been trying to figure out an alternative route in. Now, they'd finally battled more debris and blockage to get their hoses into the front entrance. They were dragging them up the staircase, to the second floor where the fire was.

Abe stuck his foot through a rotted step and cursed. He thought he felt something sway. He stopped, took a deep breath of clean air through his mask. Reese paused behind him as he wriggled his foot out of the hole.

"You okay?" Reese asked through the com.

"Fine. Let's get this over with."

Abe reached the top of the stairs. To his left, the flames leaped and smoke rolled. Ahead of him was a large broken window that was once no doubt composed of wavy, leaded glass. It was probably a lovely jewel in the old brick warehouse—before companies that didn't care about the town or the land let it slide into disrepair and danger.

"All right," he told Reese when they were in position, "hit it."

They flipped the lever and braced themselves as water blasted onto the blaze.

The smoke began to change immediately to a light gray. Abe wouldn't let himself exhale, but it was a good sign. The air was less tar-like, less toxic. So why was there still so much heat?

He was about to ask Reese the question when the rumble took him by surprise. He turned just as Reese uttered one, terrified word: "Lu." Barely a warning, but it was all he had time for. Behind them, the staircase was crumbling.

He and Reese jumped back, losing the hose as the staircase engulfed it. Flames were leaping from the wood, and that was when Abe realized that debris from the second-story blaze had dropped onto rag bundles below. They'd caught fire as well—before anyone had noticed. They'd ignited next to the rickety staircase, which had gone up quickly, and now their hose was gone—not to mention their main exit.

Worse, the fire to their left wasn't quite out, and it was starting to build again. He could see it in the lick of the flames. The thing was still hungry. And they had no way to fight it.

Abe raced to the window and smashed against it, trying to shatter more of the remaining panes. Reese joined him. Behind them, the fire was roaring, building as it consumed more rags. The heat was suffocating.

He called on the com for a ladder, coughing and praying his oxygen tanks would hold. He couldn't hear anything except the roar of the surrounding fires. They were closing in. They had to get out. *Now.* Reese was driving into the window with everything he had. Smoke was pouring through the holes they made. He could hardly see.

When they finally had an opening, he stuck his head out and managed to glimpse a ladder before smoke blocked his vision again. He grabbed Reese by the back of the neck. "Go," he said, and all but threw him out the window. The kid disappeared in the thick smoke.

Abe climbed out after. Behind him, heat seared his skin, even through all his protective gear. The roar of the fire filled him. Pain flared everywhere. He struggled to think.

He groped for the rungs. Finally—there. His foot found purchase, and he scrambled down, praying that his crew would be there when he hit the bottom. He didn't know how far he'd made it when the explosion hit. It tore through the window just above his head. His cranium was hammered, his ears imploded. He lost his grip on the ladder and fell.

In the plunge, he thought of Casey and wondered if he'd ever be able to see her again. He held on, fighting for consciousness, as the picture of her flashed in his mind. Stronger than the heat, stronger than the flames, she was there.

Love is with me, he thought, fighting back the blackness once his body met enough pain to make him think it was the ground. Love had run into the fire with him after all.

Now he just needed to ensure he made it out again.

* * *

Betty was shaking her.

Casey raised her head, and sharp pain shot through her neck. She groaned, rubbing her forehead. She felt the grooves of wood on her skin, where she'd fallen asleep with her head on the red table. Her mouth was thick feeling from all the whiskey. Outside, darkness had fallen.

"What's going on?" she muttered.

Betty pushed a glass of water toward her. "Drink this. Then we're leaving."

Casey glanced at her phone. No missed calls. "Where are we going? We have to wait until—"

"The hospital. I turned on the scanner while you were asleep."

Casey sat up, blinking against the jagged light overhead. She struggled to think, struggled to make sense of what Betty was saying. "What? What do you mean?"

"Your fireman, Abe. He was hurt. Come on, we're leaving now."

Casey revolted against the news. *No.*

Abe Cameron could not be hurt. Only from the pained lines on Betty's face, she knew it was true. Her whiskey-coated stomach roiled. She thought she might be sick.

"What happened?" she managed to whisper.

"I don't know exactly. From what I can make out, they went into a building thinking there was one fire. But actually there were two. It was the old cloth company. Oil-soaked rags and whatnot…" Betty's words faded. Her eyes shifted with sadness.

"Oh, God." Not Abe.

This was her nightmare, playing out in real time. She

thought then that her breath might leave her, that her muscles might give way.

Instead, something else took over.

Casey sat up. She felt as though her bones were infused with steel, her nerves were steady, and her mind was resolute. She was the opposite of weak. *She was going to be strong enough for them both, come hell or high water.*

Right then, she had all the reserves she needed, all the fuel to burn brightly enough for two people, not just one. That was what love did, she realized. It didn't deplete you. It made you strong and not weak.

She straightened and pulled on her coat. "Drive fast," she told her friend.

CHAPTER TWENTY-TWO

The hospital's overhead lights blazed too bright, and somehow everything seemed tinged with green. Casey knew it was just her filter of worry and fear, but nevertheless she couldn't blink away the film.

At the reception desk, a nurse in maroon scrubs stopped tapping on a computer screen and looked up. A row of charts tiled the wall behind her. "Can I help you?"

"We're here to see Abe Cameron," Betty said when Casey's voice had suddenly decided to stop working. Casey shoved her hands into her pockets to hide their trembling. "The firefighter who came in recently?"

The lines around the nurse's mouth hardened. "Are you family?"

"Not technically, but—"

"Then I can't let you in. We're limiting bedside visitors right now."

Casey bit the inside of her cheek. She feared the worst, and pictures of a disfigured Abe flashed through her mind.

"Because of his condition?" Betty asked, perhaps thinking the same thing.

"I can't really go into details," the nurse replied. She turned back to the keyboard. The typing was a cackle in Casey's ears. She wanted to hurl the keyboard across the room.

She looked at Betty, who could only shrug. Surely they weren't going to give up that easily—were they?

Casey took a deep breath. She had to see Abe. By any means necessary.

"I'm his fiancée," Casey blurted. She ignored Betty's wide-eyed stare. The typing stopped. The nurse glanced at Casey's bare left hand.

"It—well, it just happened," Casey fumbled, hoping her face wasn't blazing red. "It's all very recent. But I really need to get in to see him. I'm—we're—well, this could affect wedding plans."

She was babbling. It sounded ridiculous, talking about wedding logistics when all she cared about was Abe and being with him.

The nurse ran her tongue over her teeth, debating. Casey could only hold her breath. Finally, the nurse stood up. "Sign here," she said, pointing to a clipboard. Casey exhaled loudly. "When you're logged in, take the hallway here straight down. He's in room two-oh-seven, on the left. Visiting hours end in an hour, so please keep that in mind. Your friend needs to wait here."

Betty grabbed Casey's arm and gave it a reassuring squeeze. "I'll be close by if you need me," she told Casey.

Her hands still shaking, Casey signed in and then headed down the hallway. The flecks in the tiles blurred together.

Somewhere she heard the ping of a monitor, the grumble of a patient. A nurse squeaked by in sensible shoes.

At room 207, she paused and took a deep breath. She steeled herself for the worst. He could be paralyzed. In a coma. Disfigured by flame.

And I'll love him still, she thought, *because he's still Abe*.

Straightening her spine, she pushed open the door.

* * *

The room was quieter than she expected. The light was dim, the curtains drawn tight. A screen next to the bed danced with squiggles and lines.

She'd expected doctors assessing vital signs, hovering over Abe's prone form. She'd thought there would be nurses padding in and out of the room. But there was just Abe lying on the bed, his shape draped in white blankets and sheets. She tiptoed closer, trying to get a good look at him in the low light.

"Doc, I swear to God you'd better be working on that release paperwork. If I don't go home first thing tomorrow, I'm going to be seriously pissed."

Casey stopped. Abe hadn't moved, but she could hear him breathing.

"What, so now you're not going to come any closer? Fine." The whirring of the motorized bed started as Abe raised himself to a sitting position. "I *told* you, I'm good. I don't nee—"

He stopped when he saw Casey. His hazel eyes widened. "*Casey.*" Her name was barely a whisper.

She was frozen, taking in the white bandage on his neck, the IV poking into his arm, the dark stubble on his chin.

"Are you...?" She didn't know how to finish the question. She studied his legs, wondering if he could move them. He looked all right and had just said as much, but what if he wasn't?

Instead of answering, he opened up his arms. His eyes were pleading with her, begging her to move closer. The pull of him was stronger than anything she'd ever known. Biting back tears, she rushed into his embrace.

He groaned, low and deep, and pulled her close. Casey swallowed, feeling completely overwhelmed. Abe was *alive*. He'd made it out of the fire.

Now what? she wondered.

This wasn't the time to think, however. She refused to let her brain take over. This wasn't about being logical. Right now, she just wanted to feel the joy of being close to Abe, of knowing he was right here next to her. She took in his solid muscles, his cheek against the top of her head, his breath warm on her skin. She inhaled, catching the lingering smell of smoke.

"What happened?" she managed to ask. "Are you okay?"

"I am. Thank God for protective gear is all I can say. Reese and I were caught in a second blaze. Our exit was compromised. We had to go out a window. He's down the hall if you want to say hi."

"What do you mean your exit was compromised?"

"A staircase collapsed when a different fire started. We lost our hose and then had to go through a window. There was a small explosion when I was on the ladder—probably old chemicals—and I fell about five feet."

Casey gasped, hating the idea of him tumbling through nothingness. She glanced at the parts of him hidden under the white sheet. "Are you hurt? Is everything...intact?"

She could hear the smile in his voice. "*Everything*. I have some burns on my neck, a few bruises. I inhaled some smoke. I wasn't going to let them keep me here, but my captain wasn't hearing any of it. You just missed Quinn, by the way. She finally decided Reese and I weren't going to croak and left her post."

"And your family? Do they know about all this?"

"The captain called them about a half hour ago. I was getting ready to call you in a few minutes, but you beat me to the punch."

Before she could answer, before she could tell him how glad she was that he was all right and how worried she'd been, the door opened and three people poured in, all talking excitedly.

"When do you think he was going to tell us?"

"I can't freaking believe it."

"It's quite a table."

As they jostled into the room, Casey knew instantly that this must be Abe's family. She disentangled herself from Abe's arms and stood, smoothing the front of her shirt. A woman with silver-blonde hair and Abe's same hazel eyes took up a position on the other side of the bed and grabbed his hand.

"I can't tell which I'm angrier about," the woman said. "The fact that I had to find out you were hurt from your captain, or the fact that you're engaged and you didn't tell us."

"Mom, I'm fine, I—" He stopped abruptly. "Engaged?"

"The nurse told us. Of *all things*, Abe. Holding back from your own family? Oh, but this must be her. Casey, is it? I'm Abe's mom, Julia, and I just have to tell you, we are all so thrilled by the news." She reached over the bed, clasping Casey's hand in her own.

Casey stared down at the woman's fingers. They were speckled with paint. She swallowed nervously. Oh, God, what had she done? She couldn't just let Abe's mother stand here *holding her hand* and believing this ruse. She had to tell them all she'd made it all up just to get access to the room. "I'm sorry," she stuttered, pulling away from Abe's mom, "there's been—"

"A delay," interjected Abe suddenly. Casey's heart sputtered in her chest. She whipped her head to find laughter in Abe's eyes and a barely-pinned-back smile on his face. "We meant to tell you, but the fire got in the way."

Casey let out a little gasp, but it was lost in the collective "Oh" of understanding that suddenly filled the room.

"Damn, I thought you'd messed it up, bro." This was from the tall, lean-but-fit man wearing khaki cargo pants and a long-sleeved T-shirt. His blond hair and hazel eyes had Casey pegging him as Abe's brother. "From the way you came over to my place all hangdog about her, I assumed it was over. And then to turn it around and get *engaged*? Color me impressed." He grinned and held out his hand to Casey. "Stu Cameron, by the way. Welcome to the family. For better or for worse."

Casey managed to take his hand and smile back, but her brain was screaming at her to stop the pretense already. She glared at Abe. She hoped her eyes read *End this now*. But to her dismay, Abe only shrugged.

Before she could spill the truth herself, the older man, whom Casey assumed was Abe's dad, came forward and put a gentle hand on her shoulder. "I'm Pete," he said quietly, "and for the first time, I think my son finally has a lick of sense."

Abe erupted into laughter. "Gee, thanks a lot, Dad," Abe

said. His smile was a warm light. Casey felt drawn to the un-abashed joy of it, thinking she'd never seen Abe this happy before. But even so, pretending they were engaged wasn't right. It wasn't the *truth*.

"We can't wait to celebrate properly," Julia said. "But in the meantime, tell us how you're feeling. What happened and how bad is it?"

Abe deftly switched the conversation over to the fire, explaining the two fires and how he'd gotten out, leaving Casey bewildered and tongue-tied. With every passing minute, the conversation moved farther away from their en-gagement, making any explanation of how and why she'd invented the story more and more distant. At one point Abe reached over and twined his fingers with hers. And, God help her, she let him. The feel of him was so reassuring, so wonderful, that she couldn't bear to pull away.

Never mind that a little part of her didn't mind the idea that they were "engaged." Okay, maybe not such a little part. Maybe a big part that was growing with each passing minute. The idea of being with Abe for life didn't knock her off kilter, not by a long shot. It accomplished just the oppo-site, in fact—it grounded her to the here and now in a way that had her toes wiggling in her shoes.

It almost didn't matter that they still had a huge hurdle to overcome, one that rhymed with *kids*.

Casey pressed her palm against Abe's, wondering if they made a good enough team that no matter what came their way, they could tackle it together. Children seemed like such an unmovable barrier, though. Was it possible for them to scale it?

Casey wanted to try. She wanted to be honest and tell Abe that she loved him. And when she did, she'd force the kids issue and see if it was a deal breaker. She pictured Carter, and all the kids like him who were already in this world and needed help. Her heart ached for them. She wanted to reach out to them if she could.

Even so, becoming a foster parent might not be enough for Abe—he might need his own kids. A lot of people did, after all, and she didn't blame them one bit.

She wouldn't—she *couldn't*—hold it against Abe if he felt that way, too.

A dark, dead weight formed inside her, and at its center was worry that that would be the case. But then at least she'd *know*. If she came clean about her wants, then at least she'd be truthful and not hide behind her list forever, pretending she was doing just fine.

The future with Abe might hold hurt, same as it might hold hope. She'd just have to take a chance and find out.

"I'm actually pretty tired," Abe was saying as Casey tuned back in to the conversation. "Maybe you could give my fiancée and me a minute here before visiting hours end?"

"Yes, of course," Julia replied, one of her paint-flecked hands smoothing back Abe's blond hair. "We'll leave you be."

Whatever graceful exit they were going to take was interrupted by Betty storming into the room, the nurse in the maroon scrubs close on her heels.

"Casey, we gotta go!" Betty's eyes were bright, her skin was pink and shining.

"What in the world?" Casey asked. Her blood pounded with concern about more bad news. Had Audrey been hurt? Or even Kieran?

"Ma'am, you cannot be in here," the nurse was saying. "I gave you explicit instruc—"

"Willa's having her baby!" Betty said, ignoring the nurse and elbowing her way farther into the crowded room. She grabbed Casey's hand and started pulling her toward the door. "Come on already. She's two floors up. The other girls are already here. Let's move."

"Wait, what? She wasn't due until January."

"I guess the baby had other plans."

Casey barely had time to get a wave good-bye in. "Nice to meet you!" she called over her shoulder to Abe's family as Betty hauled her out of the room. Her eyes happened to catch Abe's, and she didn't have to wonder if there was more laughter there. She could hear it, as he cracked up loud enough to have a smile creasing her own face, too.

* * *

Casey had to trot to keep up with Betty's short, quick steps. "When was Willa admitted?" Casey asked, more breathless than she thought she should be trying to go two floors up in the White Pine Hospital.

"A few hours ago. Burk called me when she was first going into labor, and I told everyone in the recipe exchange to haul ass and come down here. I guess it's happening pretty quickly."

Happiness ballooned inside Casey. She was delighted for her friend. "Do you think the new arrival will get here before visiting hours end?"

Betty grunted. "If she doesn't, they'll have to drag me out of here by the hair. I am not waiting another twelve hours to see that baby."

Together, they huffed into the labor and delivery waiting room, where Anna, Stephanie, and Audrey were already gathered. The group of them were all standing—Audrey was pacing with nervous, frenetic energy; Anna was pulling on strands of her ebony hair; and Stephanie was rummaging through her purse until she pulled out a piece of gum with a triumphant flourish.

"Oh, thank goodness!" Anna said when she caught sight of the pair. Up close, her face was more pale than Casey had expected. Probably because she'd been through the whole process before, with Juniper, and knew just how difficult it could be. "Betty, any news?"

Betty glanced at her phone. "Not since the initial text. But I wonder if he'll just come out and tell us in person when it's all over?" She glanced at the gray door that separated the waiting room from where the babies were delivered.

Audrey sidled up next to Casey. "Hey there," Audrey said, linking arms with her sister. "How are things?"

Casey wondered how she should answer. *Amazing. Confusing.*

Instead, she pulled Audrey into a corner of the waiting room and filled her in on the fire, and how she realized that her feelings for Abe went far beyond her list. "I think...that is, I might actually love him."

Audrey responded by punching Casey in the shoulder. "See? I told you so."

"Ow. That hurt. And I don't think that's what you're supposed to say."

"Sorry. I know, I know. I just didn't think you'd take a chance on this guy, but here you are, being such a total badass!" Audrey's molasses-colored eyes sparkled. "You listened to your heart instead of to your list."

Casey exhaled. "See, that's the problem, though. I don't know if my heart can get us past the no-kids part. No matter what we feel for one another, that might just trump everything."

Audrey nodded. "It might. Have you talked to him?"

"I just saw him. We got interrupted. I'll try again tomorrow."

"No matter what happens, I'm still really proud of you. You're taking a risk—an actual, bona fide risk—and that's worth something. More than something. It's worth a lot. You're letting go of control."

"Enough already, Professor Head Shrink. I get it."

"Probably I should say it one more time, though. To make sure you really understand that you—"

Casey silenced her sister the same way she had when they were kids. She pinched her hard on the back of her upper arm, and giggled when her sister squealed.

Audrey tried pinching her back, but she deflected it with a nearby *TV Guide*. They were both laughing so hard they almost missed the fact that Burk had walked into the room, eyes ringed with exhaustion but shining, and announced that his and Willa's daughter had arrived.

* * *

Minutes later, the group was gathered around Willa's bed, gazing in quiet wonder at the baby snuggled into her mom's chest. Willa's eyes had the same tired look Burk's did, but joy made her radiant.

"Meet Calico Bella Olmstead," Willa said, her voice whispery with wonder. "I think we'll call her Callie." She peeled back the pink blanket so the group could get a closer look at the tiny red face, the curled fingers, the miniature lips. Callie was exquisite.

"She is beautiful," Anna said, blinking back tears. "The perfect niece."

"Why Calico?" Betty asked, beating them all to the question—as usual.

Willa glanced at Burk, who was standing nearby. They shared a secret smile. It was simple but powerful enough to knock the breath out of Casey, this idea that two people could communicate whole sentences with just a flicker of their mouths, or the arch of their brows. She wondered if she and Abe would ever get a chance to learn such a complicated and secret and special language.

"Calico like the fabric," Willa said, "to honor Knots and Bolts and all of you. I don't think she'd be here today if it weren't for the recipe exchange. I want Calico to be a reminder that a group of strong women with enough casserole and pie can change the course of history. Or, if not history, then at least the course of events in this girl's life."

She kissed the top of Callie's head while Casey—along with everyone around her—battled back a fresh round of tears. "Well, shit," Betty muttered. "If I had known you were going to say all that, I wouldn't have asked."

Casey felt suddenly full, though not the kind that comes after eating too much at Thanksgiving. She felt like her heart had finally thunked into place in her rib cage. This whole time, she had wondered if it had been just millimeters off, brushing up against hard bone and gristle and aching just a little with every beat. But now it was perfectly centered and beating freely—a sensation that was both new and thrilling.

She'd thought this whole time she would remain an outsider among these women, but she knew now that their similarities far outweighed their differences. It didn't matter if she didn't get married or if she never had kids, because she could feel the strength of this group's bond, and that was far more powerful.

And, sure, there could be moments when she might doubt her place in this tapestry of relationships. But she wouldn't push these women away because of them. In the end the doubt didn't matter, because she knew herself what *she* would do. If Anna or Stephanie or Betty or any of them called her at three in the morning, she'd jump out of bed and use every ounce of strength she had and every single resource at her disposal to help them. To have Callie as a living reminder of that—of what they were capable of when they stood by each other—was breathtaking.

The group took turns bending down to kiss Willa and the baby until the nurses insisted that they'd made enough concessions and the group had to go home. Visiting hours had ended almost a half hour ago.

They shared a last round of hugs, then headed to their respective cars and into the cold, crisp winter night. Betty gave Casey a lift home, smiling slightly as she pulled into the driveway.

"So Abe gets out of the hospital tomorrow, eh?"

Casey nodded. Her stomach twisted at the thought. Tomorrow. Everything in her life could change—or precisely nothing could.

"Thanks," Casey said after a moment, "for everything today. Talking, getting me to the hospital, the whole bit."

Betty's face softened. "No sweat. I'll be thinking about you. Hoping things go okay."

Casey stared out the front windshield at her house, dark and quiet and peaceful. "I'll keep you posted. I mean, the group. I suppose it will come out at the next recipe exchange."

Betty snorted. "I don't think you'll have to say much."

"What do you mean?"

Betty winked at her. "It'll be pretty obvious. You'll either have that glowy I've-had-a-lot-of-sex look, or you won't."

"Betty!" Casey touched her face self-consciously. "I do not get any such look."

Betty's eyes locked with Casey's. There was more laughter there than Casey would have liked. "Okay," she said slowly, "whatever you say."

Casey pulled down the visor and flipped up the mirror. "Do I have it now?" she asked, tilting her head to the left and the right, remembering the handcuffs from earlier in the day.

Her cheeks pinked at the vivid images that flashed through her mind.

"I'll give you three guesses and the first two don't count," Betty said, laughing.

Casey slapped the visor back into place. She could feel the smile starting on her own face. "All right. Point taken," she said, opening the door. She thanked Betty again and watched her friend back out of the driveway, swearing she could still hear the other woman cackling as she pulled away into the silent, snowy night.

CHAPTER TWENTY-THREE

*A*be signed the release form so quickly his signature was more of a ragged line than an actual name. He touched the bandages around his neck where the worst of his injuries lay hidden under gauze and tape. The pain wasn't bad, but there might be scarring. He grimaced, thinking about the scars in addition to his mangled nose. God, he was practically a beast.

He'd take it, though. He'd been lucky in that fire. Both he and Reese had. The fact that they were each going home with nothing but a few white bandages on their bodies was nothing short of a miracle.

What's more, this beast had found his beauty.

He stepped out of the hospital and into the morning, the sky turning a pale yellow to the east. It was early, barely eight o'clock, but he was still headed over to Casey's first thing.

His fiancée.

He could barely keep the grin off his face at the thought.

He'd gotten the details about its origins out of the nurse—how they weren't going to let Casey in to see him, but she'd adamantly claimed they were going to be hitched—and when the nurse had offered Abe a quizzical look about it all, he had confirmed the story, same as he had to his parents. "It happened recently, but it definitely happened. We're thinking May for the wedding."

It was a lie, as blazing white as a single untruth could be. He'd told it because acrid smoke from the fire was still rolling around in his lungs, he could still taste it when he breathed, and he wanted to pretend for a while that he had lived his life differently up until now: That he'd been bold and brave enough to give his heart to someone, and that someone had come to see him in the hospital.

It was pure fantasy, of course. Casey didn't want to marry him, she only wanted to bang him. Yet there'd been something different about her when she'd showed up at the foot of his bed yesterday. The look on her face had been so pained, so pale and drawn, it had sucked all the air right from his lungs. If he didn't know better, he'd say she had been downright worried about him. Although worried wasn't right. She had been *distraught*.

And Casey wouldn't get that way about him unless there were strong feelings churning through her. Feelings she was acting on and not running from, for once.

He hadn't expected it. He hadn't expected her to rush into his arms like that. He hadn't expected her to go along with the engagement story for one second longer than she absolutely had to.

But she had done all those things and more. She'd looked at him so tenderly, so full of affection, that for the first time he actually had hope about their future together. Finally, maybe Casey was allowing herself to feel all the emotions that he knew were there—the same ones that pounded through them both when they were in bed together.

Maybe she was done hammering her heart into oblivion. Maybe she was ready to be honest about what was happening between them.

He knew they still had so much to talk about to ensure this was the path that made sense. But after this many years staring down dangerous situations, Abe knew when things were perilous or messed up, and when they were right.

And this—it wasn't just right. This had the calm and the peace of something clicking into place with staunch finality. This was true north.

This was forever.

The only remaining question was whether Casey would see it that way, too.

* * *

Casey stared at the text on her phone.

I'm coming over.

It was Abe.

It wasn't a question.

She clutched her mug of coffee more tightly as she sat at the kitchen counter. Her body ached from tossing and turning the night before. She'd stared at her plaster ceiling for hours, catching the far-off sound of a dog barking, the slam of a car door. But mostly it was only Casey and the pressing silence, deep and empty enough to have her thoughts echoing in her brain.

She loved Abe Cameron.

She wanted to be with him.

She might not get what she wanted.

Casey rubbed her eyes. She'd been over this a thousand times. She was exhausted. The thing she needed now was Abe. She closed her eyes, imagining them back in bed, all hot skin and twisted sheets. As much as she'd love a physical release right now, the thing she needed more was an emotional one. Her heart was filled to bursting, and if she didn't find out now whether she and Abe stood a chance, it might not keep beating at all.

When she heard the Jeep pull into the driveway, she exhaled, long and slow. She didn't even wait for Abe to ring the bell. She pulled open the door and took in every one of his steps as he walked toward her, the bandages around his neck bright and white in the cold morning.

The blood pounded in her temples with a force that made her faint. Her fingers twitched, wanting to curl into his hair, wanting to pull his forehead against hers and let their lips fit together like she knew they did.

He wore an expression she couldn't place. She wasn't sure what to expect as his long legs devoured the space between them, but when he didn't stop until he was nearly on top of her—when his broad chest was against hers and his strong arms were wrapped around her—she relaxed so deeply her legs almost gave out. She hadn't felt like this since he'd left for the fire.

Maybe she hadn't felt like this ever.

They needed to talk. They had things to discuss. She knew this when he pulled her close and his mouth found hers with a heat that scalded her insides. But instead she met his need with her own, using her tongue and lips to tell him what she'd had such trouble putting into words. She'd missed him. She was so glad he was safe. She loved him.

Her fingers snaked along the corded muscles of his shoulders, up to the bandages on his neck, where they lingered delicately. Her muscles tensed at the thought of him hurt. And the awful truth that he might be hurt again. She couldn't guarantee that he wouldn't be. But she would take this day—heck, this minute and this second—and be grateful if it meant she could love him, and he would love her back.

"Abe," she murmured into his skin. They broke apart and he fixed her with a stare that was so flamed with feeling she wondered if parts of her weren't melting. "We should go inside. The neighbors might be watching us."

He smiled then, the lines around his eyes deepening. "Let them. I want them to see."

"You want to show off that you can make out like a teenager on my front stoop?"

"No. I want the whole neighborhood—hell, the whole world—to know how I feel about you." He kissed her again, deep and electric, and she shuddered with the hot spark of it. His palm was on the back of her neck, guiding her to him, closer and closer. She let herself get pulled in by the glorious undertow of his tongue mingling with hers, his teeth gently nipping at her lip, his breath warm and sweet.

Somehow, after she thought she might pass out from the sheer pleasure of all of it, Abe pulled her inside. She was dazed, following him as he led the way to the kitchen. Part of her kiss-numbed brain wondered if they might go straight to the bedroom, but then she remembered how much they had to talk about. How much there was to say to him.

The thought had ice-cold clarity chilling her. She blinked, pulling out a stool as Abe helped himself to some coffee. "I could use a pick-me-up. The hospital's java was more like tea. Weak tea. Warm tap water, really."

He grinned and Casey found herself smiling back, relaxing into the reality that he was *here*. He was in her kitchen. He was right in front of her. She took a deep breath.

"I'm so glad you're here, Abe, standing in my kitchen. When I heard about that fire yesterday, the only thing I could think of was what would happen if you didn't make it out."

Abe lowered himself onto a stool. The blond hairs of his forearms were golden in the morning light as he held his coffee mug. "And what would have happened?" he asked. "To you, I mean." There was an anxious note in his voice that surprised her.

"If you hadn't made it out of that fire, then part of me wouldn't have made it out, either. It made me realize how much I care for you. All this time, I thought being with you was just about the list. But I was so wrong. Being with you is about being with the person that makes me happiest in this world."

He reached out and grabbed her hand. His eyes tracked across her face, intent with feeling. "I care for you, too, Casey. I think I have since that first day in the elevator, even though I went about it all wrong for a while there. I know you didn't want a relationship—hell, neither did I—but this is right. *We're* right."

"That's just it," Casey replied, blinking back tears. At how easily all this could fall apart in the next few moments. "It seems that way, but it might not be."

"How so?"

"I can change my mind about a lot of things, but not about wanting kids. Not kids of my own, anyway. The situation with Carter has me thinking that fostering someone in need could be wonderful, but I know that's not an option everyone considers to be for them. Meaning..." She took another deep breath. "We may want different things in the end. And if that's the case, I want to be up-front about it now, and not two or ten years from now, when suddenly we resent each other because neither of us has what they were hoping for."

Abe put a hand on her cheek. She leaned into his touch. "Listen," he said gently, "I've always said you've been honest with what you wanted. I love that about you, Casey. Frankly, I just love you, period. You've changed what I see when I look ahead. For so long I tried to control what the future could be. But now the only thing I see is you, and it's more than enough. You're all that matters. Everything else is negotiable."

"But not *kids*. Surely you—"

"*Yes*, kids. If you're with me, then we're a family. That's enough. Fostering on top of that sounds amazing, actually. Helping kids that are already in this world would be an incredible opportunity. But only if we're in it together. That's the bottom line."

Casey's whole body trembled. It couldn't be that simple, could it?

"Abe, I just don't…"

She wasn't sure how to finish. She didn't know how to trust that he was being sincere. She didn't know how to believe him at his word.

He must have read the doubt and confusion on her face. He must have known that her thoughts were warbling with uncertainty. And he must have known that the way to tell her was through her heart, which was already beating with hope.

He left his stool to stand in front of her, his hands cupping her face tenderly. "I won't hurt you, Casey. I won't let you down. You have to believe that." He kissed her, his lips ardent and sure. His cinnamon smell was fire and warmth inside her. His honesty, his firm truth, was evident as his muscled arms wrapped around her.

"I love you," she whispered. "But I don't know if it's enough."

"It's not," he said, pulling back so he could gaze into her eyes. "But we're not relying on just that. We're being real with one another. This is bare, raw honesty. It's brutal in a way. I know I could walk away right now if this wasn't what I wanted. But I'm telling you, this is it. You're it for me, Casey. Am I it for you?"

She tipped back her head to take him in, feeling dizzy with the sensations coursing through her. Joy. Trust. *Love*. "Yes," she whispered, "you're it."

He crushed her against him then. She could feel his heart hammering though his shirt. The rhythm was a drumbeat of belief that whatever came next, they could tackle it together. She let its steady cadence infuse her with hope, with certainty, with *faith*.

His lips found hers in a breathless kiss. She wrapped her arms around him, trying to be careful of his neck and the bandages there. Fireworks of feeling were exploding in her chest. She gasped as he nibbled on her ear and her whole body ricocheted with feeling. The emotion was rolling and building, a snowball growing as it tumbled down a mountain.

As if she'd read his mind, Abe ran a calloused finger down her cheek, along her neck, straight through the gap between her breasts and down to her belly. She shuddered, clinging to him for support. "Come with me," he murmured, grasping her wrist and tugging her gently toward the bedroom.

She couldn't have argued if she wanted to. He led the

way to her bed, where a bright patch of winter light radiated on the bedspread, as if calling to them, pointing the way to where they both already wanted to go. Abe pulled his shirt off, leaving only his white bandages in stark contrast to his honey-colored skin. The sight made her ache.

She touched her fingers to the gauze. "I hate that you were hurt. I don't want to lose you, Abe."

"You won't," he said, trailing kisses from her jaw to her forehead. "You never will. Even if I'm gone, I'll still be with you."

She knew it was true as she let him peel off her shirt, unhook her bra, and help her out of her jeans and panties. She was laid bare, naked not just physically but emotionally as well. She was exhibiting her heart right along with her body, and it was all for the taking. By Abe. No more rules, no more control. Whatever happened next was out of her hands, and into *their* hands.

"I can't believe you're so beautiful," Abe murmured, trailing his fingers from her hips to her thighs. Her body tingled. "How did I end up here?"

Casey smiled. "I know. Part of me feels like I'm dreaming as well."

Abe cupped her breasts in both hands. He arced a thumb over each nipple, and her every muscle tightened. "Do you still think you're dreaming?" he asked. Hot heat spread through her.

"Mmmm," she answered as he lowered his head to suckle on one nipple, then the other. His touch was the perfect blend of gentleness and passion, tenderness and flame. "I don't think I want to wake up."

"Then don't," he said, backing her against the bed. He towered over her, his weight pushing her on the downy comforter, until he was perfectly positioned on top of her. "This can be a real-life fantasy. I'll spend all my days working to make you happy if you'll let me."

His lips found her neck, nuzzling the tender skin there. His breath was warm as he placed kisses on a delicate spot behind her ear. "You already make me happy," she murmured, feeling drunk on affection and disbelief. This man loved her. He would always love her. She knew it as surely as she knew her own name.

She reached for the button of his jeans but he pulled away. "No, baby. Not yet. This is all about you for a minute."

"I want this to be all about us."

He smiled. "Oh, it is. Believe me, I'm having a wonderful time. But give me a second here."

She could hardly refuse the touch of his fingers between her legs. She inhaled as he slid them inside her. "You're so wet and beautiful," he said, his voice filled with wonder. "I could do this all day."

"Please do," she begged as he found a rhythm inside her. She arched her back wanting him deeper, harder.

"Like this?" he asked, his other hand gently finding her clit. The walls shimmered in her peripheral vision, the whole world bent as he touched her.

"Don't stop," she begged. "Oh, Abe, don't stop."

"I will never stop," he whispered, his body firm against hers, his lips in her ear, his breath coarse with emotion. "I will always be here for you. I will love you forever. No matter what."

The words were as glorious as the orgasm that broke her apart. She flew away in pieces that scattered everywhere, like sand grains in the wind. Oh, but Abe called her back home. He was the glue, and she was mended again as her mind slowed its spinning course, as her body relaxed, as she came back to the present and settled into her body once more. She sighed, feeling spent and yet somehow filled up. "That felt...that was..." she fumbled for words. "That was life altering."

He grinned, a light box of happiness. She understood then that her pleasure was his. Her list had never accounted for that, she realized. Her list had only ever been one-sided: it was Casey taking what she could get. In her wildest dreams she never imagined that she'd find a man who was so dedicated to her satisfaction that it would be enough for him, too. Not that she would let it *end* with her pleasure. But how amazing, how wonderful, that it could.

"What about this?" he asked, as if reading her mind. He stripped off his jeans in one swift move. He settled between her legs as heat spread through her anew. "What does this feel like?" he asked as he pressed the tip of his penis against her. She groaned, clawing his back, trying not to crack into pieces all over again. Not yet, anyway. She was desperate to hang on to the present, onto the realness of Abe and what they felt for one another.

"Wait," she pleaded. He stilled.

"What is it?"

"Nothing. I just want this." She clutched his body with her thighs and rolled to her left, taking him with her. He let her place him on his back, and settle on top. His rock-hard penis pressed deliciously against her clit. *Against her but not inside her.* Not yet.

He ran his large workman's hands up her sides, across her shoulders, palming her breasts. She threw her head back and he groaned, deep and primitive. "My God, you're like a queen," he said. "You're so full of power."

She felt like a queen, somehow. That she could command him to do anything she wanted, and he'd do it. But it was more than that, too. It was knowing she'd do whatever he wanted as well. He could ask anything, and she'd give it freely.

Somewhere in the back of her mind, she knew at that precise moment that her list was no more. The things on it were gone. It had crumpled into a deep, forgotten part of her where she never needed to look at it again.

She understood without a doubt that she would get everything on her list—and so much more. She had wished for five things, but now she would get five thousand things. Perhaps even five *hundred thousand*. Because that was what love did: it went well beyond what you had imagined and gave you an entire ocean, when this whole time you thought you'd only needed a single drop.

"I love you," she said, reaching for a condom from the bedside table and rolling it on him. She rearranged her body so he slid into her in one perfect move. He threw his head back, his jaw muscles clenched, as she rocked against him.

"Oh, Jesus," he murmured, "this is too perfect."

He tilted his hips just slightly and then—dear God, then—it *was* too perfect. Casey shuddered and came again with Abe's hands on her hips, coaxing more pleasure out of her with each thrust and swell. She clenched around him.

"Casey." Her name was on his lips as he came right along with her, their physical connection a knotted, writhing thing that tied them both together. Bound, they ascended their breathtaking summit together and there, Casey imagined, was the whole of their relationship: the past, the present, the future, and all the possibilities therein. The sight of it in her mind's eye was enough to have her choking back tears.

"I've got you," Abe said, as they relaxed together. She collapsed against his hard chest, hearing his strong heartbeat there, knowing that the steady course of it had already guided her home. "I've got you forever."

She snuggled against him. It was true. It would always be true. Her heart swelled with the thought. "I've got you, too," she said, kissing him. "Forever."

"Then I suppose we should make plans to be together on Christmas." There was a playful look in his golden-green eyes.

"Christmas? I thought you said you'd been naughty this year."

"I have, but it turns out I got what I wanted anyway." She could feel his smile as he kissed her.

"All right. What did you have in mind?"

"How about you come over to my parents' place with me? Stu will be there, and we've vowed not to eat the bland food from the retirement home. You'll get a home-cooked Christmas meal."

She pulled back to gaze at him. "I didn't realize you cooked."

"Eh, I'm okay at it. You sort of have to learn how at the firehouse. Stu's even better, though. I promise you won't be disappointed."

She pretended to think it over, even though there was no place she'd rather be. "Well, seeing as how we're *engaged*, I suppose I should make an appearance."

Abe pulled her closer. "It would be scandalous if you didn't."

"The front page of the *Dane County Herald*."

"On the news board at the Lutheran church, even."

"Oh no, anything but *that*. I guess I'll have to go, then.

But…" She readjusted her position so she could look at him fully, could take in every line of his strong jaw, every strand of his dark blond hair, every rise and fall of his chest.

"Yes?"

"I was thinking that maybe Carter could come, too? That is, if his mom's not quite out of rehab and his new foster family seems strange…maybe he could hang out with us? I suppose we'll seem just as strange but, I don't know, it was just a thought."

"I love it," Abe said, kissing her forehead. "It's brilliant. We can at least ask. And there's someone else I was thinking of as well."

"Who's that?"

"It's this older woman named Viola, who calls the fire and rescue a lot. She lost her husband a few years ago, and she's all alone. I'd like to invite her as well."

Casey's breath caught at his thoughtfulness. "I think that sounds wonderful."

Abe raked a hand across his chin. "The only thing I'm wondering about is space. Suddenly that seems like a lot of people crammed into my parents' little retirement apartment."

"Oh," said Casey. She could feel her face falling. "Because I was just going to ask if Audrey and Kieran could come, too. So maybe we should have it someplace else?"

"The Elks Club? Now it sounds like half the town will be there."

Casey laughed. "No. But maybe here? It's already decorated, and I'd love to have a big family Christmas." She swallowed. "I never had that growing up."

Abe traced her cheekbone with his thumb. "As long as that sounds right to you, it sounds wonderful to me."

"Imagine," she breathed, hardly daring to believe it herself, "a huge group together, with a turkey and carols, and presents."

"We'll have to kick them out before too long, though," he said slyly, "so you can get—what was it?—your stocking stuffed repeatedly on Christmas Day."

Casey laughed. "Oh, I think I'm done with the list. I've got something even better."

"What's that?"

She touched his cheek. "You."

He leaned into her hand, and her chest ached with joy. "It seems too wonderful to be real," she said.

He kissed her tenderly, sweetly. "It's real. *We're* real."

"And this Christmas will be real."

"Let me show you how real."

Abe pulled her into his arms as a quiet snow began to fall behind the gauzy curtains, blanketing everything in sight, making the world new again—Casey's heart included.

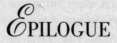

$\mathscr{E}$PILOGUE

Six months later

$\mathscr{T}$he sun was high and bright as Casey walked up the sidewalk to Robot Lit, humming happily to herself. Above, the summer sky was a bright, cheerful blue, and at her feet, poppies were exploding to life with color and fragrance.

Inside Robot Lit, Rolf was setting out pencils and paper, getting ready for a write-a-thon that afternoon. She waved and chirped good morning, feeling excited about all the kids who would be pouring in the doors in an hour or so, each of them having committed to writing for eight straight hours. She'd promised to help with snacks, stretch breaks, and anything else the kids (or Rolf) needed.

Even better was the fact that Carter was one of the write-a-thon kids. He'd said he was finally ready to try to write about his experience with the crow, only he told her he wanted to call Scotty by name. "I want to write about it like it really happened," he'd confided in her the week before, when he'd signed up. She'd hugged him, commending him for being brave, and told him she'd be there if he needed anything. She hoped the writing—plus the fact that both Scotty and Bridget had charges filed against them for child neglect and abuse and would be facing trial in the next few weeks—would bring Carter some closure. He was back with his mom, who'd been sober for almost six months now, and both of them had a light in their eyes that hadn't been there at Christmas. Casey said a small prayer, hoping the light would only continue to get brighter.

As she walked to her office, she briefly wondered where everyone was. Usually Ellie was running around helping Rolf, while Ingrid was leaving chewed pencils and cold cups of coffee everywhere as she printed off copies of grant proposals and called donors.

It was entirely too quiet.

Figuring maybe everyone had made a Rolling Pin run for fresh crullers, she shrugged and pushed open her office door.

And stopped cold.

Inside was a four-foot-tall pine tree decorated for Christmas. A warm glow radiated everywhere from its multicolored lights, while tinsel sparkled amid the needles. "What the . . . ?" she whispered.

As she stepped forward to investigate, her lungs nearly collapsed. Pulling in air was all but impossible. Because her tree was decorated with her missing ornaments.

No way. It couldn't be.

She reached out and touched the cow wearing reindeer antlers. Nearby was the snow globe with Paul Bunyan and Babe the Blue Ox. She saw the cardboard-and-tinfoil star that Audrey had made for her, and the ancient candy canes she'd collected in college. How had this happened? Who had—?

"Happy belated Christmas."

She turned around to see Abe standing in her office doorway, leaning against the frame. His face sported a grin brighter than the tree itself. The sight of him made her skin tremble. It always did.

"You did this?" she asked. "How? When? I thought you were at work?"

"I told you I'd try to get your ornaments back if I could. It took me a while, but here they are."

Casey went to him, twining her arms around his scarred neck. She'd kissed them all, each one a smooth, pale reminder that, come what may, every second, every minute with this man was a gift. Now, her lips found his, and she relished the perfect fit of their parts the way she always did. And just like always, it felt achingly familiar and blazingly new. She shivered slightly.

"Where were they?"

"In a lost-and-found office in Fargo. I got them a couple days ago."

"And you managed to do all this... when?"

"I can't divulge my secrets. It's against regulations."

She was going to argue, but she was silenced when Abe pointed to a wrapped present under the tree. It was the size and shape of a shoebox. "Santa brought you something," he said.

"Is it footwear?" she asked, arching a brow.

"You'd better find out."

She knelt next to the tree, inhaling the heady, piney scent. She giggled, thinking about how crazy this was—being in her office in June and unwrapping Christmas gifts. With trembling hands she tore open the shoebox, only to find Styrofoam packing.

"It's empty," she said, confused. "Did I miss something?"

"Look around. It's there."

She fished and fumbled and was about to tell Abe to stop kidding around already when her hand bumped against something.

She grabbed for it and came up with a tiny black box. Her heart hammered. A velvet jewelry box.

Abe crossed the room and knelt next to her. She wanted to lean into his massive frame for support. She wasn't sure her hands would ever stop shaking, but somehow she managed to lift the lid to find a sparkling ring blinking back at her.

"Abe," she whispered. It was the only thing she could think to say.

Gently, he took the ring into his huge, strong hands and held it in front of her. "Casey, I love you and can't imagine my life without you. I wanted to ask you to marry me this coming Christmas, but I just couldn't wait six more months. So I faked Christmas here. In your office. I hope that's okay."

Tears were sliding down her cheeks. It was okay. It was more than okay.

"So here I am, in the middle of June, asking for your hand. I guess I'm asking for your heart, too, because you have mine. You've had it since the first moment I met you and I never want that to change." Abe swallowed so hard she could see his throat working. "Casey Tanner, I'm asking. Here and now. Will you marry me?"

"Yes," she whispered, so trembling and overwhelmed she hoped he could hear her. "Yes, I will marry you. Absolutely."

He slid the ring onto her finger and kissed her until she saw stars. Or maybe it was just the light of the Christmas tree through her closed eyelids. Either way, she didn't care.

It was Christmas in June and Abe Cameron loved her and everything was perfect.

"Oh, I have to call Audrey," she said when they broke apart.

"No worries," Abe said, winking at her. "She's already here."

Casey turned and saw Ingrid, Rolf, and every one of her co-workers, as well as all the women from Knots and Bolts, plus little Callie and Abe's parents and brother. All of them were smiling at her. Audrey raced forward and swept her into a hug. "Congrats," she said, clutching Casey tightly. "I'm so happy for you."

The locket that Casey had purchased for her sister last Christmas sparkled in the low light. Inside was a picture of them when they were kids. Audrey hardly ever took it off.

Casey had managed to find the right gift after all.

The tears started anew, streaming down Casey's face. Someone handed her a tissue, though she couldn't say who. The entire room burst into applause and cheered until Callie started screaming, red-faced.

"I'd better not bring her to the wedding," Willa said, patting Callie's back soothingly. "She'll let you have it when the pastor asks those opposed to the union to speak now or forever hold their peace."

"I'd better stay on my toes, then," Abe said. "Make sure she has nothing to object to."

"She won't be able to think of anything," Casey said, sidling back up to Abe. He put an arm around her, strong and protective. She'd never been happier, never felt more loved. She pictured the fostering paperwork she'd recently printed out, and how she and Abe would fill it out differently now. They'd planned on fostering together, of course, but now it would be as husband and wife. The thought made her smile even bigger. Someone switched on Christmas music and popped champagne.

"You thought of everything," she whispered as he handed her a glass of the bubbling liquid the color of a holiday star. His jaw flexed.

"I didn't think of anything until I thought of you. My dad was right. Before you, I was an idiot."

"Before you, I was a jerk."

"I guess we were meant for each other."

"I'll drink to that," Casey said, smiling.

They sipped the cool, fizzing champagne while the lights twinkled and flickered and the holiday music played.

"I have an idea for the honeymoon," she said suddenly, feeling as effervescent as her drink.

"Already?"

"It's the only place I want to go."

"Then you'd better tell me so I can start planning it."

"I think you already have the details worked out. We're going to Freiburg."

Abe's eyes widened with surprise, then delight. He laughed and kissed her again.

Casey knew then that she'd been given the best gift anyone could give—and that here, next to the tree, surrounded by friends and family and wrapped in Abe's arms, she had everything she'd ever wanted.

Casey's
Wake-Up-It's-Christmas-Morning
French Toast Casserole

Modified from Paula Deen's Baked French Toast Casserole with Maple Syrup and Tablespoon's Perfect French Toast Casserole.

Ingredients

- 1/4 cup butter
- 3/4 cup brown sugar
- 4 eggs
- 1 1/2 cups milk
- 1 teaspoon vanilla
- 1 tablespoon powdered sugar
- One loaf bread, crusts cut off

Casserole Topping

- 3/4 cup butter (1.5 sticks)
- 1/2 cup packed light brown sugar
- 1 cup chopped walnuts
- 2 tablespoons light corn syrup
- 1/2 teaspoon ground cinnamon
- 1/2 teaspoon ground nutmeg
- 1/4 teaspoon ground ginger
- 3/4 cup dried cranberries

Directions

1. Melt butter, add brown sugar, stir until mixed.
2. Spread sugar mixture into bottom of a 9 x13 pan.
3. Beat eggs, milk, vanilla, and powdered sugar.
4. For the casserole topping, soften butter, combine all the ingredients in a large bowl, and stir together.
5. Lay down a layer of bread.
6. Ladle on half of egg mixture.
7. Sprinkle with half of the casserole topping.
8. Lay down second layer of bread.
9. Ladle rest of egg mixture over the top.
10. Sprinkle with the remainder of the casserole topping.
11. Cover and refrigerate overnight.
12. In the morning remove from refrigerator.
13. Preheat oven to 350 degrees.
14. Bake for 45 minutes and enjoy!

If pride goes before a fall, Willa Masterson's trip back to White Pine, Minnesota, should be one heck of a tumble. The girl who left her hometown—and her first love, Burk Olmstead—in the rearview twelve years ago was spoiled and headstrong. But the woman who returns is determined to rebuild: first her family house; then her relationships with everyone in town...starting with a certain tall, dark, and sexy contractor.

Look for *A Kiss to Build a Dream On*, the first book in the White Pine series, by Kim Amos.

An excerpt follows.

$\mathscr{P}$ROLOGUE

$\mathscr{W}$illa Masterson shifted her shopping bags from one hand to the other as she rode the elevator up to her sixtieth-floor apartment. *The highest you can go in this building*, she often thought to herself—but not today.

This afternoon, each additional second she spent ascending in the elevator's cramped, square space fostered a growing sensation that she was starving. Not literally, of course—she *had* just eaten a divine spice-crusted salmon with a ginger yogurt sauce for lunch—but instead feeling like she was hungry for affection. For intimacy.

Frankly, Willa knew, she needed to get *laid*.

The elevator stopped and the doors swooshed open. She stepped out, head up, determined to give her boyfriend, Lance, her brightest, happiest smile when she entered the apartment. It might not lead to sex, but at least it would stop her brain from pickling itself in lust-filled thoughts.

The long, carpeted hallway stretched before her. Somewhere, she could hear raised voices and slamming doors. Probably someone getting work done by noisy contractors. It happened all the time in the building.

Thinking about how much she needed a good romp between the sheets wasn't fair, she knew. Sex with Lance had never been melt-your-panties hot. It had never really even been that good. But it had, at one time, at least been *existent*. Sort of.

She clutched her bags, knowing she had countless female friends who longed for their husbands and partners to back off the bedroom antics a bit. Why couldn't she be one of them? Lance had been so persistent and convincing early on in their relationship that she'd agreed to moving in together and combining their lives after a few weeks. She'd done it, had kept taking her birth control pills dutifully, even though that one critical, physical piece between them was... broken. Or soft and limp, depending on your take.

Not that it was just the sex. Willa swallowed, knowing that whatever was—or wasn't—happening in the bedroom was actually a symptom of something else. Of she and Lance shopping too much and not talking enough perhaps. Of them traveling to exotic locations but never venturing beyond the hotel. Willa pictured the first edition book of poetry they'd bought for their coffee table, a lovely piece from the late 1800s with Moroccan leather and gilded pages. They'd spent thousands on the volume, but neither of them had ever read its contents.

Willa walked underneath the hallway's sparkling chandelier thinking that she and Lance weren't opening each other, either. A year into their relationship, and they were like that dusty book: untouched and unexplored. In mind and body both.

Perhaps it was time to acknowledge they weren't museum pieces—that they both needed handling. Maybe even by other people.

The thought didn't sting as much as bring her relief.

She exhaled and continued on—white crown molding above her and plush Berber carpet underneath her. The voices grew louder as Willa rounded the corner. She paused when she saw men in embroidered shirts swarming about. These weren't contractors; they were too clean for that. And they weren't police.

Had something happened to one of her neighbors? She wondered if Mrs. Faizon had finally passed away. The woman was at least a hundred.

Just then, a tall man with a buzz cut marched down the hallway toward her. He was carrying a finely framed work of art, and she was able to read the embroidering on his polo shirt.

Midtown Repossession.

Willa understood immediately that one of her wealthy neighbors had fallen on hard times. Her heart sank with compassion. Her corner of New York City might be wholly focused on status and wealth, and someone's loss often meant another's gain. But it never felt good to see people bumped out of the game entirely.

And then her eyes fell on the art, and her blood turned to ice.

The painting was *hers*: a sparse Andrew Wyeth watercolor she'd fallen in love with a few months ago. It had been hanging above the fireplace.

Dumbly, she cut through the cluster of repo men—one of them swept past with her jewelry box, another with an original Eames chair she'd purchased at an estate sale—and stumbled into the apartment.

Her heels echoed on the polished wood floor. Her Persian carpets had been rolled up and carried out. Straight in front of her, sitting with his head in his hands on the single couch that remained, was Lance. Standing next to him was a police officer.

"What is happening?" Willa asked. She'd meant to shout it, she'd meant for her indignation to be loud enough to bounce off the now-empty white walls and startle everyone, but she'd barely been able to whisper. Lance looked up. His dark eyes were bloodshot. His face was puffy, as if he'd been crying.

"I lost it," he groaned. "I lost everything."

Willa blinked. This wasn't possible. Lance was an *exceptional* investor. They were so far in the black, he often said, that she could buy whatever she wanted every day for a hundred years and still not put a dent in their wealth.

"There's been some mistake," she replied. A distant part of her realized she was still holding on to her shopping bags. She set them down on the bare floor.

"I'm afraid not," the police officer replied. He glanced through wire-rim glasses at the notebook resting in his thick hands. "Charges are being filed, and I need you to come down to the station."

Fuzzy spots dimmed the edges of Willa's vision. "Charges?" How was losing your own money a criminal offense?

"We'd like you to give a statement," the officer said to Willa.

A statement about what? Dimly, she realized the officer's uniform was the same rich navy blue as the crisp edges of their bathroom towels. She wondered if those had been taken away, too.

"If you'll just come this way," the officer said. When Lance stood, Willa saw his hands didn't fall to his sides. He was *handcuffed*, for crying out loud.

Sudden fear made her jaw tremble. *What had he done?*

The officer led them to the freight elevator near the stairwell, where their things were being loaded. Cramped between her dining room chairs and a postmodern sculpture, Willa stared at Lance.

"What *happened*?" she asked him.

He only shook his head and repeated the same phrase he'd used in the apartment: "I lost it."

Her fear switched to frustration, which in turn kindled sparks of anger. It sharpened her thoughts to a razor's edge. She wanted to reach out and shake Lance, to insist he tell her everything, but the police officer was right there. Best to wait until the station, she reasoned. She wasn't about to add to the mess he'd created by forcing Lance to explain everything right this second.

Instead, she tried to calm her ragged breathing and her churning insides.

Not ten minutes ago she thought she needed to get laid.

Now she understood she needed to figure out what had been going on in her life—what had *really* been going on, that is—while she'd been running around Manhattan thinking everything was fine.

The elevator doors opened in a matter of moments. The ride to the bottom, she thought numbly, always seemed so much faster than going up.

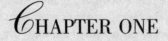

CHAPTER ONE

Two months later
Wednesday, September 19, 11:21 a.m.

Willa Masterson tilted her head back and moaned. Underneath the table, her toes curled in her shoes. Her spine was on fire.

With a hot buttered biscuit in one hand and a steaming forkful of casserole in the other, Willa was as close to pleasure as she'd been in—well, months, really.

Opening her eyes and taking a deep breath, she tried to regain some of her composure. Customers in this crowded, wood-paneled space might begin staring if she didn't stop with the sounds already. Never mind that the food at the Paul Bunyan Diner could make *anyone's* insides heat up with a shivery, goose-bumpy thrill. At least the hot dish could anyway, which was what Minnesotans called a casserole—in this case, a spinach, mushroom, and sausage concoction that had her wanting a second bite before she'd finished swallowing the first.

Willa chewed slowly, trying to savor every moment of her hot dish bliss. It was all she'd been eating since she'd arrived in White Pine two days ago. Part of it was out of necessity—there just weren't that many restaurants in town, and God knows she herself couldn't cook—but the truth was that Willa had yet to get her fill of the stuff. It was a wonder, really, considering that in Manhattan, there were five-star restaurants that could barely hold her attention for a single meal.

Lucky that the food is so good, Willa thought, taking in her surroundings. The décor was straight out of a pioneer exhibit she'd seen once at the New York Historical Society. The lace-edged curtains were yellowed with age, the fabric fraying. Peeling birch logs leaned into some of the corners, the wood tired and dusty. And the tin plates and lumberjack saws nailed to the walls were more primitive than rustic.

Willa stared over her gingham placemat and imagined ripping out the old booths—wood splintering and nails creaking—and replacing them with shiny chrome tables, the tops so reflective you could see your own face. She imagined painting the scuffed wooden floor a velvety black, and swapping out the sawed-off stump of a hostess station with a sleek podium. It would be the kind of place she could imagine in Manhattan, where all her friends would be angling for a dinner seat.

All her *former* friends, that is, since these days they'd probably rather sue her than have lunch with her.

Willa stared at her chipped coffee mug and wondered what they'd say if they could see her now, shoveling her face full of food at a two-bit diner in her hometown. They'd no doubt purse their perfect lips in barely contained laughter. Their wrinkle-free faces would stretch with mirth at the ramshackle house where she was staying, their manicured hands clapping together at the debacle her life had become.

She knew exactly how they'd react because she'd done it to others herself. She grimaced, remembering how Mercedes Whittaker's husband had dumped her for a much-younger woman. He'd left poor Mercedes nearly penniless in a brutal divorce, and when Mercedes had to move to Brooklyn, Willa had simply deleted the woman's phone number, as if they'd never been acquainted at all.

Willa swallowed a lump in her throat, regretting how awful she'd been and thinking of what a field day these women had—and were no doubt still having—with *her* wreck of an existence.

Not that her life was a mess exactly. She straightened in her seat, reminding herself that things could always be worse. Her dad had once told her that she had a solid brain for business, and a knack for getting things done. So what if she was back in Minnesota? She had a foolproof plan for her life here, and it was *going* to work.

But her gut clenched nonetheless. Part of her was beginning to wonder if she was navigating a new path to success as much as clinging to her only means of survival. Was she here because she wanted to be, or because she *had* to be?

The cowbell over the diner door clunked, and she set down her fork and biscuit, glad for the distraction. She'd expected the contractor twenty minutes ago, and she didn't like being made to wait. She was also miffed that they weren't meeting at her house. Didn't a contractor need to *look* at a project to assess what needed to be done?

Willa knew firsthand how exhaustive the to-do list was since she'd been staying in her childhood home for the past forty-eight hours. By day, she'd pull white sheets off old furniture and try to sweep up years of dust and dirt; by night, she'd lie awake in her childhood bed, breathing in the house's old air and listening for the scrabble of animal feet in the walls or, worse, close by her head. In the quiet darkness with the vermin closing in, she'd battle back tears—sometimes winning and sometimes sobbing until her ratty pillow was soaked with snot, wishing she felt more *victorious* already. She'd left Lance, after all. She'd started over. She was still standing, even if her former friends were rooting for her to fall on her face.

Instead, she'd stare at the ceiling, memorizing every crack and chip, thinking that her own life was cracked, too. She'd go red-faced with the realization of what a fool's life she'd been living in New York. Her friends had been fake, her relationship had been a joke, and her whole life had been covered with a veneer she was too frightened to shed. Until it shattered into pieces before she could stop it, and she was left with raw reality staring her in the face.

In those moments, her only comfort would be the house's persistent quiet. At least there was no one around to see her shame.

Because she'd been pacing the floorboards and staring at the walls in her misery for the past two days, Willa understood precisely what improvements needed to happen with her place. Even so, the contractor had insisted on meeting at the diner. By way of explanation, he said he knew he was up for the job—he'd been caring for the house since it had been abandoned nearly twelve years ago, after all—but he said he wanted to see Willa face-to-face, to determine if working together was going to be a good fit.

The New York Willa never would have put up with that kind of attitude. She would have snapped off her cell phone and found someone who would do exactly what she wanted, precisely when she wanted it. Spoiled New Yorkers could get away with so much. Like stealing their girlfriend's money to make bad investments, for example, not to mention screwing up the finances of every single one of their friends.

Willa was just turning to see if the contractor was, in fact, there, when a man slid into the booth across from her.

"Willa?" he asked.

She couldn't even reply. The air had gone from her lungs. The clinking, bustling sounds of the diner had receded to the edges of the earth. The world had gone still and silent as she stared into the eyes of Burk Olmstead. She'd know that stormy dark blue color anywhere.

B.C.'s Contracting was *Burk's* business. In a million years, she never would have guessed or expected it. But now that he was here, it made perfect sense. No wonder he wanted to meet face-to-face: He wanted to ensure it wouldn't be awkward for the two of them to work together.

Willa continued to stare, speechless, until the lines around Burk's eyes deepened in a confused crinkle. She realized he was waiting for her to confirm her identity.

It had been more than a decade, after all.

Willa forced herself to smile and hold out her hand. "Hello, Burk."

He grasped her fingers in a short, rough shake. The feel of his skin against hers sent an electric tingle through her body—a hundred times stronger than any pleasure the food had given her. She blinked, surprised at how easily it all came back. How her body could remember the touch of him, even all these years later.

He nodded at her. For an awkward moment, neither of

them spoke. Willa waited for him to say something—anything—in a greeting: "It's nice to see you" or "it's been a while" or "what are you doing back?" But he remained stonily silent, the hard line of his jaw unmoving. His wide, muscular forearms rested on the table, perfectly still. His dark blue eyes never left her face. Nor did they betray any emotions. They were as hard and fixed as diamonds in a setting.

She hoped her own eyes were the same, but she doubted it. She was alarmed at how undone she felt at the sight of him—just like when they were teens.

Not that she was about to let herself get swept up in old memories.

"Would you like some coffee?" she asked finally. "Or some lunch? Sorry I started without you, but I'd been waiting a bit."

Burk shook his head, instead pulling a small, battered notebook from the front of his plaid shirt. "I'm running behind. We'd better get started."

Willa couldn't remember Burk ever being this gruff. Or this handsome, she thought, taking in the tumble of dark hair, thicker than she recalled, and the edge of his cheekbones, sharper than when they'd dated in high school. The shadow of stubble across his face made her pulse quicken.

Willa, by contrast, knew her recent past hadn't done her any favors. She'd put on weight from all the financial strain and legal battles related to Lance's botched finances. She tried not to think about how her newfound curves must look next to a plate of decimated hot dish.

Not that Burk appeared to notice. He tapped a pen against the notepad's spirals. "So you're finally going to fix the old place up, eh?"

His vowels were incredibly round. "So" and "going" sounded drawn out, as if he was adding extra O's to the words. Willa wondered if she'd talked like that at some point. She must have, but now it sounded like a foreign language.

"Yes, it's stood empty for a long time, as you know. It needs a lot of work."

"What do you want to start with?"

The brusque question was no doubt the result of Burk being time-strapped, but disappointment needled her nonetheless. Did he have to be so curt? She couldn't expect Burk to treat her any differently just because they had a past. But she suddenly felt as if a long-buried part of her *wanted* him to.

No. Absolutely not. She stared at his mouth, fighting off the memory of his lips against hers all those years ago. The warm, tender brush of them. The sweet touch of skin on skin.

Forget it. She was not going to allow her emotions to sidetrack her. She knew firsthand how disastrous it could be to want something that just wasn't there.

Besides, Burk was being terse, not to mention inefficient. If he'd met her at the house, they could have covered all his questions already. They could have walked around and talked about the things that needed taking care of first. If the purpose of the meeting was for them to figure out if they could work together, why was he asking about project priorities?

"As you know, there's a lot to be done," Willa answered carefully, reining in her emotions. "In addition to fixing up the obvious things—the roof, the floors, the windows—I also need to knock down some walls. And reroute some plumbing. Probably also put some additional appliances in the kitchen. A second stove maybe."

For a moment, Burk didn't answer. Willa wondered if his face had paled slightly, or if she was imagining it.

"That's quite an overhaul," he said finally.

"It needs to be. My goal is to turn it into a bed-and-breakfast. It's about time, don't you think? I'm positive this town is ready for a first-class place to stay." Willa didn't know why she sounded like she was trying to talk the entire diner into liking her idea.

Something dark flashed in the depths of Burk's stormy eyes. There was a time when Willa would have been able to read it—to know exactly what every expression or gesture meant—but that was long ago.

"We already have the Great Lakes Inn on the other side of town," Burk said. "And I'm not sure they're exactly bursting with customers. You sure you want to open a second motel when the first one can barely break even?"

Willa's insides flamed with frustration. "It's not a *motel*, it's a bed-and-breakfast. There's a huge difference. And I'm not going to have rotting bedspreads with lighthouses on them like that dump. I'm going to have down comforters and roaring fires and five-star food. Comfy couches and beautiful grounds and freshly baked cookies in the afternoon. Plus fresh juices and teas anytime you want them. Not to mention first-rate wines. All the things they have in B and B's out East."

Burk arched a dark eyebrow. For some reason, the motion sent a shiver through her.

"Sounds expensive," he said.

Willa squared her shoulders. "It will be elegant. *Lovely.*"

"Suit yourself," he said, his eyes returning to his notebook.

Willa had the distinct impression he wasn't convinced. Which was fine, she supposed. She needed a contractor, not a consultant.

"There are a few outdoor issues as well as indoor," she said, pressing forward with her project list. "Some rotted wood on the front porch, though I'm not sure—"

Burk held up his hand. "No need to go into any of that yet."

Willa blinked. She wasn't used to being shut down like this by anyone, much less Burk. In high school, he had once driven to the next town over for ice cream when it turned out that White Pine's own Lumberjack Grocery was out of rocky road, her favorite. She would have settled for vanilla, but Burk told her she deserved to have what she really wanted. When he came back with the rocky road, she kissed him so hard that they wound up entwined together for hours, and the ice cream had melted into a puddle on the counter.

"You under a deadline?" he asked, jarring her back to the here and now.

"Not strictly. Certainly the sooner the bett—"

"Well, I'm always on deadline. And I like to finish projects quickly. If I take this on, I'll be at the site often. No screwing around. If I'm in your way, that's just part of it. I aim to get it done fast. And right. Will that be a problem?"

Willa sat back, shocked by his tone. She suddenly debated hitting the yellow pages, maybe trying to find someone else to do the work. But if it had been Burk caring for the house all these years, then he'd know it better than anyone. It would only make sense to keep him on the job.

"No," she replied.

He scratched something on his notepad, then shoved it back into his flannel pocket. When his eyes met hers again, she thought she saw a softness there—a spark of kindness. Her heart fluttered in anticipation. He was going to tell her how good it was to see her, and that it made sense for them to collaborate on this project together. *Finally*.

Instead, he stood up. "We'll get started tomorrow. Eight o'clock sharp. I was late today, but it's only because my truck wouldn't start. That's the exception, not the rule."

Willa pressed her lips together, more disappointed than she wanted to admit at his gruff manner. It shouldn't matter to her whether Burk Olmstead was glad to see her. She didn't need him to be *nice* to her, for heaven's sake. All that mattered was that he was willing to work on the house.

Or so she thought until he gave her a small smile. Instantly, her breath caught. She leaned forward, tensing with an inexplicable desire to hear him say how glad he was to have her back in White Pine again.

"You have melted cheese on your upper lip," he said instead.

Willa raked her napkin over her mouth, her cheeks flaming with embarrassment as he strode out of the diner. As she heard the cowbell clunk over the door, she suddenly wanted nothing more than to be back in New York, breathing in the dense air of the city as she threaded her way down packed sidewalks, past galleries and shops and restaurants where she could pop in and get sushi anytime she wanted. She rubbed her forehead, knowing that if she asked for an eel roll here, they'd probably send her down to the Birch River with a pole.

Taking a breath, Willa flattened her palms on the table's slick wood top and steadied herself. Two days in, and she already wanted to flee Minnesota. It wasn't a good sign, that was for sure, but New York was in the past. She was going to have to make White Pine work now. She was going to have to make her bed-and-breakfast work, for that matter.

She paid the bill, marveling at how little her meal cost and at how the waitress, Cindi, had dotted her *i* with a heart on the handwritten ticket.

People like Cindi-with-a-heart needed what she had to offer them, Willa reasoned. They were behind the times, and she had a New York aesthetic to bring to the town. People like Cindi would positively eat up the level of culture and sophistication she'd give them with her B and B.

Right. Because shacking up with a fumbling investor and then leaving town when you're on the edge of broke is so high-class, a voice inside her chided.

Willa swallowed. Her past wasn't blemish-free, that was for sure, but she wasn't going to let that stop her. And she wasn't about to let Burk Olmstead stand in her way, either.

He could give her attitude all day long and it wouldn't matter. He could yammer about the Great Lakes Inn and it wouldn't make an iota of difference.

Her job was to think of him as a contractor now, and nothing more.

She stepped out of the diner into the crisp sunshine and tilted her face to the sky. A breeze rustled the leaves of Main Street's trees. The smell from the nearby bakery floated on the air, warm and sweet.

Behind her was New York and all the mistakes in her life she couldn't fix. The embarrassment of it was right there, a tar pit of humiliation bubbling just under her skin. But she refused to crack. She blinked away the tears that sprang into her eyes. A herculean wave of embarrassment was trying to drown her in the idea that she was just a stupid, shallow socialite, and she'd lost everything as a result.

But she wouldn't go under just yet. Because ahead was the one thing she *could* fix: her house.

Or more precisely, Burk Olmstead could fix her house.

Briefly she wondered if she could trust herself alone with him for weeks on end, but then she shook off the thought and the all-over tingle that accompanied it. She exhaled to cool the heat in her body. The girl who had loved Burk Olmstead was long gone, and the boy who had loved her back had disappeared into an exterior as hard as concrete.

Which was just as it should be.

Houses needed lots of concrete, after all.

Fall in Love with Forever Romance

EVERY LITTLE KISS
by Kim Amos

Casey Tanner, eternal good girl, is finally ready to have some fun. Step one: a fling with sexy firefighter Abe Cameron. But can Abe convince her that this fling is forever? Fans of Kristan Higgins, Jill Shalvis, and Lori Wilde will fall for Kim Amos's White Pine series!

HOPE SPRINGS
ON MAIN STREET
by Olivia Miles

Now that her cheating ex-husband has proposed to "the other woman," Jane Madison has moved on—to dinners of wine and candy, and to single mother-hood. When her ex's sexy best friend Henry Birch comes back to town, their chemistry is undeniable. Can Henry convince Jane to love again? Find out in the latest in Olivia Miles's Briar Creek series!

Fall in Love with Forever Romance

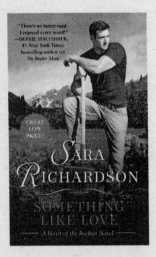

SOMETHING LIKE LOVE
by Sara Richardson

Ben Noble needs to do some damage control. His heart has always been in ranching, but there's no escaping the spotlight on his high-powered political family. The only thing that can restore his reputation is a getaway to the fresh air of Aspen, Colorado. Not to mention that the trip gives Ben a second chance to impress a certain gorgeous mountain guide. But Paige Harper is nothing like the shy girl he remembers...she's so much more.

WALK THROUGH FIRE
by Kristen Ashley

Millie Cross knows what it's like to burn for someone. She was young and wild, and he was fierce and wilder—a Chaos biker who made her heart pound. Twenty years later, Millie's chance run-in with her old flame sparks a desire she just can't ignore...Fans of Lori Foster will love the latest Chaos novel from *New York Times* bestselling author Kristen Ashley!

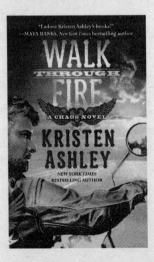

Fall in Love with Forever Romance

ONE WILD WINTER'S EVE
by Anne Barton

Lady Rose Sherbourne never engages in unseemly behavior—except for the summer she spent in the arms of the handsome stable master Charles Holland years ago. So what's a proper lady to do when Charles, as devoted as ever, walks back into her life? Fans of Elizabeth Hoyt and Sarah MacLean will love this Regency-era romance by Anne Barton.